Glam
Rock
Boyfriends

Glam Rock Boyfriends
an imaginary memoir

by Raewyn Alexander

published by **Brightspark Books**
print-on-demand & ebook

ISBN 978-0-473-26664-6
(ebook **ISBN** 978-0-473-26667-7)

Books by the Same Author

Novels
FAT
Concrete

Short Stories
What we Talk about When we Talk about Death, Money and
Heart

Non-fiction (co-authored)
Bacon is Not a Vegetable (701 Tips for
Flatting) *with Olwyn Stewart*
Sweet - A Guide for NZ Teenagers *with Jan Hedge*
The Butterfly Diaries

Non- fiction
Better Writing
Writing Poetry - fireworks, clay and architecture
Staples (recipes, hints, poetry - all everybody needs)

Poetry
AUP New Poets One
It's a Secret - (Selected Poems 1993 - 2005)
Grey Lynn Land of Bright Stars
Tiny Titles (hand-made books)
Museum of Lost Days
A Bee Lover's Poetry Companion
Family of Artists (with CD) *with*
Transistor Davis Jnr and Sandra Bell
Our Mother Flew Unassisted

Publishers - Penguin, Auckland University Press, David Ling, Earl of
Seacliff, Brightspark Books, Engage Aotearoa

Cover photographs - Raewyn Alexander - of Kneel Halt
Author's photo - Geneva Alexander-Marsters

Glam Rock Boyfriends first published 2014 (POD)
ISBN 978-0-473-26664-6 Author: Raewyn Alexander
                        Publisher: Brightspark Books
                        Address: 45 Ivanhoe Rd,
                                          Grey Lynn,
                                          Auckland 1021
                                          New Zealand

This book is dedicated to my family and friends - every one

Table of Contents

...lost my appetite then found it/in men disguised as getaway cars.
- Rachel McKibbens

It's an island mentality, a brutality cloaked by a conspiracy of decency.
- Janet Frame

Without music, life would be a mistake.
- Friedrich Nietzsche, Twilight of the Idols

Part One

Patricia

Achieving the Impossible

Our zip-trip, and music's a time machine. Rock and roll boom,
glide, wiggle; outside a blue moon appears between countless
stars. Drumming up caves of sound, more night than we knew
what to do with, dancing, we breathed each other in.
Every time may arrive on a favourite track or two. Bubble gum
bop pop and sparkle, but Mum's car bunny-hopped when I tried
to drive, under-age. A neighbour cycled furiously, his signals
frantic, yelled, 'You old enough to drive?'
Had to admit I wasn't.
'Best get that vehicle back into your parents' garage. Lucky I
don't call the cops.'
Lipstick slippy slide later, pearly smeared pink, kissing a boy at
the beach. The buttery taste of his skin. How can someone smell
so good you believe you'll never want to eat again?
Surf everything else, ride the waves of memory. Multi-coloured
towels warm, the scour of sand, and warmth soaking into our
salty wet bodies. Age of Aquarius, truth extruded to psychedelic
ribbons of light. No more pretense, everyone open and loving
they said, stroking for replies while so many purred. The way
young men made you laugh then slipped their hand inside your
t-shirt.... What came loose?
Years gone, a slide through colours and shapes, some skitter and
shuffle for groove. Purple, green and cream with touches of
yellow, my favourite floaty silk dress; English magazines and
foreign films lifted us away from rough paddocks on the edge of
town, and broken-edged roads, asphalt.
Naked actors sang the musical Hair on His Majesty's Theatre
stage. Curtains of hair about their faces, over shoulders and bare
backs. We melted and re-formed as other creatures, hybrids, and
culture nuts.
Violins and violas in The Long and Winding Road, creamy
sparkling wine revisited on a guitar riff, a ratty old rug where the
empty bottle toppled. His lips against mine, tongues exploring
each other's mouths, tasting our smooth young skin - a
compelling urge to go further. Quite some push. The heat inside.
Back of a band's van, piled in amongst black guitar cases, amps

and shiny-edge drum-kit we rode to a party after a gig.
Something rattled. Raggy carpet square on the vehicle's floor
felt like an old dog's coat. Someone ran their hand along my
thigh. 'Wild side, you wanna?' he said, 'Hey....'
Melodies from multitudinous directions, potent, we flew into the
eyes of anything against us. Youth, the scrubbed dirty world
ours. Whatever we imagined or said or wanted, that way forever
and ever.
Closeness. *A couple*, touching where blood swells, a holding-hand
world, kiss-behind-the-ear to open hours, days, and months.
Men stood tall and women clung to them in vast landscapes of
films we watched in darkness, like visitors from outer space;
music soundtracked ever after. Love a game to play as easily as a
four square ball bounced on the playground or marbles, *flick,
flick, flick*.... Win.
Rules thrown together from eavesdropping. A fall, the hurt or
ache a hit pop song.
Age, the final frontier, no matter how spacey TV shows say
otherwise. Memory, where we've never been before even if we
wrote the map. Time creased just so, smoothed a way, folded
into a jet plane to skim through the air, a journey, a trippy dip, a
doorway to another land.
Taste that ice cream, breathe in by the sea in sunshine or rain, a
certain fragrance, the perfume of roses and jasmine. A vehicle of
age, travel back on a song into the past now impossibly
reappeared.
Rewind the tape, download the mp3, slide out the vinyl, play
that album turning the better ways loud.

Lamington Days

Hands together, our footsteps
patterns along the sand, by running water,
the sun brighter in every sky I dream.
                - My Dreams by Vaughn Oberon 1963

Fidgety, I watched, transfixed, and tied myself in knots or rolled about the floor in concentrated adoration. His arm and thigh muscles taut, they appeared so clearly defined, and he dashed, agile as a flying fox, through Sherwood Forest. I'd tell him to punch my brothers if they dared jeer at his tights, or just whenever I wanted to see them cry, run. They'd be scared of me for once. Robin with his excellent profile and he spoke with the authority of a prince.

In an hour, after tricking evil men and flexing muscles between jingly TV ads, Robin Hood departed completely. No tunics crumpled and stained to wash in Rinso or quivers to polish with Mr. Sheen, we didn't disagree about whether Watties baked beans or spaghetti were tastiest. My hero demanded nothing more than my devoted attention.

Over the road from ours, my uncle was the first to get a television. We charmed our way into their place constantly, 'O aunty, we'd love to help with weeding/dishes/vacuuming/dusting. Can we do some after the TV show?' She'd laugh and usually said we could watch whatever it was we couldn't bear to miss. Robin Hood appeared on Wednesdays. We'd go along their crazy paving path to a stylish kitchen, past a blender looking like it'd arrived in a Flash Gordon spaceship, then into their carpeted lounge with rounded sofa and globe lightshades.

Punished for some sin I forget now, one diabolical Wednesday my mother grounded me. 'That includes watching any TV.' This possibly proves such punishments hardly serve as a deterrent, or I surely would recall what criminal act I'd committed.

In any case, thwarted and corralled I wept in my room, imagined Robin searched his forest and wondered where I'd vanished to. He'd surely have noticed me there every week,

adoring. Wasn't I essential? Beside my bed above the soft
candlewick spread, wallpaper against my cheek felt rough, but I
did my best to see it as his warm, muscled chest. Robin's beating
heart only inches from my ear. Urgent whispers, 'Oh my darling.
I'll see you next week.' Passionate messages sobbed at my
bedroom wall towards my uncle's house. Definitely, Robin
received my voice through his magical antenna. Surely he
missed me? Someone had to (and such a desirable candidate).
TV actors were de facto magicians, privy to magnificent
scientific knowledge, devices to get them wherever and whatever
they needed. And Robin needed me. My logic worked in
mysterious ways.
A few weeks after my time-out, Robin Hood was replaced by Sir
Francis Drake on the deck of his sailing ship, surrounded by
cannon smoke. TV shows could change without much warning.
For some reason I didn't cry if I missed seeing the captain's
endless voyages to plunder treasures for his queen. Possibly I'd
matured, now believed my mother's advice to always *play hard-to-
get*, or maybe just missed plain tights on a man.
The black and white images entertained me in quite a different
way this time. Complicated plots at a high level, rather than a
group of daring men banished to live in a forest, plotting against
the rulers of their country. Queen Elizabeth the First's pearl-
encrusted frocks also encouraged me to think Maid Marion had
no true idea about fashion's power and magnificence. I
wondered if Mum could run me up something like those jewel-
bedazzled phenomena on her Singer sewing machine. But I
couldn't imagine beaded, grand dresses suiting the local
community hall for Girl Guide meetings, nor would I easily
sweep into Sunday School wearing a crinoline, no matter how
much I wanted to try.
These obsessions didn't completely engross me. TV went off the
air early and my aunty often stopped children's visits. A gang of
grubby larrikins lolling about her immaculate living room. I
overheard aunty talking to neighbours, 'Scallywags to put it
mildly. Mud to their knees and climbing trees like monkeys.' She
laughed. 'Sounds like a limerick. Poet and didn't know it.'
Parents called us *square eyes* if we got too television-crazy, too.

Our health warped by technology. 'Get outside and play. Have some fresh air.'

Lush, rough lawn spread over a few acres, the local park in our street. A tree-filled gully at the back where boys said they caught eels. A few pieces of playground equipment but mainly just a big open area.

When a gaggle of local kids gathered any larger than eight or nine of us someone suggested Bullrush. In barefoot, hand-me-down splendiferous excitement we rallied for battle. One muggins in the middle chosen, after much debate, to try to grab other kids who ran past. The mid-grabber compelled to remain there alone trying to catch the rest. We pounded past them at intervals, when they called for particular children, always calling the slowest, smallest kids first. Gradually a raggle-taggle gang formed in the centre to grab more and more. 'Run, run....' we screamed to the targets while they tore over the grass. Bullrush banned eventually, but no one ever got hurt much as far as I recall, even if some did hit the grassy ground and roll over and over, groaning when tackled.

Scraped knees, stubbed toes, bee stings and prickles, these painful accidents were everyday life. 'Ow, I've got a prickle,' someone cried out, hopping and grimacing. We'd crowd around to see the damage, try to get the pricking thing out with a grimy fingernail. No one wanted to go home and see their mother dig for it with a needle. I always knew when it was summer, because my big toe would get stubbed on the huge stones along our street. We didn't have tarseal for about ten years. Bare feet anyway.

Children raced around, organised games, played on the equipment or pondered enormous questions like how long would it take to climb to the top of the frame for the swings? And could we walk along the pole at the top?

Some wondered about torturous things to do to insects and small animals : guinea pigs, cats, kittens and so on. Wing removal, or strategic placement of firecrackers.... I usually protested during those conversations. Budding sadists learnt not to make such wicked plans anywhere near me.

Feats of strength and mayhem against each other appeared

more acceptable. Into attack-mode in seconds - soldiers, indians
or cowboys brandishing off-cuts of wood nailed into the shape
of guns. An underlying delight in violence simmered constantly.
It only took one or two keener than the rest for battle ideas to
catch and we'd rampage. Ecstatic release while we whooped and
tore after each other, shouting descriptions of damage, 'I blasted
your arm off. It's pumping blood everywhere.' We'd yell, squeal,
race along between houses, over the road, streams of children
between two and ten or so years unsupervised, gathering rowdy
force. Slavishly copying films and TV shows, soon adding our
own versions of moves and plots with extra daring.
Quieter huddles whispery by the high brick wall sealing the park
from view, (as far as the family with the tennis court were
concerned). Subjects of gossip or conjecture oblivious on swings
or up a tree, where we soon joined them. More often than not
forgetting whatever tittle-tattle someone'd cobbled together for a
run through scandal, to see if it rang loud enough to affect
anyone else.
Magical talismans everywhere. 'Just let me hold a buttercup
under your chin.' A yellow patch showed on the soft skin there
like with an upward-shining light. 'That means you like butter.'
Clouds formed shapes of animals and things. Those forms
sometimes revealed the future. 'A dog, that's a dog, that cloud
there. My dad'll get me one. You'll see.'
Split daisy stems woven into flower circlets for our fairy queen
hair. Holes in the gully held goblins and elves. We concocted
potions from grass clippings and gravel. 'This is the ancient spell
dust of long life and happiness. I command you to arise,
Princess.' Rhymes chanted, stories remembered, fragments of
conversations hinted at what we need to know and have, to be
grown up. 'Tinker, tailor, soldier, sailor, rich man, poor man,
beggar man, thief.' Girls counted cardigan buttons to see who
we'd marry.
I hung back when they played this game, the girls in a somewhat
organised gathering. Rituals and chanting drew most of us
together, the sounds attracted people, few boys however since
they didn't ever want to marry it seemed to me. Boys liked to
run and climb, free enough to take off whenever they pleased. I

tried not to get involved, because I did my counting in private, and knew what the girls would discover. My mother made long cardigans to keep my kidneys warm. A beggar man or thief usually turned up for my husband. Despite other girls' wrinkled noses and sympathetic noises, I told myself I did not care. My healthy organs, protected by Mum's knitting, could withstand our difficult life, I felt sure.

Eventually, enough nous to put the notion to Mum that a *jersey* could feel warmer. 'A pullover, Mum?' I asked, all innocence. They lacked buttons, and therefore safety from the dreaded fortune telling would be mine.

Always ready to help with practical matters, bless her, Mum duly knitted pullovers, but placed tiny buttons along the shoulder for the snug necklines to work properly (chests also needed protection). Destined to find a soldier or sailor, by that count. They'd bring in a regular pay packet, I consoled myself - and a man like that would be away at war or on boats, often. Ample time to watch as much television as I liked, to climb trees, and see my friends too.

No jersey or cardigan buttons were ever named *outlaw, artist,* or *film star*. For a while I tried a new rhyme. 'Tinker, tailor, soldier, sailor, richman, poorman, beggarman, thief, outlaw, film star, artist, musician,' I'd say, feigning innocence.

The interested huddle of girls stepped back at least one pace. If anyone particularly nasty stood there they'd sneer, 'Artist? That doesn't rhyme. She's *making things up*.'

One tall rather stupid girl called me names, 'Faker. She's a rum one. Mark my words.' The echo of her mother's fake posh accent through her meanness. A flock of ducks flew overhead, and I turned to watch them pass.

But usually those skeptical girls drifted away as if I wasn't there at all. Non-conformity meant I no longer belonged. Fitting in mattered almost as much as knowing how to play various games really well, and being able to swing your swing 'over the bar', beyond the limit of the frame at the top. It made me feel dizzy, so many different rules that other children decided we needed to follow. A welcome break to have them ignore me for a while.

An apple stalk twisted off to the chant of A B C etc., gave your true love's first initial. Falling for Aston, the local accountant's son, meant I tugged right at the start on the stalk, loudly saying, 'A,' without much luck. Twisted barely at all towards the end and then, the start of the alphabet once more, but often ended my chant on an O or a W. The broken stalk my unbearable truth.

Soon said those letters to myself while I twisted, so sharp-eyed girls couldn't say I loved Wacko Willy, who hit people - including teachers; or silent Olaf Peterson. What my mother called *slow*. Handsome Aston refused to play Bullrush with girls. He learnt different manners to many of us at his quiet dinner table, in a house with two reddish brick columns beside the front door. His parents away for the weekend to a motel rather than a camping ground (where we went), and they hired a gardener. My best smiles saw Aston's glance slide away as easily as dew down a blade of grass.

But I longed for someone to call me beautiful. The first step towards having someone else was a compliment. I knew this from television. Then people saw more of each other and held close, discussed plans for the future together. Perhaps we'd watch TV, discuss the stories and this hero would protect me from frights. I recall that need, I felt as desperate as if being hunted. No other child in our family much liked to talk. The boys always in action and I had to keep up, or stand away, or be pushed around. My brothers' Chinese burns stung when I said things they couldn't understand or agree with. They shut me inside the dog kennel if I insisted they were wrong; other incidents involving darkness and pain followed. They swore me to silence with threats. In any case no one liked children who *told tales*, so adults rarely listened to our complaints.

People now say we had so much freedom in the 1950s and 60s, wistfully imagining it was better, but being shunted outside to fend for ourselves wasn't really being free, even if we often perhaps felt gloriously released for a few moments. Our childhood usually ruled by whoever took charge, many times they were simply bigger or louder children, and they could freely treat me however they liked.

No *tell tale tit*, either. Few adults wanted true stories about neighbourhood torture to interrupt the six o'clock news, their coffee break, nap, or housework and gardening.

I needed a protector and companion, this grew clearer every day.

A breeze of him at first, the smell of grassy outdoor air replaced by Lifebuoy soap and fresh sweat, then his warm smile. Wham, he sat so close to me. Robert Hughes brushed his thick, dark fringe away from his eyes. So chatty at lunch-time. My mother's lamingtons and caramel square went down Robert's red lane, *grin, bite, gulp,* then he simply dashed away, refueled for rugby or cricket.

Few boys lingered for conversation or plans. Always with some scheme of their own.

Distractions crowded in as easily as weather. Girls hissed remarks or tossed chants together, peculiar bouquets of fresh words, a few with thorns attached. You needed to seek out a friend, often some hid near the trees or in a cloakroom. When school bullies got their juju on, the air felt more metallic, and an urgent need for shelter appeared as if drenching rain had started falling.

Other girls began energetic games, flung themselves about as if they had too much energy and they had to get rid of some or burst. They hurtled across the playground, touched or tigged someone, 'it' for Tiggy. 'You're it, *you're* it. Catch someone, run, run!'

The target they caught was the next one to chase everyone else. The outcast desperate to be absorbed by the group again, to run in a mass, across the wide open school field.

Or we battled for marbles with the boys, in the dirt. Romance paled next to the idea of winning. Victory mattered enormously when we were ten. I called, 'No Changies,' just as the best player placed his prize black marble on the line.

His face collapsed, he remembered distinctly and with deflation he hadn't shouted *Changies.*

If I won, his black marble would be mine to keep and he knew I played well.

The game as important as a championship, every broad area of concrete basketball court we played on excluded except where my marble had to roll, to hit his off the chalked line. Noted little bumps and oddities, what extra force could be needed to keep my marble on track. Ignored him strutting with his chest out, trying to intimidate me. One of his friends hissed a bad word, I refused to hear it.

Lined up. A crowd watching. My thumb in place to flick, my eye steady, everything a part of everything else, in synch. Nothing existed except the moment. A tiny sound, thumb hitting my glass marble. Too late now, I'd done everything I could.

Watching as if we needed to know this outcome for our very survival. My ordinary green clear marble flew across the rough concrete towards his rather smaller, rare, black marble and hit it. Mine.

Triumph all through me as if I'd just eaten something hot and spicy, I grabbed the marble and swept away. My opponent tried one last ditch attempt at persuading me not to, 'Look, I was going to say it. It was just that....'

'Mine. No changies,' I shouted in delight and bluster, while a few sycophantic friends luckily hedged me in. A mass of girls around the corner where the teachers sometimes were. Away from the marble games for that day, and some days afterwards.

Forever lost any chance of a kiss from that hero or his sticking up for me when my brothers loomed in sight with fancy new torments. But I possessed a rare, black marble as dense as night without a moon. Held up it did nothing but gleam, unable to be seen through even in bright sunlight. My own mystery. I possessed the unknowable, and imagined cherishing a husband the same way, as if he were rare.

Mum kept Dad like he was a prize. As soon as Dad stepped in the door we needed to be quieter, and dinner was often a little tense. She obviously thought Dad could break or be stolen.

But marriage meant a man and a woman would be together forever and no one would dare hurt them. The spell so powerful. White dress, black suit, flowers and horseshoes, '...something old, borrowed and blue,' special garments, rhymes and music.

Glorious feasting, speechifying, witnesses everywhere and the whole kit and caboodle captured in large photographs, placed inside padded or beribboned albums, some with gold lettering.

Proof - the couple lived charmed and protected forever ever after, story books said so. Clever German ceramics and expensive stainless steel baking dishes, gifts to furnish their house, tokens they needed to care for, always.

Marriage looked like *No Changies* in the 1950s and 60s. A known and trusted pattern people followed, a dance they did safe and secure. Each taking the same steps others took. Almost identical wedding photos framed in hallways or living rooms all along our street. Mum, Dad and children, as enduring as the melamine picnic tea cups and saucers we used at the beach, although far more special and complicated.

Even at the Cole's, five doors away behind knotty, dark pine trees, where everyone knew he hit her, and at Svenson's where he barely spoke English and ate strange food (even if his wife was from the same small town as my mum), together forever no matter what. They'd vowed. It was like swearing to cross your heart and hope to die, only far more lofty and important than our childish determinations. Even if people angrily strode out sometimes and shouted from the street, faces red, eyes creased to dark specks; fierce words spouted like they could catch the hedges and buildings alight, or we heard acid phrases like venom; they soon returned to their houses. Families belonged together and they'd sworn to stay. Even people who went to jail returned, fitted into places kept for them, a father again, a husband (not that anyone near us did this but other children told such stories).

Young marrieds, each pair neatly dealt out with family groups on the edge of town, as various as characters in a kiddie pastime. Happy Families a popular card game then. People matched. Then they wanted to stay in those groups, to win, to be the best, to show they belonged. One red-headed, freckly family, another darker with black hair, next to a mousy quartet who wobbled when they walked - except for the father - he strode along almost greyhound-like. Then us with hazel or brown eyes, fair like Dad when he was young, but we tanned easily like Mum with her Spanish grandfather. Bunches of people, blooming in the fresh air and fed with excellent food from our gardens.

As fascinating as any insect or bird, people appeared everywhere. I liked to try to make sense of who was who, what was what, and where I could belong in the picture this made. In town (with my mother), to buy shoes once every six months, or more often to buy lengths of fabric for clothes she ran up for us, or to see about a present for a new baby, other people were dotted about everywhere. Young couples sometimes with faces so happy (like in religious pictures), old people bent and twisted or slow (a few sprightly but grey-haired), or young men without a girl - vaguely like Robin Hood's Merry Men (except those groups rarely appeared cheerful). A few mothers with shopping bags and children, often dragged-down looking but sometimes bouncy like the heavily made-up, cheery women in advertisements. Girls shopped in giggly clusters or cruised along, looking superior. Bodgie and widgie types slouched and some sneered, or a few laughed, loud, like someone could want to notice and join in. They looked like they played something like *Changies,* or at least had code words. Teens and early-twenty-somethings in black jackets, tight pants and skirts, slumped or strutted by flash Chevvies, Buicks, and Fords near city milk bars. Eyes slitted, or extra-round stares like in a comedy, play-acting innocence. Some startlingly beautiful, various versions of Elizabeth Taylor and handsome Elvis lookalikes.

Such black or blonde hair, the widgies, where did they get such dramatic looks? And could my dad grow the hair on his face long past his ears, or sideburns like those bodgies? I tugged at Mum's hand, turned and stared back. Mum told me, 'They'd have you soon as look at you. Stop staring, it's rude ….' and sometimes, 'I'll leave you here, shall I?'

When I didn't keep in step and just gently hold her hand it distressed my mother so much she wanted to abandon me. For a few minutes, walking obediently in step I'd plan what I'd do if she did walk away. What shop could I go into, who could I perhaps ring on the telephone? My steps quick and my face as clear of plotting as possible.

One day, my mum mentioned a woman who'd lost *her* marbles. Her 'poor husband.'

I wondered, *Couldn't adults buy replacement marbles?* Such questions

best kept quiet. It was soon apparent from when I could first talk
in complete sentences that many things I uttered were too
strange for Mum or her friends to fathom. Their little giggles felt
rather like they poked at my tummy, as if I were a cute dog
doing a trick. Sharp humour kind of prodded me away. They
couldn't help it, I decided, on one of my late night wonders of
wandering taken in bed. In the quiet dark thinking luxuriously
alone about all the endless puzzles of every day. Time alone
such a relief.

A sound splash, whiffs of perfume, sweet tastes, light sponge
lamingtons coated in chocolate icing, rolled in desiccated
coconut; tiny club sandwiches layered with lettuce, tomato, ham,
creamy butter on white bread, crustless; flaky pastry egg pie with
finely chopped parsley; piece de resistance home-made
chocolate cake filled with raspberry jam and whipped cream,
chocolate icing sprinkled with icing sugar through a lacy paper
doily, so the top of the cake appeared lacy too. Transported back
to the family lounge, *clink, clink, clink* of cups on the tea trolley,
afternoon or morning tea, a trill of voices. Women talk
simultaneously, '...those children, this sewing, the prices of, the
ways to, colours chosen, the new and old, you'll never guess....'
And whispers about people absent.
My mother proclaiming, 'Little ears present,' or, 'Big ears
flapping.'
Their hissed tone riveting. But, prompted with a reminder that
we children could hear (even if we sat as still and quiet as garden
ornaments), local wives stopped murmuring about drunken
neighbours, or some relative that had disappeared or done the
dirty. Rearranged their crisp cotton poplin, big-skirted frocks,
smoothed down bright rose patterns or geometrics, swung along
onto a new recipe or a particular child's recent accomplishment
or waggishness, 'O you'll laugh....'
How astounding we were in our raggle taggle, grazed knee, silly
question fresh and apparently empty-headed curiosity. We
offspring gob-smacked and uproariously amused our parents,
going on what they told others, while they also insisted we *be seen
and not heard*. Soon telling us to *speak up. Cat got your tongue?* A

grown-up changed in a twinkling, peculiar as any magical creature in a book - but you could touch, hear, and smell them. Many stunk of tobacco or strong drink, some worked with cars and had an oily odour, others worked in offices and ink stained their fingers, mothers usually smelt powdery and sweet. Adults emerged from their various atmospheres, in charge, and told children their bellybutton kept their backside on, or a father was off to get *a wigwam for a goose's bridle.* Some grown-ups pretended to steal your nose, but when you touched your face everything seemed attached the same as usual. I wondered why they wanted my nose, what would they do with it? Wear two? *Laughter.* The rhyme of four and twenty-blackbirds inspired this activity. One bird in the song pecked off a maid's nose. Our mothers' extraordinary bravery on display out there, hanging up laundry with pegs, refusing to let any birds scare them. Eventually, experience revealed that grown-ups lied; difficult to decide what to believe in and what was nothing much at all. I possibly in the back of my mind decided to invent what I liked to believe in too, after all, it seemed to be the way of things. Friends mostly didn't know much, nor cared to try to figure oddities out. They cared who could do a spider bent over backwards like Madeline Sparks, or how many marbles someone owned, or if they could devour some of my lunch; no time to talk about what things really meant, or who to trust, or if truth even existed. Some just stared at me like I'd admitted I liked cutting worms in half, when I asked questions about truth or the universe. Others simply never heard my queries. It made for a distance in my life that yawned at me sometimes, as frightening as a dark cave.

At a young age, I stuffed pants and a jersey with other clothing, imagined someone beside me while I drifted to sleep. The form gave me enormous comfort. My insides could finally rest, forget to stay alert, my jangle-jingle of thinking subsided. I hugged it and imagined the cloth was warm.

The best thing about going to the doctor a gentle hand on my body somewhere, a pat on my chest or back, a soft hand on my arm. Someone touched me with care. Blessed. I'd wish and wish that feeling could last. Doctors specially trained, gentle. I admired them like they were someone holy.

My dreams troubling, even if I did make a scarecrow to keep
away my flapping fears and screeching woes. About the bed,
bright insects and twisted faces floated in darkness, my own
scream-fest, but I said nothing. Suspended and animated like a
film in the air playing, when I woke up. After brother-induced
shocks, or just out of the blue, these visions haunting me since
before I could talk. I sometimes think now - I must've wondered
how I would also see other objects, like my plate at meal-times
or my parents around these bright, moving objects. Usually by
morning the lurid night visions had gone, always replaced by a
kind of background whir of memory, flickering coloured
pictures in mind, constantly diverting and strange a layer over
and through everyday life.

Many years passed until I realised not everyone suffered
haphazard pictorial intrusions. Then I learnt that telling others I
could see things that were not there could make them suspicious
of me. Silence a fine protection. When no one knew what you
could see they readily decided you were like them.

Nowadays rough moments have been smoothed over with hours,
weeks, years of talk and supervised drawings, exercising phrases
and theories as if they're tools weighted for wet plaster, swish
and smooth. The material of my existence changed and cleared.
Previously, my flashbacks were the way the world was and it
couldn't have been any different. None of us can undo events
once they've occurred, life is not knitting. I'm writing the pattern
of it now, though, I need to condense the way things are in mind
into words, into finite forms.

My bumper sticker solution to understand why people
mistreated me, their ignorance often coming from their lack of
ability to think or feel, so Forgiveness is Freedom. Others say
things like, 'My life wasn't so bad,' or 'What's done is gone.' They
behave as if they're not ever looking back again. Some kind of
bond between us, mutual recognition between the neglected, the
abused, and bullied - calling ourselves braver names like
survivors, or sensitive. A league of characters in a vivid, and, at

times, horrific play, but stepped into a finer story now. Grown-
up, matured, we know better, walked past all the open windows,
didn't jump off the bridge, left those pills in the bottle, aren't we
lucky?

The best thing about marriage obviously, in any case, was that
you had a massive party, dressed up like movie stars, got a house
and had someone to talk with, just about any time, every day.
This had to be a real advantage in life. But how to achieve this
marvel?
To solve the puzzle of how to meet someone who looked good
in a suit for the wedding photographs and also who knew the
fine art of conversation, there were very few clues. I started
gathering information as best I could, anyway.
'Meeting someone' was discussed by older children, teenagers or
20-somethings at family parties. This appeared to be the first
step. 'Gail met her fiancé at their local rugby club,' my second-
cousin proclaimed to a group who were all ears around her.
After making sure this man Gail now was engaged to had a job,
was tall, didn't seem to have any awful friends or a truly
suspicious past, everyone discussed where *their* local rugby club
was for some time.
Territory as important as the scenery in TV shows and movies,
people had to have somewhere they knew well to perform in.
My dad went hunting sometimes with friends for ducks and
possums. Women also hunted, but they did it with knowing
where to look and being attractive.

Days and nights had slid past, the toddler who sang, 'I've got a
white sports coat and a pink carnation...' disappeared, along
with the six or seven year old girl who sat in the top of pine trees
to think, and sometimes, to play General Whippersnapper for a
bunch of grubby-faced children left to their own devices out-of-
doors, day after day.
A tanned youngster who swam fast, talked a lot and laughed
through aftermaths of tantrums like she'd only ever been happy,
eventually I looked far older than I really was. Dressing up for
the flicks, one of my favourite 'intensities', took all my focus and

crowded everything else away. I loved saying I had *intensities*, to
sound arty and famous. Many of my friends didn't really get
what I meant however, and one said, 'Intensities, like in tent
cities? You going camping?' Laughing, away she went.
I refused to give up that name for my favourite pastimes, but
never said it aloud again.
Our three picture theatres in town mostly not too flash (one a
flea pit, old and shabby), true, except for a gorgeous mock-Tudor
arrangement of two-storey building, with circular glass ticket
booth inside, sweeping curved stairway to the Upper Circle and
plush Persian carpets. Incongruously set by the concrete block
Munis (our municpal baths), a picture palace to start dreaming
on before you even entered the place. Mainly white with
distinctive black boards outlining the planes of the building, a
steep shingled roof, and stained glass windows by the Sweet
Nook which sold lollies, potato chips, ice-cream and drinks.
Sometimes I dreamt of that cinema as if I lived there. My hero
carrying me up the curve of staircase. Both of us laughing,
dressed in film star splendour of some description and far taller
than any human being usually appeared.
I suppose someone had a construction firm and they somehow
wangled payment with our city rates, a friend on the council
putting forth the proposal. The council pulled it down to replace
with some plain and serviceable office building. No one would
ever dress in slipper satin and peacock feathers to be carried up
their stairs. As disappointing and tragic as a death - the mock-
Tudor cinema, our very own palace for everyday people,
destroyed without a trace.
In 1959 a beauty queen from Australia visited New Zealand.
She was asked when she returned to Sydney what she thought of
the place and said, 'I don't know, it was closed.' People in charge
seemed to prefer to appear bland. Destroying beauty and magic
their fearful crime. I didn't want to meet any of them. The
evidence of their heartlessness appeared in how early everything
shut in town, how tense people appeared to be in public, and the
authoritarian manners of officials.
Troubles evaporated watching movies, however. I escaped into
crazy sense, more attractive than any everyday. Arabian tents

hung with tapestries, huge castles where couples in sumptuous costumes spun across mirror-like ballrooms, swept on to exotic islands and across wind-blown deserts, over-acting to match big orchestral numbers, cutesy child actors with animal stars....
Bizarre cartoons beforehand, rinky dink music and chuckle-tracks, lovely make-believe arose as easily as breathing.
With the grand Tudor place destroyed, I simply took my disillusionment to one of the other two theatres. Both more like serviceable halls, one old and one new. Inside, darkness, then miracles filled the silver screen. On Saturday cinema afternoons, older boys slunk along in the dimness, slid into the seat next to us, slipped an arm around our shoulders. I hissed to one, 'I'll slap you if you don't go away.'
My furious glare scorched him. He laughed loudly but moved quick smart.
Once I was a wild girl who threw rocks at unknown kids who dared to enter our local park. We rallied the whole street's children for war. I wasn't afraid of one strange boy in a cinema. But I obviously wasn't ever going to *meet someone* with that attitude, either.
In the mysterious realm of make-believe come to life, flickering projections, leather seats, various patrons sitting comfortably, sometimes the torch of an usher flashed to show someone late to their seat, or to spotlight an unruly teen. But what I wanted never really appeared clear. Maybe the boys who sidled up to me didn't care about my wishes, only closeness, however I wanted a version of Robin Hood - or at least Francis Drake. None of the boys at the movies vaguely resembled anyone famous or heroic. They often smelt strongly of cloying hair oil or body odour, or both, some with peculiar hair-styles too long in front which they flicked about, and almost every one smiled like they believed that was all they needed. Presumption as unattractive as their personal grooming.
Rebuffing cheeky lads who wanted to snuggle in the cinema nevertheless a thrilling game. We girls told stories about this one or that, laughed at their ineptitude or showed off how many boys had approached us, then what we'd done to make them go away. I secretly wished I'd find one I didn't want to refuse, but

over and over again refusing them appeared the best choice.
On the screen, gorgeous women who attracted the most
stunning men, those heroines who spoke the best lines all looked
like someone had painted them, too stunning to be natural.
Obviously more glamour could influence someone else with a
true sense of conversation and finesse, at least a boy able to
show off with class, good humour, something more than
bravado.

When I wanted to learn to draw a cat or a rock, or to write a
funny rhyme, I tried over and over again until whatever
appeared on paper seemed close to what I'd imagined. A
neighbour who collected lovely china inspired me. Try and try
again. They learnt what was good and what was not by trial and
error, 'You have to go out there. See what's around. Then
gradually you learn. Train your eyes. It's easy for me to spot
quality now. Practise.'
The bunches of wives in their best frocks at my mother's
morning teas often declared they were *staying the distance,* and *not
giving up*. One would be all awhisper, the others drawing in close.
Hard to catch the remainder of their plans. Talking about
husbands, marriage, and other mysteries of grown-up-land.
Schemes and wiles meant winning perhaps, but I only knew how
to play Snakes and Ladders, marbles, Tiggy, or card games like
Snap. Every one difficult to win. Marriage could be a
combination of every known game and even more of a
challenge.
Girls muttered snatches of wisdom gathered from
eavesdropping, or the nonsense answers grown-ups tossed to us
as if we were pets on the scrounge. 'When men and ladies fall in
love, they're together.' No one called women *women* then except
as a kind of insult. We had to imitate *ladies* to find romance.
Easy peasy to find pat answers in our cookie cutter minds -
recognise a pattern, make a copy, try it out.

Swimming club was a great social occasion, much like the
movies. Some chance after races or training to impress, to find
romance, even if our eyes were red from quantities of chlorine

in the water. We chatted with teenagers from other suburbs, perched on bleacher seats high around the chemical-scented public pool.

My mother's blue eye shadow in a gold case - it arose at the flick of a little protrusion, golden glitter in the hard stick of dark blue. I took it, telling myself this was only borrowing. The make-up itself as thick as a crayon and difficult to apply til it warmed a little on my skin. She'd never miss the small, tubular gold case. Mum only wore eye make-up to go out somewhere special, not every day. I tucked it into my duffle bag.

After we'd done our training, we went to change. Dawdling, I told my friend I'd see her out there. Didn't want her telling me off for trying make-up. She was so bossy sometimes.

Hair in straggly rat-tails and the changing room concrete giving off a damp smell, I applied thick blue eyeshadow. Glittery sheen heavy on my lids, but I hoped the blue somehow enhanced my dark brown eyes, albeit with red chlorine rims. The mirror in the concrete bathing sheds rather smeary, but I surely appeared as fabulous as any movie star.

Hips swaying slowly like a screen idol who paraded around a far more glamorous pool with a saxophone soundtrack, I sashayed along the wet concrete pool surround, and eased up to the weatherbeaten wooden bleacher seats. Didn't say much but posed rather with one hand behind, leaning back, a mysterious smile. We got on quite well for a good half-hour with the others. My so-called best friend snapped later, 'Everyone asked me what on Earth you had that awful make-up on for.' She flicked away. Her wet hair showered me in drops of water like the weather'd turned bad.

All I could do was stammer, 'I d-d-don'know why.' By then, I didn't. What did please me however was learning better. Blue crayon-thick eyeshadow did not suit and I needed something for my particular colouring.

Plebeian swimming club people as uninterested in glamour as they'd be in being told they had to stop sports altogether, too. I needed to avoid them.

A bewildered girl from the edge of town. A horse paddock over the road. Children wandering the neighbourhood. My uncle

had got a TV we loved to watch. But what did I imagine could
happen for me apart from more of the same?

No idea then that high sensitivity meant that many other people
would often think me strange, ad finitum, sometimes ad
nauseum, unless I was of use to them. Also, most highly sensitive
people were introverted, not extroverted - they avoided
attracting attention unless it was essential.

But I loved to know more, and it felt good to get others to
believe they could achieve too. Many times I worked with other
children and their writing, described how to express themselves,
passed on hints, watched them grow in confidence. Not that they
often thanked me, but some people don't realise we can lead far
richer lives if we're grateful. Many preferred quick fixes, fast
gratification, the easy way, curiously.

School lessons never as complex and hurtful as learning received
at the hands of my peers and brothers, or from a few sadistic
teachers and adults. Being hit really taught me how to scream
loudly as if it truly hurt, so they'd stop sooner. A swerve so they
missed sometimes, or a tip forwards so the wallop didn't connect
so hard - also fine lessons to learn. Perhaps I deserved
punishment for wrong-doing, but I usually forgot whatever it
was I'd done to break a rule. Pain and humiliation engulfed me,
instead.

Our everyday existence - plain speaking, ordinary, rarely
dressing up, but with thousands of day-dreams. Mainly, our
neighbourhood of half-finished streets, new houses, and
farmland nearby appeared predictable. We had to entertain
ourselves.

In the city centre a half hour drive from home, many new
buildings butted the sky, the grand Post Office an exception, a
Victorian palace. People's messages mattered so much they were
treated like they'd been written by royalty. The domed ceiling of
the Post Office and our one glamorous picture theatre were
important architecture, almost as grand as romantic movie sets.
But my favourite ballroom chandeliers and various dreamy
cinema visions of mansions, sleek cars, resorts carved from
marble - those did not exist in our flat, quiet town.

Soundtracks, snacks and a completely different world up on the screen my blessed escape, living as someone else, believing this new story could last forever. Dissolving in celluloid visions any clue to the tracks which led back to home. No one could ever return me to spankings for a wrong word or something spilt by accident (I did benefit from hindsight eventually, connected pain with some misdeed even if the hurt far outweighed the crime, to my mind).

Knowing I never wanted any child of mind to suffer like I did. My legs stung while I waited under the flamingo painting in the hall. They hit you then they banished you.

At not older than five or six, I learnt to look like I knew better with silence. Plots to run away carefully planned beside that tall, pink painted bird. A known escape route did more for my good spirits than any idea of punishment being alleviated, if only I could 'behave' myself.

If we copied the way adults talked to us we got spanked. If we laughed when *they* did at something we didn't quite understand that meant we were *cheeky* and we got spanked. It was hitting. We were not allowed to hit anyone, but they were. They hit us at school for gazing out the window, for day-dreaming into the air, for lateness, for wearing no shoes, for singing too loud or not singing at all…. Hit for being children, plain and simple, but suggesting this earned a whack for *impertinence*. Enormous words brought in like guards, proof of their power.

Mysteries crowded our days, our blind world, nothing seen properly. In our mute, flat district, new people from nowhere arrived in their car, usually followed by a truck crammed with new things. They moved into our recently created street as if they'd always lived there. Smiled, kept complaints down to a dull roar, or behaved like troublesome things were invisible. When someone stole my blue rabbit then left this distinctive creature in the Cole's compost heap, my mother said it was probably not mine. She wouldn't listen to my saying, 'It's the rabbit my second cousin made me, *herself.* How could anyone else have one the same as me?'

Nobody much talked about things going wrong, except to deal out punishment swift and hard for interruptions, annoyances, and cheek. Few people discussed where they used to live either.

When children sometimes whispered that they missed someone back there in their old town, it apparently needed to be a secret. 'No point in dwelling on the past,' a mother would say in passing.

'What's done is done. Time to look ahead,' a father could agree. Words crowded in, they bundled important feelings and questions away with new meanings. Adults could change the scene with a sharp sentence, they cut out new pictures of the past to put in place.

My head full of jangly jagged things, clang, clang and pointy, I found taking pills Mum used for headaches dulled the edges. Life distant and fuzzy for a while. After pulling out the bottom drawer where newspapers were stored, I stepped up without rustling the papers with my toes if it was full. Then I slid a knee onto the cool bench, opened the high cupboard, smoothed and stretched myself up those shelves to the top. Finagled the bottle open in a few seconds, silently, with practice; I palmed the necessary pills, closed everything quietly on my way down and stood a while to get my breath. Two taken with water, sometimes three, a saving blur.

Company also helped with forgetting everything else. Crouched by the brick wall in the park to talk about earnest matters - how sore one's knee was after falling over, or who was invited to someone's birthday party, or what someone's mother could possibly mean when she said, 'You, girl, can't have a new dress, not for all the tea in China.'

We didn't think tea had anything to do with clothes, did it? If it did, how could we get some tea to swap for clothes we loved? A quiet girl who rarely spoke spat the word, 'Nut-cases,' at us, and ran off to climb a tree away from the crowd.

In the vast park, we clambered and bounced and swung on playground equipment our fathers had built. The poetry of our mutterings entertained the grasses, insects, and thousands of fairy-folk. I told everyone these magical beings inhabited the whole green area, including the gully. Invisible friends mattered hugely to me then. I populated my world with them and with a luxurious future, easy, pain-free. Imagination I could count on, always.

New words appeared to puzzle over. A father five houses away
looked darker than everyone else. Some said he was a Marrie.
Then he was gone, left for *the sticks* my dad said. I proclaimed to
my friends, 'He lives in a house of sticks piled together, like red
indians live in teepees.'
Someone else's wife looked like a Marrie, golden skin, dark hair
and eyes. Soon I discovered there were these people called
Maori who lived mostly in the country, and she was one. I asked
her about them. 'O you don't want to know about all that old
stuff, dear,' she told me.
One day her daughter explained her mum was adopted and
didn't know her real parents.
Week after week, more and more questions and discoveries.
One of the determined, crazy Cole boys dug into the clay bank
of the gully. We stood below amongst damp ferns and sodden
soil. Some of us shouted encouragement or directions, 'Make it
bigger. We can all get in then.'
In the ferny, damp gully, I asked, 'Isn't it wet and cold in there?'
Solid lumps of orange clay piled out behind his long, dirty, bare
legs. My worried comments kind of fell flat. Excavation debris
tumbled down the steep bank. Huge lumps of slippery stuff
plopped in the creek below. We moved out of the way after a
fair-sized clod hit a little kid on the arm and she squawked.
Someone shouted a strangled noise. I looked up. No gaping hole
there in the bank any more. The entrance had half fallen in.
The boy still inside with legs kicking.
Three boys scrambled up to the collapsed cave mouth, tugged at
the Cole boy's legs. One small lad full of orders, 'Grab him. Get
a spade.'
'No time, stupid,' the strongest one yelled, desperate to get his
friend free.
Muggy air pushed in on us, seven or eight locals mostly younger
than the 10 year old now buried in the clay. We watched from
under the gully trees, hot and damp. It'd rained only that
morning, now the sun blasted down. In sticky shade we could
see the boy's legs seemed to move less. My breath felt thick. How
would we ever explain this to Mr and Mrs Cole?
The bank enormous. Someone scrabbled further, over the lip of

the gully above, brothers from the corner. Two dark shapes
against a dappled sliver of sky.
A Svenson brother soon skidded back down with them. Tall for
his age, he swore continuously and dived for the collapsed cave,
cursing - some of the foulest words ever. No one told him off,
then with a strangled scream the Svenson eleven year old
dragged the Cole boy out by the heels. Both boys covered in
sticky orange clay and spluttering. 'Only just got him out before
he was buried so long he suffocated,' boasted the Svenson's
eldest.
The Cole boy looked so pale he was almost transparent.
They were a lanky, translucent lot the Cole children, never got
sunburnt or went brown. I sometimes wondered if they were
part fish.
After that excavation disaster I said, 'Everyone has to ask the
fairy folk first before we do anything. I'm the one to talk with the
fairies.' Ambitious ideas, which so many of us invented, now
needed to run past me.
'We could set fire to one of the fir trees for Guy Fawkes. Pine
cones on them. They'd really burn. It'd look neat.' Proud
inventor, little Jeremy stood arms akimbo showing off his
fabulous idea.
I replied, 'O yes. The fairy folk know all about those trees. I'll
just explain it to them.' I promised to relay a message, later
saying if the fairies would allow Jeremy's or anyone's latest
ludicrousness or not. Usually, I created a diversion, saying a fairy
told me a story. Explained elaborately how treasure was buried
in our own park, if only we knew the secret chant; or I made up
some game to play so they forgot what they'd said earlier. 'Fairies
like singing. We can each say a line for a song. The fairies could
leave a present for us.' Sometimes I left little dolls made of twigs
and leaves - fairy thank you gifts. Smaller children loved these.
Our supernatural guardians were held in high regard.
We never told an adult any of those loopy theories or plans.
Who would listen? We were far more reassured by the fairies
watching over us.
I behaved like the only child I wished I was at every opportunity
and managed myriad smaller children something like pets.

Youngsters responded with obedience or some manner of quiet, if I just pretended they were *much* smaller. Fairy entertainments assisted too. 'Shhh, the fairies are watching and they don't like noisy fighting.' From about seven years old, I'd cultivated a fine troupe of wide-eyed innocents to occupy my time (they needed stories, or trees and rain explained, that kind of thing). These tiny tots too silly and annoying for my thoughtless, brutal siblings to want to be near us. Thankfully.

I explained rain as, 'Angels crying, for all our little hurts. You know when you fall down, boom?'

The littlie would nod solemnly, sometimes with their bottom lip quivering.

'Well, the angels cry for those hurts. So we don't have to remember them.'

Trees were, 'The earth's laughter. Dirt can't talk can it?'

Wide-eyed shaking of their heads.

'So the earth laughs with trees. A little plant is a chuckle.'

Demonstrations of chuckles often needed to follow. Then we'd all be laughing, rolling over the grass, kicking up our legs in the sun.

My background plain to some perhaps, or *as clear as mud* like my father used to say as a joke - no matter how much anyone carefully explained something. Young 1950s married couples settled in with offspring along our new street of twenty-five weatherboard or brick houses, like an ad-exec-approved collection of same-age hopefuls in a brochure for real estate. Children found entertainment wherever possible, preferably out-of-doors, were not to bother the adults with anything, unless it made them laugh or had them crow, 'There's a good girl (or boy).'

Setting the table correctly inspired approval, as did saying *please* or *thank you*, and, also, spelling difficult words. My ability to reel off the letters for *manifestation* my father marvelled at, as if I'd built a TV from wood shavings and appeared there on a foreign show, with new vocab exact.

No adult ever appeared in our child-ruled park for long, except for the man on a tractor with a machine behind it who mowed the vast expanse of lawn. Other grown-ups' disembodied voices calling some inside for lunch or dinner. But in the park we rampaged, laughed, jeered, cried, imagined and plotted. We ran, skipped, jumped, slid, see-sawed and swung. We climbed, we lay on our backs and watched the clouds, lay on our fronts and observed insects in the grass. Older kids showed the young ones how to make daisy chains. We all knew to stay off the road if a car came.

Money arrived from somewhere, somehow, with magical qualities and could be turned into food, toasters, radios, trips to the big city, cars and clothes (no one had a television for many years early on, anywhere in the country, but eventually those too could be paid for). Now and then an adult gave us a coin to spend. Perhaps 'being good' was our job?

To complicate general fascination, in my last year at primary school, he appeared. Or he'd always been there, but I noticed him rather more than before.

Curly reddish hair and a slow walk like an actor who played not-so-good guys, but not always the really bad one (not as scary as Robert Mitchum), Ryan Caesar. His name could've appeared in the credits of any major motion picture and stunned the audience with its majesty.

Ryan also one of the chosen, privileged, a boy who went home for lunch.

Once Ryan walked in the school gate at 1pm, I ventured from my cubby behind the gardener's shed and casually called, 'Hello Ryan.'

Lots of Michaels, Peters, Johns and even a few Anthonys, but no other Ryans.

Sometimes he said hello weakly, with a puzzled expression.

Usually he ignored me, then raced towards the straggle of boys playing games on the enormous paddock, which teachers called *the playing field*, behind our classrooms. On the scrubby grass, children made up teams for soccer or rugby, occasional cricket or chasie, various versions - some ad hoc, invented that day.

Once my daily humiliation ended, when I'd said hello and Ryan sloped off, I wandered about. A group of girls, mean-mouthed or hard-eyed, suddenly behind a shield of silence when they saw me. I knew to take a wide berth there. What I liked was one or two, maybe three girls at a time, any who smiled nervously or called out my name with something like pleading in it, or just happiness.

From old chocolate boxes, we traded what we called stickers (but the cellophane packets we bought the embossed, joined pictures in were clearly labelled *Swaps*). We had to focus for this intensity, with each of us determined, and as tough as the razor strop our parents threatened us with at home. Also, trade needed the guile of a kitten sneaking up on a butterfly, just cute enough to seem innocent. Then *gotcha*. A successful trade allowed no deep romantic thoughts, nothing too friendly, but encouraged these on the surface of things, because they were beautifully distracting. We daren't be overly snobby, or the crowd would move away. It took experience to make sure whatever was swapped also benefitted the trader, or girls could lose a huge angel sticker for inferior, common flowers or nursery rhyme scenes, or (as mentioned), have the whole trading group up sticks and take their fun somewhere else.

Luckily, energetic teachers set up four squares painted together on concrete. Another, more physical pastime took place there. Players bounced a large, multi-coloured ball without touching any painted line, bounced it to another player, and they bounced it on inside the lines to stay 'in'.

Anyone with chalk in a pocket, or an eye for the best pale stone lying about, could draw a hopscotch on the concrete. If we got the wobbles or the giggles, lost our hop, then we were 'out'. My other foot would always come down to steady me (not allowed), when I tried to pick up the stone thrown to a particular distant square. Tired after about halfway through.

In winter, we skipped, and the celebrated girl with the dad who worked the sand barges brought a lengthy rope for *long* skipping. She chose who skipped, 'Altogether girls, this fine weather girls....'

American skipping arrived later, a loop of thin, white elastic held between two standing girls' legs akimbo. The third girl skipping made cat's cradle patterns with her feet.

On storm-ridden days girls huddled inside by radiators to chat

and read (boys sullen, inert, no running or play-fights inside).
But if the sun grew hot we girls lay around under trees,
camouflaged by shade. Few boys teased or showed off. The smell
of baked earth and old leaves somehow reminiscent of
afternoon teas of my mother's. The hot beverage also gave off a
heady aroma.

Talk inevitably turned to who liked whom. Convincing other
girls you liked *no one* required enormous skill. Any admission you
did like someone meant long minutes of swearing select girls to
secrecy first, then blushes and a reluctant, carefully timed, shy
admission.

Usually, in no time your secret quite ruined. Girl after girl fell
prey to tittle-tattles. The boy inevitably got told. You both fell
into a pit of boiling embarrassment. Love turned into something
akin to burnt pudding. The boy almost always made some nasty
remark to the bewildered girl, or he was furiously grumpy. All
boys shunned the girl. Feelings bloomed an outline target for
vandals.

No film romances for us in real life to escape the humdrum,
often scatter-brained, casual world of school, home and
neighbourhood.

My pretense at having no romantic ideas so professional I
could've been an actor at a young age. Girls pressed me for my
innermost desires, 'Tell us who *you* like, go on. We won't tell.'
'O I can't think about boys. I'm writing all my fairy stories at the
moment, in a *book*.' Even if I had scribbled a couple in the back
of last year's maths book, this subterfuge did make me feel guilty.
It made me think about my secret, and I didn't want to. Secrets
weighty, I preferred them to slide away into this deep pool
inside. Ideas best left alone simply submerged way down, dark
and silent, like a rock or a ripple of sand. With too many secrets,
however, the pool felt like it could rise then and swamp
everything. Every time a new secret slid into the darkness the
level crept up. Sometimes weight needed shifting out.

A rainy day mid-week, and so many people shut inside our
school. But two of us found the cloakroom empty and sat by
coats hung on pegs, some a little damp. Moira and I nibbled on
home-made cakes from our plastic lunch-boxes. She smiled.

'Mine's Louise cake, what's yours?'
'O, this is Mum's chocolate slice. Secret recipe from my Gran.
Want to swap half of each?'
'Okay.' No hesitation.
This girl didn't snitch or snap either. Moira Jenkins could
possibly be trusted. 'I really like Ryan,' I blurted, in our
seclusion. Felt like I'd set off a firecracker.
Moira's eyes widened. 'So do I.'
Whispers ensued with some consternation, damp cloakroom air
about us. Cakes forgotten.
'I *know*,' I smiled, 'we'll share him.' Mind cleared, I felt like I
could bounce with happiness. We arose to get back into the
classroom, by one of the heaters, polishing off our cakes now as
we walked.
'Oh, but how would that work?' Moira asked.
'Well, we can both like him.' My smile perfect, a mask. Any
thought of complaint shunted away with cheeriness, just like the
adults who grinned away trouble in our street.
Ryan barely spoke to either of us, anyway. Maybe Moira shared
my realisation. Immediately, she mentioned, 'It's Ryan's birthday
this coming week.'
'Let's buy him a present.' Planning ensued. We'd give a gift to
Ryan when he arrived back from lunch. 'No one else will see it,
and he could be happy to get a present,' I said.
We both loved the idea of seeing Ryan happy.

Moira and I stood in clear sight on the school driveway the next
week.
Coloured pencils seemed safe, they could look as if his mum
gave them to him at lunchtime.
He walked lost in thought, then slowed down. Us girls ahead in
full skirted dresses with too-tight bodices - we grew so fast that
year. We grinned and offered the bright cardboard packet.
He blinked.
We babbled on about Happy Birthday.
He took the gift, nodded briefly, put the offering in his shorts'
pocket. Kept on going like he did every day. If anything he
walked faster but somehow looked much older. It was like he'd

turned into a middle-aged man who didn't like talking to giggly girls.

I gaped after him.

Both Moira and I shook a little in strong sun on the asphalt driveway by the little wooden shed, where free school milk for every child had once been delivered each morning. So much history to do with that one spot, toings and froings, and now this peculiarity. Neither of us touched the other but we stood close. We watched Ryan disappear to the back of the school, where everyone had to play if not in class.

The day was sunny and clear.

He never spoke to nor looked at either of us ever again.

The action of being accepted or rejected is continuous, and we surely learnt about rejection that day. It wasn't that we exactly wanted to catch him, however, we just both felt that reaching out with our small token could've lightened our lives and his, perhaps. Lately, I see some people live more in a bubble than others, and also, we were told in time that girls do not chase boys.

Moira and I barely spoke with each other much either, for years. Something buried and forgotten, well gone, before we shared anything close to a confidence again. Our differences apparent. I'd risk anything for love (Katherine Mansfield unknown to me then, but like her I still prefer to face the most difficult truth, to see what eventuates). Whereas Moira grew more likely to keep her ideas and feelings hidden, unless she felt reasonably sure of the result being favourable.

Gradually I gathered people all held different viewpoints, and life rarely matched any TV or movie plot, but it took a long time to realise this was something to whole-heartedly accept.

In and Out of the Frying Pan

That girl, the girl, true girl,
rising from the waves.

My Aphrodite, come an' say,
how'd you stay afire through all those storms?

- Electric Azure 1970

My aunty handed over a small wooden box with a leather
handle, like a tiny suitcase, one spring day. 'It's a surprise.'
Inside, after opening the little clasp, all these small tubes of
paint.
'They were your grandmother's. Gran Florence's oil paints. Nice
wooden box, isn't it?' she said.
Colours in metal tubes, some smeared to mix long ago on the
tan wood and now dry. The little leather strap on the outside
well-worn, each brush stiff and properly cleaned. A whiff of
turps. My grandmother once touched these. She'd chosen paint
to work into a still life painting now hanging on our wall.
An uncle showed me how to layer strokes. 'Colour and shapes
mix together. The eye makes different shades and tones blend,
even if they're dots or dashes of paint.'
Variations of trees daubed on creamy paper from a pad of
genuine Art Cartridge, for an entire summer. Painting engrossed
me. Everything else disappeared. Gran Florence also knew this
joy.
A while later, I gathered I mainly liked to play in my serious
moonlight with words. Scanned a book so fast my mother said
she was scared to watch me. By my teens, I'd read volumes
about writers who took true Risks (yes, with a capital letter),
travelled alone on sailing ships to find a lost love, left the country
on a dream, defied their parents, eloped with lovers... A few
absorbed so much information they traveled the world giving
talks to let words free. Notable writers created odd but
recognisable characters : a Cheshire cat, Long John Silver and
Tom Sawyer, Jo in Little Women (also a writer), the gawky Anne

of Green Gables - an orphan, but clever and amusing. Every
one on paper with something about them reminiscent of people
I'd met or wished I knew.

Writers solitary, tapping away on typewriters, scrawling in
notebooks. Artistic license a gift, it had to be used or get wasted.
Hiding a wonderful birthday present in a cupboard would be
almost as bad.

Finding out about the world required Risks. Climbing trees and
inventing fairies no longer adequate. Behind the fear which this
idea produced lay the unknown. I planned to explore it.

A plate of bloody steaks on a table above a chilly bin full of ice
and beer at a barbecue and this stranger beside it smiled at me.
Surely a Risk, he held my eyes like a man in an ad for chocolates
or perfume. I smiled back.

Older, he wore a suit as effortlessly as friends back home wore
their jeans. 'I'm so out of place,' he muttered and broke our
gaze, eyed my summer frock and sandals.

I told him his suit looked cool, 'You could be a model in an ad,
like at the movies.'

This appeared to really please him, but he kind of hid his smile.
'You could be a model too.' His eyes played over my face like he
knew me from somewhere, and wanted to recall who I was.

I wondered if this man had any idea I was a kid from out of
town; was he just being kind? Or was this a taste of Real
Romance?

My silence encouraged him. 'I'm Hampton, by the way.' He
talked softly but with authority, 'You suit white. Your golden skin
and that dark hair, the contrast.'

I smiled shyly. 'I've been sunbathing. My mother's part-Spanish.
We tan so easily.'

'In Havana, Cuba - you know, in the tropics, men wear white
suits. They're to repel the sun's rays and keep people from
overheating.' Hampton then segued on to books he'd read, films
he liked, and cars he'd owned.

I kept on smiling and nodding. Occasionally, I kind of hummed
as if almost singing, to be agreeable.

Eventually Hampton asked, 'Would you like to go out to dinner some time soon?'

Secretly, I hoped his conversation wasn't always an endless list of
marvellous things he'd done or owned, but also, felt pleased to
think I'd eat at a fancy restaurant. 'Lovely. When?' My white A-
line mini-dress with inserts of cut-out daisy shapes around the
neckline (borrowed from my aunty for the barbecue), new dark
eyeshadow, and pearly lipstick - these made me look *so grown-up*.
I wished I felt older too, and smiled to cover my confusion, but
maybe he liked the fact I couldn't think of anything to say? An
older woman would comment, offer her own ideas. I'd seen
them do so. But any disparaging opinion I stuffed into a dark
corner of my thoughts, like a cheeky child who had been
punished for one too many heedless remarks knew how to hide
their bright ideas.

My aunty believed in girls being independent. She didn't mind
me going out to dinner with friends. It wasn't a terrible lie. He
was *one* friend. New. But (I had to ask myself), what made
friends? Perhaps he wasn't quite there yet but soon he could be (I
fooled myself).

Risks sometimes meant making things up or letting things be a
little more than they really were. My mental notes growing so
complicated, meshed into dark clouds. I hummed songs I liked
to stop thinking so much.

Cream expensive furnishings and delicious aromas, Burt
Bacharach's *What do You Get when You Fall in Love?* tinkled with
background almost-grooviness in the place Hampton took me to
the next evening. Frosted globe lights floated above white linen
tablecloths. Most patrons rather like my grandparents - grey and
small. Even if the luxurious setting oozed safety, I could appear
like a silly girl. This led to a decision to move as little as possible,
like someone in a film if they don't have many lines.

Hampton in the leading role. He pointed out the tablecloths
were real linen, as if I needed to know. For those few seconds I
suspected he seldom patronised these places himself. But in a
moment Hampton explained why it was best to order the
crayfish and appeared so in control, I almost wanted to leave just

to see if he could tug me back with unseen strings. Without waiting for an answer he read the wine list to himself, the folder held high, his face obscured. My idea of a rare steak blinked out and *he* told the waiter what we'd eat and drink.

The waiter smirked for some unknown reason. I then felt like a little kid out with her dad, and hoped the waiter wasn't smiling that way to get at me somehow. Although Hampton was nowhere near as old as my father, he just behaved like he deserved to decide everything. But the man at the next table ordered for his wife too. I copied how she looked at him admiringly with her head low, except I regarded *Hampton* in that way. I turned into a cat. Difficult to tell what cats were thinking - that same blank expression, except if they relaxed their eyes did close a little, or they'd purr when truly happy. Cats also purred randomly. If I purred, Hampton would...what? I giggled. Hampton glared at me, and as if his eyes made a noise like *shhh*, I fell silent.

A clever writer like Mr Lewis Carroll could tell me this was definitely a Huge Risk, allowing someone like, well, like *him*, the writer, *a grown man* to make decisions. What other activities would Hampton then prescribe? I needed to Beware; (capitalising important words was so fashionable in those teen years). My thoughts raced. A warning signal in mind, Beware was yellow. Highly visible and a little icky.

A movie script would call for the woman in my place to do something about now; not an extra in the background any longer. I ignored that Beware sign. Hampton's foot against mine under the table, I moved my shoe toe gently against his shoe, like a famous actress did in a film, once. He nudged me back. Our footsie a Definite Risk. What nudging each others' feet actually meant had eluded me, but a warm feeling developed, like I could laugh about it later. This felt as dangerous as reaching through the bars of a zoo cage to tickle a tiger.

A mix of emotions as if on a fast ride at a fair; the glittering eyes of carnies, girls screaming from garish lit carriages zooming through the air. I moved my foot away.

My skin still tingled, but it felt like I needed someone, a friend, to make sure things went okay.

Instead of mentioning anything about my unease, I chattered on about a favourite film. 'Loved the music. They...'
Hampton asserted, 'Sounds silly.' Instantly described a far better one.
No one took much notice of us.
Eventually we ate crayfish the way he demonstrated. Pinching the sides of the tail 'til it crunched. I did this but it seemed cruel. 'The poor things.'
Hampton reminded me they were *cooked*. 'With smaller ones you could just break off the head, then suck the meat from the tail.'
'O, shrink.' I blushed, my face so hot I could've grilled another crayfish in front of it. Hated myself for using kiddish slang, too. No adult said *shrink* when they felt embarrassed. 'I'm used to cutting them. Uh, guess we have finger bowls because of all this man-handling?'
'Man-handling? Now?' His smile lit up his eyes, almost like a teenager again.
Busy with the main course, I hoped my hot face didn't mean more blushing. Was this our very own racy movie? But I never liked Diana Dors, the way she shoved her chest at people.
In a major motion picture Hampton could be a know-it-all college graduate who visited a small town and learnt to be real. We were *real*, my friends and I back home, especially when anyone offered glib insults, horribly real like a slap. We were *wonderfully* real. Hampton needed lessons in *real* even if he did know how to buy a fancy dinner with glasses of wine, out on the town.
Mum often said *out on the town*. Then I imagined taking him to meet Mum and Dad. Mum smiling bravely, like when we had to go to hospital for tests (but then found I only had some virus). Dad polite but cold, like when he had to talk to the neighbour about making sure he kept the hedge trimmed at the beach when we holidayed there. The man that everyone knew had just got out of jail. *Too* real. *Beware.* As strange as the drunk who shouted at the bus-stop near breakfast-time. He stunk of spirits. Mum took me home, said we'd forgotten her list, but I knew it was in her bag.
Despite the delicious food, I almost walked from the expensive

place. Wine-blurry thoughts, like with painkillers I'd
surreptitiously taken at home now and then - a soft effect, fine,
just fine. Still, it seemed better to leave. Rude to walk out,
certainly, but how ridiculous and dangerous to stay? I'd wobble
on those high heels, though - could stumble, fall. Walking alone,
dressed up....

Easier to silently research Hampton with mental notes in case I
wrote movies one day, packed with danger. Not a film starring
Diana Dors. I'd be Kim Novak or perhaps Elizabeth Taylor, or
Sophia Loren. Stars who could play me grew more and more
gorgeous. Food almost went up my nose when I laughed,
imagining Elizabeth Taylor climbing a pine tree. She'd never go
up our knobbly stick-riddled things, and Sophia Loren in our
clunky new street with stones on the road? She'd look like a
pedigree cat on a junk pile. Kim Novak in our great big paddock
of a park? Even if she wore jeans, she'd look like an orchid with
a bunch of common old daisies.

Hampton sighed, mentioned the food didn't make *him* laugh.
My face fell so I covered with a cough, saying, 'Hope I'm not
catching the flu.' Made myself look composed. Children where I
came from learnt this skill early, or suffered a smack. Our formal
evening like a tense sticker trade at school when I was much
younger. If I didn't keep my secrets, let them slide down deep,
I'd be shown up for the youngster I pretended *not* to be.
Hampton looked like a bodgie then, such a sly look in his eyes.
Unable to think of him in a temper without the sound of
something breaking. Then once more, with the thought of a
walk along city streets through the evening alone, I decided I
liked the pale restaurant enough. Anyway, grown-ups kept
secrets, important private ideas. Good Training for Maturity.
Certainly, much hidden securely from my brothers who'd made
a career of wrecked dolls and shredded fluffy toys. The bullies at
school, too. Many of us learnt how to pretend around them so
they were never annoyed. Men had tempers. We had to watch
out.

I also wriggled with something like glee at the idea of not telling
Hampton my true age, even if this felt frightening beyond just a
thrill from telling a lie. Secrecy intermingled with intense love

affairs made the best movies. I sipped more wine. Fantasy
needed a flavour of mystery; a recipe or.... no, *a formula*, yes,
definitely - this was scientific. In a haze, surrounded with genteel
people, none of whom looked like they'd ever tricked others, I
half-believed my parents could understand my reasoning if they
were ever told what I'd done.
Also, in films like West Side Story and Romeo and Juliet, those
young lovers cared so much and kept on together, even when
others tried to stop them. Hampton and I, our kiss in the
moonlight, his whispered promises, perfectly lit. *True love keeps
people together, lifts us from dull routines like a blessing ensures goodness,
love takes couples to starry rendezvous,* I told myself.
I only recalled the fevered beginnings of those films. I hadn't
figured out that if those young characters truly loved each other,
and asked their parents to end the feud - persuaded the families
to be friends, those lovers could've stayed alive.

On the radio at my aunty's a philosopher explained, 'Evil is
attractive. It's easy to like.' They also said it may eventually grow
to appear more rewarding to choose decent, kind actions
instead. '...because evil only attracts more evil and then it undoes
itself, often in a terrible manner. We tire of the mess, the chaos.'
Listening to that show with only half a mind, thinking that
nothing was all bad, I hurried to get my make-up on another
night, preparing to go out.
The city a golden swarm of traffic and people here and there.
Street after street of artfully lit shops and places to eat. Decor,
music, and food - everything swam together under genius
direction. Holiday Auckland - Hampton took me to Italian
places, steak houses, a Swedish smorgasbord, then a Chinese
banquet on the top floor of a hotel. Visiting the world with our
appetites. Fragrant pizza, mozzarella cheese, oregano, garlic, fat
black olives, mushrooms, tomato; a pepper steak sizzling on the
plate when it arrived - the knife melted through it, green beans
and mashed potato on the side; pickled herrings at the
smorgasbord as beautiful as funky jewellery, crisp lettuce, fresh
tomato. Dark rye bread and I exclaimed, 'It's delicious. Looks
like nothing on Earth I've ever seen but I love it.'

Hampton laughed with pleasure. 'I love how you enjoy what I show you.'

Wontons at the Chinese place, fascinating parcels of crisp pastry, quickly deep fried with a filling of vegetables or spicy meat. Fluffy white rice, crisp stir-fried carrot, onion, cauliflower, cabbage, sliced bamboo shoot. Dumplings steamed then served in delicious sauces and the soup, 'O it's like a painting, that moves. Everything floats and makes a picture.'

Again, Hampton laughed. 'You say the most amazing things.'

My aunty breezed replies to my plans. She'd smile. 'You'll be fine. Glad you've made friends.' Aunty never asked who the friends were. Just went back to her book, crossword, or telephone call.

After our fourth or fifth lavish dessert that week, this one dancing with blue brandy flames, I wished aloud, 'Fish and chips on a park bench could be fun some time.'

His cracked laugh seemed to dismiss the idea, but Hampton next took me to Mission Bay. A takeaway by the grand fountain where multi-colours gushed against the sky and beach backdrop.

Later, a tangerine sun disappeared behind gloomy ranges ahead. We drove and he stopped for ice creams at a dairy. Wallet in the glove box, Hampton asked me to get some cash. When he'd gone

I sneaked a look at his drivers' license. Only 15 years older. *Not so ancient, hardly a crumbling ruin, not so scary,* I thought. Except the difference in our ages was more than my whole age, my entire lifetime.

My heart *plop plop plop*, like I'd been running, but no bright yellow Beware sign flashed in my mind. I just breathed slowly, like the time I got stitch running cross-country at school. Told myself it was fine to go to his place. My aunty knew I'd gone to Mission Bay, and I'd told her Hampton's full name. I'd just never said how old he was, that's all.

While Hampton had asked me my age, so he could feel sure it was okay for me to drink during our swish dinners, I'd never asked him the same. Now, knowing he was so much older, even if I stood tall I really *felt* my just-turned 13 years, and guilt, too, for

lying. I was 21 as far as he knew, or pretended to know. I had to
be that old to be permitted alcohol anywhere in public.
Everywhere we went I wore my fashionable aunty's cool clothes,
and lots of make-up. Possibly I appeared around 18 or 19, and
most restaurants just let us drink with dinner. Only one waiter
had asked to see my driver's license. When I said I didn't drive,
they'd politely refused to allow me wine with our food.
Parked in the suburban street now opposite the Busy Bee Dairy,
waiting in his car, I noticed a bus had just pulled in ahead. Plain
two-tone green and yellow, the bus half-full. Everyday, ordinary
life, each passenger just themselves on public transport heading
home. A few people alighting from the bus held rolled up,
sodden towels or striped beach bags. They'd enjoyed a swim
some place. I'd liked to have gone swimming, and imagined
catching the bus, a bumble to the end of the line. I'd pay to
return to the city. It'd only be one more bus ride, later, from
there to aunty's place. Safe.
I could climb out of this vehicle and back to something easier,
any time, do it now. Not late yet.
On flatter land below me the view stretched on and on, rooftops, roads, and trees. No one could ever know all those people.
The enormous city swallowed most of us, gone. No idea what'd
happen next. Overwhelming, it felt like being drunk, but
promising - even though part of me wanted to run.
In Hampton's car, on an ordinary street at the end of the day, I
just floated in my mind like I'd walked off into the sky. For a few
minutes, I wondered - *What stops me leaving?* Hadn't I wished to
be free of my brothers' torments, of teachers and adults hitting
us, of punishments and strangeness? But now here I was with
this man, this older man who could definitely hurt me. We told
such horror stories at school. But what shape could a solution
take? No idea if any way out existed, or what to do to fit this
mystery, open it and reveal the core motivation so it was easily
dismantled, made into spare parts. If someone told me they
could stop it all, would I agree?
Hampton strode back across the road, sat down, leaned over me
in his car and kissed me with his mouth open, warm and slightly
wet. His tongue slid into my mouth. I did my best not to open

my eyes in shock. The kiss quick, like he wanted to make sure he could.

He handed me my treat. 'Got a present for you at home, too.'

My bottom lip felt a little sore, like it could be bruised. I just sat there.

We drove, listened to some soft rock radio station that I tried to ignore.

As certain as a ride at a fair, like I'd paid money and had to stay. A niggly feeling ensued, but I just sat there. The realisation arrived as surely as if someone plopped a cold wet towel over my head and shoulders - it was doubtful anything good could happen from then on. I fought the urge to openly wipe my mouth, looked out the window and put my left hand to my lips out of his sight, scrubbed with small movements the way mice clean their noses. Then I ate my chocolate dipped vanilla.

Inside his huge, dark, many-windowed house that was surrounded by massive trees, Hampton opened champagne and produced a gold box. 'Just for you.'

The box looked like something my mother would sniff at and call *cheap and nasty*. Inside, a pair of black patent leather stilettos lay like strange fish on tissue paper. Hampton beamed. 'Try them.'

Tissue paper soft. Shiny shoes. My stomach ached as if his black and grey furniture pushed at me.

Hampton believed he deserved more than a quick, wet kiss in his car. 'Try on something else too?'

Soon my body would dislocate and fly off in different directions, legs one way, arms somewhere else, my head rolling and spinning out the window. The house isolated, no bus home would rumble past now. And Hampton could get nasty if I asked to leave. But I wanted to know how he saw me. What 'something else' did he have for me? Curious, I smiled, also hopeful I'd devise an exit soon.

The bag of clothes he handed over felt light. A negligee like in a corny old spy film? Hands clammy, I undid the fancy, expensive packaging. Fabric inside smooth and silky. The maid's costume frilly, and so short I almost shrieked with laughter, but instead skipped away to change in the bathroom then sauntered back. Managed the high heels rather well. Did a few silly poses in his lounge. Flipped up the teeny skirt to show my frilly knickers. Pouted at him.

He eyed me from a leather chair by the fireplace.

I pretended to dust the bookcase, looked the other way a moment and gazed out over vast trees and ferns on his property, endless tracts of wild bushland. When I looked down at the frilly skirt and giggled however, I fell backwards, cried with laughing on his black leather sofa. Kicked my legs in the air. Asked him through the tears if he'd like to catch the flu and I'd wear a nurse's outfit? 'Ooo Hampton, let me get you a Disprin and kiss it better ....' My laughter and prattle stopped as fast as a bag of sand hitting concrete, when I took a good look at Hampton's face - as dark as the hills he lived in.

He insisted on driving me home and spoke in this far-too-even way, as if every word had to seem heavy to stop him screaming. 'Just get in there. Change. Now.'

I snapped, 'I never asked *you* to wear any special clothes.'

He snarled, '*I know* how to dress, thank you.' Hampton shouted, 'Show me some respect.'

I retorted, 'A maid's costume hardly shows *me* any respect.'

He shouted, 'Do you have any imagination?' His hand slapped a low table and a streaked blue, red, black and yellow vase on it jumped, then toppled. It fell to the carpet and the art glass shattered against the table leg but he ignored it.

I yelled, 'A cliché is hardly creative. Only wanted a laugh, to go out for dinner. You're much, much older than me. You do *know* that, surely? Or are you just a *stupid dirty old man*?'

He shouted, 'Do not tell the *entire* neighbourhood *my* business.' Tempting to scream that it was his *business* then, being a dirty old man? But I didn't.

For a few long seconds, Hampton's face was like a collapsed balloon, more wrinkly than usual and his eyes glazed. I hoped he now really considered how young I sounded and behaved. Great that he mentioned the neighbours. People could hear us, see us. He knew that. In a chair, Hampton covered his eyes with one hand. He whispered, 'It's the shoes, anyway. I love the shoes.

Wear them again?'
In disbelief, I snapped, 'High heels are hard to walk in, Hampton.'
He wondered aloud if we had that much in common after all. Opera or ballet fantasies, where I'd wear a fur coat through the city, like a movie with us starring in a love story that could *only* end in a white dress and a dark suit, a gorgeous chandelier reception... childish fancies dissolved as easily as cake disintegrates in a rain storm at a picnic. I babbled, 'Sorry, I really am sorry. O Hampton.' My hands flapped. 'Didn't think. Couldn't we stay friends?'
Hampton drove me home in complete silence.

After a day imagining he'd miss me, I left one wan message on his fancy imported answer-phone, and said I hoped he'd call me. I risked leaving aunty's home number (this was years before cellphones).
My charade of playing older, telling myself I was only researching romance and taking risks for inspiration – something more exciting than playing Gin Rummy with my aunty or shopping with her for new pantyhose, or more than my love for the city and fancy places. So much tangled together like junk jewellery left in a drawer opened and closed, tossed about. My desperate need for affection remained, but I'd lost the man supplying a close second to that (any attention at all).
Hampton seemed to have given up on me.
Cried myself to sleep a few times.

My summer holiday ended and I caught the bus to our smaller town, south.
When the bus pulled in, people waiting stepped forwards, faces brighter when the person they knew disembarked. They walked away to snug cars, their cosy houses. I did the same when my mother found me and we drove home. 'Yes, it was fun, Mum. The city's got lots to do.' I described swept-up shops, answered questions about my aunty (my Dad's sister). 'She's still into crosswords, yes. Does a huge one every week in a magazine.'
Behind small talk an immense nothing of something

unexplainable.

Only just in my teens, the stories I later told to friends about this older man sounded too loud. I whispered. 'He wanted me to, y'know, dress up, and go to expensive restaurants. We drank wine. Then, well, he took me to his place. It got a bit uncool.' One friend gasped, 'He hurt you?'

'No, no, nothing like that. I just laughed at him. I....'

'You stupid idiot. He could've taken your virginity. Ruined you forever.' A few were scathing.

Others didn't believe a word, 'As if a grown man would believe *you* were 21, as if. Little liar.'

My better friends hinted I'd soon get over it, 'Think yourself lucky he never hurt you.' Pushed aside their disbelief and envy enough to feel sorry for me. We'd go to the movies or the park, stopped talking about my escapades. Memories worn vaguer, and time diffused poisonous possibilities.

Strange dreams about dark hills recurred, however, and I'd awaken gasping for breath. Terrified, like the way I should've been at the time, instead of pretending nonchalance. Streams of fragmented memories unrelated, but to do with hurt and humiliation, flickered through my mind - at some times more vividly than others; flashbacks, oddly enough whenever I smelt Jaffas. He ate them in his car, the interior scented with orange and chocolate.

When I was older, working in sales, a return to Auckland city sounded exciting. Our manager as delighted as a tourist on a free trip. Our training proved useful. She wanted to reward us, insisted we try this new place. Six of us walked into the Thai Palace past gold screens. A red wallpapered room opened. This restaurant near the city's most exclusive shopping area with the funkiest expense.

Right after I'd sat down Hampton walked in, with a tall woman on his arm. They eased into chairs across the restaurant from us. My newly blonde hair was by then long past my shoulders - unlike my darker, shorter style before, and I wore specs. My face had slimmed down. I doubted he'd know me after eight years, but didn't stare.

It felt like secretly watching a play I hadn't paid to see.

Every ten minutes or so, Hampton spoke to the blonde woman. She arose to slink past tables to the bar, then back with a toothpick, a serviette, or a drink, as if she starred in a fantasy getaway travel ad. Hampton kept glancing at her shoes, high, black Loubotin heels with trademark red soles flashing while she walked. Hampton gently rubbed the fingers and thumb of one hand together as if imagining he touched something sumptuous, or signalled something to do with money.

His companion only a little older than me, in her twenties, with brown hair to just below her ears, similar to how I once wore mine. In profile, a tilted nose like mine, too.

A chill across my chest as if a draught of cold air entered the room and found my heart. I looked away. Delicately sliced, spiced vegetables (arranged to resemble a tumble of lovely flowers), on saffron rice, and every forkful delicious.

In a well-fed haze after ordering dessert, I considered my slim dark friend who I hoped would be my boyfriend soon, one year older than me back home. His jeans and overalls on weekends, the way he laughed loud and long. He rarely minded whatever I wore, most often just said I looked great. I hadn't found a matching Hampton. But he found a look-alike me - a doll to dress up?

As sudden as someone slamming a door, I recalled the editor of the school paper (and captain of two sports teams), from years before. We all felt a little afraid of him. Risky before I thought the concept needed emphasis.

In my arm a tremor again, like someone ran a chilly finger along my skin just enough for me to know they touched me.

My best friend Blossom went to this boy's house. Later she told me, 'He has dolls. Blonde hair and specially made clothes.' This control-freak told Blossom that his future girlfriend would wear those outfits. He asked what size *she* was. My friend left as soon as she drank the promised strawberry milkshake made with a real milkshake maker. Brimming with the story, she'd raced to my place.

A few days later in Auckland, on our business trip, I shopped nearby.

The way she laughed with little *pfff* sounds made me turn my head. Hampton and his friend browsing a designer store. Easy enough for me to lurk by the accessories and watch them.

A shake of his head and Hampton kept saying *no*, every time she held up a top or dress with a smile. Instead, he chose dresses without consulting his girlfriend, checked the size and took them to the counter. His lovely companion kept on admiring racks of beautiful fashion, dress-hangers clicked against each other. He bought women's clothing, then handed the bag to her.

Spinning on his heel, Hampton walked back and also purchased a necklace of long bronze chains.

The woman gazed about the store and met my eyes. She looked a little like a lioness, large eyes. Except, her eyes widened even more in fright when I smiled a little. It felt as if I'd looked into a cage, saw someone in there and they knew they had to let me know they were trapped and to leave them alone, without making a sound.

Soon I surmised my friendly look truly scared her, but of course I had no real idea why she looked that way. You couldn't have friends around a man like Hampton, surely? They'd criticise him or he'd try to add them to his collection. Quickly, I examined catches on five or six extravagant beaded purses.

In a haze of Muzak, the couple walked out.

I wandered over to the clothes the woman admired, wondered if she left a note in a pocket, but each appeared flat, sewn up for retail presentation. Nothing remained of her, no space where a garment was taken because she chose it, no bus ticket or other ephemera dropped, not even the lingering scent of her perfume. Along the street outside, traffic flowed then stopped, flowed then stopped.

Oddly, I wanted to follow, tell Hampton who I was and maybe flirt a little to see.... The thud in my stomach told me I was more foolish than I'd ever been, to think I should ever associate with such a man again. He'd paid me attention once for a few weeks but it'd felt like a training session for an elaborate circus act. I kept thinking of one of those cages on wheels - they still had those then for circus animals - brightly painted - red and yellow, touches of gold and blue, some black.

Hurriedly, I chose a couple of beaded purses and spent hours wondering why I bought two of them. My manager liked the one I gave her, but for ages I wished I'd kept it.

Caught in Music

It could've been bliss to hold you like this,
but when I awake I discover your tricks.

   - Lyana by Tom Banton 1970

On the sunny side, afternoon warmth through the window,
riding along only two from the back. Daydreaming in the rattly
bus with its particular syncopated rhythm - like I was small
again, carried by a large woman on her hip. Gazed out the
window and thought whatever I pleased, I idly designed a few
outfits I wanted to sew - imagined what I'd look like with an
afro.

The bus pulled into a stop near the end of town. A few people
got on, swayed, grabbed hold of upright chrome poles to swing
down and find a seat. With a haughty stare he swept along and
plopped down next to me. 'I hear you're having a birthday
party?'

'Uh, yes. Yes, I am.' I stared at this older boy, tried to recall his
name. Quickly looked away. He was talking to *me*? Remembered
I'd given him cheek sometimes, on late-shopping Friday nights.
Oddly fun by the bright shops to see him sneer or snipe back. I'd
laughed; but now felt unsure.

'Why don't you invite me?' He dragged his dark reddish hair
back behind one ear, with a single hooked finger.

Made me feel like a furry animal in a pet shop. A potential
owner wanted a good look at me. My stomach flipped. Usually,
on my bus ride home from high school, I sat with my girlfriends
- but none of them that day stared intently from a few seats
away (they usually loved intimidating outsiders). What could I
say by myself to create distance between us? His name, snippy
and quick - like he didn't matter. *O Mark, my party?* Yes, that was
it, Mark. But would he like my crowd of friends? He'd probably
criticise. They'd mutter. My happy birthday could be more like a
funeral, or just a flop.

I'd also seen him once or twice at the Saturday afternoon movies
and around our local shops, most often only in passing. Mark,

always with older teenagers, nose in the air like a general or politician in a play. His lofty expression for some unknown reason provoked me to drop smart remarks into the conversation when any chance appeared. Handsome nevertheless, nice wide mouth and large blue eyes (even if he rather slitted them half-closed at times), long, quite thick auburn hair just past his ears. Good looking, if his arrogance could be ignored, and stylish. Our isolated pale suburb in a prone town surrendering to the enormous sky. Everything seemed to have to be the same as same could ever be. But stylish people produced the promise of adventure, excitement, or just plain pleasure with seeing their attractiveness and daring. Mark wore a co-ed school's dress code, casual mufti with long pants. They allowed their 7th formers longer hair. I silently noted details to record them later in my diary.

Sitting close to someone intriguing who wanted an invitation to my birthday party? Entranced, even if against the bus window my shoulder felt cold despite sunshine streaming in, while the vehicle lurched along.

Tabloid press didn't get delivered to our house or anyone else's nearby. Scandal wasn't daily fodder. No one ever sat me down either and explained good looks could indicate that the latest charmer (who I maybe noted as if they were a rare bird), had relied on how attractive they appeared to others to make an impression, so they didn't develop good character. No such conversations at home and if I ever attempted to start one elsewhere, about what people really meant, or what certain behaviour could lead to, friends and acquaintances shied away like scared horses near a snake. Information readily available in movies, magazines, and many books usually promoted the idea that someone attractive needed to find somebody else who'd look good with them (perhaps for wedding pictures, later). Simple.

Younger girls sat behind us on our bus trip home, under strong sun in the blue sky. A summer like many others was made plumb new and astonishing by events that day. Many eyes and ears on alert, a disbelieving silence. The girls watched and listened, as closely as cats lurked in bushes and waited to pounce on noisy blackbirds rustling something up in fallen leaves and mulch. A sensation.

I did invite Mark to my birthday party, almost right away. The countless thoughts that'd crowded in on me were easily dismissed by my decision to take a risk (which by then had diminished to a word usually unworthy of capitalising - surely proof of my maturity).

My dad had said numerous times that teens with shaggy haircuts were cavemen (as if they hunted woolly mammoth and grunted), but this boy talked fine. And I doubted he'd ever used any kind of weapon (*except those blue eyes,* my cheeky aunty in Auckland would say).

Mark made me think of fast drums and *taboo,* a strange word my aunty muttered when viewing certain items on TV news. Through years of sameness and nowhere conversations I'd wanted to feature in a startling broadcast to the nation. Maybe soon stepping inside that TV at last, where happily ever after occurred over and over again until the credits rolled, official writing - lists there on the screen a special seal, the proof of quite an authentic tale.

Our bright orange phone at my parents' could've melted. Furious chat zipped between my girlfriends and I for the weeks we endured to my party. 'Who is he?'

Opinions varied from, 'Arrogant idiot,' to, 'Plays in a band, I think,' and, 'Peculiar,' to, 'Much older than us. Why does he want to come to your party?'

On a rounded vinyl chair, curled up with the phone, I smiled my stay-happy-think-the-best smile and refused to consider any answers to pointed questions about why Mark wanted to attend my birthday, except, 'He likes me.' Never uttered those words, simply stated, 'I don't know.' A touch of worry in the tone; people could think I was naïve. This felt better than anyone realising I *wanted* peculiar, arrogant, older Mark at my party - that I loved the idea of him appearing in my actual house. (Not that I realised my attitude until later, while writing this, in fact). Passive aggressive was a term I'd never heard of, and excitement overrode difficulties, quandaries, or syndromes. This behaviour appeared as easily as a teenager exuberantly bounded into a

room and claimed it as their own, as if no one else had ever
spoken or existed there.

On a dizzy day pre-party, I dusted, vacuumed, retrieved odd
and distasteful things from inside the sofa and chairs (old socks,
half-eaten biscuits, a piece of hardened cheese, three wooden
spoons my brothers hid from Mum so she couldn't hit the boys
with them, a bread and butter plate with a big chip in it and
various hairclips, pencils, pens and combs), used the long broom
to clear cobwebs from the high ceiling, and polished everything
possible. Shopped with Mum for soft drink, potato chips, and
fresh white bread to make club sandwiches. I baked a chocolate
cake and Mum made sausage rolls, too. The kitchen smelt like
the best bakery ever: fresh, sweet, buttery and delicious.

My parents' huge lounge held easily enough room to dance,
linger in corners, and lounge on the settee. I gyrated for three
minutes without music in sheer delight, high-kicking, with my
arms as snaky as an undersea creature fighting free of a net.

My heavy wooden 50s gramophone painted with bright swirls
(70s paisley), took pride of place in a corner where no one could
tread on the records. People would strew them on the floor no
matter how careful some could be. Ten 45s stacked on the silver
spindle played one after the other: I'm a Believer, Wild Thing,
Build me Up Buttercup.... People toted in albums too: Procul
Harum, The Moody Blues, The Beatles, The Doors, Cream,
The Supremes.... Vinyl records slid from printed cardboard
sleeves like ancient tablets of religious significance, holding
secrets to eternal life and ecstatic wonder.

Later than everyone else, Mark arrived in a powder blue shirt,
collar fashionably long over grey and cream herringbone coat
lapels. Slogans and captions from fashion glossies easily attached
to everything he wore. Myself, a great beaming idoliser, in
gobsmacked delight. Mark could've walked out of one of my
British magazines (six months out-of-date by ship. After a
wharfies' strike they'd be a year behind, for a few issues). But
here he stood, in real time, as stylish and provoking as living in
Swinging London itself.

Every other guest appeared even younger with Mark in the
room. My long legs and arms grew extra joints, so gawky, but

the beguiled smile remained.

For a while we listened to music and danced, with the lounge light on.

Someone soon turned the light off. Wide beams of illumination fell into the room from the kitchen and hallway.

My parents had disappeared next door to, '...yarn with old Roly' and all my bully brothers were staying at friends' places in distant suburbs. We were supervised, but not too closely. I think they all wanted to escape our music.

After offering me an aniseed drop (from a bag he carried constantly), Mark murmured, 'I've learnt how to meditate.' He held my eyes and sat cross-legged on the floor of our lounge.

I copied him, because I felt silly standing by myself even if it was weird to sit in a pretzel shape while everyone else was in motion. The party rocked on around us.

For a half hour, Mark sat eyes closed with me following suit. I peeked now and then to see if he'd moved, couldn't believe we posed cross-legged like in some newscast about gurus to famous rock stars. As close to being on TV as I'd ever felt, but not as enjoyable as I'd hoped. Meditation more like discomfort. Human macrame woven into something I didn't understand. But surely it was *electric* to be with Mark? I wanted groovy, didn't I?

On Mum's new broadloom, in the barely lit lounge surrounded with friends, beloved music boomed on as loud as we could get my ancient record player cranked up. I resolved to learn to enjoy these strange encounters. As an artist or a writer (I had to be one of those), it was vital to be more open-minded. Artistic people didn't shut themselves in a bedroom forever, hiding from the unknown. We took on fate without fear so we'd have something later to write about. I imagined a tattoo in future with a globe of the world and *fate without fear* written underneath, wondering if birds flying over the top of the map would be too much.

Another aniseed drop accepted from Mark, he replaced the bag in the pocket of his herringbone coat. We seemed to have stopped meditating, but remained cross-legged.

Just as Build me up Buttercup reached the first verse for the third time, asking why they got built up only to be brought

down, the lights went on. My father stood there. His shapeless
pale pants and plaid shirt so unfashionable. Hands on his hips.
'Right. It's 11 o'clock and I've promised your parents that you
children will leave now. Home time.'
I wanted to cry but instead struggled to my feet from the floor.
Standing didn't make my shouted rhetoric more persuasive, 'It's
not midnight yet. You told me it could go 'til then.'
Dad insisted, 'This party has to finish. Now.'
People drifted off into the night, most took their music with
them. With a cheery wave, Mark bounced out the door like he
had springs on his feet.

A phone call the next day, Mark and I talked for over an hour.
Nutty as a tea cosy worn as a hat, or even stranger - like wearing
the teapot itself on his head, he spouted nonsense or snatches of
lyrics from songs, interrupted his own opinions like he possessed
two personalities elbowing for attention. He also called people
snide nicknames behind their backs, but I kept silent about those
because they seemed too unfair to comment on and I felt afraid.
Believed that if I disagreed with Mark, he could aim a few
barbed comments especially designed for my particular
neuroses. Fear often consuming my life for most of my years, this
didn't seem unnatural - to take defensive steps. Like watching a
television show - it didn't feel like he'd respond favourably or
change one iota if anyone objected to his judgements, either.
Finally, in any case, I surely moved away in some regard from
our wide mowed lawn, tidy flower-beds, our scrubbed house, my
rowdy brothers and their childish, sometimes far too rough
games. Not their readily available target any longer, not easily
tidied up into something surface scrubbed and never mind the
rest; now I knew someone so peculiar he would definitely put
quite a few people off bothering me - and he dressed as
fabulously as I did.
To look good even if feeling worried, scared or sad was
achievable. Fashion spoke for us, it pretended and distracted,
wonderful protection. In league we both looked even better. A
victory.
A half hour through tree-lined suburbs, past rose gardens,

clipped shrubs, prize camelias and tidy lawns. One late summer afternoon, for the first time I walked down a quiet street some distance from ours. Invited over to his place, how different could Mark's house be?

Live music flowed from a pale yellow bungalow with white wrought iron along the front porch, all set back from the road. Easy to guess the house was Mark's before seeing the number. His father a short figure on saxophone in the lounge by the porch. Cruisy notes jazzed over neighbouring properties. Flashes of his red and yellow tartan waistcoat. Then his mother played cello in a studio practice room at the far end of their hedged, but rather empty, garden. Lawn alone stretched in all directions with a rotary clothes-line in the middle of it, without laundry that day.

Both stopped practising as soon as they realised I'd arrived. Slim the pair of them, but Mark's mother taller than her husband which made me think that was why he wore brighter clothes - to stand out. She wore a navy frock with teeny flowers all over it and he a rich blue cable knit cardigan over his waistcoat and dark green pants. They shook my hand, said my name, made eye contact in this really penetrating manner as if they needed to know more about me, and soon.

Taxidermy birds eyed our small gathering in their roomy lounge, a fantail on a branch, a kahu on the top of the piano, and a pair of ducks (drake and hen), on a slab of wood above a couple of rows of important-looking books with gold embossed spines. Mark's dad commented, 'My little hobby. Do you like birds?'

'You hunt them?'

Everyone else laughed and he replied firmly, 'Certainly not. We can't hunt natives. People bring them to me if they find them. They know I have this hobby. Relaxes the mind.'

'*My* dad likes to play cricket.'

All three of them laughed again as if I was a comedian.

'O but, erm....' I didn't want them to laugh again, and tailed off. They all looked far too merry, like actors in a comic play.

Mark's mother at last appeared kind, smiled warmly. 'Few musicians play contact sports, nor any with a hard ball like cricket. The hands, we have to be careful. Alphonse and I love tennis however, perhaps we'll have a match sometime?' Mark's mother murmured on, 'You live over in Bether Park, don't you?' 'O yes, by the park.' I smiled too much. My eyes roamed for something which wasn't them trying to assess me, or stuffed birds. The eyes glistened as if the inert animals could chirrup or fly away.

'Okay, come and see my records.' Mark showed me his room out to the side of the house, on top of the double garage. With a view of the suburb around them, it smelt faintly of lavender cleaning products. Furnishings brown or dark orange, with pale wallpaper and a blue stripe in it. Music on the stereo within seconds. He took me in his arms. We kissed as if at any moment we'd dance around the tiny space, waltz or foxtrot. But the tootle squawk from his metre high speakers sounded nothing like what those dances would require.

Mark explained the music was someone called Miles Davis. Then he kissed me again, as if he couldn't quite believe he was permitted so close, his full lips tender. We kissed each others' faces and necks, warm skin, hands under each others' clothing. The silk of our bodies, breath faster and faster. A pleasure, this heated encounter transporting, blessed closeness. Everything we needed to know. Together. Parents and their ideas faded away like photos left in the sun. Invincible youth and delighted touch, addictive certainties.

Mark rarely visited me at my house and I spent many weekday afternoons, Saturdays, and Sundays in a haze of music and caresses at his place. A far superior stereo to mine, his own room sound-proofed above their double garage. More privacy and better entertainment than our household crammed with brothers and lunks of friends, who glared and punched people's arms as proof of friendship, or in annoyance, or just for something to do.

Escape. My delight about this unexpected freedom and kind attention remained carefully hidden at home, but once free of our place I could laugh and stride about like a real girl. Satisfyingly close to someone else, their warmth as tangible as clothing I'd put on, feeling safe, wanted, cared for, and the novelty produced wonder.

For weeks, I also tried to play the drums in Mark's garage (with egg cartons over walls and ceiling to stop the sound travelling far). A stick insect (no pun intended), peculiar angles and easily tangled up in myself, while quite foreign to the scenario and the instrument. Mark explained in the end, 'Not everyone *gets* music.' He played almost everything he picked up, except brass instruments which I suspect he pretended to be unable to play, to annoy his rather dictatorial father.

I studied, lived, and dreamt of the road code (a formula for freedom), driving up and down and around our long driveway, then the big patch of gravel near the house (training for liberty). After trying my father's patience with some driving lessons he guided me through (proof that mobility worked wonders), my driving license was passed the next year. The day I turned 15, I could also drive a car.

I drove Mark to band practice sometimes twice a week. My mother allowed me to use her yellow Morris Minor. Perhaps she'd started to feel some sympathy for me by then, but Mum also appeared more and more tired. Life could gradually wear you away, like water against a stone. She gave up her craft lessons, the sports she liked such as lawn bowls, hardly visited anyone. The car unused except for a weekly grocery excursion. Mum murmured by way of explanation, 'You're young. Y'have things to do. Take it. Enjoy these years, girl.'

Outside various community halls, I'd wait, smoke, and daydream. One had an unsealed carpark edged with unkempt grass. I listened to versions of Cream's latest, versions of rhythm and blues songs, or something Mark's band invented, sounding like The Rolling Stones in their shambolic enthusiasm. Music from the other side of the vastly distant rest-of-the-world slammed and jammed over dust and raggy grass, tossed around the overgrown hedges and peeled-paint suburban houses nearby, bounced off buildings 'til the sky stood well back.

I sometimes wondered what I was doing there listening to songs about stations with black curtains, but it was such heavenly music. In awe of their ability to play any song, and what else

would I do? At least I wasn't getting roped in to help my mother
clean, do laundry, or cook - which she seemed to tackle day and
night. Nor was I fending off my increasingly larger and more
boisterous brothers. Still too scared to report them to Mum or
Dad. Anyway they'd only scold me for complaining.
At home and miraculously left to myself, in my room with music
blaring, I wrote in my diary, painted huge murals on discarded
boards (long-legged, big-eyed girls copied from fashion
magazines), or sometimes with friends wandered with our talk
along nearby endless streets of houses. *What if... where could we...
what happened when...* But band practices opened the doors of a
huge room full of fresh, loud, penetrating, essential mystery.
Musicians accepted me, too. No one ever behaved like I
shouldn't be around. These young men joked ceaselessly when
they weren't playing - good-natured, confident, discussing every
ring-a-ding thing. If God existed, was there an afterlife where
the greatest musicians jammed as loud and as often as they
liked? Who'd make up this super-band? What would Mozart
sound like on lead guitar? Did sex have to be secretive, or could
we read wild magazine articles aloud to each other without
embarrassment? What did we think about oral sex, group sex,
open relationships, anonymous sex, erotic books, and food sex?
Vegetarians could save the world. A fallout shelter to protect
against the nuclear threat fitted easily into a house hallway.
People dried certain things, smoked them, weeds, herbs, and
other plants from the garden or the kitchen, hazy exits. Suburbs
burst with psychotronic potential.
Many times, nevertheless, I wished someone else could hang
about to take the band home from building their noisy dream.
The same song practised fifteen times then they boom-banga-
boom launched into it again. One more time for fame to push its
way in. Immersed in hope and music.
Who would help *me?* How did I turn into a writer, an artist?
I stepped in time, zoomed my boyfriend about. At first I said
nothing much against his ideas. Mesmerised, living in a juke box
stocked with only sounds we adored. He made me feel wanted
and so good after our dishevelled pleasures; understood with all
his heart that wearing the best, most up-to-date clothes possible

was an absolute necessity, too, possibly more important than food.

When I said, 'I'll be a famous writer one day,' Mark and I had known each other a year.

In a second, his face hardened. 'You're still stuck on kiddy things like Lewis Carroll.' On and on he went, barely taking a breath between stabbing opinions. 'Writers require intelligence. Originality. Something to say. Entertaining words. Go on, make me laugh, make me cry. Go on.'

Instead of allowing insults or ignoring him, I insisted, 'People have their own tastes. I'll find an audience, a readership.' My sophisticated phrases surprised me and I shut up then.

He sneered and walked out, left me alone for a few days.

Soon it grew easier to give up discussing anything I liked or planned with him, unless prepared for a fight. Some days I felt like a clear glass jar people fancied then (in the early 70s), ornamental, shaped with a spire on the top. Fashionable folk filled them with coloured water. Mark liked my looks and wanted to fill me with whatever colour he thought best that week, that day, whenever.... One day, after much silence, I'd been under attack for weeks, and finally shouted, 'Do you watch your father stuffing animals people find dead in gardens, and think you've the right to fill me with whatever *you* think best, because of your dad's creepy imitation of life all over the house?'

'Whaaat?' His eyes darkened. 'I'm nothing at all like my father. How dare you. Get out.'

Unaware then that at times when people argue, they simply want to control you, keep you on the back foot. It isn't that they truly disagree necessarily, they simply don't want anyone else to feel comfortable, or to develop understanding near them. Fear breeds more fear.

How do we learn softness and calm, if we've never known it? I wondered. Mark's parents and mine, they kept this strange distance from us.

I read a foreign sociology magazine article one day years later and kept the clipping in my diary - Bullies like to know what people are doing and when, so such tyrants can believe that no

one is about to sneak up and frighten *them*. The sadistic
propagate fear and so relieve their own terror, worries often kept
hidden. Fear makes people feel tiny, inconsequential. Seeing a
friend's success or plans for a change alarms a bully, because it
makes them feel even smaller. They hate popular people, despise
happiness, feel they'll never have it, so why should anyone else?
Also, when people close to them grow happy, a bully may believe
anyone joyful could ride off on their fine deeds, and leave the
bully alone with their self-loathing. They'd rather hook others
into the scary thrill and diversion of disagreements, run others
down so they're less likely to leave, are more likely to want to
stay and fix things, make things better. Like a drug dealer
peddles addictive substances the bully touts anger and
frustration.

I remained caught up in the mechanics as if tangled in a
machine. We argued foully many times, I couldn't tell you now
what about. My eyes swelled after crying for hours; someone
had wrung me out like a dirty old floor rag. My brothers too had
brutalised me; no one much listened when I complained. And
with Mark our drama felt like high passion that meant love,
somehow. Wasn't it?
Perhaps his excellent stereo played so loudly that I felt I didn't
have to be silent any longer either, could unpeel my stay-happy
smile and snap back. When Mark laughed at me, I teased him in
turn about his latest band break-up or took apart his opinions,
crushed them as easily as smashing an egg. 'You can't tell the
future, Mark. I can make plans. I'm allowed.' *Splat.*
I'd refuse to stay there a moment longer when Mark insulted me.
Off home I stomped in a fury, ignoring him for days, in my turn.
The music drew me back as much as the promise of making up.
Miles Davis, Blood, Sweat and Tears, James Taylor, Charlie
Parker, Coltrane...so fantastically beyond the bubble gum and
pop I'd bopped gladly to before. His vast array of albums to play
- magnetic - and Mark, too - his soft lips, unpredictable
utterings, strong profile, and his fascination with me. New
recordings arrived every week from overseas, building Mark's
Best Record Collection Ever in Existence. And he kissed softly at

first, wonderingly, then harder with purpose, and his hair always
smelt so clean. He touched me in this tender way as if he
thought I could break, then slowly grew more forceful, as long as
I responded. Yes, those lips, especially dramatic when he sneered
or kissed. We formed a glamorous darkness full of musical stars
to inhabit. A universe of two, like a song.

Anyway, when the soothing effects of romance didn't always
make me forget, I told myself that an older boyfriend would of
course have some funny ideas. I'd just *secretly* not agree, for peace
- when I had to, or when I couldn't face another argument.
Risk not without cost. Adventure's price stood high. My Dad
paid massive amounts for shooting gear and a boat, his
beekeeping too. Mum shelled out for shopping holidays. I paid
with time and something like my heart for romance, for
closeness, for at last feeling wanted - like someone did not want
to lose me. Unconventional territory - leaving home without
going further than four long streets away, then three smaller
roads, around a few corners - another world and me the centre.
A wrinkle in the ironed fabric of predictable everyday. Easing
into its shade - smaller to fit, although at times it felt like I grew
as enormous as the sky or the heavens, luxuriating deep into a
fold. Fridays and Saturdays, some weekdays out at night, we
drove all over the city or to neighbouring towns. Mark's many
bands - one after the other - struggled to get on the map they
imagined awaited. They played gigs in pubs and clubs, at
celebrations, and in parks sometimes. One gig at the lake took
place with barely any lighting. Music roared through dark trees
as if a monster had awakened. Ugly orange fashion haunted me
that evening - about five girls in shapeless dresses too bright for
their sallow skin.

In high heels and make-up when they played pubs out of town, I
stood tall. Walking in with the band created credibility. 'A whisky
and dry,' I'd say, to sound sophisticated. While Mark's group
played the soundtrack beginning the latest glorious film, starring
me, in a sumptuous version of star-life. We shimmered. Half a
glass of whisky and my hyperbolic fripperies appeared effortless.
Mark's parents allowed him to order tailor-made suits and he
worked part-time in a menswear shop. My mother at times

assisted with sewing the latest styles at home. She was an expert seamstress, keeping us all clothed. 'I'm not sure this skirt should be so short,' Mum would murmur while I cut away the hem and pretended not to hear until it was too late.

Arm in arm, Mark and I sashayed through town on a Friday night when everyone who could afford it showed off in front of our main department store. Loud colours, round-toed platform shoes, fitted coats with enormous lapels, swathes and bounces of hair, funky jewels, nonchalant fashion plates. People admired us. Some glared, furious. Others appeared bewildered.

For a long time I slid aside the idea that Mark thought he mattered more than anyone else (including me). Glided the uncomfortable thought out of the way like moving items in my room to hide a scorch (from when I ironed on a chair and carelessly melted the fabric). Youth's screens and cushions, privacy put together with hormones and imagination, the furniture of not-knowing.

Years of training when watching people smile and agree, smoothing things along. If I ever tried to say things were not good enough or I felt scared, alone, worried, someone would tell me, 'O rise above it,' or 'Stop moaning.' It took years to learn to find help elsewhere and then to step over any metaphorical slime; meanwhile I muddled along otherwise, albeit in fine feathers.

Pretense served meanwhile, and disguises. Fashion magazines offered valuable tips and pointers. Good legs - fine with a short skirt. Big hips - don't wear a fussy dress. Great eyes - lay on the mascara and eye shadow. Thin hair - get a perm. A warm tint also coloured many ideas, emphasised Mark's best qualities, his looks, clothes, stunning musical taste, amazing talent with any instrument, devotion to me (albeit part-time), and so tall (a good head above me - reassuring in some primal way).

One five piece he joined played up and down the country for a short while. The band then recorded. Their single made it to the top twenty for one brief week, they recorded a performance for TV. After one gigging weekend away, a new face appeared at his address. Blonde curly hair; a violinist, he said. She used phrases I could only guess the meanings of and when she laughed it

sounded like tiny bells. Usually, soon after I arrived, she left.
My imagination hyped into full technicolour drama, inevitably
encouraged by the stream of 1930s, 40s and 50s movies from
TV throughout my childhood (many played Sunday afternoons
even then). Throughout my formative years these fancies reeled
on without adult conversation to explain the ridiculous dramas,
outlandish comedies, and unreal musicals were not true life.
Certain fanciful details appeared clear - dramatic confrontation
was a method of improving relationships. Reality never fitted
the plot of any motion picture, but I half-believed movies
showed a world we'd inhabit if only we knew the code - wore
those clothes, spoke better words, and appeared really well lit.
Yes, excellent lighting and any gorgeous costume could truly
help supply what I needed.
Dressed in my latest extra-short, chocolate-brown mini-skirt,
giant hipster belt in tan, with a cutaway sleeve, ribbed, cream
polo neck top, pale textured tights and dark brown platform
shoes, I simply needed to demand the truth. Love would find a
way. A cool super-spy about to discover a fabulous secret, I
lavishly applied creamy pink lipstick, brown eyeshadow, and
elaborate mascara - as if preparing for a close-up. Night best for
the awkward question, neither of us too sharply defined. So I
asked about this girl, what he thought of her.
'Yes, I do like her. A lot.' He didn't flinch after this admission,
just glared at me.
The idea he could like someone else made me tremble. 'What
does that mean?'
'Just what I said,' Mark's voice as cold as inside an empty freezer.
'So, we need to break up then.' Pulling down my skirt, suddenly
far too short. I tried this statement the way someone would, in
desperation to stay somewhere, assert they'd rather die than
leave their own country. But I'd foolishly grown dramatic far too
quickly in this negotiation.
Only fifteen years old.
A tall teenager in clothes imitating young adulthood, but inside
as childish as believing in fairyland. Barely able to understand
relationships, even if I did secretly see myself as invincible and
that the world had to love me - or else.

We resolved to break up.

This caused us both to cry.

In a cloud of emotionally-induced hormones I felt drugged, could not stop sobbing and wailing but had to drag myself home, eventually.

Then like a criminal to the scene of a crime, revisiting the drama, I returned to Mark's the next day. Those old films I'd put so much credence in, they showed how when destined lovers got together again after they'd argued, they always realised their true feelings and reconciled. Violins de rigueur, a snow storm or soft rain to really set the mood. My Mum's little yellow car didn't have a radio however and that sunny morning appeared far too cheery. I imagined a soundtrack anyway. Beethoven. Da da da duuummm.

We sat in his parents' lounge. Light streamed in the huge picture window over their enormous Persian rug - reds, black, cream, and green; stuffed birds arrayed about the place, glass eyes catching the light. Mark's mum and dad out for the day. Two teenagers on the floor, our backs against the edge of the tweedy sofa. Court of the Crimson King played loud and we sobbed our hormone-drenched hearts out. Surging music packed our world into sound and threw it to the sky.

Exhausted by the break-up we'd endured for almost 24 hours, we now resolved to stay together.

I never saw the blonde girl again, her bell-like laugh only an annoying memory.

He grew his hair even longer. I gave him three metres of black and white striped ribbon on a whim which he wore in his pony tail (more of a shaving brush really). Ribbons streamed down his back.

Dressed as unlike our parents as we possibly could. Freaks metamorphosised everywhere. Previously clean-cut plain people now tattooed with esoteric signs from India, hair hennaed bright as copper, headbands beaded to imitate American Indians, both genders in floaty clothes. See-through (so nudity appeared likely at any moment), naked and dancing through a park at a concert. Outlandish garments, some like bright toys - jackets, pants, bags,

tops, and hats in every colour - sometimes ten or fifteen colours
together. People spouted philosophy borrowed from Persia,
Tibet, China, India, or Thailand. Protest marches surged along
spiked with placard demands, and thousands chanting. Flaunt
and flash, while people smoked, shot up, snorted, and imbibed a
bewildering array of substances read about or heard of. And
music, film, books, and fashion changed drastically forever -
altered for the expanded and bent minds of a psychedelic,
weirdo, freak, and head generation.

Mark liked and cared for absurdities the way some men tended
exotic flowers - lilies or orchids - and I'd grown aware that
ridiculousness did fill most waking hours even if so many refused
to admit it. Blandness too had an absurdity about it, the
apparent fakery. We embraced ludicrous like an old friend
returned from overseas with a new religion and haircut, and
expanded on the theme. A propensity to follow silliness as if it
mattered felt intoxicating. We called this free.

No longer believing we had to do as our parents wished, to
follow in their footsteps or improve ourselves according to
tradition. But choices sometimes appeared too easy or plain
nasty. Like in a horror movie when the girl sees her lover's hands
grow hairier and suddenly he's a wolf, my boyfriend did make
me gasp with fear at times. Then I'd kind of float away, as if it
wasn't happening to me. For years I believed that everyone did
this when frightened.

Quite an effort, but I shifted my fractured attention to
conservative, shallow aspects - his kisses always made me feel
great. Mark said he loved me. Vital currency - the magic phrase,
'I love you.' Doubts removed with a few words. Love equalled
survival, brilliantly, somehow. Passion did not always mean love,
but again, these truths appear with hindsight. Such a cut, a
retrospective view appears to slice away treasured illusions when
hope's no longer necessary.

He still expounded at random on the benefits of meditation,
sang nonsense songs when people asked him reasonable
questions, and asked obtuse queries at inconvenient moments. A
nincompoop, my sensible aunties would've said, but they'd long ago
moved away.

In a bank one afternoon, Mark asked the teller, 'Do you ever find a fish in your mirror?' The whole place felt colder after his voice rang out with this nonsense. I withdrew my money at the counter where everyone did this and hurried away, with him in tow. Learning to live with difficulty had to be part of my maturing process, I told myself when I turned sixteen.

Mark soon kicked out of about three or four bands in succession. Or they agreed to dissolve, melding into the general pool of musicians to form a new configuration, without his foolishness.

Then one summer night, the latest collection of hopefuls he played with performed a great gig at a local hall. The echoey place overflowed with people. Music so energising the whole building lifted off the ground and we could fly unassisted anywhere we wished - to the mountains of Russia and on to the Arctic, floating above the ocean or into the outer stratosphere. People beamed with joy, danced and showed off - a blur of floating hands, gyrating bodies.

Other girls and women flocked to talk with them and flirt as soon as the band stopped playing. A big old community hall, wood-lined and wooden floored, the stage down the far end rented for the night and not far above the crowd.

Mark no longer determined to keep me by his side, no-matter-what, in the teeming mass of grinning teenagers.

We later went back to someone's place in my car and sipped coffee from coloured mugs (bright orange inside, dark brown outside, I'd never seen anything like them). Extra-still, I hoped no one noticed how astounded I felt by the entire evening. Their mother lived on a commune and crystals hung from coloured threads in the windows. So peculiar - a window bejeweled. 'This is our town house,' one of the girls explained. She smoothed down her long paisley dress.

We'd sauntered onto a Rolling Stones movie set (not that they'd yet been in a film). I wanted to languidly drape myself over a sofa like a fashion model, instead of not knowing where to stand or sit. My height loomed enormous next to the tiny girls who lived there in their delicate, print maxi-dresses. Each simpered and handed over drinks, filigree copper rings on their slender hands.

When Mark said he wanted to stay, but I could go home, he stood just a bit too close to the eldest daughter. He told me again I had to drive back alone.

Young and full of bravado, I was determined that nothing could harm me. Paralysis wasn't planned. My legs simply would not work. I couldn't go. I think most of me collapsed in emotional shock.

Mark had to carry me to the spare bed and he slept there too. Anger in every word he spoke, but then he took me wordlessly and pounded away for a good twenty minutes. I'd previously calculated silently that I wasn't ovulating and so didn't refuse him. The darkness seemed dull for some reason, like there'd never be light again. We both nevertheless soon fell asleep.

Next day, I reeled with grief and worry about losing Mark anyway, and also fretted that I'd really annoyed my parents. Drove home in a state of extreme nervousness and eventually staggered into my parents' house.

Mum and Dad turned to gasp at me when I walked through the kitchen door. They looked like I'd died and come back to life only to say it was a joke. I'd tried to ring them the night before, they didn't hear the phone. 'I just couldn't walk properly. Thought it best to stay there. Not to drive.'

'Did they offer you a drink?!' Dad yelled the question at me.

'Coffee. We had coffee.'

'Drugs,' he hissed at Mum and she went pale.

I couldn't explain it was worry over Mark that had affected me. Grounded, for two weeks. No car either.

A sunny day. I ate some breakfast, then immediately walked over to Mark's (the long way - in case anyone followed). But Dad drove there, sneered at my boyfriend with his ridiculous long ribbon in his hair, and took me home again. In the car, Dad's words through his teeth, 'Do you want to give your mother a nervous breakdown?'

'No.'

'You are grounded. What do you see in that freak anyway?'

No answer to that.

In some covert manner, I liked Mark precisely because he was a

freak and so was I. No words for such an explanation, this
situation not mentioned in any magazine. Throughout our stay-
happy-smile neighbourhood locals discussed proper and and
pleasant situations, but almost no one ever said anything about
peculiar. We were normal. Saying you liked weirdos would sound
like Russian or Martian.

Dad's electric blue Valiant glided through our suburb of 1960s
house after house more or less the same with tended shrubs,
roses, freshly painted fences, clipped hedges, and pretty
pathways. Along towards home, me with my misery about me
like a cloak, swathed in its rigmarole for company. At only
sixteen years old, purple prose was as natural as swooning over a
lead break in my favourite song. Everything always seemed far
more important than anyone else could ever possibly imagine. I
swam in a vast sea of consuming emotions or burned in strange
fires, alternately.

For two weeks with seemingly endless grounded time alone, at
home after school or on the weekends with books and records
for company, I drew chaotic amalgams of black lines. Poetry
written chockablock with jungle and eagle metaphors. In the
supposedly safe place where my parents remained determined to
keep their rebellious daughter. I refused to allow my brothers
into my room, fitted a lock. Their own distractions to see to
anyway, out of the house with sports and girls.

Eventually, I stopped sulking and managed to join in
conversations about preparing dinner or watching television.
Tension eased as definitely as an aroma fills a house when
someone bakes a delicious cake or lights incense.

Sins supposedly diminished by enforced isolation, I was allowed
to drive back to Mark's place on the weekends. We lazed about,
made love, and listened to brilliant music again. Our own
universe regenerated, expanded, and hung with ever more
brightness.

Just as sunshine makes plants grow, the way he kissed my eyelids
and my neck, his hands soft on my back and mine around his
waist - closeness encouraged me to feel more alive.

Pushed into a corner for so long; but now someone really cared
for me. Even if it was flawed and strange (Mark cruelly taunted

me at times), I clung to our intimacy. It kept me alive. Starved of affection, people like me seek closeness as if it's food. Now, I imagine he too suffered from a lack of care. Some of us live so much of our time in the cold dark, even when it appears we're walking in sunshine - fed properly, dressed fine, smiling.... Many of us learn how to look happy, but loneliness is such a horror. That lack of self-worth, too - sometimes I felt like a paper doll someone tossed aside, flapping in the breeze, skidding over the ground, growing soggy under some piece of rubbish. When anyone admired or wanted me I felt stunned, grateful, and unworthy. Then I worked hard to try to find ways to stop them seeing my uselessness lurking close by, like a shadowy sibling.

At Mark's, invited for Sunday dinner; late afternoon, his rather thin but determined mother sat on a chrome and vinyl chair by the kitchen bench with her eyes closed to play cello. Beef, potatoes, parsnip and pumpkin spat and crackled in the oven. A domestic recital, her lone, large instrument sumptuous, accompanied by fat almost catching fire in a hot cooker; a suburban kitchen with pale mushroom and peach Formica, deep-green painted cupboards and swept up 1960s gold handles (biomorphic, perhaps a design-tribute to Jean Arp). Soaring, sonorous music caused everything but sound to dissolve and her fingers danced on the dark wooden neck, the bow strands of light above the deeply golden wood body, stroked this way and then the other, drawing out moaning notes.

Through the open doors to the lounge, Mark's dad's taxidermy in frozen gothic poses with their hard, shiny eyes. But those dead birds didn't disturb me when his mother played her cello. Their tiny Pomeranian, its fluffy teeny legs by her feet, stared with big eyes while Mark's mother made walls, kitchen appliances and Sunday dinner cooking all disappear. Music opened the walls and ceiling, cello notes welcomed in the world. Our collective human joy took on sound - subtle ways we felt and thought, pains and worries, too - a teem of sensations all beautifully recognised, ordered, and celebrated in her music. She expertly stroked those strings week after week in a reverie. Mark's mother made human beings appear worthwhile after all, no matter what we did, with her cello recital and practise.

Drawn to make admiring comments; in reply to me Mark's
mother mentioned, 'They ask me every year to join the National
Orchestra in Australia. Once I was asked to play in Germany.'
She set her thin mouth hard. 'I'm from Australia, Canberra. My
parents are from Berlin.'
When I asked why she didn't go ahead and join, this woman
asserted, 'Because I have a family.'
Enthralled, I thanked goodness she never did fly overseas and
join an orchestra; her instrument sang so exquisitely. I wanted
my experience to be as lovely and transportive too, even if life
could also feel so sad. Gorgeous sound cleansed away everything
except pure appreciation. Swept into the unknown, where great
music came from, I swam there ecstatic.
When the spell wore off, however, I felt leaden. We were both
weighed down with what we had to do, were supposed to think
and say. No room for our ambitions. Family, a magic formula for
security with locks in every syllable. This genius musician
refused public acclaim for them; her family overrode any
transportive music or her obvious, extraordinary talent. A
husband and children quite cooled Mark's mother's desire to
play with gifted others like herself, to be part of either of the two
supreme orchestras who'd offered her a place.
Self-sacrifice the greatest proof of love a mother could display.
Grander than the elaborate lace making she did at night, doilies
and runners to place under her husband's menagerie of death.
Finer than delicious food cooked and served without complaint.
More important than endless cleaning and mending done with a
family of six, such as they had (even if most were away at
boarding school on fancy scholarships and barely ever home).
She threw off fame for them, she'd taken off layer after layer of
beautiful clothes and left them on the ground, to wear plain dark
frocks and cheery aprons instead.
Inevitably, I practised patience for when my own family would
appear. In order to keep someone near I needed to do what they
wished. What Mark wanted, we did. We went to the cinema,
dances, and to town, all at his suggestion, in ways he preferred.
If he wanted me to drive then I did so, if he felt like a walk or
the bus, I obliged him. Couples held hands, stayed together, did

not wander off and talk to anyone else. Mark made it clear I
wasn't to ever leave his side when we went anywhere. Also, I
wasn't to ask about his friends, all of whom could visit whenever
they liked and stay for as long as they wished.
My glare, or a stare and my chin out, could state disapproval
more blatantly than anything spoken. Mark grew annoyed, 'You
glare at them like they're criminals or something.'
'They were talking about drugs. They're illegal.'
'Never ever discuss this with anyone. Got me?'

We walked home from a gig one clear, still night when I stayed
at my friend's for the weekend. I'd said or done something Mark
didn't like. Never did find out what it was. He refused to answer
my questions. Soon he gripped my wrist and dragged me almost
all the way. My mind a whirl of maybes to try to find a way free.
Maybe he invented an invisible, unspoken, never-to-be-proven
reason alluded to, a shadow following that only he could see?
Maybe Mark was insane and needed to be seen by a doctor?
Maybe I found these people who hurt me because I needed the
familiar pain? Every dark awfulness I possessed inside me grew
larger and larger, dense stupidity and ugliness surely my fault.
Pulled fast with my wrist aching, torturous, but he wouldn't stop.
My skin burned, the bones ached, I cried and begged him to let
go. He tugged me along mercilessly through a still evening.
We walked for an hour this way through dark suburban streets.
Houses tucked up with curtains and blinds drawn. People
watched TV or read, talked together in there, refusing to listen
to sounds in the street. Nothing to do with them.
*These stories are not any one else's concern. No one wants to read them -
what if they feel helpless, sorry, or maybe in danger themselves?* I think
sometimes, now. I'm still trying to keep all this hidden you see.
Why bother when you could pretend what happened never existed? But
some ghosts demand to be shown, they grow so large in secret
places otherwise, they bulge and push. *Always tell someone else when
you've been hurt,* that's what I think now. Some won't listen or
believe you, but keep on saying what happened and how you feel
until someone can sympathise, or assist you. People need each
other.

My brothers at least never drew out their cruel games, didn't observe results in this exacting way. They liked a fast reaction. Blasted off fast as far as possible from my tears.

The whole time I sobbed and pulled away from Mark throughout sixty or so minutes walking. (For about thirty or forty years of my life I could judge time to within a few minutes, easily). No car stopped, no one leaned from their vehicle to shout or ask if I was all right.

By the time we found my friend Alice's pale weatherboard place behind a neat hedge, blind hysterics saw me race into the kitchen. I pulled out the heavy stove set into an alcove where once a coal range had stood and hid behind it. In there I sobbed incoherently.

They told Mark he had to go. 'Look at her. You can't stay here. Sorry. Go. Now.' Alice and her boyfriend, sleepy and annoyed, locked the back door, and the front.

In those days people often slept with the house unlocked. Not this evening.

Any idea of either learning to step into a daring world where freedom ruled, or just giving in and accepting that family had to come first, those plans were quite destroyed in those terrifying minutes. All I wanted now was to have some semblance of a mind returned to me.

In the spare room in Alice's parents' house, between the crisp cotton sheets of a strange bed, I resolved never to speak to Mark again. Jabbering thoughts tumbled about and I drifted off eventually.

The next day, sun filled the room through the window to the left of my bed and there - in the doorway opposite - Mark held a white tray like in an advertisement for orange juice and eggs. Blue and white striped china, he'd made me breakfast in bed. My friends let him bring it in.

Warm in the sunshine and refreshed from a good long sleep; I tried to recall when he'd ever fed me before, except with aniseed drops, and failed.

He could change.

The tray balanced on the bed on my lap, sunlight covered us

both. He sat down, face soft. 'I love you.' In daylight, his blue
eyes so different to those black holes in space the night before.
I'd obviously overreacted to his relentless grip on my wrist, his
refusal to let go, dragging me along. A mistake, people often got
things wrong. Mark convincing, his violent behaviour was over,
'No idea why I did all that. Never again, I promise,' such a soft
voice.
He promised. I had to believe that. It'd be unfair not to.
Hungry, I ate the entire tray of breakfast and felt much better.

The scintillating brilliance we lived inside returned anew, more
impressive. Yet also awfully familiar like a tacky fairground ride.
Once enjoyed, but now the trick of it all too obvious, the rusty
struts and wonky wiring. Whizzing about now often lacked the
old charm and exhilaration.
But somehow, even with disappointment lurking, loyalty and
patience appeared. Perhaps it was through habit or invention, or
a little of both. So many older married women in my street, they
too learnt to accept their lot. Mrs Clark with a broken nose still
hung line after line of laundry every day at their place to flap
and dry in the breeze. Every white flag of it proof she'd
surrendered and not escaped.
In my diary, I wrote - Some things need to stay the same. Some
people have to stay in my life or it could be so strange I'd be
truly lost. People need patterns we recognise, can only alter
partly, slowly, towards anything more fortunate.
Stumbling around with bits of language trying to build a safe,
known place to dwell. Excuses appeared more easily than I
could run up a new skirt or trousers on my mother's sewing
machine. If annoyance or worry bouldered in, I laboured to
keep these feelings away, pushed and pushed, tumbled worry
down the hill.
Paths to choose like a game, was that life? Coloured counters to
represent yourself, some dice to roll, then win or lose? Random
luck everywhere, but various clever plays sometimes altered the
outcome. I could predict tomorrow well enough to feel secure
about a choice, occasionally. But how could anyone go play a
new game without knowing the rules? Did peace and quiet and

security even exist anywhere? Reasons to stay put : safety, familiarity, a version of security (even in chaos I recognised something known). At the back of my jumbled fancies a dreadful, empty longing - like a bare cupboard everything was supposed to fit inside, neatly arranged. But I never seemed to find a way to clamber over the mess inside to shift this and that someplace more meaningful.

Underneath or behind my life, daytime cast unreal shadows, places I could fall into. As far as I knew, this, too, was a normal state of existence. *Everyone* put up with this lurking fright. No one talked about it because they didn't know how to change anything to play along better, obviously. Every other day, sometimes when things were fine, or at other moments after I'd been shaken by a brother's threats or an adult's over-the-top admonishing, I imagined the road would turn into a war zone. Wrecked buildings everywhere, streaks of fire in the sky, and any second I could slip into a sudden hole or a bomb could drop without warning. It grew difficult to walk about outside alone for too long, fractured pictures in my mind provoked terror. My thinking was dangerous, newness incited spookiness, open places appeared too unpredictable.

Meanwhile (when I felt safer and a group assisted with this), my friends and I purchased swirly 70s fabrics in lurid shades, worn with ever more clompy shoes, longer false eyelashes, madder hats and stockings. Truly groovy music mapped the way to fabulous wonders. Wearing extreme fashion we were permitted entry without question, and flamboyant clothes protected us from fading away.

I loved trying on clothes at home, lounged in my finery, imagined myself in London on a black velvet chaise longue in a Chelsea flat bedecked with ostrich feathers and Biba wallpaper, silver and black Art Deco nouveau. Increasingly likely to stay inside, dressed extravagantly, my imagination furnished me with excursions.

Rituals redefined everyday life. Repeated fancies like curling my hair and styling it pushed away the ordinary, hurtful world. Art and writing answered almost everything we wanted answered too. I sketched to-order psychedelic posters for other students at school, featuring boyfriends' names written over and over fifty different ways. They paid for this work, and lessons washed over me while I doodled. The school tuck shop did well from my earnings throughout those years. Food, the great placater. Sequestered in my room to create in my spare time for hours, while my mother appeared in the doorway at intervals with suggestions, 'Be lovely to visit the Laceway sisters, wouldn't it?' or 'I bet you could ride your bike to Bonnie's house before dinner. You love a chat with her.' It seemed that Mum wanted to get rid of me. But I refused to go anywhere unless I thought of it or I had to go (like to school). I withdrew into drawing and my diary entries. Mark liked me staying at home too, and encouraged all my artwork. He never knew about the diary. No one did. I hid it in an old box marked 'envelopes' in a corner of my cavernous old wardrobe.

Friends nevertheless joined clubs. They took me along occasionally. On the edge of their perky groups, I'd imagine a BBC voice-over for a TV documentary, 'These gatherings of young people spring up. They tend to share a common interest. Let's see what these two over here say, when we ask them why they attend these weekly meetings....'

I took to carrying my sketchbook, drawing while I listened to their endless talk. After their president said he liked my art, I designed a surreal mural for a local youth group's house. Daliesque eyeballs on long stalks sprouted leaves, musical notes tumbled out of lilies and other flowers, fish swam through the air towards long-haired maidens holding guitars. A few club members asked odd questions about what I smoked and looked disappointed when I replied, 'What brand of cigarettes?' I knew what they meant but didn't like their knowing tone, and I didn't take illegal drugs. Like Salvador Dali, I was the drug.

The youth club collected for charity, cleaned up community gardens.... I suppose my parents thought they'd have a positive influence. Their dads belonged to Lions and Rotary. The term *pillars of the community* was mentioned. Curious, that anyone thought of people as a construction, as easy to identify as a building. Society was a bewildering mix of personalities, each with their own agenda and beliefs. A feat of luck and determination that we ever got anything done. The individual so often put so much before sharing with others, working together, in my youthful opinion.

Eavesdropping while mural painting, I registered the club members' talk about playing rugby games to raise money for charity. Ideas flowed on by. When someone suggested a dance, a social, I attended. But the boys smiled too much, it was like getting trapped in a toothpaste commercial for three hours. They played ad-land music too, light, innocuous, not very loud. No one with extraordinary looks, except for one young man in profile with short brown hair. But his cruel blue eyes made him repellent, a massive bird about to pounce on an insect and eat it.

Weeks later, when I'd almost finished the mural, an older girl with super-curly hair asked, 'You all want to come to my flat? Have a coffee?'

The worthy meeting of hopeful, useful youth were away home early. 'Sure,' I replied.

My two other friends also agreed, Heather and Justine.

'Told my flatmates I'd invite my girl friends from the youth group to meet them. They're all Christians like me. In a band too,' she talked while we drove in Mum's yellow car, making for a rather run-down old white house backed onto a shop near the edge of town. Coincidentally she lived just down the hill from our school. We trooped along a dirt driveway and up onto the small wooden back porch on a lean.

Inside, bare lightbulbs lit the kitchen and an adjoining living room. Piles of band gear, guitars, black vinyl-covered speaker boxes and amps in the shabby lounge, and a few worn, brown, art deco sofas and easy chairs around the room. Joe and Pete in jeans, long hair past their shoulders. Pete, the fairer of the two, bounced when he talked, his gold earring glinted. They appeared genuinely happy, to my surprise. I thought religious people just pretended to be joyful. Both worked part-time and studied at university : social sciences, psychology, and sociology. Mind science. All my movements slowed. Could they know my thoughts by how I held my shoulder bag or how I sat down?

'You girls want a drink?' Joe made everyone instant coffee. 'This is Led Zeppelin's first album. It's just released.'

'Lead, like the metal? Is that a joke?' I asked. 'A heavy air balloon? The cover in my hands I frowned. 'Not spelt l-e-a-d, though.'

Joe smiled, nodded. 'Play on words I guess.' He turned up the volume.

Led Zepplin's guitarist had definitely plugged into the vast Milky Way, glittering grand mystery transformed into sound. I couldn't stop smiling, but felt like I'd betrayed Miles, Coltrane, and the rest back at Mark's place. I also tried to imagine what Mark would think of this hard-edged sound. Such thoughts kept scuttling away into the melee of ideas seething around in my mind's passages and caverns.

Hard rock, they called it. This made me laugh too. 'Rock *is* usually hard.'

Joe's face really lit up. 'O, it's a term for music. Jazz, classical, folk, rock, but hard rock is like this - with more edge. A more forceful sound, more drums, more lead breaks.'

'I've never heard this on the radio.'

'Ha, we call the radio a time machine running backwards.'

The one-and-only local station played imported pop and old-style music, like most did. My Mark played jazz, blues, and more esoteric music. At Joe's place music slapped my ears from the inside. We beamed, danced in our chairs, cracked remarks about tracks and chuckled. I liked their instant coffee and how everyone smiled so much.

Based in town behind an old-fashioned shoemaker and repair shop, in a run-down villa, their half-a-house, their flat - a new place. Often we popped in after school. A game of cards, a can of juice from the corner dairy, a few sneaky cigarettes and endless cups of coffee. Jokes, laughter, earnest discussions about movies and books. When we knew exactly what was going on we'd be better off. Joe and Pete would save the world and we'd help them.

They decided to call their band something religious '...but it has to be cool.' Days of writing lists tacked up on the old-fashioned rose-patterned wallpaper so everyone could see them. Finally, they chose Sky Pilot. I painted Pete's bass drum skin, which

faced the audience, with a vicar's surprised face, clouds, rockets
and stars burst from the top of his bald spot.
Church meetings took place in this high-ceilinged Victorian
wooden hall near the middle of town. Everyone was at least ten
years younger than my parents. Some my age - sixteen - and
others in between. Candles flickered in glass jars on the floor,
shadows leapt. 'Attended by guardian spirits,' a girl with waist-
length hair murmured. Wearing jeans, Indian embroidered tops,
coloured t-shirts... figures sat on the floor, wandered in and out.
The minister padded about in jeans and a t-shirt, with bare feet.
People sat cross-legged while candlelight danced across our
faces; muttering our human music.
When they passed the collection plate, if anyone needed money
they could take some. One time, this skinny guy in raggy jeans
took four cents for milk and waved the empty bottle to prove
he'd be going to the dairy later. Everyone laughed kindly.

Usually, I liked to put on my make-up just before I left the house.
Mark stood in the doorway watching one night. I burbled on
about how meditation could change people, 'Really, it can.'
His face thunderous, which puzzled me, until I realised I'd raved
about one of his favourite subjects as if he'd never mentioned it.
I layered mascara, silently. Then he droned on about a new
mantra, 'I've explained all this before. Don't you listen?'
I told Mark, 'Your idea of meditation's staying the same. But I
want to do something to make the world a better place.'
He laughed. 'What could *you* ever do to change anything?'
I waved my mascara wand, and shouted, 'What would you
know? I *am* going to change things. People change the world
every time we take a breath.'
He sang a ridiculous song from a comedy show he liked.
I shouted, 'You could meditate on what it could be like to be a
decent human being.'
He sang on louder and smirked until I ran out of steam.
My noise gave him a boost. It was so obvious that I almost
screamed, except he'd have loved that.

Mark also told me the next sunny day on his parents' concrete

driveway, 'As soon as you're 17, I'm marrying you.'
Until then ebullient, I wondered at his certainty and blinked in
the strong sunshine. Didn't men *ask* you to marry them? A wife.
Would he take me away? I wished for a while never to get old.

Finally, Mark gathered the idea I'd met new people and wanted
to meet them. We caught the bus into the city centre. Through
the main shopping area by coloured neon signs and blazing shop
windows, down a side street past big furnishing shops, printers,
and speciality places, then around the corner from a closed up
lunch bar (dark by then). Along the potholed dirt drive to the
rear of the old villa behind the shoemaker's. We called in to Joe's
early on a Friday evening.
Mark'd just bought the latest Melody Maker newspaper and
held it rolled up like a king did a sceptre, sailing along with his
nose in the air. We strode up the rickety wooden steps at the
back, our steps made a noise. I knocked. Joe let us in. I made
introductions in the big lounge.
When no one paid us that much attention after an initial chat,
Mark muttered, 'Let's go.'
We'd only just sat on the sofa. I said, 'I'd like to stay, but you can
go.'
He just glared at me.
'Walk along that short way. Catch the bus. I'll catch it later.
They're making us a coffee. They're just in the kitchen,' My
voice light, I smiled.
Mark jammed his rolled up newspaper hard into my face. Left
so fast it felt almost like he never existed, except for my
throbbing face. His exit noisy, however, slamming the door. The
others, in the kitchen where they *were* making coffees, rattled
about in confusion. Joe eventually looked in at me.
The paper had hit me in the nose and mouth, but I'd drawn
back so it didn't bruise. It hurt the way accidentally banging into
something when groping in the dark gives a jolt of pain.
Frightening more than anything. No one had ever hit me in the
face before.
Joe's arm around my shoulders was welcome and unusual. A
warm hand on my back. I tried to recall someone doing that

before when someone hit or hurt me. No one ever had. But it
felt like a teacher I knew who would place her hand on my
shoulder – on the rounded part nearest her - if I grew agitated
about some mishap, or the way a doctor patted my arm for
reassurance or gently placed a stethoscope on my chest. A touch
which *gave* me something. Nothing was taken away.
I cried, and Joe comforted me.

Confused, in a ragged state over Mark's attack and distanced
from the pain in my mouth I watched from afar, hovering up
near the ceiling somewhere. Involved with someone who would
hit me, and Mark'd hurt me before. Why did I ever ask him to
my party, all those years before? *Stupid.*

Now I can admit that Mark looked so good that long ago day on
the bus - tall with brownish-red hair longer than any other boy.
His confidence a secret power. *I* wanted to just sit down and ask
for what I wanted, too - like him, but it hadn't quite worked that
way. He'd ambushed me, so disarming. Why had I taken any
notice? To be kind to myself, I say performers get attention, he'd
have persuaded me to do what he wanted even if I didn't care
for his looks and swagger. A dramatic two and a half years we'd
known each other, and I was already accustomed to savage
behaviour from those brothers of mine.
You don't have a lot of clues at fourteen - or I didn't - not sure I
had many more at sixteen either.
Nevertheless, no one else in our backwater suburb in a teeter-
totter edge of the world country offered such riches of sound, a
glorious release into the finest original music. Not even my rich
uncle (who played Louis Armstrong and other popular artists
imported for his hi fi), owned wondrous albums like Mark's. I'd
never have heard those fantastic tracks then in any other way.
Mingus, Miles Davis, Parker, Sun Ra et al. Rich, coruscating
compositions. *Life music* Miles Davis called it, 'I never heard the
word jazz 'til some white man mentioned it. My music is life
music.' Those musicians made me stronger.
Also, I'm reminded now for some reason of something my dad
told me once, on a rare occasion when we had a conversation.

He crunched into an apple. 'See that bruise there, on the fruit?'
'Yes, Dad.'
'I don't care.' Then he chewed it up, flaws and all, a satisfied
look on his face.
Many years later, I imagined talking to my father when I was
drunk one night. I said, ' I don't eat the bruises, even now I'm
older like you were when you told me that story. It was like,
"take the good and the bad," I guess you were saying. But you
can eat more or less the whole apple, you know. The pips and
the core, everything but the stalk.'
I imagined Dad laughed and said he'd never thought of that.

Bellybuttons and Changing Names

We were King and Queen Imagine
glitz reign for infinity.

The stage rich but you've run away,
this play-dream fool again, again, a-gaaain.

- Fool Dreams by The Cool Waters 1971

In wonder weird inventions and revamped faves, we paraded in
our get-ups, eyed each other with frantic intentions - romance
wannabes, stars of the future. The central Woolworths
department store, the fabulous retail jewel in our main street,
close to the virtual palace of the domed and pillared Central
Post Office. Outside, every Friday night, various dramas would
build and subside, build and subside, as if we were trialling soap
opera storylines.
Youth is its own excuse. Over the two years we went around
together (as local idiom had it), Mark and I socialised like those
insects who only have a day to live and have to mate or wreck
the chances of their kind of ever surviving. Urgency and
appetites ruled.

At thirteen, before we'd met, I'd often swung myself alone
onboard the bus, away to town, on Friday nights. Alighted,
coolly showed off what I wore that week along the most
crowded strip of footpath, our main shopping centre. This
involved carefully eying each window, as if one day they could
display something cool, or I maintained a stare along the street
as if someone I knew and loved would appear at any moment.
Sometimes they did.

Movies were our magnet on a Saturday afternoon (I'd
abandoned swimming club due to its inability to keep dreams
afloat). Mum and Dad dropped me off at the cinema one time
with a friend, Katy, on their way to see relatives (picking us up
on the way home). Katy and I whispered together outside,

furiously trying to decide who could be worth a smile, then a giggle. Without ever discussing this we instead muttered over other matters, our eyes every which way. A few minutes of daring to make eye contact with boys before our escape into the dark reaches of the theatre.

Youth club dances loomed monthly. We whirled and swayed hour after hour. We called it dancing but in the barely lit darkness our jiggling could've indicated mere nerves. Conversation limited.

I realised, years later (awake for one of my late night wondering replays-of-Mark), that he liked to take me to parties, to other bands' gigs, and into town where we stopped to chat along the street, as long as I stayed close. Perhaps my company made him feel safer. If I stood beside him then people could be more likely to stop to say hi. With me there they didn't find Mark so peculiar that they grew lost for words. For his part, Mark played many gigs but rarely socialised, unless his sneering comments to almost anyone encountered were considered that.

With his snatches of nonsense songs and crazy quotes from invented or famous people, and the obvious insults he'd blurt occasionally, too, he was a bit touched. But I didn't find his oddness all that difficult. I could usually think of some smart aleck retort myself, or I displayed obvious disbelief with laughter. Mark often scathing then, disagreeable and sniping at me, but we did converse quite freely. His words hurt less than what I'd already suffered at the hands of my brothers for years at home, without anyone intervening. And Mark and I were peculiar together, he matched me. At the time I imagined I was normal, except later I could see how my difficulties attracted other eccentrics - we belonged together because we couldn't see how to fit in anywhere else. (Although I must also say I have never met an ordinary person. We all have our quirks, but some have more than others).

Usually, I'd sulk if Mark was too cruel. Then he'd have to placate me with particular music; he possessed a knack with that stereo. Made an effort too, attempted pleasantness, like someone unsporty managed to aim for a tennis ball occasionally. He did this, however, as if playing a role. Mark only acted or attempted

the kind, gentle lover, as if rehearsing, it seemed to me,
eventually.
I loved asking questions once I felt happier nevertheless, and
Mark knew so much about music and other matters, showing off
knowledge - his peacock display. Face animated, somewhat kind
and entertaining, but Mark never kowtowed to me in public -
nor to anyone else. He got me away from my oppressive and
rather unexciting life, in any case (even if my siblings did still try
to introduce terror at every opportunity). The challenging
avenues of Mark-land - like a real estate ad, *avenues*. Perhaps any
major life shift is like moving house. Our days together held
some rewards. Difficult to forget them even if Mark did end it so
painfully and abruptly at Joe's with his Melody Maker shoved
into my face.

When Mark and I were a couple, I imagine my parents hoped
I'd find him agreeable enough and then settle into married life
and provide grandchildren. Everyone loved babies. It was when
we grew up some people found us disagreeable, with our own
minds, instead of supposedly blank little folk who adults could
drape with their invented, impossible, and sometimes pitiful
dreams and designs.
Invited to the big city eighty miles north for the weekend by a
friend, I packed every piece of fabulousness I owned. My new
white patent platforms looked like front end loaders, only shiny
and gorgeous. Then clompy brown brogues with a chunky heel,
a yellow paisley fitted shirt dress - my folk-singer-turned-rock-
star look - the maxi skirt made from maroon velvet that mum'd
kept for years (true vintage, not pretend), voile blouses with puffy
sleeves, and 1940s grey wool baggies Mum couldn't see herself
wearing again (but o she wished she could). I had to Promise to
Take Care of Them. A few little tops crammed in, just in case;
weather hotter up there, people said. Only the best underwear
(ten changes for two days). Make-up vital, putting it on for a half
hour prepared me for leaving the house. Anyway, the orange
vinyl make-up case also pushed in.
Two nights in Auckland city, the Big Smoke - home of
grooviness and wonder, where no one was ever bored and life

took on extra wow just because. We would die of pleasure. After the first evening, we'd have one full Saturday including a second night and a good half day on the Sunday, before the train departed for the two hour or so trip home. Others could laugh at my enormous swag for such a short journey, but fashion's a truly serious, monumental business, requiring dedication for maximum frivolous fun and glamorous beauty effects.

I was still at high school, but my parents permitted travel with my then-boyfriend Mark on the train. They'd travelled themselves as teenagers for holidays. Mum seemed glad to see me enthusiastic instead of in my room reading or drawing, alone.

Off to see Kim, a new friend we'd met at the beach. Invited to stay at his parents' in a suburb called Kohimarama. My mother wiped her hands on her apron and looked impressed when she heard where we'd be staying. 'O, yeees?' Mum said with this rising inflection.

We sat at the table to talk. Mum really listening. She asked repeatedly, 'Kim lives with his parents?'

I kept agreeing, and eventually we were on our way. Bona fide, supervised and safe.

After the train trip, we disembarked in the elaborate, cavernous Auckland Railway Station. The Ladies Restroom a time machine, with wooden built-in benches in one anteroom where ladies could wait and feel more sure of not being molested or bothered by strangers. Lovely old white tiles for the entire toilet area. Further on near the exit archways, grand echoes. Mosaic floors in pale terracotta, grey, and cream throughout pedestrian ways to and from trains. A high-ceilinged, brick and mortar monumental place; altogether something more suitable for India than the temperate North Island of New Zealand. This especially from the outside where large Phoenix palms waved in the breeze in avenues leading to the entrance, a curved road swept past.

Our largest city an enormous, armoured animal, the sky appearing smaller.

Mark knew what trolley bus to catch from the station to the

built-up city centre. The trolley bus clacked and rattled, attached
by long antennae-like poles at the back to wires overhead.
Sometimes blue sparks flew off into the night at junctions.
The green and yellow trolley bus soon clicked and whirred away.
We walked up a hill to The Bellybutton. Bright psychedelic
swirls : green, purple, yellow, orange, and white on the front
window. A clean white interior, plain pale wooden furniture, and
patrons in the latest clothes at ease with this vegetarian
restaurant innovation. Some passers-by stopped, stared in,
shocked by the cafe's fresh style. I stared at them in amazement,
wouldn't Aucklanders be more accepting?
Inside, bright posters on the pale walls. The scent of spices and
incense overwhelming. Rather dizzy, I surreptitiously held onto
the edge of a heavy plain pine table. In the late 60s nothing like
this cafe existed in our home town. Usually, coffee bars or tea
rooms were furnished with dark chairs upholstered in orange or
brown, or someone crammed them with frilly country-cottage
décor. Those catered for suburban mums out shopping, tourists
and office workers, and sometimes labourers (but the latter
normally patronised a bakery or lunch bar for takeaways to eat
on-site wherever they worked). Sausage rolls, meat pies,
sandwiches (ham, corned beef, egg, cheese and onion), and
cakes (custard squares, neenish tarts, Louise cake, chocolate or
caramel square, slices of sponge with jam and cream filling,
dusted with icing sugar on top)... food in orderly fashion behind
little hinged, plastic windows - display units. Restaurants offered
steak, fish and vegetables, with salad the most exotic thing on the
menu, and creamy desserts heavy on sugar and fat. Meat, cheese
and butter the main feature in every eatery - but not this one.
So we walked in. Kim grinned from a table in The Bellybutton
with a few beaming others in florals or jeans. His long dark hair
flicked back. 'Groovy to see you both, cool. Just a natural high,
here.'
Talk so hip it felt difficult not to gape. When the others spoke
amongst themselves he lowered his voice, 'Look, Mum says you
can't stay at our place. Only got one extra bed, you see? She said
you aren't married so you can't sleep there.'
I'd lugged my immense suitcase along (no wheels on cases in

those days). I imagined if we had to camp out in a park perhaps
my extra clothes could make a tent. The humour in this wryly
kept me going, silent thoughts pumped up with silliness to
bolster myself. The boys chatted, Kim asked, 'Good trip up
here? You must be so glad to be out of your hick town.'
Mark murmured something.

My glare must've registered. From then on their jokes sounded
strained and rather weak. Mark and Kim tried to pretend I
wasn't annoyed with our host's put-downs, hoped I'd just go
along happily with whatever they decided as long as they fed me
pap. In a sullen cloud of wishing to be somewhere else, I didn't
trust myself to speak.

Mark looked so much older than either of us, taller, and he'd
grown a moustache. Kim commanded, 'Go buy a bottle of
vodka. That mixed stuff you get. Go on.'

Kim and I left alone together on our wooden cafe chairs, with a
couple of smoothies in tall glasses. His friends went to a film. At
other tables, couples or groups of friends. Lights bright,
everyone young, but to my hot-faced embarrassment I had little
to say - even if Kim babbled on at first, mentioned what he'd
been doing that week. I just grinned, and said, 'Sure,' or 'Cool, '
but it sounded hokey - hard and flat, nasal. City people
pronounced some things in new ways, 'Cig-*a*-rette,' they said,
lightly. 'Ciga-*rette*,' we out-of-towners said with a hard, dull end
to the word.

Quiet observations – half-amusing - distracted from the
alarming idea we'd soon sleep on the street.

Mum would ask questions on my return about the house we
stayed in, she'd be storing each one in her encyclopaedic mind.
One of Mum's favourite topics - other people's houses… 'Their
curtains were sheers were they? Then the heavier fabric, was it a
pattern or...? The carpet new and patterned, or *plain*? Did they
have a new stove, a dishwasher?'

But we'd done it, a scene, a trip. Young and by ourselves in the
city without a home, no curfew, making do. *Reading* about
someone washed up on a desert island, however, was far more of
a thrill than feeling like we'd soon be sitting in a gutter wishing
for somewhere warm. Nonetheless, definitely a true change from

the suburbs of nowhereland. I stared into space.

Musing over the past seemed far safer than thinking about the future, and I lived as if on a merry-go-round that whirled every which way - as my normal existence. Unpredictable, flickering images from the past appeared at random. Some memories shocked or worried me, others brought a smile. These flashbacks were everyday noise and chatter - I had no idea then that they were Post-traumatic Stress Syndrome. I thought everyone experienced such visions, but no one else spoke of them. Neither did I. The silence of the cracked. Some people call anyone with mental health issues all kinds of names. It's like thinking a sports star can't break a leg, believing clever people don't suffer inner torments or damage. Later, I chose to call the condition a syndrome, like some health professionals do, the word 'disorder' more common but also more damning.

We'd met Kim at the beach, anyway, only that last summer. Cheeky with holiday insouciance and my outwardness (more so from associating with eccentric Mark), I strode along the only shopping street. About six stores, awnings on a lean, and a gas station in those days (with mini-golf next to a trampoline rent-by-the-hour place) - small-town quiet. Mark tried to shut me up with urgent hisses, but I just said loudly to groups of teenagers, 'There's a party on the beach.'

A few people did follow through the gathering night, away from the local shops (closed up except for bright takeaway bars), along a raggedy side street towards the water, and down through the dunes.

They groaned and muttered at the lack of a blaze on the sand and young people singing with guitars, like a Cliff Richard film, but I said we could *make* a bonfire. 'Come on. Get some of this wood together. Who's got a match?' My laughter sounded forced.

One tall guy said, 'You told us there was a fire, already.' It sounded like he wanted to hit someone.

I didn't want to gather driftwood by myself, but made a half-hearted attempt in order to get away from his angry voice and to see if anyone would follow my lead.

No one did.

The Little Red Hen in the children's story would've understood, except this wasn't harvesting wheat to make bread; soon nine or ten pieces of dry driftwood piled up. 'Anyone got any paper or want to get something dry? You know, tinder?'

No one moved. No one spoke.

Sand cold under my sandaled feet in the dark. People snapped remarks. A few walked away.

A disparate bunch remaining talked on the dim beach a while with surf shhhing in the background. This tall boy's American accent obvious, 'Tonight reminds me of a time when we went camping and no one brought anything to cook on.' Petey, he said his name was, after he told his story. His ginger afro and pale face apparent in the moonlight while he drawled on.

We loved America, which poured forth impressive, startling films, vital music, splendiferous cars, fashion, and ideas to our glamour-starved shores.

Petey had told us, 'Pop just went all caveman and decided to set an open fire.' Another family nearby told them off and invited them for dinner in their camper, with a gas burner for a barbecue. The way he spoke in a half-laughing sing-song made people smile.

His friend Kim cracked one-liners, or what sounded like poetry, 'Beach party, surf's up, night swimming with the stars....' and he sprang about. 'Lovely to be here with you fine people. Who's from out of town?' Everyone laughed. None of us were locals. The small crowd close. Kim and Petey, egged on with questions and compliments while surf pounded under a full moon sky. Mark never made one nasty remark nor sang one silly line from a song no one else had ever heard of, so those of us who stayed on the sand did have a pleasant party of sorts for a while.

With the next day sunny and clear, we packed ourselves into Petey's tiny car. A promised ride back to our town two hours away. Kim kept up amusing remarks in the back seat of Petey's orange Mini, as if going for the prize for silliest teenager. 'Vegetarians will save the world, except our farts are worse than anyone else's. Suffocate everybody as soon as they're saved. O

the irony.' Not so much what he said as how he said it - that grin,
those flashing eyes, his tone. For a while he pretended to sleep,
then Kim leapt up, pulled a funny face. Any sudden movement
quite difficult in the tiny car, this made his behaviour even
funnier.

Laughter cosy, the two of us in the Mini's back seat, safe. Mark
wanted more room in the front, had said his legs were longer
than mine. It felt like moving into calm water between the
breakers, smooth surface and soothing noise, beside Kim. But
that was where Dad said never to go, the rip would pull anyone
out to sea in the calm places. Undertow.

Guilt mixed with desire and happiness nevertheless kept me
woozy along the road home. Hours through snaky roads of the
bush-covered Coromandel, along the flat Hauraki plains past
vast paddocks of grass and clustered herds of cattle. We whizzed
by little old shops which sold everything imaginable to local
farmers, and white net curtained coffee bars designed for
peckish holidaymakers. In the little orange car I held my tongue,
made sure I looked at the back of Mark's head at least every few
minutes. Being a little fuzzy 'round the edges felt good, as long as
I didn't try to kiss Kim or do anything like lavish him with
compliments and questions. I could nurture this lovely feeling,
believing the world a great place, without an enormous effort to
believe in the idea, after all.

For some reason, Mark liked him too and asked Kim to stay at
his place one weekend.

Duly, Kim arrived from the city in these great tight jeans
(imported like all blue jeans of any note were then) with his
brown hair much longer. He looked like an Indian from
America. With his usual sass Kim led the conversation. Mark
and he rattled on about music and art. They didn't mind
explaining things to me.

Most men and boys in those days wore their hair more or less
shaved at the sides and so very short on top you could see their
scalp. Screeds of bullet-headed males teemed through school,
work, shops, streets, featured on pages of newspapers and
magazines, in films; clean-cut and severe, every size and shape

but in uniformity, army-neat and tidy. Also, many dressed the same as others - en masse sedate conformity - troops of suited men, many also in trilby hats. Frocked women with Queen Elizabeth curly shortish hair. People's conversations, hairstyles, and food, too, rather bland and careful. Children looked like small versions of adults, often. Teenagers barely invented. If anyone did wear something extra-fashionable, the style remarkable (probably bought from a local expensive boutique or overseas), they were often, 'Showing off,' or 'Up themselves,' or 'Flash, too flash.'

Flamboyant meant suspicious, extreme styles drawing attention (how dare they). People who discussed anything in-depth, critically analysed politics, music, art, films or behaviour, anyone too individual or interesting was an odd-ball, a weirdo. Sit still and agree with the others, be virtuous. Active people needed to focus on sport or paid employment, housework, gardening, particular clubs, or volunteer activities - nothing else. To stand out or expound, to look in any way outrageous or provoking meant, 'rocking the boat,' and no one wanted to get wet.

My dissociative condition meant I didn't register disapproval all that readily (I know now). My father also told us we could wear what we liked and he enjoyed loud discussions after dinner when we grew older, usually inspired by his shouting at the TV news. His encouragement provided a safety valve. By that time it was a variety of sport in our family to talk about news and ideas. None of us children quiet. I also loved the latest fashion; adored discussions and had developed a thick skin.

Mum tried to calm us down, worried we'd lose love over our raucous talk, or come to blows inside the house, but we never did. She didn't mind what happened outside – indoors, however, Mum disliked anything messy. Dad and I both loved making things and, also, discussion - when it mattered (rather than small talk). We certainly disagreed about politics and other topics, with enthusiasm. The world shifted, my father at last conversed with us. We passed some milestone or the other during those heated discussions.

My friends and I took freedom of expression to a previously unseen level. Few parents agreed with Union Jacks cut into hot

pants, lacy tops over bare breasts, lurid colours worn five or
more at a time, men in pants so tight you could see their
anatomy, body paint, towering platform shoes, afro hair, or
ironed straight hair to our waists, fists full of rings, peace signs,
yin/yang symbols, headbands like American Indians wore (and
some took to living in teepees), ethnic jewellery instead of fine
gold and diamonds, tattoos, henna painted skin, enormous false
eyelashes.... Older people only took on any fashion after it'd
been diluted and reconfigured to appear acceptable to them.
We'd copy things on TV or album covers the day we saw them.
In a frenzy, cutting out copies on our bedroom floors. Sewing
machines ran up such concoctions. We dressed like our idols and
imported fashion magazine models before shops ever thought to
offer any way out, far gone, wild and wonderful designs. Not
that we ever said 'way out' or 'far gone' - advertisers used terms
like those, not us. Some also discovered or founded little
alternative places, imported or made outlandish styles. And we
dressed that way because we thought it made us look good.
Men and teens with hair that just covered their ears even a
fraction were such a contrast beside sharply defined males'
severe haircuts. I wanted to stroke some as if they were cats.
Many in time took on this softer look. Sensual. Everyone's hair
grew in particular ways, the manifestations startled many. The
straight-laced, upright and sedate - their plain dress and super-
tidy hair proof of innate goodness or obedience, and therefore
decency - were threatened. Some driven to shout in public or
frown at men with longer hair (people they didn't know), in the
street. 'You there, sonny. You. Boy or girl? Ay? Ay? Get yer hair
cut.'
Many bars and restaurants refused to allow long-haired men or
casually dressed women inside - they *lowered the tone.* Prim styles
provided a certain gravity to any proceeding, but people
flaunting their sensual and individual side suggested far too
many possibilities for them to pass.
Various students at parties sounded off. 'Only 40 or 50 years
earlier, any woman laced into a tight corset was called decent. In
enduring these instruments of torture, many fainted or grew to
have health problems.' This social science major laughed, coldly.

'A woman not forced into an hour-glass appearance appeared more voluptuous, out of control. This threatened belief in rigid obedience, a preference for a lack of individuality and refusing to consider kindness as worthwhile. We must keep on with preferences which encourage a healthy lifestyle, be open-minded.'

The world held many opinions, they teemed, as if thoughts were a kind of tropical fish. Some parents and school teachers believed we were out of our depth. Surely sinking to criminality and ill health; long hair, modern styles, overt sexiness, and obvious joy - all evil. Wrong to delight in our youth. 'But surely they did the same thing when they were younger?' A professor talking this time, taking a break from playing his sitar at a gig, 'Your parent's fashions reveal the guilty truth. Old photos. Daring baggy suits, tight topped dresses, plunging necklines on evening gowns.'

Luckily our father didn't demand we wear out-dated things, and Mum often ran up new styles on her sewing machine then showed me how. But a handful of relatives and others openly ridiculed my bright red tights and cut off jeans, covered in multi-coloured embroidered decals. Or they screwed up their faces at the ankle-length, floaty dresses in delicate Liberty prints we true fashion leaders wore, just when coloured mini skirts in every material possible appeared on seemingly everyone, everywhere. Bewildering - almost every woman in an entire city wearing a skirt at least at mid-thigh or higher. But as soon as anything gained mass approval, true fashion leaders rejected it.

In any case, Kim, like a bright flower in an entirely green garden, drew my attention. A live wire, my dad would've called him. Kim knew, 'This guy who paints with only discarded food then varnishes the results. You've gotta see his work. Art, man, fine art reveals so much.'

My mind expanded so fast it creaked and cracked, listening to his expansive stories.

Once, Kim went out with a girl who spoke only Russian, and a coffee bar owner called her a communist and chased them with a kitchen knife. At school, Kim took over an entire classroom as a protest, for a week. 'Until they promised to build a music room. Those fascists had no right to refuse to teach us what we needed to know.'

We listened, wide-eyed, exclaiming. We wanted to be a part of Kim changing things. So it seemed natural that when Kim had asked us to go to Auckland that time we went.

Going over when we first met Kim and how captivated with him we'd felt - memories crowded my mind while I sat dejectedly in The Bellybutton Cafe. The food smelt tantalising, but we had nowhere to stay, I didn't want to lug a suitcase wherever we went next and, now, conversation flagged. But we'd only been in Auckland two hours. Not as scintillating as Kim made out, with his, 'O Auckland's got tons of great places to go. The coolest....' I didn't say a word against the place, however, waited at the scrubbed wooden table with him in The Bellybutton. My silence spoke volumes.

Kim muttered things like, 'We'll be fine. I know a place near here.'

I turned into an ember - an intensely furious, quiet teenager building steam for whatever lay ahead.

In Auckland, on the bus from the train station, I'd seen so many shiny shops and streets crowded with cars. Everything glittered and shone, buildings towered above on and on, it was much bigger than our town's one main drag. I felt unsure - could I catch a train home if I had to, by myself? Usually I knew exactly how to get home. I murmured to Kim, 'Hope it's close. My suitcase is heavy.'

Mark strode in with the bottle of vodka in a brown paper bag, a victorious look, eyes shiny. Now I realise he'd probably already had a drink. Looking back makes everything seem so much easier to understand. At the time it's breath-taking action. We three left the cafe.

Down the hill, across the main thoroughfare at Victoria Street with trolley buses zinging past, then up the other side. Kim said workmen had started on new grounds for the City Art Gallery, 'We could probably sleep there. I've done it before.'

Coloured lights glowed all around and I tried to believe my fashionable platform shoes, sheer pantyhose, and shirt-dress mattered, but I wished I liked wearing jeans. Hoped the place we headed for wasn't too rugged.

We walked and turned right into Kitchener Street, the enormous trees of Albert Park looming above to the left. I hefted my suitcase and wobbled behind the boys on my high shoes. A few little shops to our right, all closed. Late shopping was over at 9pm. Across the road lay lengths of wood, bags of cement and other construction site mess. Kim spoke quietly, 'They're building a fountain and so on.'

I clambered over sawn timber and across shallow ditches, hoping my heels wouldn't break. Cooler air whispered about but it wasn't cold. I staggered, worried my dress would rip. My big glass rings kept hitting against concrete or other hard materials. Taking them off, I swore to myself by half-built garden walls. In fashion shoots, they sometimes posed a model done up to the nines with a backdrop of half-finished or ruined buildings, but no one had paid me to model anything.

The boys muttered to each other and laughed quietly, taking swigs from the bottle of vodka mix, visibly more relaxed in the shadows. I glanced about but no one seemed close-by. No one near trees in the park above, nor in the rather dark street a short distance below. Mark and Kim, in dark tops and jeans, blended with trees and the exposed earth, and the slab of concrete we'd finally relaxed upon.

Half of the large bottle of vodka was gone by then - a ready-mixed, orange, sickly concoction, called Screwdriver with a cartoon drawing of a partying Cossack on the label. They occasionally passed it to me. Soon Kim hissed, 'I saw someone lurking in the trees.' He muttered, 'It looks like some older guys just settled over the wall. Probably drunks. They want to sleep there.' He grimaced. 'They could get violent. We have to go.'

We hunched over and scuttled away, me dragging my case. Two heads popped up. The men over the wall must have heard us. One, in a long dark coat, clambered towards me. 'Hey girlie. Whatcha got?'

I'd lagged behind. The boys didn't hear the old dero. The vagrant's stench made me feel like throwing up. I held onto my suitcase handle. He grappled with the thing. 'Fuck off. Leave me alone,' I shouted.

We fought. My hands hurt and my arms ached. I imagined the drunk could hurt me, there'd be blood over my face in a photograph. A front page story in a stupid Sunday newspaper. My parents horrified. I grew short of breath and someone hit my arm. I yelled again, 'Fuck off!'

My legs weak as ribbons. Impossible to see the boys properly in the darkness. Huge trees overhead blocked streetlight, and we were surrounded by building site disorder. They'd walked off without me? Mark loved to stride onward for hours with his chin out, hands in pockets, nostrils flared. He could've gone ahead and never checked behind.

My hand tight on the suitcase handle. The old drunk tried to prise my fingers off, again. His hands slimy, wet, and rough - but weak. He stunk of booze. I kicked at him. He groaned but would not let go. 'You got a bitta fire in yer, girlie. Betcha go off. Do yah?' He leered into my face.

I turned away, sobbing now.

'Hey, leave her alone.' Kim, a huge dark shadow. His voice menacing rather than loud, 'I've got a knife. I'll cut you, you stupid old man.'

The drunk let go, staggered back into the building site. He muttered something but we were truly gone before his fragmented words quite reached us to make sense of them.

Kim grabbed my bag. 'Let me take this.'

Mark had a few things in a duffle bag and hadn't assisted me with my luggage, not once. He'd not exactly dashed to my rescue, either (Kim did), but Mark hugged me when we got clear of the rough ground and street where the old man had tried to steal my belongings.

After we rushed away, I trembled and gagged. We now stood in a hidden area, high concrete walls on three sides. Boxes and bins on the footpath side obscured us from passers-by. 'Just walk.' Kim grinned.

'Where to?' Mark sounded disdainful.

I sat down. 'Those drunks could follow us. My arm hurts.'

'You didn't need that huge case.'

'For God's sake, you bloody idiot. We were staying at a house.

Not living in the street like, like....'

'Good to get moving again soon,' Kim tried a less cheerful tone, looked apologetic.

'Yeah, it'd be good not to sit next to rubbish bins. Great scenery.' I turned away from them both.

A cold corner of the city, long after shops had closed on this Friday night. Hardly any nightclubs existed, no funky little bars or cafes that were open late. New Zealand closed down early, except for isolated takeaway places. On the edge of civilisation, on the slim chance we could make our own fun, we were stranded in the biggest city of Nowhereland.

Eventually, the vodka we'd glugged down affected a slump. I fell somewhat asleep in the mild summer air with the cheap alcohol's fake warmth.

Some traffic noises here and there, occasional footsteps passed by; I woke up first, rubbing my arms and legs to chase off the chill. Concrete and old rubber, the city greeted me with its perfume. Still dark but Kim told me it'd be dawn soon. He wore a watch. We sat there enclosed by this u-shape of walls, on chilly concrete.

'If we walk home now, we could hang out at my place. Catch more sleep through the day.'

'I'm going to arrive at your place with my suitcase?' My voice childish, high.

'Yeah, well, why did you bring that great big thing anyway?'

'Thought we were staying at your *house*. Remember?'

Silence.

About fifteen minutes after easing out of our hiding place and then walking through the closed up city - expensive, blank, and enormous - observed by a few delivery men in trucks, we walked along the waterfront. Five or six cars cruised past, but most of Auckland slept. Nowhere was open for food early in the morning, few shops were lit, and people lived in the suburbs then - except for street people : bottle-os and tramps who generally hid away in the quieter inner-city hours.

Near Kim's place, after a half an hour - a good long trek, we passed a line of old wooden boat sheds all joined together, with high double doors for each one. Painted pale sherbety green and blue, they looked pretty but worn. 'Come on,' Kim grinned, 'let's sleep in here. One of my friends has a dinghy kept inside for their boat. They told me the lock's broken. Look.'

Despite my protests that it seemed wrong to be going into someone's shed, we ended up inside, clambering about again. This time, we climbed up to sit in one of the small row-boats on the top row of dinghies, stored on wide wooden runners.

Glamorous new places, clubs and restaurants, parties to wear the best clothes at - all those wonders had been imaginary. No band played, no music nor people dancing, no one to talk with about what they were wearing or where to go next to hear some even better band play and to dance ourselves. My sullen mood as heavy as the dark harbour outside.

The boys made themselves comfortable on two rowboats' narrow wooden seats, rocking about and making a racket, thock, thock, thock on the broad wooden shelves. I couldn't see how to sleep in the thing, nor in any of the others. 'Seems wrong to me, to get into someone's boat like that, Kim.'

The boys behaved like they'd landed on a desert island without me.

Auckland's railway station only an exotic memory. The road we'd trudged had taken us far from the city now, with no recent landmark familiar. A train held heating, cushy seats. It chug-a-chugged along, rocked and swayed a comfortable beat. But every crowded street muddled into every other. Startling. Tall buildings blurred. My thoughts were disjointed, and I felt like I was missing vital pieces of information. I kept remembering that smelly old drunk grabbing, as if I'd never forget his rancid breath and crazed stare. If I walked out and tried to get back to where we'd arrived there would be few people about to ask directions from - and someone could bundle me into their car, against my will. What then? White slavers roamed the city, they hunted for lone girls, we talked about them at school all the time. No choice but to steam silently in the rather chilly, extremely early morning.

At least it promised to turn into a warm day, the sun had been strong on a clear horizon already, when we'd entered this refuge, and the night hadn't been inclement, either.

We dozed fitfully awhile.

A noise, footsteps, then someone rattled the boat shed door, stomped in and we all held our breath. Mark and Kim's faces completely visible but shadowy. The sun had come up, shafts of light filtered through cracks in the unlined boat-shed walls.

The man below could raise his eyes, investigate, or want one of the boats we sat in.

Kim suppressed a giggle and I wanted to hit him, but just glared his way instead. We listened while the boatie slid out their little rowboat below us and set off for a yacht moored in the harbour. On the road again soon afterwards, we eventually found Kim's parents' place. Along the way I'd completely lost the power of speech. The boys probably glad. My complaints had grown more and more inventive, '...If we keep walking my legs will turn to stubs. This isn't your suburb at all is it, Kim? Some kind of torture Auckland inflicts on people. Walking in circles like lab rats....' Our glamorous weekend now one of those moralistic stories about people who went to London thinking streets were paved with gold, then ended up robbed and injured in the dirt. All my reading hadn't made me so clever. I grimly trudged on, trying not to cry. My enormous suitcase heavier and heavier, but I made the boys carry it by simply refusing to go on unless they did so.

My secret love for Kim was a store of fuel too, hopeless romanticism uplifting me - even if I found his jokes rather silly by then, and his lack of a plan almost a reason to go home as soon as we arrived. Again, a fool had appeared, and I adored him. Kim had let us travel all that way without explaining that we had nowhere to sleep, just so he could see us both and show off his supposedly wonderful city.

His lectures on the wonders of vegetarianism started to pall along with everything else. But then he smiled and made some wry remark, like, as we plodded along in weak early light, 'I told you Auckland was a fun place....'

We cracked up laughing. The way he said things. Throughout our walk - an ordeal - when Kim made me laugh I forgave him. Click. Just like that. His smile and the quick way he moved like a sleek cat; I almost ran a hand along his long, freshly washed brown hair.

That sitar-playing professor I'd listened to before, if he was there he'd probably say, 'Human beings, we make decisions based on all kinds of ridiculous premises. That's why we have forgiveness. Without such a concept, how could humanity go on?'

Kim's place was a mid-green weatherboard house in a well-kept street with many trees. We climbed up some concrete steps by a white-painted wrought iron zig-zag rail. Into the kitchen, which was in pale colours and smelled of lemons. His grim mother tried to look stern enough to make us leave, but Kim charmed her, too. 'They stayed somewhere else last night, Mum. Just calling in for something to eat. I'll get it, you don't have to do a thing.'

I tried to smile and say something polite, but maybe she could smell that cheap vodka on us. One hard stare from this woman and I looked away, made myself invisible - or close to it.

Instead of chatting with his mother, which I'd planned to do, I hung out down the hall with the boys in Kim's small room. I lay on the top bunk and they sat on the floor. This phrase-popping, hip-looking, evangelical vegetarian slept in a dark green room with proper, new, wooden drawers and a built-in wardrobe. His homework was done at a new plain wooden desk below a small cork notice-board on the wall - a couple of magazine pictures neatly placed there with drawing pins, just so. Kim so often told me how useless our town was and how great Auckland was, what joys awaited, but his city meant disappointment and ordinary suburban life - except for his continuous spiel.

For an age, he ran through the food innovations he introduced to the family home, 'Wholegrains - totally excellent for your body, mind, and spirit. The oneness of all things needs respect.' Held on my knee was a plate piled with various cooked grains that had been chilled, bean sprouts, a wholemeal wafer and some kind of brown sauce. He explained everything on my plate, and why it was better than meat and three veg.

'Wholefood feeds your body true vitality.' His art, he assured us, really improved since he changed his diet. 'Once your vision clears, creativity knows no bounds.'

Later, I fell asleep off and on, lolling on his top bunk between

talk of vitamins and oil pastels, a lulling drone from Kim. He sat
on the floor cross-legged and Mark dozed on the bottom bunk.
When I awoke after one really good nap, I could see Kim
stretched out on the floor, asleep. Curtains were drawn but
enough daylight filtered through to see he was just a boy. Like
when bright house-lights in those days went on inside the
cinema after a movie, illumination dispelled most of his charm.
Then I fell asleep once more and later what I'd seen and felt was
just a dream.

Finally, after a good rest, I washed my face and brushed my
teeth, did my hair, reapplied make-up, and changed all my
clothes - invincible and scintillating once again. Looking good
one step towards feeling great. We made for the city but I had to
take my suitcase. 'I know,' Kim beamed. We dropped the
massive thing at the bus station in Left Luggage. A handy place
– cases could be left there for a fee, once a upon a time - before
suitcase-bombs shattered public places worldwide too many
times. Kim said, 'We're going to Albert Park. It's A Happening.'
We caught a bus to the city.

Bright sunshine, blue sky, electric music loud enough to hear
before the park hove into view. People happily drifted towards
raucous electric guitars, loud drums, and two people singing
rock. De rigeur to waft or dance towards the stage, some
bounced. In blue jeans, tie-dye, and flowery things, young
people and the young-at-heart thronged the lush, well-tended
park. A colourful crowd was scattered over tended lawns and
beside regular flower gardens - crowds of teenagers, freedom-
lovers, political activists, hippies, and yippies all relaxed, snaking
their arms and talking in animated or aloof fashion. A bunch
danced and bright fabrics caught the breeze.

The Progressive Youth Movement had a low stage with their
own flag flying. One speaker, red mouth wide, railed against the
government. His long, wild black hair tossed with every
emphatic point. Another, whose stringy blond hair whipped
about when he laughed and flung up his arms, insisted socialism
had to work or we'd all suffer. Tim Shadbolt was compelling -
his grin, that drawl - every word clear and magnetic. So much of
this was news to me. I tried to gather as much as possible,

distracted with culture shock. Another speaker used his hands to
keep the audience watching. They splayed out against the sky, or
he figured the air as if moulding shapes from it, words as clear
as the faultless blue. A teeming mass listened, applauded,
hooted, and cheered.

The PYM ranted on and on (with music in between for the main
attraction) in our town too, by our lake, but the Auckland
Happening swelled to easily ten times the size. Eventually we
couldn't see the grass or the smaller trees and shrubs much at all,
there were people everywhere.

The Move played, their guitarist in black and white calfskin
pants, and the singer's long silk scarf floated on the summer
wind. Air salty from the sea nearby with hints of gasoline; traffic
streamed past the crowded park and nearby university grounds.
A girl with curly hair (which fell over a long filmy dress
patterned with tiny flowers) danced by the stage and waved her
hands in the air. She kicked her long legs, twirled, swooped, and
skipped into the air. I tried not to stare; wished I was her.

Myers Park was a good ten minutes walk away. It led from the
central city up to Karangahape Road. That green space had
previously been the only legal place to stand and speak to the
public, the story went, but it got too small. Hippies appeared
from nowhere and everywhere. They moved on from reading
books about politics, and meditation classes. They found esoteric
clothing in India and South America, and brought with them
fresh attitudes recycled from the ages. They spoke up, out,
sideways, and often. Revolutionaries rejected conservative ways,
favoured instead free love, open debate, protest, cultish
behaviour, and foreign ideas like Eastern philosophies. Youth
and liberals - a few casualties of stricter places - copied their
style and soon amassed in park gatherings. The city, a nation,
the world - transformed in mere months. One day an ebullient
crowd gathered in Myers Park to listen to people like Tim
Shadbolt. A core group amongst them said they were sick of
talking about how they needed a bigger space. A mass simply
marched through the city. Took their Happening to Albert Park.
Months before Mark and I visited, these activists had taken over
the orderly flowerbeds, collection of trees, and manicured lawns.

Freedom-loving hippies, weekend wannabes, politicos and earth-shakers, sightseers, and soothsayers enjoyed the music, poets, and political speakers in the landscaped gardens by the university every weekend. A statue of the rather aged Queen Victoria looked on.

Our smiley friend Kim as attractive as any light in darkness. People kept stopping to converse with him. In a print dress (tiny pink and green flowers on cream), a girl with a pretty woven sun hat who had surely just stepped off the pages of a British fashion magazine (my finest compliment) appeared '...fresh, groovy, and so very now. This cute floral with a long flirty skirt....' I wanted to write fashion journalism, to move to Auckland immediately, and discover where you bought clothes like hers. Difficult not to goggle like she was an exhibit in a show. For a few moments I suppose I felt like what half my town did when they saw me in my latest finery every Friday night, parading.

My year-old platform shoes now too clunky like bricks on the end of my legs, out-of-date, overly formal. Most of this crowd wore flats or sandals. Nearby, I moved my legs sideways out of her line of vision. We relaxed on the grass, well back from the crowded main stage. I'd certainly grinned all my life, but now the great smiley-smile of positive vibes took possession of me. Petey the American appeared with his sister. 'Such a cool day. This crowd, what a groove,' Petey's words rolled. With the friendly Americans we were surrounded by teenagers dressed in the latest gear. Excellent live music was everywhere - and free. Of course Kim loved this place.

At home, the only foreigners were the Dutchman who owned our local shops (but didn't talk to me), a fierce-looking man called Svenson in our street (who built boats but didn't speak much English), a few Irish and German people dad befriended (who did talk to me but they weren't young), plus an Indian teacher at our high school - and she spoke with an accent like mine, even if she did wear a sari sometimes. Some Maori people lived in a suburb nearer town in my home city by the railway station - their accents more like country people - and one Maori woman lived in a street near us, but she spoke like Pakeha. She

was, I'd noticed, however, kinder than the rest of the women (all
Pakeha) in our street. Almost everyone else a pale New
Zealander, with nasal twangs demanding to know what on earth
I was wearing, or simply glaring, rarely sympatico.
Heavy suitcase gone, at ease after true sleep, the weekend
evolved. Sunshine, political ranters, live music, excellent fashion,
masses of people quite different to anyone in our city…. We
wandered the park day-long and enjoyed every second. I wanted
to move to Auckland and live there.

That evening velvet soft, we rode the train home – with nowhere
decent to sleep, we couldn't stay any longer. Swayed along for
miles and miles for two hours or so, chugging through the
suburbs and factories of Auckland as buildings grew
progressively smaller and further apart. Wide open countryside
soon greened everywhere, with only occasional small towns or
settlements in sight for brief minutes, six or seven times. Smiling,
we conversed mildly, or dozed.
The Happening, the sunny day, people we met, Kim's smile, his
laugh....

Within a week or so I started wearing jeans - even though they
never suited my curvy figure. No one made women's jeans, or if
they did, we didn't know how to order them from America or
Australia. I copied the way Kim tied his house key to his jeans
belt tab with a leather thong.
The next time he came to stay at Mark's, I flicked the key in his
general direction - showed him I'd caught his fashion. Kim
stared askance. 'Can't anyone be an individual these days?'
So hot I could've cooked something on my head. Blushes were a
reminder that I could stupidly invent a story to suit any situation
and fool myself, but too often considered people were kinder
than they really were. The idea that someone would not want to
be copied never entered my head. Fashion all about imitation,
wasn't it? It took hours to gather Kim stood *against* fashion, and
this stunning idea kept me quiet for some time.
At Mark's while we listened to music, or around town (at the one
cafe we'd discovered with a good jukebox), Kim raved on more

than usual about our useless town. Did concrete and ceaseless traffic, crowds, and endless busyness exude a special atmosphere which transformed people to feel more sure of themselves? Conjecturing while hoping that Kim really liked me, it was apparent that he didn't - not much, anyway. My balloon of hope deflated and disappeared.

In the usual haze of adolescent confusion I cried after he went home, and admitted to Mark I thought I loved Kim.

'I thought so,' Mark muttered.

Why I admitted my feelings to Mark I couldn't say at the time. Now, I think I hoped he'd dump me and I'd finally never again feel his overpowering, hard-hearted push. Kim was more inclined to criticise places than people. He also didn't linger on anything he didn't like about my behaviour, on and on, as an excuse to flatten me with words. He only mentioned the key I'd worn the one time. His merriness was such a welcome change. In any case, fantasies about Kim quite disappeared. It felt like when I adored someone in a TV show or a film and then it got switched off, only Kim didn't act. He just was. Then he was not. For some reason I didn't have Kim's address, so I couldn't write or call. But I did wonder how I could feel as happy as he'd seemed to be. Pitiful to me now - the scraps of information, the glimpses of behaviour, the hopeful plans I patched together as a kind of security blanket - a sense of there being possible ways to change without anyone else's help. For many years I thought everyone had to live that way, to manage without another person on their side. You just tried to sneak clues, find treasures, then needed hours alone to imagine how they could work in your own life.

With my brothers so snide, continual insults from Mark, and my parents somewhat distant, to stay hopeful I developed a rich imaginary world. In the mundane routine of school, bus rides, suburbs, home, dinner, sleep, school, and weekends doing the same things with the same people, I struggled with inventing ideas to inspire me. Real events were often painful, they dulled or shocked me - but most simply evened me out to this humdrum blur.

I had no idea why Mark wanted me to stay as his girlfriend and found few reasons to stick around. The whole masochist/sadist dynamic in love affairs was as foreign to me as a coal mine under the earth. I also had no idea that people could oddly enjoy such unbalanced relationships, or that bullies have to always have a target. I didn't want to feel pushed around and belittled, but lived in a twisted picture. Other people perhaps cannot imagine the trapped feeling, where there were in fact no walls or locks.

Our Auckland friend Kim impressed me the way a great view from a high building gets people thinking they could move to an apartment. Then the actual move looks too expensive or difficult, or someone remembers they get vertigo. But while Kim was around, Mark didn't hurt me so often, not as obviously at least. He refused to help with my heavy suitcase and other by-the-way things like that, but nothing right-in-my-face mean.

Mark often insulted his family and friends, like his dad, 'Shut up old man, you're stupid.'

His father just sneered at him, in reply.

To fellow band members once he shouted, 'This is not music, it's an obscenity. Fuck you.'

Along the street, Mark sniped at a girl he knew without pausing for breath, 'You look like a fool. Join a circus.' He drew a sludgy line of foul words around people then pointed it out like their own doing. To argue with him or even to try to laugh about it became too wearying eventually. But familiarity is a pattern we know how to fit into - even the ugliest or most painful routine may seem preferable to the discomfort of having to learn better. Some of us may have no idea there is anything else.

The images keep on arriving. I try to make sense of it all (to get free of anywhere, surely we have to know what the place holding us looks like?). Mark in a swamp, on a house-boat that was falling apart. No way to get out of the stinky water. He couldn't walk along the road and up a hill to see more - couldn't believe in wider possibilities than sarcasm and arrogance. He needed company in misery at the bottom. Now perhaps it's easy to see what he was like, back then it was a place I simply couldn't escape.

Maybe I provided him something close to goodness. Mark smiled softly every once in a while, as if he really loved to see my face close to his but couldn't allow himself to be that vulnerable for long. Music more like his true love, lost in those songs.
I kept on thinking I could get free though, no matter how many times many older women made it clear that it was our duty to suffer so men could be happy.

Years later, I ran into Petey's sister again, when I took a school trip to the Auckland museum. 'How is your brother, and that friend of his - Kim?'
'Oh they are with Baba now...' She smiled wanly, said the guru's full moniker.
They'd both joined a religious cult and changed their names.

At Ngaruwahia Music Festival (our own Woodstock and the first of its kind in the country) I sat on a sunny hill. A farm venue, above where the stage was set, beside the scarf-draped booths selling beaded, fringed fashions, or offering services like tarot readings. A band thumped and wailed through their set. The crowd wafted by in silky dresses, embroidered tops, blue jeans, long skirts, or next to nothing, sometimes nude or in bodypaint. Smiling or calm, contented, and many danced in drug-induced undulations or frenzies while others meandered about in a trance.
A slim figure walked into view below and he laughed, tossing his dark hair.
I sat up straight and stared.
He approached a group of people below the hill. Everyone there was animated, smiling excessively, hugging each other, and exchanging greetings - like they needed other people to see their joy.
Since I believed my heavily pregnant self wouldn't make a grand sight if I sailed into view, my long full dress billowing, instead I called his name. He smiled and joked with the group of people only 20 metres away, not far. I'm sure he heard me. 'Kiiim. Kiiim. Kiiim.'
Not once did he even glance my way, and (if I read his lips

correctly) I think he said, 'I don't even hear it when someone calls my old name any more.'

Their collective laughter rose up like the sound of water flooding everything else. Down through the music-filled, sunny air, I could've made my way over to say hello. It had only been a few years since we'd seen each other. Getting up would feel ungainly but I imagined the walk downhill and could see how to maintain grace if I took a diagonal.

I wondered how I'd explain my huge belly and my unmarried state - the yet again odd relationship I'd found myself in. So much happened without planning, and often I felt so sad I cried for hours.

Over the last year or so, I'd read stories in the tabloid press about teenage religious cult members. Not allowed to speak to families, nor to old friends. But Kim's friends appeared unrestrained in the crowd of music fans. The band played on - a fine cacophony. People were in synch with the beat in the warm sun on this cheery day. Me, I felt like I wasn't allowed to talk to them, as if I lacked something to make myself heard. I was faced with his apparent boundless delight on the bright hillside below with his beaming new friends.

He'd stepped into a new persona, taken another name, gone somewhere I couldn't follow.

Love Shack

Got all the light behind us now
sun and moon on our side.

You and I found our place to dance.

Never mind what anyone else may say,
for all time ever long we'll own these days.

- Timeless in Rock by True Rock 1972

A rolled up Melody Maker newspaper in the face when you're
feeling quite pleased with yourself and you're expecting only a
cup of coffee from the people you're visiting is a shock. My (at
that instant) ex Mark stomped out of the room, long reddish
hair flying like a war banner after his brief attack. I'd wanted to
stay at Joe's place and Mark had wanted to leave.
Tears ran down my face. The rather bare and dishevelled lounge
felt cold.
Joe appeared from the kitchen where'd he'd gone to make coffee
and asked, 'What happened?'
'Said I wanted to stay here, Joe. And, a-and he pushed that
stupid newspaper into my face.' I held a hand to my mouth.
Tears didn't stop and my voice sounded whiny.
Joe was over to my chair in seconds, kneeling down. After an
examination to see if anything was truly damaged, we decided
coffee all 'round could solve everything.
A jug boiling, cups clinked together, with laughs every other
sentence.
Mug of hot instant coffee in hand, I ran details of what
happened over and over in my mind. Although I'd been
provocative and quite uncaring, saying he could go home alone,
I paid little notice to that detail - since he'd *hit* me. Ammunition.
Another battle. Mark frequently took my answering back
(offering extra information or disagreeing with his assertions) as
an onslaught. He tried to shut me up with his own rants. I was
quite a captive by the time I'd befriended those city flatmates at

Joe's, but they presented a way out. Mark now was exorcised
with kindness and beautiful noise.

Far from tidy houses tucked up in spick and span gardens on the
edge of town - exurbia - where tousled farmland met manicured
urban sprawl. Now in our city centre. Traffic noise, an
impersonal atmosphere, anonymity. Faded cream, brown, black,
and blue denim - the dominant colours of their flat in a
converted house. Bright friends, angles and wangles. Life
boomed.

Joe and Pete lived near the town centre, two streets back from
where a Woolworths department store offered stands of goods
with uniformed assistants in the centre of each island. DIC was
a swept-up version of the same establishment, only with more
clothing and hats, and posher counters. Hallensteins sold
menswear, suits, or casual walk shorts, and coffee bars offered
glass jugs of Cona coffee, warm on a metal stand.

We stood at a counter and asked for what we needed, served by
a trained retailer, everywhere we shopped. Almost nowhere
massed stock, displaying it on the shop floor for people to touch;
shop assistants presided over displays of goods instead.

No supermarkets existed in the whole country. The Hamilton
Art Gallery was a large tin shed run by a musician who sang in a
band on weekend evenings. Book shops looked like libraries but
were even more conservative. And, curved over the one, two,
and occasionally three storey shops and buildings, the enormous
sky of an immense river valley and surrounding dairy farm
plains dominated with colour and weather.

Only one stage on the bus to university from their place, my
latest friends were lucky, even if the walls looked grubby and the
cream-ish carpet had holes near every doorway. One bedroom
wall had a child-sized hole to the outside, roughly mended with
off-cuts of wood. But no one else was about at night, nor on the
weekends (with no Saturday trading). Band practise rocked until
dotty hours, uninterrupted. Black leads, speaker boxes and amps
- beige, black, and gold woven synthetic cloth over the speakers;
Fender guitars, Gretch drums, sometimes a Gibson guitar
(everyone admiring when this instrument first appeared) - I
learnt the best names to revere and those to take little notice of;

hefty microphones, and chrome stands. High ceilings shook with music. High inhabitants did too, and we believed we'd take everything higher - where enlightenment awaited us. Telephones, newspapers, and television, with some radio for publicity, massive waves of word-of-mouth, the fans... fame built slowly. Few music magazines ever mentioned a New Zealand musician. When musos departed for another country they were expected to make it there or return home and painfully rebuild the following they'd enjoyed before, often from scratch, or give up.

A phone connected. 'We only use it during the night to ring out. Think it's a forgotten extension from the shoemaker and mender's out the front. Don't want them to remember it's here.' To voodoo the anti-gurus, one afternoon Joe wrote a song about people on the other side of the wall, eavesdropping. Teens drifted about in orange print Indian tops, embroidered muslin pink, purple, reds and blues, white frilly shirts, paisley and pop, sexy boots, beaded jewellery, and glop make-up. We rocked pop off its proper perfect perch and it had to learn to fly acrobatics. Long hair meant so much in the early 70s. 'Clown outfits, beardie weirdies, o you complete sluts, you impertinent yobbos....' the staid and afraid a chorus, sometimes they hissed, other times they shouted, occasionally they spat the words. Our shrieks of disbelieving laughter.
Maybe the quiet shoemaker and his staff *did* stand with glasses held against the wall - spies hoping to hear an orgy, or mysterious noise they could turn into whatever they imagined. We spent our time in talk, playing cards, smoking cigarettes, loving music, and other enjoyments.
Conversations swelled and ran like rivers. Rinsing off parents' prescriptions for a healthy existence, we swam in peculiar waters. Joe and his friends studied philosophy, sociology, and psychology. They discussed discoveries, and dug into words as if they'd grow new ones. Sometimes they did. Shadows moved elsewhere. Music was a tornado, a flood, as startling as a hail storm. But *we* believed we were gentle souls searching for peace and love if you read our badges and slogan-printed shoulder

bags. Few fights or disagreements, usually - gently, albeit uproariously, enjoying ourselves. Dreaming of when NZ songs would play on the radio. Joe wanted to perform overseas. Flip colour slaps, ballyhoo rebellion, once upon a lull of a time - a generation who'd never known a war we had to go to.
In the midst of mind-altering whizz-bang and furious fashion statements, a stray black cat appeared on the bare dirt yard and driveway every few days. It peered towards the back steps. A huge area behind Joe's had ground turned to dust by years of vehicles going and appearing. Surrounded on three sides with the new, grey rear walls of 1960s concrete block buildings without big windows facing away from the street. The dirt area was used for parking, and sometimes we sat out there on lounge furniture dragged from inside to enjoy weekend sunshine. Anyway, when the cat appeared it was clearly visible. The animal sniffed around our circle at a good distance or stared, but skittered off when anyone approached. 'Here puss, puss, puss. Awww, he's run away.'
Joe and I spent weeks coaxing the black and white moggy closer with tasty offerings from filled rolls we bought around the corner from the bakery, or sardines from a tin. We purchased cat food. His sleek dark coat proved we'd changed his scraggy ways after two or three weeks, but we wanted to stroke him. 'Always wanted a cat,' said Joe with this wistful look.
We decided someone dumped 'our' cat and then local shop owners and businesspeople shooed it off. City traffic would have scared the animal, and rarely a kind word spoken to it. The cat shied from our touch as if we were those others. Shrieking guitars and the crash of cymbals from Joe's, a stereo at full blast - this maelstrom of rock and roll bouncing around the enclosed back yard (gouts of noise echoing from the high walls) probably also put the stray feline shy.
We persisted with soft voices and tasty this and that, relentlessly. When a new bass player appeared, having moved from New Plymouth, he discovered Kentucky Fried Chicken - newly arrived in the country. Stacks of bone-filled boxes out the back in what we imagined were old stables could've tamed the cat just that little bit more.

I asked the new flatmate why he didn't throw his empty
containers in the rubbish bin. He said, 'An Everest cardboard
mountain, to celebrate fried chicken, of course.'
My laughter perhaps had him thinking I approved.
In any case, there were no rats out there - maybe the cat always
saw them off.
One day I walked down the drive and there was Joe standing out
the back. In his arms was the black and white cat. Joe couldn't
stop smiling.
This attractive moggy allowed us both to stroke him but never
permitted anyone but Joe to pick him up. Joe crooned, 'Beauty,
there's a beauty. His name's Pirate. I've named him Pirate.'
The cat soon streaked towards him as if they'd known each
other for years.
But his cat would only stare at me, green eyes cold, when I
called. I only ever touched Pirate's shiny dark back once or
twice, never anywhere near his head, and only if Joe held him.
Maybe the animal heard me asking their bass player why he
didn't throw the fast food boxes away (marking me as some kind
of traitor to catness).
Between taming the black and white cat and my visits to talk
over many cups of instant coffee, Joe and I explored various
territory. I'd ask about psychology and he explained patiently,
'Positive reinforcement is when a child is rewarded for doing
well. There's no need to hit or smack kids. If they're rewarded
instead for good behaviour, they're more likely to keep on with
doing the best thing.'
'How long have people known this?' I stared at him, wide-eyed.

Joe so kind - how he'd waited and hoped with that cat, and fed
the animal anyway, even if it didn't seem friendly. He also
explained so much to me.
In the rather run-down lounge, we'd sit around playing cards.
Talk burbled and raced. It felt unreal, as if at any moment it
could evaporate. But every time I drove my mum's car down the
bumpy driveway, stepped out, then up the three wooden stairs to
the little back porch and knocked on the door - there they were -
talkative, beaming, friends of mine.

It was Spring, the air warm-ish, with a jump in it. We sat playing
cards. Joe and I side by side on the sofa, our thighs touching. I
remember Joe just turned to me in a lull and leaned forwards,
still holding onto his cards, and kissed me - soft and inquiring.
I kissed back.
We were boyfriend and girlfriend.
Simple.
You'd think men followed me around waiting for their chance.
Maybe some did. I'd never overly thought about it and didn't
actively search for romantic company every waking moment. I
may have been careless, or perhaps arrogant, but I wasn't full of
wiles and schemes. Being young, my sense of what could be
good long-term depended on how much joy I imagined when
thinking ahead.
Mostly I welcomed night - in my bed to sort through the day's
events in silence. So much didn't lead to any kind of
recognisable pattern except something as complicated as paisley
(like my favourite shirt-dress). The mysteries of life took up most
of my night-time imaginings and reckonings.
Every Friday evening thereafter, anyway - replete in my latest
fashion find, with curled long dark brown hair or it rearranged
in some novel way, make-up piled on - I drove over to Joe's.
Ready. We'd go hear his band play or to the flicks, or sometimes
just walked around town.
I would bump down the potholed driveway in my mother's boxy
yellow car and park around the back, clomping up the wooden
steps in my platforms then knocking excitedly on the door. Joe
would open the door, take one look at me - often appearing
quite different to when I'd last appeared. His eyes would widen,
he'd gasp as if horrified, then slam the door in my face. After I
screeched for him to stop being so mean, or knocked again,
pleading or some such, he would always open the door and
laugh at his joke. For months off and on he convinced me he
really felt shocked by my appearance, (sometimes I suspected he
was joking but then he'd try another tack, another trick).
Their new bass player demanded, 'Why aren't you
complimenting her about how amazing she looks? Are you
crazy?'

Years later, that bass player told me Joe only pretended to be shocked, that he wasn't really amazed by my fashion sense. He fooled me over and over. But their bass player could've wanted to turn me against Joe, waiting for his chance, like Joe had done. We learn as adults to be suspicious of one another, don't we? It's survival.

However back then, being young, the sunny side of the street would instantly cheer me up, and I'd be singing, '...all you need is love', '...always thought I'd see you again', '...somewhere over the rainbow'.... My mother also keen on quoting songs or singing a few lines. She knew so many lyrics. But I'm not sure Mum ever realised the mayhem I sought for fun. What reason was there to tell her? No words existed to explain to my mother the attraction of hairy students and their rock band. Nothing like them had ever existed before.

Why hadn't I taken up with friends who older people accepted and could see were well-behaved? If Mum had asked such a thing, I would have had no answer except, 'I don't know, I just like those other people better.'

Drawn to a man who teased. But then I realised years later that Dad always liked a difficult joke. Dad would ask for a bite of my sandwich, then he'd bite and bite and bite, 'til my lunch would almost all be gone. Any crying on my part and he'd walk off chewing, victorious. Mum and Dad's friends teased me unmercifully, too, when I was little. They'd shout, 'There's a cat in the room. Where is it? Where's the cat? Where?'

In hysterics, I would run, frantic - looking for the animal - dashing about on my tiny legs. Two years old or so, in bewilderment - as if at any moment I'd break into pieces and fly into the sky, out the doors and into the wide world. The abject fright of nothing making sense, adults screeching with laughter at me - a tiny child alone in the middle of the room. Tears rolling down my face, my mouth a grimace. Panic tasted metallic, the fear of even the air itself growing wrong somehow. The room would tip and morph. My tiny tummy contorted, water springing into my mouth, I'd gulp and cry. They would just roar at my discomfort, poking at my innocence until it broke and ran.

How I learnt my place in the world.

Years later my mother murmured one day, ' That man. He'd fool you. They'd laugh. I hated how they did that.'

I wanted to yell at her, 'Why didn't you stop them?' But I knew she didn't have the firm words for such an act of defiance. Only, later, this admission of failure, her complicity and cowardice, her silence.

In time I believed I'd escaped those cackles and jibes, the tricks, their pretense and hatred of anything gentle and kind, but so many people often reminded me of home in some obscure way. Familiarity.

We soak up what's around us.

One afternoon I told my mother Joe reminded me of Dad and she said, 'Yes, well, your father's a bit like my brothers, too. Funny, isn't it?' Mum grew up without a father, in a family of five brothers.

I laughed coldly when she told me about Dad being like her brothers, but Mum didn't even smile. She simply tidied the shelf of spices and dried herbs in packets, the line of cups in the glass-fronted shelf, and the fruit bowl, like she so often did. Sometimes she chanted quietly what to do that morning, a list of cleaning and order. That morning however she turned back briefly and said, 'Don't let him be rough with you, will you, love? Boys sometimes don't realise.'

Birds then unaccountably flew about in my mind. Flocks of gulls at the city dump, and the screeching they made. My uncle, one of Mum's brothers, worked there when we were younger, while he trained at the local technical college.

On the tiny bookcase her old photo album sat between an Atlas of the World and a book called Knitting with Nature. After what she'd said, the pictures of Mum with her five brothers (when she was younger), made me feel a bit shivery.

Mum also said to her friends at one morning tea that she wished she had more girls herself, and sisters, 'I'd like to have had a sister.'

Sky Pilot disbanded and their new bass player along with Joe were asked to join Howl (named after the famous Ginsberg poem). Fascination with the Yippie trial of the so-called Chicago Seven in America inspired them. Ginsberg had recited his long poem, Howl, in court.

Soon, two groups with the same name existed since the original Howl won the Battle of the Bands. Prizes were such currency. The drummer went off with one version of Howl, and their singer with another. Joe played in the singer's band. But sometimes the other Howl's fans appeared. 'Hey, hey slag-face. Tell your boyfriend he's useless. Call that guitar-playing?'

The initial address directed at me always an alert as to who they were; Howl had already told laughing stories about the base level of their anti-fans' insults. Behind a mask of make-up and superiority, I'd glide past them in my finery and pretend they were part of the wall.

They lurked to jeer outside only - they wouldn't pay to enter the club, or any pub. Eventually one would've slugged back a bit too much cheap grog from the boot of their car, and they'd get seen off by bouncers, the police, or both.

Soon, the drummer's group went overseas, and Joe's band ironically took over any fans remaining at home. I pretended I'd never seen them before when they appeared at gigs, inevitably arrayed along the back seats or in some dim corner, at first. Bookings racked up and Howl employed a manager. 'A tour 'round the country,' Joe laughed in disbelief, 'it's happening.' Their drummer had to choose between his well-paid job or superstardom, and chose to stay with the bank. 'They're going to promote me.'

'We can't be named after revolutionary writing and have a bank manager as a drummer anyway,' Joe joked. 'Those Yippies threw money onto the floor of the New York Stock Exchange. Watched brokers scrabble for it like little kids after lollies. What would they've made of *him* playing with us?'

Their new drummer walked in for the first practise, put down his drums, dragged back thick, long black hair past his shoulders, and regarded the bedraggled room. There were two old sofas, one with springs showing, the other pale but stained and worn, and four armchairs in a similar state. The carpet was

rarely vacuumed, and, stained with spilt coffee, it appeared a
dull grey instead of cream. The walls smeared with who knew
what, some posters tacked up but many were falling down, their
drawing pins lost to vibrations which shook the place daily.
'Quite a shack you've got here. Yeah, it's a real Shack Attack.'
Soon everyone called the place The Shack Attack, then
shortened it to The Shack.
Sometimes, Joe looked annoyed - the way people do when a car
alarm sounds in the distance - when someone called his flat a
shack, but never said anything against it. Amiable best describes
Joe, or shut off, two definite favourite moods.
Girls clip-clopped in stacked shoes along the footpath in flocks
like lovely, noisy birds. Young men followed them, too, of course.
Sometimes when I stood outside a club waiting for a friend it
seemed like the entire town appeared to hear Howl. Nightclubs
were packed with beauty, sweat, frenetic dancing and crazed
voices singing along.
Swanning about, dressed up on weekends, their stereo or band
practice played accompaniment to whatever my latest fantasy
held at The Shack. Many days I still wished for travels to
amazing worlds, but most of the time it felt like I'd walked into a
movie I wanted to star in forever - no plush furniture or
gorgeous gardens but the music and talk gathered me into
something sumptuous, revitalising - and I belonged there.
With the earnest dedication of gamblers in a Western, we threw
our attentions into interminable games of Last Card, then 500.
Players stood to turn three times and undo their bad luck, the
rest of us jeering in disbelief, or winners leapt into the air as if
we were playing for money and they'd won enough for a car.
Cups of instant coffee blasted our repose all day and jigged us
back to waking mode late at night, refueling constantly.
Occasionally someone produced a plastic sandwich bag of green
stuff, rolled into a package. Dried leaves looked like mixed herbs.
Pungent and potent - grass, dope, weed, and smoke - a drug
that'd been around quietly for decades. But we popularised the
stuff. Dull ideas seemed to transform with just a whiff. Thinking
expanded with only a puff. Keen smokers were its finest
promoters. 'It'd be a happier, more bountiful world if only

everyone would light up.'

The fanciful words they used bothered me - I'd seen propaganda posters before.

'Do you smoke?' meant something entirely different now, no longer talking about the ubiquitous cigarettes so many people inhaled in houses and flats, on buses down the back, along the street, on beaches, in parks, at parties, in offices, clubs, pubs, restaurants, morning, noon, night, and anywhere they pleased - puff, puffio, puffity.

Almost every adult smoked tobacco, and many children did, too, surreptitiously. Men were often drunk and disorderly but usually didn't suffer any consequences except a headache, unless they were unlucky enough to get arrested for fighting, or end up in an accident. Sparkling and hazy days segued effortlessly to blend in with various smoky times. Our fresh young ears and eyes, bodies and minds ready for anything. We plunged in, took deep breaths....

The boys intently rolled joints like craftsmen, working on these objects as if they'd last. Patchwork assemblages of cigarette papers glued together with delicate licks. Each mastered the art of getting their creation just so. Fat and long but also easy to keep alight to the very end - the roach. New implements and sensations, new words. Roach clips disguised as jewellery hung from people's necks on leather thongs, little tongs to hold the roach for every fragment of the drug to get smoked. Licorice and other flavoured papers were available from head shops, boutiques, or arty crafty places, along with pipes and particular posters and psychedelic books. Shoulder bags, too, printed with tokens of our in-group razz (the marijuana leaf icon) and Ban the Bomb (a circle with lines inside it like a crucifix with upward struts, upside down), round yellow smiley faces, paisley, yin and yang - black and white in a circle - two fingers raised for peace. These accoutrements indicated someone called a head, or someone who wanted others to think they were one. Heads smoked dope.

It felt like illicit seances at school, while sitting in a circle and toking on a rough or expert joint of marijuana. I believed, sitting there, something grand could be revealed. The more supposedly cool of us commenting, 'This takes you somewhere else, really, somewhere else.' Doors of perception opened to every indulger. Drugs not merely a spree, no, they'd save the world from greed and war. It was so easy to go along with this - an adventure promised, and a world changed for the better, eternally improved with our wise application of substances.

'He's a head.' The new drummer knew everyone who smoked. 'I see them, I know straight away.' He was so out-of-it one evening that he flattened himself against the wall of The Shack and glared at a toy truck someone had left on the floor, as if it was a monster. 'I'm so whacked. O I'm so whacked.' His eyes goggled, he gasped for breath and his hands tried to grab the wallpaper at his sides.

The others roared with laughter at his antics.

I didn't like this much. It was as if they were like the teasing adults who laughed at me when I was young. For all those times I kind of felt distanced from the action, as if I watched from afar.

Mark, my ex, had taken me to a farmhouse when I was only 15, and we'd dragged on this odd cigarette passed 'round. Soon, I lay down and slept, dozed a while on the floor. Someone muttered, 'She's crashed.'

Later I supposed that was also marijuana. They called it something else. Different places had names for their own plants. Barrier Blue, Coromandel Fire, Northern Wild....

The smoke tasted good, and at first made me smile, but it soon amplified what already appeared to me as a vivid, inspiring, or, at times, frightening, world. Overwhelmed, it felt like someone turned all the brightness and volume up, without telling me. Then I'd feel like people secretly hated me too. No matter if someone smiled, they lied. Anyone could at any time turn nasty. I'd shiver in a chair or leave the room and walk about alone somewhere until I felt better.

Paranoia was about as entertaining as being punched or kicked. I usually slept well so I didn't need zonking to relax. After a few tries of this wonder drug, I usually refused to smoke. 'No thanks,

not tonight.'
Others giggled or roared with laughter over nothing much,
uplifted. Listening to their conversations as an unstoned, straight
bystander, I tried to follow their apparently brilliant sentences,
their streams of scintillating words. No one ever seemed to go
anywhere with their thoughts, however. But they'd sit in awe of
each other, gaping, or in stitches. The whole process reminded
me of people lost in the countryside. Of course the trees and
flowers or some wild animals would appear intriguing. But the
people lost were, when all was said and done, nowhere they
wanted to get to.
Groups of rather hairy people were, from then on, many times
seen peering at some perfectly ordinary mannequin in a shop
window, laughing at some quirk or angle only they noticed. Or
they whispered together in the shadowy environs of the small
park in the centre of town, soon collapsing into uproarious
laughter. Ravenous appetites then took over.
Heads with the munchies descended on late night takeaway bars
and open-air burger joints, these furnished with long counters to
serve punters conveniently on the footpath. Red-rimmed eyes
and giggles marked many patrons as different. Dope produced
rapacious hunger and heightened the taste of food. Snacks
devoured with groans of pleasure, exclamations, and delighted
grins.
When one place called itself Wacko burgers, many patronised
the place. The guy behind the counter so full of hoopla and
wisecracks, many believed he too was stoned. This added to the
growing reputation the place gained as the place to go for late-
night snacks.

'Whacko got me whacked one night,' Howl's drummer solemnly
informed everyone years later. 'Best heads I ever had. So I was
right. I knew. Spotted him the minute he set that place up.'

A few others soon relayed agitated or dreamy stories. 'Tripping,
man. You won't believe it.' Lysergic something or other, LSD, a
hallucinogenic. 'You see things which aren't there. Visions of the
secret life of nature, man. It's going to change the world, the

galaxy, the universe.'
Sensational articles appeared - teens on acid believed they could
fly then threw themselves from buildings and died. My friends
scoffed at these tales, insisted LSD (or Acid) was fine, 'It expands
your thinking and the things you see. It's beautiful. Beauty - we
need more of it.'
Contemporary art, album covers, music, fashion, and films
developed with more vibrancy, sharp intense colours, swirling
shapes and a surreal aspect. The world of dreams and
imagination truly, visibly, overlapped everyday-land. Strange
psychological story lines also appeared in this heady climate,
books in new languages. Droogs populated A Clockwork
Orange and committed ultra-violence. Strange lifestyles
permeated The Onion Eater - people ate raw onions, as if they
were apples, at the dinner table. Then Miller's books explored
human nature in more depth - such straightforward sexuality,
pushing for more free speech in fiction writing than ever before
with Tropic of Cancer. Interviewed, the author said, '...cancer
symbolises the disease of civilisation, the endpoint of the wrong
path, the necessity to change course radically, to start completely
over from scratch.' The Female Eunuch by Germaine Greer
revealed what I'd noticed wasn't an isolated circumstance,
suburban life and marriage pressures disempowering women
everywhere. Gloria Steinmen and other glamour-pusses like Jane
Fonda raised my awareness of feminism to mean more than
academic arguments, to relate to more women than the severely
unfashionable, and impressed the need to empower women
everywhere - even those with apparent privilege. After one of
my rants at a party a young man sought me out and gave me the
SCUM manifesto. He stated, 'I'm worried you're going that way.'
Written by the woman who shot Andy Warhol, describing the
start of her programme to eradicate chauvinistic men, it was
hardly an inspiration. He could've kept his strange red and black
pamphlet. Murder's so unattractive.
In our youth, though, we were so often open to anything that
meant we could believe ourselves original. The year Woodstock
the movie appeared, a local drug dealer, Breaker, saw the film
every single night. Someone made him a fringed, white leather

jacket, like Hendrix wore in the film. In perpetual sunglasses, Breaker sat cross-legged on the lounge floor of another friend's flat. A carved box from India in front of him, incense burning on ceramic holders in corners. A temple to hedonism. To buy drugs (dope, acid, heroin, pills).... people needed to behave like Breaker was a king and they were lowly subjects. Each approached and hunkered down, sat cross-legged, and waited for him to speak. Breaker intoned wisdom, 'The universe speaks in colours.'

'Colours, man yeah,' the customer replied. Disagreeing with Breaker or adding anything extra could see you leave empty-handed.

With a low monotonous voice (self-deluded), unaware everyone could see he was out-of-it day and night, Breaker would wave his hands grandly. Every hip phrase crammed in. 'O the grooviness, you gotta know babe. If the universe could, we know your cool and the true star shining voice. O land of wonder, glory true, now sky kiss.' Breaker carried a dark cloud with him, too. I sensed it when he stood near. Took me almost no time to decide not to speak with him, nor to listen when Breaker tried to talk with me, but I spied on him from the hallway when he did his deals. I like to say lately I needed information about what to avoid, but he also appeared compelling.

Most of the time our circle didn't do much but talk, listen to music, and smoke cigarettes. Cups of coffee fueled our hype. When the mood took us we also enjoyed each other. Naked, transformed, desirous, vocal, energetic love-making; our involved kisses, visions of glorious wild beaches and spinning planets. Colours pulsed, morphed, and writhed. Later, we'd dream a Saturday afternoon away, sated. Soon we'd pile out of bed, dress up in flares, satins, fake fur, and beads - an eager crowd, away to a Howl gig. O finery, such pretties, driving parents insane - so like the Bowie song because we inspired it.

Months went by, a year, then the second Christmas I bought presents for those Shack flatmates. Almost like another branch of the family in the ramshackle flat in town.

I grew to feel like I'd always known these people.

One day a while later, Joe asked, 'When did you last have your period?'
I just shrugged, 'Not sure, why?'
He said, 'I think you could be pregnant.'
When I held onto metal outside in winter, sometimes I almost dared not let go in case my skin got left behind. This felt like that. The moment before he spoke, I didn't want to listen but words came at me anyway, torrential sudden weather, and me not properly dressed. When in doubt, do nothing, I decided. Told myself everything was the same as it was, refused to engage my brain, mind a parked car.
A dreamy feeling then, with hormones and denial as a buffer. Between morning sickness bouts for months and months, which I hid from everyone possible, nothing had changed - even if I did see a doctor. The growing foetus didn't alter my appearance at first; I was still a schoolgirl. In uniform, a girl laughing on the footpath or gazing into space at the bus stop. A teenager from the inside looking out, however (particularly with secret worries). This was more terrifying and exhilarating than anything before or since.
Plans of mine bloomed when I was intoxicated with a belief in my own autonomy, and brimming with soothing hormones. Solitude seemed necessary, and to enjoy myself, in that order. Apart from gastronomic deliciousness and imbibing, fashion had been my great love before - but now a widening belly caused a style crisis. My life after giving birth nonetheless looked as far away as another planet. Men had landed on the moon only six years before. It looked empty.
Following years of battling class schedules to get more time for writing and art, I finally gained permission to work in my own small art room at school all day - desperate to stay there. A tiny space where mainly only one of us worked (the other art student attended more classes for bursary exams, whereas I'd wangled it so I was only studying for an art qualification).
Plans arrived as fast as a heater warms up. Terrified, I sucked in my tummy and wore my largish blazer done up constantly to the end of that final year, with a rather stand-offish attitude. Most close friends had left school. Not one of the ostensibly well

behaved other seventh formers socialised with me. At lunchtimes
my art room offered a fine hideaway. Our teacher called in to
see work, I remained turned towards the art on a wide bench, so
she didn't see my bulge. Before and after school I nipped out to
my car and drove myself to and from without any company.
Screenprints, water colours, drawings, and sculptures.
Completely absorbed in colour, shape, and form, I disappeared
in my work, abandoned my attendant worries. Instead I became
the ocean, the sky. I turned to an infinite inner world. In my art
room, so much dwindled - how my brothers hurt me, the way
my parents ignored me, what to possibly do when my baby
arrived, the cruelty of school bullies, and teachers telling me to
sit and listen. Ogres, monsters, and nags vapourised. Art rescue -
working alone. Lovely pages, drawings, paintings, carvings, and
more appeared day by day.
The only other person told about the baby was my oldest friend,
Bonnie. She thought, 'Your mum should know.'
I swore my friend to secrecy, 'Every girl who falls pregnant gets
kicked out of school. They disappear like criminals, overnight.
No trace, no names, no talk. Vague stories surface about their
visiting an aunty.'
'I suppose so.' Bonnie looked like she wished she could tell.
Fallen pregnant they'd say, like I'd stumbled over a rock. Those
girls disappeared, with stories awash with tears or bolstered with
swaggering bravado. Their names were passed around in
whispers, manipulated like satiric puppet shows. Some admitted
their terrible secret to a select group, no one allowed to tell.
Inevitably a few leaks hissed. Like paint splatters the lurid colour
caught, excitement being so rare and gossip immensely popular.
The girl's disappearance, tears, and fragments of terrible tales
added together - hey presto - the scorching truth burnt peace
into ashes. Tragedy was as vital as food to teenage girls and
many of their bonehead parents.
Hiding in the art room with no one to shunt me off like an old
railway carriage to unload an item, then slide me back to the
main track as if nothing much happened. At times it felt like we
were machines that someone else owned.
Pregnancy turned me off smoking, drinking alcohol, and all

other drug-taking - even the painkillers I had still sometimes
sneaked from the top shelf. In good health with a real glow, I felt
fitter. All the while my tummy grew rounder and I stood
straighter, to pull the bulge in. Good posture and creating art all
day, it proved to be one of my best years ever.

To my complete delight I stayed at school to finish my art
qualification.

After school ended I was at Joe's one afternoon. He took the
magazine I was reading out of my hands. 'We have to go and see
your parents. Today. You have to tell them. No more avoiding
this.'

Months of my airily saying I had to finish school, then get
through Christmas and summer, but no more plausible excuses
existed around my keeping this secret, even if the festive season
was yet to appear. My supposed mystery now an enormous
bulge.

Smocks were ultra-fashionable (I'd sewn so many of them and
led the way), and for every hour possible I spent time away from
home hiding over at Joe's or at other friend's places. But a
pregnant belly is difficult to conceal. Backstory crowded into my
mind while I sat there and Joe held my eyes. 'Suppose so.' I
slumped.

Someone had placed iron weights on my legs but somehow I
managed to walk. We drove over to Mum and Dad's, with me
still thinking of ways to avoid this talk. For years, I'd been
accustomed to never discussing much. What would I say? If I
stood there saying nothing maybe the awful hour would be
delayed? What could anyone do to change things after all or to
help me?

Walking into the house felt like wading through thick mud.
Mum sounded surprised to see I'd brought Joe over too, but she
could've been faking it. Nevertheless, my denial still worked - a
blank wall appeared in mere moments. I told myself Mum just
didn't expect an extra guest for dinner, no big deal.

Our cheery kitchen had blue and white tiles, white frilly net
curtains above the sink, and blue and white gingham curtains.
Mum's china bird collections were on display. The boys older
now - less likely to break them with shenanigans. The kitchen

arrayed with ducks, geese and hens on the sideboard, windowsill, on top of the fridge, and on the walls. My terrifying news didn't fit the cutesy decor at all.

While Joe coughed loudly in the lounge (audible through the door at intervals) I carefully set the table, then offered to peel spuds and did so with complete attention. The air felt heavy. With everything for dinner completed, I began with a deep breath to launch my admission, 'I've something to tell you, Mum.'

My mother just said in this matter-of-fact voice, 'I know. What are you going to do?' She turned to me and wiped her hands on her yellow apron, then went to sit at the table like we'd have a chat now. As still as one of her many bird ornaments, I stared in amazement.

Relief - someone had opened the roof and walls. Anything could happen now. It'd be fine. 'I'm having the baby adopted and I don't want to talk about it.' The hardness in my voice surprised me as much as it did my mother.

'O, I see.' Up from the table as smartly as if someone had just raced into the room with news there was a fire, or some other emergency. Mum rattled cutlery and pots in drawers and cupboards.

In my mother's extreme busyness, she seemed disappointed. Her silences often appeared potent, meaningful, a talent developed in our house of shattering noises. My brothers produced racket and whirr, bluster and shouting, wreckage, and derision. Mum and I were perpetually under siege unless Dad was home, when the roar died to a rumble, with only occasional flurries of disruption and random brief outbursts. Dad would always laugh along with it.

Mum and I developed ways to find things out fast, rarely getting a chance for long talks.

My brothers wanted our mother making things for them, tidying after them, or waiting for them to ask something. Each boy shouted their involved stories to Mum - with actions to emphasise the most lurid details, and bellows of laughter too. If I dared comment, there'd often be a thumping or some kind of shutting into a cupboard, later. 'Stupid girl, shut up when I'm telling Mum stuff.'

They treated me like a boy. It puzzled my brothers that I didn't want to fight and never grew as big as they were, muscled and shoving, rowdy as a hail storm on a tin roof. Few adults ever corrected their behaviour or commented, and no one insisted that they needed to be careful with me, either. What boys are told this nowadays, and who told boys that they needed to care for girls then so they believed it? Naturally, they thought violence was permissible to some extent. How I forgave them involves some awareness of their education.

After my mother grew up without a mother of her own in a house full of men, she too didn't know what a girl was supposed to be treated like, perhaps. Reasons are a comfort too, without them I'm lost in fright again.

I never wanted to believe Mum simply didn't like me and didn't care what they or anyone else did to me. How was that possible? Really? Mothers loved all their children, didn't they?

She and I so were different, however. Mum liked to be careful, I loved adventure. Mum followed fashion after many people took it on, I liked to be the first to wear something. Our mother rarely argued with anyone at home, but I did - even if it meant I got hurt. Maybe she thought I deserved to get hurt if I couldn't follow her sensible example? But, rarely, I hated to think it but did so anyway - I thought it was that I refused to do what she wanted (to be more girly and quiet), so she wanted me punished for that. I cried enough as it was, so tried to ignore anything that would make me even sadder, it's only now I see how things perhaps worked.

You may, dedicated reader, be finding this hard work, reading about my agonies and worry. Let me mention then, that some may say there is no language for victims so others need to tell their story. But once we are mended, we who were hurt and damaged may tell these tales, ourselves. Sometimes scary stories are based on real things. Why can't we talk about them then as fictions, as concoctions, but realistic? There's a safety in narrative, after all. Understanding matters.

The house in any case soon was filled with my brothers, in from work, and I wanted to leave after the admission about my baby had finally appeared. Mum said, 'You can at least eat something.'
The entire meal dominated by noisy eating brothers, followed by them their telling work stories.
I didn't have to convince Joe we should go as soon as we'd eaten the mashed potato, fried steak, and liver in gravy, peas, and cauliflower cheese - which Mum had cooked to perfection. 'No dessert thanks, Mum.'
'Yeah, she's watching her weight,' the eldest shouted after us and the other boys laughed.
Sitting at that long wooden table with the whole family felt as overwhelming as the pressure before a thunder storm.

I didn't think to leave town or hide my condition like so many girls did. Our furious household taught me that people who believed they could get away with cruelty would be nasty, no matter what you tried to do to stop them. Better to do whatever you thought best and bear the results.
In competitions held in nightclubs and halls all over the country, then at a final show in the city, Joe's group, Howl, won the Battle of the Bands that year, again. 'We've got gigs booked solid for three months over summer.'
 They got new stage clothes, tight hipped, coloured velvet flares, embroidered loose tops, and high shoes. I sewed his stage clothes, so Joe could splash out on a new amp. 'It's got a better sound for what we play.' Much knob twiddling and discussion, then endless practising. They had painfully lugged gear in and out of vans and cars previously, but with some of their prize money they bought a bus. Once the massive thing was parked in the middle of their bass player's enormous lawn we begged, borrowed, and stole about twenty paintbrushes.
In day-long sunshine, passers-by stopped to stare in the quiet suburban street. An old school bus, it was now covered in a tumult of lime green and purple coils, and enormous white daisies across the rear, every yellow centre a smiley face.
By this time Howl played in resplendent colours. Quant crayons

in hand before every gig, I drew bright psychedelic patterns over
their cheeks, foreheads, and eyelids. Enormous orange, purple,
red, and blue flowers copied from a Jacobean wallpaper design
sprouted in embroidery over the front of their bass player's
white jeans. Joe favoured a deep maroon silk for the shirt I made
him, with billowing sleeves and a long cuff with twelve covered
buttons. A plastic toolkit opened to many little compartments,
stuffed with eyeliners, Mary Quant coloured face crayons, nail
polishes, and more. 'It's so you guys stop pinching my make-up
for gigs.' I beamed when I presented it to them for Christmas.
Howl's tour bus was bright green and purple. Everyone they
knew embellished it in one weekend.
Tripped Out Lightworks, in an orange van, set up early in halls,
sports stadiums, and clubs. Swirling brilliance across the walls,
floor, and ceiling. There was no pain when their music played.
Bulging mega-pregnant in long floaty dresses (the latest maxi-
length was also an affront to the majority still in miniskirts en
masse). Women openly stared and whispered behind their hands
in the street. Showing their envy, to my mind, if I ever noticed -
my fashion sense far outdid theirs even when I was the size of a
small car. Short-sightedness was an asset too, with the gawpers
and sniggerers out of focus. Joe stopped, glared at a couple of
young women around 28 years old one bright day. 'What are
you staring at? What?'
They stopped whispering and staring, and looked away.
In a haze of hormones, I gazed about. 'Who? What were they
doing?'
He said he was sick of it, the gossip.
I just laughed. It was a gift to stay cheerful. Stoppers, stunters,
and stiflers - perhaps they were compacted once, and had come
to think it was normal? In my diary I wrote - Forgive ignorance
and ignore their pitiful ways. In times long past it was helpful to
have everyone conform to a large extent, doing what almost
everyone else did. Safer and easier to gather food and to hunt,
throughout prehistory. Obedience and quietude also means
rulers may manage the mass of people more readily. But
conformity reduces the potential for brilliant outcomes, the
many need not try too hard to believe excellent only means

treading water, barely making an effort. The few, however, must strive for innovations, and always to love one another, including those who try to shush them.

I had to think there'd be no synchronised swimming in fabulous costumes allowed if some people had their way, no champion diving or marathon channel crossing, no mermaids, nor turning into sea monsters either. Away from paddlers and splashers; sometimes in deep water, and scared, too.
Most pregnant unmarried girls who didn't hastily marry sneaked out of town to have the child, then gave up their babies for adoption. Secrets and shame the punishment for sin - pain of separation. Pressure - an entire family determined things had to stay looking the way they painted them. Or, the rebel grew invisible, out of the picture. In the early 1970s girls who were *caught* left town fast - as soon as they started to *show.* But I stayed, even though I announced our child would be adopted.
Saying I'd adopt meant others didn't talk about my pregnancy much. Used to neglect myself, I didn't know what to do with anyone wanting to get close and discuss my future, or the baby's or my well being - realising this all now as I write this down. With friends we earnestly went over many kinds of puzzles, scenarios, and dreams, also sharing an enormous ignorance. Most conversations were simply teenage fantasies, dissolving into giggles or stunned silences. Only Bonnie knew I was pregnant, anyway, for ages, in those circles.

The adoption people worked in a pale green office in a plain government building with worn wooden furniture, fake leather seats, and a desk piled with paper. I barely breathed in the disinfected atmosphere. Noting the walls were bare, except for a framed portrait of the Queen, I asked myself, *How did these people know what was best for my child?* My chair was too large, it was difficult to easily rest my elbows on the arms of it. *Giants usually sit here?*
A curly-haired woman behind the wide wooden desk told me with a grin, 'Young girls have such beautiful babies.' Her eyes rolled and she clasped her hands to her chest like praying.

One glance at my horrified face and she hastily instead talked about papers and procedure. 'This is the form you'll sign.' She handed it over the desk to me.

I didn't take the paper from her. My body felt frozen, but my mouth seemed to be sneering.

'Of course, no need to take anything just now.' Her smile forced. Stony-faced by then, I felt pleased to hear nothing could be decided 'til after I gave birth. I got out of there fast.

My friend Bonnie asked how the meeting went.

'Gave me the creeps,' I replied. 'They talk about babies like they're new furniture. Going to look so lovely in the specially painted room.'

We never discussed it again. The decision in the back of my mind like a stack of clothes I used to wear and could do again. Looking out a big set of windows over the quad at school, in my small art room, I sequestered myself with pen, pencils, and paints. Pages and pages of work; mother and child compositions, the whole alphabet with coloured pictures for each letter, illustrations of children picking apples....

Quick thoughts as fast as tiny fish, some good to catch. A few times I struggled with concepts or materials as if they were an octopus trying to crush me, but alone and absorbed I continued. No one stood there to jeer or complain if I took too much time. In the art room I found myself swimming in many directions most of the time. Solitary freedom was as important as eating good, fresh food, listening to excellent music, and laughing with my friends. Examples of careful drawing, painting, sculpture, and print-making soon made up a portfolio for my exam.

Friends distracted me with plans, days rolled on and on, and Howl's fan-base grew. The bass player's best friend arrived from Rotorua with his doberman, Vampire, and he guarded the van full of gear which travelled behind their lurid bus. A soundman had charge of the mixing desk. From one tiny place they visited on tour the legendary Vannie travelled with them, too, and drove the boys around when they got to other places; doing this for months, without pay.

'Fans. You gotta have fans. Talent, hours of hard work, fans, money, promotion, and luck. In that order,' their soundman told me one night. He wanted to manage Howl, perhaps hoping that he sounded businesslike, and that I'd put in a good word for him. It seemed to me that listing general ingredients for success wasn't professional. The big picture instead appeared complex, interrelated. And he put money so far down on the list. Did he think those guitars, drums, keyboards, and amps were just given to people?

Joe's band managed themselves. They had lengthy meetings before each practise. Someone usually wrote down whatever they planned to do next in an exercise book. Mostly they earnestly talked through ideas, made reasonable decisions, and each completed whatever task they were assigned. Someone called the promoter, another arranged for a poster design, someone else took an amp to be repaired, or wrote a song.... Their goal was to keep playing music, and not do anything else. Every musician's dream.

No one was permitted to smoke dope before playing or get drunk. Altered states had to wait until afterwards. One practise every week, at least. No one was allowed on stage except the band or people in the crew. Someone had taped a list of rules inside a spare leads' suitcase lid.

Purple, green, orange, yellow, and red lights swam and flashed. The sound system caused its own earthquake. People packed hall after nightclub after pub after party - yelling for more. Every weekend, Joe and I had relaxed on his bed in a daydream - before the band's success mushroomed. Many times we drifted into reveries. I mentioned one time that I had half-dreamt a huge bird in a blue sky, 'It flew, then just glided there in the cloudless colour.'

With a smile he said he'd just been thinking the exact same thing.

Those were the early days in The Shack, when Joe had a cleaning job and went to uni. When he only dreamed of fame. Before he fell in love with so much attention. Before the band built up a snazz of fame.

As excited as I was to see them playing to packed fans, I also missed those earlier, calmer days. My tummy grew and grew, while I seemed to be shrinking inside, and the world expanded. Eleven people lived in a grand old place near the lake. I'd been to school with one of them, Keira. 'Come over and see our new place. It's great. Mike got it. You know him? Sings for Peachy?' A cover-band vocalist with a gorgeous, flexible voice who often opened for Joe's outfit, and a few others who lived there were also familiar from around town.

One day I did visit with my bulge. I talked with Mike, 'It's awful at home. It's like I'm still a little kid. Thought I'd be working by now or at varsity. My brothers are such a pain.' I sighed.

'Move in here. We've got that sunporch. Have a look at it.' Mike grinned. He worked on the road, promoting farm equipment to the whole district. Mike could sell sand to desert nomads.

A narrow wood-lined room. It had many windows, each with lots of tiny panes of glass, outlined in black lead. Full of light and warm; the wood rimu, golden red, and tiny shelves built-in where I could just imagine my jewellery and trinkets would go. Took no time to decide, then move in.

We each had one job to do every day - keep a shared room tidy, or do dishes, or cook. I peeled the potatoes every evening. We didn't eat pasta or rice. New Zealand food meant meat and three veg for dinner - roast, steak, stew, or sausages with carrots, peas, and potatoes.

It was such a relief to be away from my brothers, even if the new house was also rambunctious. But no one ever tried to hurt me there. Two flatmates were insanely silly, making fun of everyone, without exception. I wasn't singled out.

No one ever took drugs around me, my tummy growing ever larger by the day, but I was aware of their habits. Most believed marijuana harmless, in any case - it didn't make people violent and had no bad side effects except paranoia and a propensity to overeat, as far as we knew. High tar levels and a danger of becoming psychotic, the lethargy and depression - those effects hadn't registered yet.

One night, six of us sat in the large lounge on big easy chairs or the sofa, and someone turned off the overhead light. 'Hey. Turn that back on,' I protested.

Someone in my sunporch, also accessible from another room,

giggled and whispered.

Tall Pete with a candle under his chin loomed out of my
sunporch by the lounge, his great frizz of blonde hair about his
face like a ghostly mist. Mike, with his dark, crinkly, strange hair
and spectacles leapt out - a monster - from behind him. Roger
sat on the old pedal organ (remaining in the once grand house
from the old days), lifting his hands dramatically into the air and
crashing them down on the keys over and over again. Spooky
organ music wheezed on. Mike and Pete in grotesque Gothic
moves, slow motion miming around the lounge, completely
dead-pan and violent, lit only by the candle under Pete's chin, a
flame wavering and dancing. Shadows leapt about the walls.
Mike 'murdered' Pete in slo-mo with a knife he mimed holding,
his face monstrous. Pete 'died' about ten times, kept almost
subsiding then reared up again.

  The rest of us contorted, laughing, on the big sofa and chairs.
We were lucky kids I see now - good-looking or charming, well-
fed our whole lives, and educated, connected with a wide group
of friends. Even if some of our hearts were broken regularly and
we worried about money, our car running properly, pimples,
dumb hair, or whether boredom was something you could die of,
after all. We did each others' fashion styling and helped with tips
for other necessities like getting the best rock concert tickets,
effortlessly. Weekly, I ran up mad frocks, tops and skirts on my
sewing machine in a few hours. We talked up varied weather -
our own atmosphere, loved to dance; escaping routine with
music into a specially-branded heaven for young people only. We
floated above overly-neat houses, tidy aprons, and manicured
lawns, conformity, and expectations. We bathed in massive
glorious noise from bands like Joe's, we became part of the
molecules of it. Never-before-heard penetrating sounds, friends
and I swam through new day-glo colours and surreal
conversation. Anyone who stood against our pleasure was
scattered to the far reaches of nowhere.

One night someone knocked loudly on the front door and
shouted, 'Police. It's the police, open up.' Everyone except me in
the lounge (who had until then been reading or staring into
space) flew up and out of the room, upstairs, or out windows.

The three storey, eight bedroom house was in an uproar in
seconds. Nine people in action (Keira still at work). I stood in
tense silence like a cartoon character in shock, hands fanned,
listening to cisterns flushing over and over again in the three
toilets we had. Loud knocking kept up at the door, pounding
now. 'Police. Open now.'

Frozen, every sound and sight registered strongly. I took in the
dark wood frames of the many paned French doors between the
lounge and the hall, the neatly vacuumed mid-green carpet
(Richard was so diligent), the large armchairs - a pleasant dark
green with an embossed pattern of leaves....

'Ahahaha,' loud laughter from the front door. 'Did you get a
fright?' they shouted when someone finally checked to see who
knocked there, outside.

Pete, usually pale and amused, tall and gangly - he tangled up in
fury then leapt in the air, red as a stop sign, screaming at the
jokester who'd managed to get as far as the hall, but not the
lounge, 'You complete and utter fuckwit. You are never to do
that again. Hear me?'

'Sorry man, thought you'd know. Uh, I....'

'We've all flushed our stashes. Some of us had a lot of money
invested in those bags, man. You have to leave. Right now.'

Soon I sat down again, but it worried me every time someone
knocked that it really could be the police. Didn't want anyone
arrested, nor to be caught in some bust myself when I never
even took drugs.

Outside Joe's place one night close to that scare, Breaker the
dealer wobbled about in an embroidered, brown leather shirt,
coloured beads clicking. He drawled, 'Go to Mike's place maaan,
they've got the real shit there, maaan. Horse, get some H.
Mmaaan.' His eyes glazed, pinned.

Howl's bass player had questioned him tersely and reported
back to us, 'Some foreign guy is selling heroin super-cheap at
your place. He gave Breaker some. Gave. Him. Some. Heroin.'

Everyone's head swiveled to regard me like I knew the story.
My thoughts scrambled but I managed to hatch something. 'O,
uh, Mike's let this Polish guy stay. He can barely speak English.

He's in the basement. His girlfriend, no - his wife - she wore this amaaazing calico wedding dress. She let me wear it, uh... '
They glared at me.
I took a breath. 'Yeah, anyway she's gone back to Auckland.'
I watched the others. They all frowned and some muttered.
My mind clicked into survival mode. 'Look, go tell someone sensible. Not Mike. He's charging that Polish guy rent, I bet. Just tell, uh...'
Between them they worked out what to do, roared off in my car, and then returned. Joe laughed coldly. 'That *visitor*? The local schoolboys from over the road were down there with him. He was selling smack to them. Did you know?'
'God, no. I didn't even remember he was there 'til just before.'
'They've told the guy he's out. Seems sorted.' Joe stalked away, played his guitar acoustically for a while, and shut everyone else out with his concentration.
How different life seemed from when we were younger, that evening. It took three cups of coffee to thrash it out, the rest of us talked on until we'd reduced our alarm to mere specks of memory.

Some things didn't change, even if the world now spun concurrently in many configurations. A dull ache or two one midnight, mid-March. In the darkness of my little room, alone. My stomach contracted, a pulse of pain every twenty minutes or so - on and on - for hours, with me dozing occasionally. By 4am I felt sure it could be time to get going. Labour pains - these aches meant birth was imminent. The baby would arrive with me alone in my room, terrified, in early hour darkness.

One flatmate, Pete, had already worried aloud days before, 'Shouldn't you be in hospital? I mean couldn't the baby just slide out while you're walking around?'
He made me laugh. 'Babies let you know when they're coming.'
'They call first?' Pete loped away to his stereo.

The darkness was denser than usual, like it held me down. Would the child survive if he did just slide out in my single bed, with me, alone? I struggled to stand, to get help immediately. I staggered into the lounge, through the glass French doors to the hall. In the dark, I waited until I could see better. Then up the stairs, gripping the dark wood bannister to haul my weight on, to knock on my flatmate's door.

Richard had said he'd go get Joe when the pains started. In the dimness after I opened the door his head popped up from the bedclothes. 'What time is it?' he asked groggily.

'Sorry. But I've had pains all night.'

Richard dutifully drove in my car to seven streets or so away (No one could ring in on Joe's mysterious phone, and cellphones were non-existent until a good fifteen years later).

The morning was as clear blue as a dreamy picture book. I lay in bed and wondered when the real pain would start. The pangs were less intense than when I'd been alone. Joe hung about, pacing and peering. He lost his excited edge when I said I wanted a peanut brownie and a cup of tea.

My twinges died away by 7am.

Soon, the whole flat knew I'd woken up Richard to go get Joe in the early hours, for nothing. A hullaballoo then a fizzle – with nothing even vaguely resembling an ache or a spasm.

Back to flatting life as usual. Weekday mornings in a busy kitchen. People clinked plates for cereal or toast, a few cracked remarks for a laugh, frissons of interest over someone's new job or album. The hubbub would be gone in a half hour or so, with everyone off to work. Most days, at home alone (and colossal), I read books, drew pictures, answered the door to travelling salesmen or the occasional visitor who wanted to drop something off or chat over an instant coffee. People called by often, rarely bothering to ring first.

I slept at intervals throughout the day. Pregnancy demanded regular oblivion.

By late afternoon various people reappeared from work, some as early as 4pm. Josie, who drove a truck for the rag factory, showed off a new acquisition, 'All the signs of the zodiac. Embroidered 'round the hem. So gorgeous, isn't it?' Her first pick of the day's haul. We'd swap any news, listen to music, wonder about this or that, and start getting dinner ready. Every night we ate at a long table in the dining room, together. Up to eleven of us at a time, more with guests. Mike and Pete were inventive between mouthfuls. 'Mike, Mike,' whispered Pete theatrically, 'don't you think that girl's getting a bit fat?' He pointed at me.

Mike, without looking up, just muttered matter-of-factly, 'O I think she's pregnant, Pete.'

Everyone grinned inanely.

'But Mike,' Pete, agape, put down his cutlery with a clatter. 'She can't be. She's not married.'

Then they both looked at me in horror until we all laughed. Sometimes I'd try to persuade visitors - who popped in rather too often to eat with us - tried to get them to wash or dry the dishes, without much success. After dinner, with the dishes done, we'd lounge about in the living room or depart for people's rooms to listen to a new album. Most of us read books voraciously too. I ploughed through new books A Clockwork Orange, The Onion Eaters, Portnoy's Complaint, Fear and Loathing in Las Vegas, The Day of the Jackal, The Godfather, The Left Hand of Darkness and so many more. We swapped favourites and discussed them with glee, sometimes in puzzlement, or awe. I drew pictures of imaginary lands and places, where we could live forever with art, music and literature as available as bread, butter and milk.

For a while it seemed like I'd never stop being pregnant and would have to wear a whale costume, performing at the local lake as a sideshow and learning how to dodge harpoons.

Days later, dull, deep, throbbing pains started in my belly late at night, when almost everyone had gone to bed. I wondered if I should tell someone. But in the darkness with only faint twinges I decided to wait until pains truly took hold. No more false alarms. The bed seemed far too narrow. My stomach dully ached, more and more. I dozed but my pains surely felt sharper, and closer together. When they got so bad I couldn't stand the stitch without making a noise, I grappled my way up the stairs once more, and opened the big dark door, 'Rich. Richard. It's happening for real. I'm sorry.'

'Oh no, not again,' my friend moaned in the darkness just before dawn, but he smartly got out of bed, dressed, and we were off in my car.

This time, I grimaced and wailed convincingly, completely forgetting I had a sense of humour. On the small bed I contorted and writhed, wanting the pains to stop and hoping that they wouldn't get worse.

Joe looked concerned, but also strode about in excitement.

The labour pains were so severe by 9am that I announced to the various people who'd lingered to witness their first birth pains (agony as entertainment), 'Have to get to the hospital. Right now.'

One girl visiting us, Petunia, had developed a phantom pregnancy months before, which many whispered about. She kept mentioning things like, 'The doctor says I need iron supplements now.' But her belly stayed flat, her figure sapling-like. This day, Pet swanned about in a lovely pink quilted, floor-length housecoat, circa 1920. She'd carefully brushed her long black hair until it shone in loose waves over the pale shiny fabric - gorgeous. She sat close by me and watched my every contorted look, absorbing my groans and utterances as if researching for a play.

Three of the others also hung about besides Pet. As I was about to give birth, the idea of an uninvited audience felt like I was in a car crash and they were rubber-neckers, but I tried not to think about them.

This entourage wandered on ahead from the car to the hospital, my friends dressed up as if we were going to a gig. Annie wore a lovely long green dress the colour of bright moss which buttoned up the front, lower buttons undone so the hem flowed out behind. Another was in a rainbow long sleeved t-shirt, and the most subdued, Keira, favoured shades of puce, magenta, and deep maroon, a layered dress to her knees. Pet, in her pink housecoat but now wearing elegant golden sandals, looked back, regarding me longingly while I struggled up the footpath to the maternity wing door. Wide curved steps led to chrome-edged glass way ahead. My breaths short while I walked the slight incline; I wanted to shout at Pet that no matter how much she wanted to, she couldn't take my place - more was the pity. The labour pains were consuming me each time by then. I bent over, grimacing, with each contraction.

The hospital, across a black asphalt forecourt, loomed huge and pale, with official signs about the doors. Some bell button needed to be pushed. This information however I only faintly recalled - instead pushing open the doors, I announced loudly, 'I'm in labour!'

Various gaping faces in my line of sight bulged and gaped. Nurses in white rushed forward in soft soled shoes, seeming to glide. 'Didn't you ring the bell, dear?' one asked me.

'I forgot what one. I forgot,' I wailed, and someone held my arm. Nurses bustled everywhere like piles of white wrapping paper crumpled fallen from a shelf or animated in a wind. Starched uniforms crackled. Their nylon-clad legs shhhed. I wanted to scream.

A wheelchair appeared.

The largest nurse regarded my magical mystery friends in their fanciful garb and asked, 'Is anyone else here about to give birth?' Everyone shook their heads.

'Sorry, only family are allowed to accompany the mother.' The nurse eyed my friends. Two stepped forward, including Petunia - by then crazed, her eyes rolling. The maternity nurse held out her hand to stop them. 'Only the father now. Family time.'

Joe was permitted to enter the maternity room with me, and the others went home.

Alone with the enormity of what was about to happen, Joe and I.

A poured concrete building from about 70 years before with functional cream and green walls, the maternity wing had shiny linoleum floors which smelled of disinfectant. I'd been born there. Everything was spartan and scrubbed. Joe and I discussed how strange the whole institution appeared. I reassured him I felt fine, 'Just sudden pangs occasionally.'

A nurse popped her head in, 'Timing contractions?'

We had to admit we'd stopped doing that with any diligence.

'Could we have some magazines?' I asked hopefully.

We leafed through Women's Weekly magazines and other fripperies - media that we'd barely glanced at before.

Hours passed.

Pains needled back and kept on. 'Ooo, really uncomfortable.'

'They can go on for 20 hours or more.'

I gasped at the nurse who'd told me this. 'What?' Wondered how I'd missed that fact.

Joe and I had read every magazine in the whole prenatal ward, about thirty each. It was mid-afternoon when the agonies started in earnest. I couldn't believe the pain felt so intense, and moaned, groaned, and writhed. A nursing Sister strode into my room and spoke loudly, 'Stop all this nonsense. This noise. You are upsetting the other mothers.'

A shot of pethidine to dull the pain and I zoomed away from all the action. I fought it, hard. Sister again appeared in her white starched uniform and winged white hat over her neat dark hair and fierce brown eyes, looming, 'You are hysterical, do you know that?' Her face so close to mine I could count her eyelashes.

With my breath in short bursts, I struggled on the bed, wishing I could scream that if she gave me such strong drugs that I felt like I was about to pass out then it was her fault I'd freaked. My voice appeared lost. Nothing emerged when I tried to speak. Bad dream territory.

Eventually I listened to the nurse telling me to breathe (like I'd learnt in antenatal classes). These exercises did help me withstand the rigours of labour.

At 10.30pm that evening, our son, Coltrane, arrived in a wild haze of pain-killing injections and all-enveloping physical effort. Hysterically pleased to hear my baby was a boy (which I'd always believed), I couldn't stop laughing. The nurses and other theatre staff gaped and frowned, alarmed at my dramatic reactions. But they'd filled me so full of drugs and labour had taken so long that I had no control at all by then, turned into a jelly-person - with only sound to prove that I lived.

The doctor marched out to Joe, who was not permitted into the birthing suite (no fathers were), said, 'It's a boy.' Then the doctor walked off.

In the room where we'd earlier waited for something to happen, I lay drowsy in bed and Joe sat on it beside me. A nurse, all smiles, swept in with a bundle, 'Here, hold your son.' She put the baby into Joe's arms and he gazed into his dear little face. Joe softened, holding our baby so carefully - like our little one was a bubble that could break with the slightest pressure.

Through the door came the sound of other mothers moaning. They cried out just like I had and it didn't bother me one iota. I silently cursed that nursing Sister for telling me to be quiet earlier.

Coltrane was soon taken to sleep off the shock of being born, in a plastic hospital crib, with other babies in the nursery.

Exhausted, I drifted away to dreamland more easily than ever in my entire eighteen years.

Joe drove my car home as arranged. Back he went to weekend gigs and weekday work, to people calling over for coffee, practising his guitar at every possible moment, and band practises. My flatmates, too, dressed each morning however they thought best, went to nightclubs and pubs on the weekend, or some Thursdays. It was easy to picture them.

Everyone and then some watched Monty Python on late-night Sunday TV, crowded about the lounge at our place. Such perfect insanity. Silly jokes over breakfast and the preparation of shared evening meals. I wondered who peeled my potatoes now. I recalled the graffiti Dragon's guitarist wrote inside the kitchen cupboard about Mike, with fondness - instead of revulsion. I didn't even mind thinking about how they pinched my jewellery and scarves to wear on stage. (They stayed at our house when they played in town).

The shiny lino in our ward looked too clean, like it wanted to shrug me off. There was no one much to talk with - except visitors, who couldn't stay long. The hospital put 'Mrs' before my name at the door of my room. One flatmate read it a couple of times, 'What's this?' he demanded from the doorway.

'O they make us do that.'

His indignant expression increased. 'They can't make you. Stuff them.' He got out a pen, scrabbled 'round in my bedside cabinet where I kept sketchbooks and writing materials, and wrote my full name (without a title) on a slip of paper and slid it into place.

People visited as if we were invalids. We were stuck in bed for 24 hours after giving birth and bathed there, too, with a sponge bath. In pretty flowered pyjamas and sheer, pastel, or bright nighties, new mothers did their best to laze about. Most flaunted specially purchased pink or lemon housecoats, quilted synthetic versions of the vintage rayon or silk lovelies my friends like Petunia lately wore as stylish dresses. Other women set their hair in pink or cream plastic rollers with little white stick-in pins to hold them tight each morning; preparations to create wavy hairstyles for their visitors. I brushed mine, wished it was even straighter and longer.

My baby was fed by nurses. I didn't see him unless I walked down to the nursery and looked at his little clear crib through the big window. Every day, three or four times, then five or six, then seven or eight, I stood there regarding him. One nurse told me, 'If you're giving him up, just put the baby out of your mind.' I wondered how you forgot nine months of pregnancy, then the trauma of birth pains and the stunning after-effects - the miracle of a child to hold.

Some days I walked up and down the ward hallway, over the shiny floor, and stared out the big window at the end, imagining everyone else out there at work, playing music, and laughing. Their voices silenced; I walked way to the other end and back again, over and over. Hospital was a prison.

The adoption woman had bustled into my room waving papers like a letter I'd been desperate to receive. 'Hello dear, how are you?' She sat by my bed.

I stared at her. After all the pain and the astounding revelation of birth, nothing could compare to its intensity and importance. Officials seemed as necessary as something forgotten at a bus stop. A broken umbrella - and best left that way. The day after I'd given birth, and there she sat.

The papers she rustled in my direction seemed nonsensical. I didn't take them off her.

The woman pulled her chair even closer, close enough to touch the covers with her plump knees under their floral frock. She dragged at her chin-length bob with manicured hands and snapped, 'Just the forms to sign now.' An upbeat tone, her grin a little faded but supposedly real, then she sighed.

In weariness and shock, I felt like the bed and the room looked foreign along with her. What were they all? A bed - what was it? The walls - what use? This woman - who could she be?

My unwanted visitor cranked up fake-cheery talk again, truly pretending this time, 'Look, it'll just be a signature and things can get rolling.' She kind of ballooned above me, powdery, large in her voluminous frock which was tight at the neckline.

My parents walked in for a visit and interrupted her spiel. She raced away, 'Oh, hello. Ah, yes, lovely, your mum and dad here to see you. No pressure, no pressure.'

We three united for a change, staring after the officious woman with her sheaf of papers and neat bluebell fabric over her big backside. Soon she was gone.

No nurse ever simply appeared with Coltrane, like they did with other women's babies. Gliding in on soundless shoes, nurses with so many infants. A parade of babies, every few hours.

My walks to the nursery to gaze through the window at his tiny face in the plastic crib felt like a penance. But whenever I tried to decide what to do next blackness swam in my mind. My floppy belly was worrying too. I was deformed. What happened to my slim tummy - and why did I feel so ancient now?

Health professionals believed that isolating a mother and baby from each other was for the best with adoptions, the birth mother expected to go on as if nothing had happened. Human brains apparently were as easily changed as a blackboard, dusted of chalk. After enveloping agony (worth every groan for some reason) and hardly being able to walk for days, I wondered when amnesia could possibly set in.

The birth itself consumed me. I relived every detail. For ages I'd stand by the big nursery window and watch my son in his little crib, too, sleeping - or sometimes with his eyes open. Swaddled babies didn't move that much, but he moved somewhat. I stared at his dear broad face and large eyes, his tiny body.

Three women in our long hospital room brought their babies to feed at four-hourly intervals. I sat in bed reading the First Whole Earth Catalogue, which Richard had presented to me. 'Just to borrow.' It offered respite from the intensity of hospital, where

every minute bulged with meaning and possible tears. Pages,
printed words, information - books were always so trustworthy.
On first sighting the large, strangely pink-covered A4 book,
nurses peered at me aghast. 'Not reading a romance, dear?' one
said.
Another squinted at the cover and shrieked, 'It's a hippy
encyclopedia.'
'Make your own compost.' I beamed at her. 'And this is the best
place for a nuclear fall-out shelter.' Proudly showing them
articles, as if I'd discovered their contents myself.
Nurses raced off with the book in hand to show someone a
page. The nuclear fall-out shelter design for your hallway proved
to be a favourite, and the odd things it was possible to smoke.
'Look at what they say here.' Muffled giggles and exclamations
followed, while a bunch of nurses scooted down the corridor to
read further.
Amongst this light relief, naming my baby took place. A nurse
appeared one morning with a bald command. 'Use the first
initial of your surname. Pick a name starting with that letter for
his first name.' the anonymous nurse insisted, and then swept
from the room with one last assertion, 'Easier to go along with
these rules.'
She left and I gazed after her, wrung out as if nothing could ever
stop me feeling like a husk.
I chose something that I hoped sounded momentous, but
eventually a spark of annoyance built and built until I could've
set the place on fire with a thought. 'Mustn't get too attached,'
another nurse said in passing, when I mentioned, 'I want my son
to keep his real name - which I've chosen.'
She'd tried to smile.
All through my pregnancy I'd called the baby Coltrane - didn't
she know that? I knew he'd be a boy - and he looked like a
Coltrane.
Locked up in hospital, I had no right to speak, nor do much else
under my own steam. I just smiled that fake happy smile I'd
learnt so young. They needed this trick, I could see that now.
Adult-land would be a vast melee of brawls, shouting and
attacks if people didn't pretend to be happy when things went

into infuriating or bewildering territories.

Milk would not, however, stop coming into my breasts, then soaking my clothes. I bled as well, and would for some time. Then, whenever I thought about leaving my baby, I cried. Fluid everywhere, and me trying to swim in a dressing gown. One night I walked along the dark corridor, tears streaming down my face. The nurse's room had a light on. I walked in. A nurse put down her magazine. 'Hey, I know you from school.'

'O, uh, yeees,' I peered at her, 'Margaret. You a nurse now?' Grinned.

'Yeah, well, had a baby. Had to leave school. Went nursing after he was adopted.' Her voice flat. Then she perked up. 'So what's the story with you?'

I recall the conversation in the dim nurses' station room like it went on all night. Temper and thoughts poured forth, on and on about the silly name they made me give my son, 'How can they make me name him something else?'

'That's insane.' She frowned and leapt to her feet. 'I named my baby Christopher, you know. He's yours. Name him any bloody name you want. Come on.'

Along the shiny linoleum corridor I went as fast as I could and Margaret loped on ahead. Her soft-soled shoes and my slippers barely made a sound. Way down the end of the ward, the night nurse and I sneaked into the semi-dark nursery. Super-spies in a uniform and a brunch coat.

Rows and rows of little bundles in clear cribs on legs with wheels. The nurse fetched a blue tag from a cupboard, and a pen. We both grinned and soon fastened a new blue cardboard heart to the crib - his name, Coltrane. All the windows in the place had opened to the stars.

My baby's tiny form slept, with his own name – finally, in the plastic crib they wheeled babies around in.

My mother visited day after day and kept begging me to let her have my baby. Why she didn't promise to help *me* care for him, instead, was a twisty-turny thought. It kept spinning away from me. Had she set me up to have the child she couldn't? (Mum often said she wasn't allowed more children for the good of her health). This idea shocked me so much I closed down on the

subject like a magician closing up his magic chamber where the
beautiful woman had climbed in, folding everything down. Only
a flat surface remained.

Incredulous, because for someone who rarely shut up, no words
existed for those thoughts and feelings colliding with each other.
In a fog of something like the worst music ever heard, a week or
so later, I left hospital in a deep blue crushed velvet skirt I had
once loved. It miraculously fitted again, even if it felt like a rag.
I wore a thin cardigan, too – clothes that had been too hot to
wear when I went into the maternity ward one sunny morning
shortly before. But a freezing wind blew strong. Huddled up,
arms folded, I walked fast. Sitting in a car, I answered people
who spoke, but felt like nothing. With winter's arrival, chill
weather felt like a part of me.

I went to Joe's place to stay, explaining, 'My flat's always full of
people. I need some privacy.'

Joe had taken up some other work, with the band getting less
gigs as winter approached. So he was out during the day, and so
were his flatmates. I slept a great deal, or lay on his bed staring
at the ceiling. A black circle the size of a couple of suitcases
moved around and around the ceiling wherever I shifted my
gaze.

I forgot to call my parents, imagining they wouldn't care, and
just lay there wishing life could explain what to do - as if it had a
persona. As if God really could be a fatherly old man who gave
wise directions aloud to girls who slept with men they weren't
married to (and had their babies anyway). Maybe God did
punish waywardness, burdening us with impossible days. But
what could I do? Did I have to surrender? What did Coltrane
need or want or...? I'd already almost completely given up food.

In the hospital I'd refused to eat much. That after seeing my
baby belly slide to the bed like badly cooked pudding when I lay
on my side for a sponge bath (in bed for a day after having my
baby). Soon, I nibbled one slice of toast for breakfast, and took
only salad at the end of the day. Tea kept me half-awake and
somewhat hydrated. My will was prodigious and I determined to
return to the size and shape I knew before - the girl who loved

dressing up again, who looked good in almost anything.
Elastic-girl had put on a smile after her brothers Chinese-burned
her arms for ages. Sooo cheery at school, too, after no one at
home had spoken to her directly about much for days. She could
look like she wasn't even pregnant and finish her last year's
education without a soul guessing her secret.

Giving birth was even more dramatic - and so stupefying, but I
expected *something* to appear as normal, afterwards. Except for
how someone took my young, firm body away and gave a
foreign, fat, saggy one back. This terrifying metamorphosis
happened in days, as far as I could tell.

Pregnant women hid at home, or swathed themselves in
maternity frocks for vital public appearances, but rarely went
out. No one ever discussed anything about the expectant mother
where I heard them - not her feelings or exercise, nor how she
wanted things to go or what she thought - certainly never the
changes women went through. People simply cried with glee,
'When's the baby due?' The bulging woman once possessed a
bunch of talents, friends, relationships, dreams and plans, now
she was the carrier, carer and nurturer - nothing else to think
about.

Maternity was a mass of smiles and dates, accepting baskets of
baby clothes and powders. It was a time to paint the spare room
and buy a bassinet. Doctors told you what to look for when you
went into labour as far as timing the pains and how to breathe;
never mentioning extreme pain or floppy stomachs, or feeling
like you now meant zilch. No one told me how protective and
defensive - even horrified - I'd feel about my mother or anyone
else wanting my baby, either.

At only 18 years old, people usually did explain things to me :
school rules, how to drive a car, what we were having for dinner,
what exams we needed to study for, safety for sports…. Secrecy
around pregnancy and sex flummoxed me. While recovering, I
suspected people didn't care or wanted me to suffer. So many
called an unplanned pregnancy a mistake. But every single birth
is luck - pure chance - a mistake if you like, every blessed birth
on this planet - no one can decide exactly when they will get
pregnant and be *sure* it'll happen. Conception depends on things

we can't see or control. So to call a baby a *mistake*, lumping it in
with a misspelt word or a dress cut too small, or using salt
instead of sugar - this made even less sense than fake smiles and
not ever complaining.

Anyway, I play-acted the young mother who didn't mind stretch-
marks, a floppy tummy, and leaky boobs. Eventually, I'd get used
to it, surely, and also slim down fast on minuscule morsels of
food a day. Refusal to eat. Focussed effort. Proof of power.
Regained, my body would soon be mine again.

At Joe's, I had nothing but one piece of toast and five cups of
tea a day. This took concentration, and I barely spoke to anyone.
Ignoring hunger is a dark art and not recommended - it's like
wanting to be dead and refusing to admit it. But in a few days,
feeling empty in a new way, I brightened.

The car started the first time, and bumbled along well known
city streets, passing home town landmarks and street signs. Trees
were turning gold by the lake and in the older parts of town -
inner city suburbs with huge oaks. Drifts of brown and gold
leaves lay over grass verges and the grey streets.

In my old flat, our three storey stucco 1920s house on a slope
near the lake, the wire coat-hangers in my wardrobe zinged. I
found an embossed cotton sundress from size 12 days. It was
white embossed cotton with a blue and green giant paisley print,
a few touches of yellow here and there. It had wide straps and
big buttons to hold them in place, criss-crossed at the back, 40s
style. The zip took a while to get tugged up but soon I'd dressed;
a fitted waist, then the A-line skirt to my knees. My old life
returned.

My flatmate once told me I could wear her fur stole, so I tried
that on, and some heels - even if she wasn't home. *Click, click,
click,* the heels sounded as smart as a clever machine; back to
The Shack.

Late in the afternoon I danced down the road to meet Joe, home
from his day job. He walked upright but not in a hurry, long hair
now way past his shoulders and flared jeans tight around his slim
hips. I grinned and he smiled uncertainly back in the mild warm
afternoon, a few clouds above. His head tilted, unsure what I
was doing springing along the road, when that morning I'd

barely been able to move. We drew close enough for me to
speak, 'I'm keeping our baby, Joe.'
He just smiled. 'I thought you'd do that.'
We walked back to his place with me blathering on, '... I will
have to stay at Mum's, I guess. I mean Billy's in the room next to
mine at the flat, he'd hate a baby being there. He hated Jill's
dog.'
Joe just smiled and nodded. At his place he wandered into his
room to practise his guitar.

Back at my flat, a note had said the adoption people wanted me
to call. I did, and told them I'd changed my mind. The woman
sighed, then tried to sound cheerful, 'Yes, well, dear, lots of girls
do that these days. I wish you all the best of luck.'

For a few months the air bristled with stories like a dog on alert.
The scandal probably helped draw a few more nosing around to
see what the band was up to, who knows?
The moment Joe kissed me - all that time before in his lounge
after Mark stormed away - I'd entered a whole new sphere of
attention. Life with Mark beforehand had given me only a
glimpse of popularity. His bands rarely stayed together long
enough to find much success. With Joe, I'd noticed real
admiration from strangers as much as their jealous jibes and
vicious whispers.

Joe said nothing about us. It frightened me how easily Joe could
lose interest. He'd be either amiable and kind or blank,
withdrawn, playing guitar.
Our glamorous life was slipping away, like when we stayed out
too late at some club and the sun rose while we were going
home. Shiny satin suits and heavy make-up may appear foolish
then. I'd hoped we'd live together in some nouveau-glam-
gingham version of a cookbook illustration, but with a really
good stereo. Coltrane and I could go on tour with Joe and Howl,
surely? But because Joe never spoke about our future I did my
best to forget I'd ever dreamt of such a thing.
Week after week I still visited The Shack. Joe and I talked, slept

together sometimes, and listened to music. So much was the same, but it also felt like we'd been to battle and back again. Parts of me so battered and changed I thought they'd never function again. At 18, I was weary and confused, love kept me going but it was like my spirit failed me.

Pushing against popular opinion's like struggling out to sea in heavy surf or fighting to stay upright in a strong headwind. You have to battle smoke, bad dreams, hot air, and the gossip. No one changed simply because I resisted their tacit demands. If a girl had a baby and wasn't married, then the man did not help her - she had to find a way to care for the infant herself. Any charity was accepted gratefully. She was, after all, ruined for life. It was as alarming as ink blots and stab marks all over a poster of fluffy kittens. I received half-whispered hisses, odd looks and sighs, and some remarks as blatant as a slap in the face. 'You've made your bed now, girl. You chose this, deal with it.'

In a blur I fetched my son from the maternity hospital, energised. I was still barely eating, but the decision to keep Coltrane felt like such a lift.

Exurbia had sprawled on without me. I went up the drive to our old house on a flat section covered with trees and plants, behind a hedge by the roadside. Away from my noisy flat packed with friends, and away from independent living with a stereo in every room. Neighbours, friends, and family provided second-hand crib, pram, blankets, a few toys, and swags of clothes, while Mum bought new nappies and outfits for best. Inundated with baby supplies in merely a day.

Settled with my parents. Out the window was the same view: houses across the road, a glimpse of trees, the asphalt street with concrete edges, green grass verges, gravel footpaths straight to the corner shops one way (and the awful burger bar), then to a park the other. New houses stood across the way, Mum told me, but we couldn't see them from there. So quiet everywhere. Amongst this samey same of sameness I kept up my one slice of toast a day with many cups of tea, maintaining total control of what I took off my plate. Anorexia seemed like a drug I'd discovered, although I had no idea of its name - but controlling my food made me feel better. My secret. Something powerful.

I'd not allow anyone else to notice or question me. I believed I felt in charge, losing weight, and there was no one to say it was wrong. I fooled myself that this meant good health.

Not eating while surrounded with food feels like trying to breathe only a little, or attempting to simply see straight in front, never deviating. I forced myself to not be attracted to the full refrigerator, didn't see the brimming fruit bowl, and forgot Mum's tins of baking. Always thinking about not eating - every waking moment. No space or time to think about anything else, either - such a relief. People left me alone. No one mentioned my not eating, my weight loss, or my barely speaking to anyone. After a few weeks, I'd lost four stone. I fitted old clothes with some room remaining and took a look at myself in the mirror, naked. My ribs stuck out. My hip bones did too, and my collarbone. There were livid stretch-marks around my hips and stomach, as if some rampant beast had attacked me once upon a wild night. Thinness. Frightening. It was the first time I'd looked at myself in a mirror for two weeks.

That day I ate lunch for the first time in four weeks. A sandwich without butter but with ham and salad, and a little mayonnaise. Ate so fast that I got hiccups. I had to hold my breath a few times to make them stop. Pains jabbed in my chest and I clutched at myself. Was it a heart attack? Did eating put me in shock? Burning and something was torn inside. I tried to breathe easier, coughed and spluttered. Pounding in my head. Black spots danced in front of my eyes.

No one entered the room. I prayed someone would help but no one appeared. I tried to breathe again, choking, and must've fallen off my chair, because soon I awoke with my face and arm aching, on the floor. My legs hurt, tangled in the chair I'd been sitting on, which had fallen at an angle.

It took me a few minutes to feel like I could sit up, to gingerly touch my arm (where a massive bruise formed later) and set things to rights. In the mirror my face looked okay but it hurt for days afterwards with any movement.

I raced through food at times, as if I thought it would be taken off me. Other days I'd forget to eat, then cram in two or three

meals' worth at once. My weight's now yo-yoed all my life.
Sometimes I felt dehydrated, my mouth dry, but could not make
myself drink any water. My mind left my body to itself quite
often, refusing to make the prompts needed, to register and
cause action. For some reason, too, I need to write this all down.
Perhaps once it's in words I can move along and away from the
chaos, the pain and fright? I ask myself such questions. Maybe
someone else will see my story and realise they're not alone in
their bewilderment and will get some help. If I'd felt like
someone was on my side all those years ago I could've been
happier, managed everything with more ease, known closeness
and comfort. Surface pleasures and fun I seemed to enjoy - they
masked such pain and emptiness, but what I found was the best
I could do at the time.

The millions of women with eating disorders whom I now know
about make me feel like someone's poured concrete over us all,
made us into statues. Halted but alive. Now there are helpful
websites, support groups, school counsellors... but back then
people praised us for losing weight, or ignored women's more
particular needs for the most part.

I had to keep on thinking it strange how no one mentioned my
not eating, nor said anything much about me. Had I grown
invisible? The baby - everyone talked about Coltrane,
perpetually. 'O where is he? O the little mite. How much does he
weight now? Did he have his inoculations? How do you fold
your nappies? Here's how I fold mine. This is a lovely set of
booties. Who made them?'

I murmured answers to the barrage. Everyone sat at the end of
a long tunnel, far away.

My mother did half-heartedly help me learn to breast-feed for
about ten minutes. Little Coltrane, bottle-fed from birth, didn't
like the idea of grasping a nipple. He swung his head about,
cried, and spat.

I cried, too - slow tears of frustration. I decided it could take
days, and waited for Mum to explain. She just sighed. 'O it
doesn't seem to be working.' Mum never suggested we call
anyone like a midwife to help, or that we try again. The bottle
stood in for me just fine - and she could feed him, then. Anyone

could feed Coltrane. Sometimes I noticed Mum fed him without asking me or even mentioning it.

Not Elastic-girl now, but Gone-girl again, as far as my family were concerned.

Writing this, I realise I had depression, but no one ever mentioned that word. They later called it Suburban Neurosis for a while, as if women simply grew neurotic about living in a house. Outer suburbs were vast deserts of houses, with no libraries or community centres - nowhere much for young mothers to gather except in each others' places, and certainly no organisation, in our town, to assist unmarried mothers. Adult company, apart from other parents, was scarce too. Every dwelling in our street held young married couples with teenaged or smaller children. All of them adults who were older than me.

Since I was still young, slim again, reasonably fit, and with a wide circle of friends, I beetled away in Mum's car at every opportunity. Off to a gig - good and loud - to dance, drink, smoke, laugh, converse, and laugh some more. Cigarettes no longer repelled me, without the pregnancy, although I wished I could give them up. With Joe and other friends we played cards, chatted, and laughed. There was a great deal of noise but a kind of silence too. There was no mention of certain things - and no comment on how I'd vanished, either. I no longer truly existed - of course no one would see what I was going through.

In glint-edged days and long sunny spells with warm, muggy air, lawnmowers hummed through suburban hush - summer eventually came upon us. Girls wore skimpy frocks and went about with bare-armed boyfriends. Kids cycled, skateboarded, and loped everywhere. The family trooped off to the beach, away for the summer.

Coincidentally, Joe's band also played in that coastal town of hopeful seagulls and dedicated sunbathers. Their lurid green and purple bus went on tour ('Howl' swirled in gold and blue-black across the side), ending up ensconced in the carpark of the gigantic sports' stadium. Fans readily noticed who'd play there. A three-week contract meant I'd see a lot of Joe and the rest - mainly hair and trousers by then, their flares up to 20 inches wide - and we'd all grown our lovely locks for years.

Some of the stage clothes I had run up for Joe looked rather faded by then from too many washes, or they'd shrunk, and sat a little too short in the wrists, or at the ankle. DIY glamour oddities. One foot in farmland and the other in stage lights - we can look that way when I shuffle through old photos. At the time we behaved like we could only ever be cool, however, blessed with youthful chutzpah.

A cruise through salt fresh air for a few streets in my mother's yellow car, and into the stadium carpark. On mornings of balmy seaside calm, I knocked on the door of the bus or just walked in if the door was open, calling, 'Hi, how are you?'

Once or twice their drummer made jokes about blondes in Joe's bed. 'Who was she, an angel?'

My hair was long past my shoulders by then, and black - so it wasn't me he talked about. Every crass hint was audible, but I managed to make it look like I didn't hear or care most of the time - smoothing my hair, or sitting on a seat to smile at whoever. And Joe snapped asides in an off-hand tone which shut their drummer up just fast enough for me to be able to look like I believed he was only joking.

Lately, there's a clearer line between those who respect women and those who do not. Back then (with feminism only recently mooted again as a fine philosophy), many men I knew treated women as objects to be admired or derided - according to how we looked. Few questioned this stance.

And hadn't I been set up to think that men could tease and torment me, by how they treated me when I was young? Adults tricked me and laughed at my distress, or ignored us children.I learnt my place. We rarely look for the non-existent. I see this now. Back then it was simply chaos - I lived amidst a mess.

Their singer and Joe often openly admired the various beauties who lingered, wishful. Infinite beautiful girls in bikinis (none with stretch-marks), their futures as blank as a new page. As long as Joe and their vocalist only muttered comments to each other, or Joe's eyes just casually ranged the lovely young women who sauntered by or passed remarks, I pretended nothing important had happened.

Then, when I saw Joe lean in close and whisper in an unknown o-so-pretty girl's ear and she simpered in response, when they laughed together for a whole break at a Howl gig, and when he walked off outside with another one and didn't come back for a half hour, or someone mentioned he hadn't slept in the bus all night, then I did shout and complain, 'I can't stand it. What about me?'

Joe didn't look at me or say a word, but he'd sit, apparently hearing my complaints and questions, like someone waited for a train whistle to stop. In time I steamed to a halt. Then Joe, already half-gone, walked away - a slim, tall man with long dark hair, disappearing.

One of the others almost always said something to try and cheer me up. 'You're looking great today, love. New shoes?'

Frequently, I drove off fast. I'd take a long walk on the beach, enjoy a swim, or write in my diary - long questioning loops of sentences.

The sun was gentler then, pre-ozone hole - New Zealand's light not so intense. Blue and gold days by the ocean passed amid tanned holiday-makers - multitudinous shapes and sizes in bright swimwear, shorts, or draped in sarongs or caftans; fresh air and surf. They would take the air, make sandcastles, go in for a dip, and find fresh local food later for lunch in a bach or caravan. Few grand houses were to be found anywhere near the ocean (or even in the cities, then) - plain living instead. Beach life calmed the populace down.

Little Coltrane wore a peaked cap with a sunshade on the back, like in the Foreign Legion (we joked), at the beach with the guys. We were grouped on brightly patterned towels together in the sun. I took bits of bark out of Coltrane's mouth. He wobbled on his nappy and squinted at the surf racing in, a short distance away. In an hour or so I'd take him home - even with liberal applications of sunscreen toddlers didn't stand the outdoors for too long, and he needed a drink, and a nap. Some days I'd walk away from the band on the beach, their voices rising before I was out of earshot - Joe's amongst them. They made comments on girls walking by, accompanied by someone's low whistle.

At night, hundreds packed into the stadium - they danced,

drank, laughed and shouted to each other over the boom of
music. Light show gloop and swirl, spun colour across the vast
ceiling and walls, over the crowd - scattered galaxies and
bubbling brilliance. Music stirred the best-ever generation, the
beat on and on, the most free. We were sunshine, moon and
stars. We'd conquer hatred, greed and want, bring love to
everything and everyone - everywhere. In synch, long hair
shaking, hips swinging, I'd wonder how I could ever beat the fact
that I had to be home in time to give Coltrane his bottle.
Sometimes I let it slide. Mum always remembered (and never
mentioned) my not getting home on time. It started to feel like I
had had a baby for her. Someone pushed me right outside and
left me there for good, this time.

The fantasy I harboured about Joe realising he needed Coltrane
and I (surely he wanted me to live with him) - that notion wore
away to something like a picture left in the rain. In time Joe and
I spoke even less. Panic started up, like when something acrid
simmered on the stove. But it changed, too. Hard to define or
control, it was a weight inside. And the air itself was heavy - as if
all we never ever said turned to toffee, cooling - perhaps burnt.
Was love all we needed or had I got it wrong? Were all those
songs and poems and stories mistaken? Didn't Joe realise I
needed him? I wasn't sure I even knew how to explain. Raised
by books, magazines, movies, and TV shows, I suppose I hoped
someone else would write Joe some decent lines to say.

Maybe Joe and I needed someone – *anyone* - warm to believe in,
so our loneliness wasn't unbearable. Possibly neither of us really
understood what closeness meant. Few ever showed us any
kindness to a great extent, and we didn't learn much afresh from
each other. There was just so little to share.

In the bath or in bed, and sometimes while driving my car, I
burst into tears. In my diary I wrote - A huge blue space follows
the unwanted, the rejected, the deeply hurt, the misunderstood,
and the abused. At any moment we can step into that cold place
and disappear. Familiar to us, it feels falsely safe, but few others
follow, it's too cold. So we don't take any risks, we don't reach
out to appreciate someone else, we don't carefully state how they
could stop hurting us, discuss ways to make life better, and rarely

do we leave. We just soak in that blue instead. A familiar chill.
The lucky ones who know what it's like to enjoy closeness, they
think we're weirdos. No one wants to hear our story, it's not fun
like a horror or vampire movie, too real.

Soon Joe moved to the Big Smoke – as dad called it (like a
cartoon), a good hour's drive away. A vast city sprawled across
an isthmus like a sun-loving animal trying to catch as many rays
as possible. Joe stayed with a famous band there in their
Ponsonby villa; played in a 15 piece funk machine. They
practised a short walk from his new place. Four players in their
brass section, three singers....

In fits and starts, Joe journeyed back, staying at his mum's house,
six suburbs away. He'd call me, I'd drive over with Coltrane.
We'd talk over coffee at his mother's red marbled Formica
kitchen table. Cream Venetian blinds beside us, half open, let in
a little daylight. A radio on the kitchen bench played pop music
quietly. A long way from The Shack's worn furniture and
overflowing ashtrays - our dishevelled haven where big, albeit
dirty, windows allowed light to pour in and the stereo boomed
rock. The age of Aquarius was still dawning, but the suburbs
remained buttoned up, sedate, and brushed clean - in a version
of old night, a spruce shadow. How upbeat we tried to sound,
then talk often dragged as if we needed more air to float what
we said, wanted, and wished for.
Joe's mother delighted in seeing Coltrane, she'd play with him in
the adjoining lounge. The sound of them laughing.
Our baby grew. Soon a rather plump toddler, he beamed at
people as if they'd just said or done something brilliant - even if
they were just standing there. Such a charmer.
My brothers left home. Only Mum, Dad, baby Coltrane, and I
lived in the (by then) rather worn-looking white house (built
around the 1930s). It had broad front steps that rose to a
concrete porch on the west corner, and windows that opened out
sideways - caught in place with a brass lever arrangement. Mum
often polished the catches but they rarely shone enough for her
liking. Sometimes I took to the brass with a cloth and acidic-

smelling Brasso. Exertion, and the obvious shine after working on the latches provided a deep satisfaction. Mum loved to see me cleaning.

Friends moved away, mainly to the city. Some travelled overseas or to universities. Distractions dissolved like mist in the sun. Our town dreary with wet weather and fog prevalent. I drew pictures, designed clothes, or drove Mum's car about the place just to see streets I didn't know, and went op shopping. Wheeling past familiar houses memories floated through my mind; some old school friends' parents still mowed those lawns, trimmed that camelia, repainted a letterbox... But we'd grown and everything appeared as ordinary as a plank of wood.

Coltrane laughed and crowed when we sang or spoke to him, and his toys and equipment reached gigantic proportions. Rearranging baby things and washing nappies took hours every day. Mum said to me one morning, 'You learn a lot after a few children. Gets easier in time.'

I stared dumbly at her - did she think I'd have more?

Joe sometimes called to visit, to see Coltrane. We'd talk. Occasionally we'd meet in a motel and take our skin to familiar places. We disappeared into kissing and touching, sex a true pleasure; afterwards - for days sometimes - such peace and elevation. Joe had this hollow where his hip bones jutted a little, then his skin smoothed down to his flat stomach. I liked to admire and stroke him there. He seemed an angel with long dark hair, just like always, even if we were older. He seemed to have such a soft, kind face when we lay close. Nothing and nobody completely good or totally bad, after all.

One evening we called in on an old friend recently returned from Australia, and played cards. Talk flowed, jokes, smokes, a few beers, and our friend's anecdotes, 'Aussie, the work there, maaan. I played five nights a week at this place, local. A restaurant. Drove trucks on days off. Made a bundle but it all went up my arm. Had to come back here to get clean.'

We lived on the edge of the time before almost everything people loved to do for fun was found to be bad for us. We left our friend's flat, and walked into a still, clear, sweet-smelling

early summer night. Jasmine curled through their hedge by the
gate. Into town by various office buildings, a few shops, and soon
- with not one other car on the road - Joe and I wheeled past
The Shack. There it was - an old villa converted to a shop at the
front – with a 'Shoemaker and Shoe Repairs – Made-to-Order
and Mending' sign above the door along the guttering. I
wondered, 'Maybe someone new lives behind there, now?'
A shadow ran along the footpath by the cruising car. 'Joe, Joe, it's
your cat. Uh, Pirate.' I slammed on the brakes, parked, wound
down the window, and called softly, 'Puss, puss, puss, heeere
Piiirate....'
No another car in sight, no other people anywhere.
We'd worried about that stray after Joe moved out. We hadn't
known what to do. While the cat did, in those days, allow Joe to
pick him up, we couldn't imagine getting him into a carry-box to
take to a new flat in another city, or to the SPCA. It had been
ages ago, but now there he was again.
Both of us were out of the car in a blink and down a driveway
to a factory behind some shops, calling his name. 'Piiirate,
Pirate, puss, puss.'
Smoothly running, his coat glossy, Pirate trotted up to us without
hesitation. His purring much louder than the sparse traffic
passing at that late hour.
'Someone's been feeding him. He's okay.' I laughed, and almost
cried, with happiness.
Pirate let me stroke him too, and pick him up - for the first time
ever. His muscles felt strong under his black fur. Heavy and
warm in my arms, the cat rumbled against my chest. Joe and I
grinned and exclaimed, as delighted as if an old friend we'd
believed dead reappeared quite well and full of stories.
Joe took Pirate. The cat rubbed its cheek against Joe's chin,
purring even louder. Joe stood there in a pale blue jersey, the
cat's fur (black, with flashes of white) against his chest.
When Joe let Pirate go into the night, he ran down a dark
driveway towards factories. He then turned to look back a
moment, as if saying goodbye, or fixing us in his mind - then
Joe's cat disappeared into shadows.
All the way back to Joe's mum's where I dropped him off, we

talked over and over about this chance happy meeting. The pair of us laughed like we'd each been given a gift always before only dreamed about.

The next day Joe called in to see Coltrane, and I took their picture with mum's camera. They're both in strong sunlight and their faces look a little washed out.
Some photographs, I regard them now and feel like they should tell me more but the people in them are only a moment - caught as they once were - images on paper, and no words appear to enlighten me.

Months later, Joe hitch-hiked the few hours to our child's birthday. We had a cake with one candle. I let Coltrane blow the candle out many times. Joe told me later, 'You're only indulging Coltrane. Letting him blow the candle out forever. Spoiling him. The candle is lit once, blown out once, then it's over.'
It was all I could do not to spit out a nasty remark. Joe did almost nothing to care for his son and I only wanted the birthday to be fun. Now he had some criticism? 'O stop it. It's a party for a birthday.'
Any plan could disintegrate as fast as a biscuit dunked too long into tea. For years, I wanted to escape the suburbs, but all roads led back to the old neighbourhood. Living at my parents' again after my brief, liberated time flatting with eleven people my own age. My hopes for Joe and I to get together once more were obviously ridiculous - he didn't approve of how I behaved with our son, he wasn't respectful, and he didn't seem to understand how to stay close any more than I did.
My brothers worked at various occupations, went flatting then returned, off and on, to stay with our parents - supposedly to save money. They did nothing around the house. I helped mum cook, clean, hang out laundry, and wished the enormous sky could transform into elsewhere - any place I did not have to do such mundane things all day.
'Come and work with me,' A phone call one morning while I gazed out the window, mist thick over the road and trees outside. My friend Heather (a super-music-buff) from school, had

auditioned to work in this great shop. 'I answered fifteen million music questions. Got the highest score out of hundreds who applied. They want me to choose a friend to work with.'
We worked so close to bone fide stardom. They paid us to talk about music, play music, and sell vinyl - along with eight-track tapes, but almost no one bought those. We wandered the packed record bins, and chose whatever we liked to play on the excellent shop stereo. I was a part-time shop girl in the town's first-ever record store. Customers listened to their preferences, using three double sets of cushioned headphones along a high bench, with bar stools. An innovation. Many had no idea that if they talked with the padded headphones over their ears they'd be shouting. All grins and wide eyes, people listening roared, 'It's really great, ay?! That's the best track, that one!' as they sang along, out of tune. We'd watch from behind the counter and laugh surreptitiously while their friends tried to tell them not to yell.

Joe's old bass player knocked at Heather's door one night, years after he'd moved on to another band. We smiled to see him again, with his broad grin and spiral curls to his shoulders. 'Hi, these guys are living here now,' he said, indicating two thin strangers behind him - one in platform shoes and velvet pants, the other in a bright t-shirt and blue jeans. 'They wanted to know if I knew anyone they could meet. I said you liked playing cards, Heather. New resident band at Lord's. Scott's the singer, Pete's the guitarist.'
We stood around grinning by the door. 'What's your band's name?' I hoped it'd sound good.
The guitarist smiled. 'Electric Rain. From a Dylan song. Chimes of Freedom.'
'Dylan?' My voice reedy. I prayed they didn't play folk music. Strange for a club band to like Dylan, who I'd barely heard of at that stage.
Their singer, wild-eyed in a t-shirt printed with French swear-words, red on yellow, spoke huskily, 'Sooo, you play 500?'
There we played and all the while with non-stop talk about places they'd been, '...The Cabana in Napier, totally cool. Crowds great, people who run the place *so* friendly. Pub tables

get taken over by the different ships. Kind of a friendly, well, *usually*, rivalry. The ship girls make such a noise....' We churned through lists of music we liked, and what they planned to play at Lord Love's, our sole nightclub, 'Guess Who covers, Thin Lizzy, an' Elton, uh....'

Guitarist Pete's shoes were higher than any of mine - red platforms under vibrant red velveteen flares. He told me he bought them in London. Playing cards in Heather's flat, laughter and talk in syncopated rhythm. A few hands of cards turned into a three hour extravaganza.

A mixed crowd soon congregated at their flat for five hour card games, in great billowing fugs of smoke. We built fanciful obstacle courses made of fast food containers for invented games with marbles. I started projects drawing psychedelic doodles with my treasured rotoring pens. Their mid-yellow house was close to town. Streams of fans, friends, other musos, drug dealers, the curious and the furious dropped in most days and four evenings a week there.

We danced nights away at Lord's for the remainder.

To our chagrin, the promoter had named the club - Lord Love - and he relished it. A stand-in statue stood by the front door. Beau Brummel, this sculpture was, or so the owner insisted, 'Grooved up for the 1970s. He loved fashion, we love it too. It's cool. He's lord of fashion.'

People over 30 claiming words like *grooved* made us feel queasy - and we never said that. But live music attracted us, hungry for excellent sounds, so our disdain had to be hidden. Upstairs at Lord's (as we called it), nouveau Victoriana decor - the bar embossed silver across the front, with filigree decoration at the back. Round wooden tables stood set about the large, wooden dancefloor, and a sweeping staircase led to upstairs mezzanine seating. An enormous rectangular stage sat at the far end of the cavernous place. Once upon another decade my parents met there, when it was called The Peter Pan Ballroom. Nightclubs don't get old, they simply change their name and are reborn once more.

The other reason Electric Rain wanted to meet us was to

discover where to buy dope. We did know a few places - even I did - which was strange considering how little I thought of the stuff. Information about illicit substances was shared freely in our circles and we still believed marijuana wasn't harmful. The law was wrong.

Years before - when I'd first tried smoking grass - we'd sat in a circle on the floor of a room out in this place my then-boyfriend Mark took me to, with long-haired farmers who grew their own. I'd passed out. I kept recalling this incident in fear. I'd been powerless - unable to move - and it didn't feel good afterwards at all. I hid my doubts usually from the others - belonging mattered more than my opinion.

By the time Electric Rain arrived in velvet hipsters and slogan-loopy t-shirts, people smoked so many variations of grass, dope, weed, heads, or Buddha sticks that I'd lost track. Coromandel Crash, Hallowed Heads.... Rumours floated as freely as aromatic smoke, 'They lace it with horse tranquiliser. Don't buy from him. He's a rip-off. Get the other stuff.'

'Those heads are hallucinogenic, tell you what. Opiated heads, man, they give you out-of-it dreams.' 'He sold mixed herbs to the Devil's Outlaws - the bikies? You should've seen his face after they'd dealt to him.'

Dope still didn't rip me any likable way, but stoners loved the stuff - they drifted here and there, half-connected to the world. Their eyes went droopy through nonsensical conversations, or they laughed at nothing. They devoured entire kitchens of food without a qualm in a few minutes, drove at about ten miles an hour, and shivered in paranoid delusions in gardens and on balconies....

There were trips, too - on a tiny ticket of blotting paper, sometimes with a fun stamp on it. LSD warped the manner of things into shapes no one ever dreamt existed. Peculiar frontiers discovered without ever leaving your batik-draped sofa. Heady propaganda rang true for numbers of friends who entered surreal other realms with enthusiasm. But Howl's drummer told me, 'Don't *you* ever take Acid. You're already too far there.' He laughed. 'Yeah, not far-out, she's *far there*.'

My some-time occupation became to stay straight, and care for those who were tripping. Somehow they believed I wouldn't freak anyone out. But they certainly did grow timid and fragile - unable to enter a dairy to buy an ice block, horrified at a dog running towards them, or blissed out by the sunset so much that they tried to walk into it across the road - without watching for traffic. Flip-outs were carefully baby-sat, meaning I cared for their substance-altered selves - successfully, I suppose - no one was lost on my watch.

A few scrawny, whiny people were also into heroin. We believed it looked obvious who was shooting up. The drug seemed to make people ill. Teen Challenge's clean-cut members distributed Christian literature on the streets to describe the evils of drugs. But, observing a junkie, it was usually blatantly obvious that heroin did no good. Often disengaged and ghoulish, and they told such lies. Addicts without a job or who weren't dealers were likely to rip off everyone in their vicinity. We learnt to avoid them.

Keira, from my old flat, worked in an office with accountants. She drove a late-model car, wore new clothes - even on weekends - looked rather like a Bond girl - tall, curvy - quite stunning. She rented a house by the river, with a pool, with her boyfriend Pete, who practised law. When I went over there one day, unannounced, I thought Keira and Pete appeared nervous. In a few minutes this drawly girl in a floaty Indian embroidered skirt appeared at the door. She stage-whispered, 'She cool?'
I supposed she meant me.

Then Keira and Pete sequestered themselves in their bedroom with this woman. Some kind of drug deal. Nothing else produces that manner of hush.

Heather told me when I asked her, 'O yeah, they've been tasting for ages. Didn't you know? Suppose they can afford it.'
Many people took heroin, and some looked like they rarely did much but enjoy a beer. Not everyone fitted the archetype.

Band manager, Timothy, of Electric Rain, held eye-opening opinions, 'All drugs should be legal, sold in plain grey wrappings from plain grey shops. No advertising, easy to get, cheap, guaranteed pure/of a certain purity. All profits to rehab. Anyone

over 25 can buy. Illegal drugs waste time and money. Police
should be doing something useful, not busting us. If people need
escape or adventure, they'll find a way.' He'd hold court for
hours while rolling enormous joints, using up to ten cigarette
papers. They called him Ten Skin Tim.
Bags and boxes of substances were sold for years from the boot
of his extremely smart, ultra-conservative car. He parked down
alleys or around the back of nightclubs, where it was difficult to
see him from the street. No policeman ever questioned him.
With short sandy hair, a dark, carefully-styled suit, and a plain
tie, Ten Skin Tim blended with straight, everyday people like
when a soldier camouflaged himself. But he made no war,
except perhaps on everyday sensibilities. Someone mentioned
once he could wear something more,'...cool. Y'know, jeans or...'
'I'm a manager. Whatever your job, look the part.'

Heather and I worked at the record store - blessed, invited
everywhere, we heard everything and saw more than we wanted
to, but raced through days and nights in wide-eyed excitement.
Friends and foes, wannabes, and the already famous threw
parties, fell in and out of love, and sneaked into the local school's
swimming pool near Midnight Rain's flat for night-time
swimming. We shopped for fashion at a couple of funky places
emerging in back-streets or in tiny spaces on the main drag –
boutiques - like we lived in Paris or London. For brief moments of
transcendent cool it was as wonderfully hip as anywhere - we
were looking the part to live funky.
Electric Rain on stage - a photo come to life from Melody
Maker - so polished the audience half-believed they were
certainly famous. Many punters, after a couple of Bacardi and
cokes, could almost recall their last album. Expert covers
pounded through a superb sound system. The crowd fantasised
international idols stood there in true sweat and genius, satin
pants, perfect jeans, monster shoes, and celebrity hairdressing
(long shaggy cuts), thrusting hips, eyes flashing or
transcendentally closed - hour after hour of bliss.
Most bands played covers. Original Kiwi music hadn't appeared
in sufficient quantity to be given such a name (even if Split Enz

did eventually play with Howl, at a gig where locals threatened
to riot because they'd never heard the original music they
played). Electric Rain performed alchemy. They took someone
else's music, played it perfectly, and also made themselves into
stars.

Inspired, I decided I was grown-up enough to go flatting again,
when the band was evicted from their fun yellow house (for too
much noise). Coltrane and I lived with Electric Rain in a pale
blue house close to the city and by the lake. Towering dark trees
crowded in on the place, which was damp, cold, isolated, and
without a washing machine. But I thanked my lucky stars,
moon, and sun that I'd escaped the suburbs again.

We'd had to lie and say we were married, the singer and I,
although baby Coltrane looked nothing like him and I wasn't
romantically involved with any of them. Landlords did not rent
houses to mixed groups of unmarried people very often. Mike
had only got our big house (for the eleven lucky people I flatted
with when I was pregnant) using his gift of the gab and dressing
like a bank teller, as if he could afford to live there alone, or with
some lucky woman. He only looked so respectable because his
strange wiry hair wouldn't grow long, and he wore a suit for his
sales job.

Way away in the city Joe chased stardom with various bands. I
hardly ever saw him. We rang each other once a week or so at
first, but toll calls were expensive.

Electric Rain's drummer, Logan, and I spent evening after
evening sitting up later and later by the fire. Just the two of us.
Night-time so quiet. My pen drawings easier to make at that late
hour, they absorbed me. Finally he murmured one night, 'I'd
really like to sleep with you.'

Free love and open conversations as everyday by that time as
breakfast, lunch, or dinner, and I smiled. 'Okay, sure.'

We sat there for a short while longer by the fire until it died
down. I finished my drawing, then went to bed. I imagined
there'd eventually be some kind of sensual overture from Logan.
He'd kiss me or touch my arm and we'd embrace. Our dance

began slowly with his suggestion, then....

He told me he was puzzled a few nights later, 'I thought we'd go to bed the other night.'

I laughed off his blunt assertion that our getting together needed to be up to me, but then realised he meant it; so I sneaked into Logan's room that evening. He'd only just gone to bed and turned towards me in the dark when I whispered his name. He threw back the covers of his bed and I slipped in beside him, both of us naked. To hold someone else close felt warm, reassuring, and the secrecy excited me - my skin tingled. His closeness and the scent of his skin caused my breath to quicken. Hardness against my thigh, his large hands over my silky thighs and back. Our breathlessness and moans hushed at first, then louder but not too much so.

We kept our affair a secret. I'd sneak along into his room at night when I thought everyone else we flatted with was asleep. It still puzzles me why I fell into this arrangement. Loneliness? Desire? Both? So many we knew quite often slept with each other without much ceremony. Liberation to enjoy, the children of the revolution. Magazines, books, and films brimmed with slogans. Some media got banned - it scandalised millions, could apparently destroy outdated ideas with words or images, as if language caught memory on fire. A friend of ours who'd just finished his social science degree explained one night, 'We may argue that women's liberation and the contraceptive pill made it easier for men to prey on women. Perhaps supposed freedom's like a blind to hide inside for a hunter. But it's more likely as society grew more affluent, many amongst youth decided we deserve to enjoy more pleasure than the generations before ours.'

I wasn't sure I liked the way he leered at me. Although throughout my youth I did often follow what I thought could make me feel good, as if I at last deserved to feel that way.

The insecurity of knowing whoever you lately fell in love with could also sleep with anyone else they chose, however, felt like a twisty trick. New fashions appeared every three months, new ideas were expounded in magazines, on TV, and in films, and fresh romances did relays with the famous at intervals too, we could imitate them. Did all those necessarily follow?

Equations for persuasion didn't have to make sense. What mattered was getting what we wanted. Of course we also knew everything. Young. Beautiful. Popular. Talented. Brilliant.

One night, I quietly opened my door to tip-toe across to Logan's room as usual, but found the fire screen and some other things in the way. I closed my door and went back to bed.

The next morning, Scott - their singer - snarled across the breakfast table, 'No sleeping with flatmates.' Scott stomped off with his breakfast, to eat in his room.

We made peace somehow, but soon our landlord discovered we weren't genuinely a married couple with a boarder. We were evicted and told, 'You groups of mixed people. Not trustworthy tenants.'

Some fire burst inside me, I shouted, 'You're the ones who aren't to be trusted. We paid every week on time. Never wrecked anything. You broke your promise to us.'

A woman took my arm and showed me out of the real estate office. 'Please dear, you are making a scene.'

I stood there on the footpath with the eviction letter still in my hand. Inside the office, I could see the agents behind their desks apparently writing important documents or calling people. My long purple and green paisley dress swirled in a breeze. I strode away. Peace, out.

The 70s, 'If you remember them, you weren't there,' or so an old joke goes.

I felt superior because I survived. So many didn't. Drug overdoses, suicides, car accidents, illnesses - one boy contracted meningitis - we think from the river where we once loved to swim. Others fried their brains - idiot drug casualties or paranoid husks whom no one could talk with properly. 'Jeebies man, you gotta have them then the heebies never mind.' Manic laughter on the street one weekday from a half-recalled acquaintance babbling nonsense. We tried not to talk with him for long. Art and music casualties, too, so far immersed in jargon and supposed coolness they couldn't converse with anyone outside their own tiny circle, or anyone.

Office workers swerved to avoid us.

Many found God, Khrishna, Jehovah, The Great Goddess...or grew fanatically involved with health food, anti-nuclear protests, politics, organics, craftwork, intercultural communication.... Pick a cause, it was almost certainly born in the 1970s - or popularised then. Cults and communes formed like mushrooms, popping up overnight. Weary conformists deserted all-mod-con suburbia for a version of a hundred years ago - no electricity or piped-in water, no underground sewage system. Saving the world with organic food and free love. In-groups and cliques protected the delicate, the fervent, the born-again, lost, found, nutty, and charismatic. The goal was to be the most enlightened, the hippest, new human who wouldn't make terrible mistakes like those who came before - brave new versions of homo sapiens - raving, confident, and stylish. It wears me out now thinking about it.

The way we fell into bed with each other perhaps made for more pleasure momentarily, but how empty a great gesture may also appear. Casual sex often held little meaning and its delights faded fast. Our talk lacked resonance when not worked in with attachment, mutual respect, and at least some knowledge of the other person beyond what they looked like. Others disagreed. Fast food became more popular, cars ran quicker, people also travelled overseas with less difficulty - but these trips lost their glamour to some extent. Convenience reigned, however, not always royally.

Liberation meant thinking for yourself, didn't it? Not allowing some man or woman to scheme to conquer then leave you for the next body to rub up against. Truth unpopular then, and probably now. Disillusioning, but I hadn't yet gathered that an ideal's never perfectly realised in action.

Believing we were never-before-seen wonders of the world gave us energy. Children of the revolution founded record shops, vegetarian restaurants, recording labels, nightclubs, boutiques and fashion labels, wellness centres, meditation and yoga schools, changed the way some children were educated, discovered ever-increasing startling music, developed therapies for better mental health, improved physical fitness, and other

self-improvement.... The alarming generation for peace, love,
and rock and roll.

While I stayed in my home town like a time traveller who'd lost
her way, Joe and I talked on the phone the way many distant
lovers do. A run-through of news. He asked after his son. We
talked about music and films, books, and made a few plans like
making cat's cradle patterns with words. Sometimes I drove or
bussed to Auckland and stayed with him. Fun at times on the
surface, but it also felt like clinging to debris after a shipwreck,
with the alternative being letting go into a great sea of
nothingness.

The movie of my life then on fast forward, with schooldays over.
Fashion in rapid flux : geometrics, paisleys, brights, then
whoosh, everything black, and thigh boots, ankle boots, high
heels, textured tights, coloured tights, long socks, fake tans....
Someone joined a cult, overdosed, found Jesus did save, left
town, started a band, went to university, had an affair with their
lecturer, built a teepee, tattooed their back, refused their meds
and went on the run, married in peach silk on a beach in Bali,
ran amok at a gig, or invented a gadget to out-widget anything.
Boundless information teemed and swarmed, science-fiction
realities shimmered into our streets and onto screens from
magazines and conversations. Less time to think, and an impulse
to stay with commotion, razz and snazz.

Joe and I, we drifted apart, as people say - as if humans are
continents through the ages, or flotsam and jetsam in the ocean.
Floating humanity, adrift in time, memory, and space.

My temper such a muddle. Joe sometimes refused to speak and
just practised his guitar. I threw my cork soled clogs at him a
couple of times. I don't think they ever connected, but what did
love have to do with that? A grab bag of odd sod reasons and a
broken mirror to see myself in. I never quite got the complete
picture. Pieces appeared missing - fragmented images and ideas
at times sharp, cutting - some as pointed as a weapon.

Rage consumed me. It was like being drunk on emotion.

My conscience as poorly formed as a half-sprouted seed.

My brothers had doubtless taught me to be violent. It didn't
seem overly strange to lash out, I see now, screaming insults if I

couldn't get what I wanted or needed - romance, conversation, or promises. When the rush of emotion subsided, feeling guilty I'd stuff the nagging guilt into dark places inside. Wadges of awful stuff in there - extra weight, worry, sorrow, and remorse. A leading man calmed women's tantrums in films with a look, a word, or a kiss. I wondered why life didn't match those movies I loved so much. They made so much sense. Life didn't.

At not yet twenty, I lacked the skills to plan or negotiate; discovering that the smile-and-agree strategy some adults used only faked happiness. Anger and violence at times did make fear scarper, but it always returned, usually bearing more fright than before. Abundant worries, nightmares, ridiculous imaginings - days and nights populated with horrorshow and bad memories piling in. Absence of fear was a fantasy through clouds of exhaustion after crying for hours, exhausted, after I'd raged. My temper went riot crazy for infinite expanding, boiling minutes - relief from feeling terrified and powerless. I hid my weakness underneath bravado, make-up, fancy clothes, swagger and strut, whenever I felt I could fail or appear vulnerable. Raged against the times before when no one cared enough to stand up for me, or perhaps fury simply served me passion. Better than deadening myself inside, or possibly I believed if I didn't scare people away they'd hurt me again - and I'd had enough - ample sufficiency - of pain. I haven't described all that happened to me in this story. I don't want to revisit some of the more dreadful events. Suffice to say there were strangers and some supposed friends who pushed into me - who treated me like a toy they wanted to wreck, who did nasty things no girl - no one - should ever have to experience.

Occasional tantrums released me briefly from the certain knowledge that uselessness and ugliness - my own undesirable self - lurked inside no matter where I went, no matter what I said or did. It took decades to realise this, and the shame at how I'd behaved felt overwhelming.

I've since tried to avoid belittlers and bullies, steered away from abusers, or make it clear they do not affect me. I never want to feel worthless again.

Despite his crass playing around and some of his dominating

moves I'll never discuss, I was cruel in my turn to Joe, too.
Nowadays, I could find him and apologise but I doubt Joe'd do
much except say, 'I thought you were sorry, ages ago.'
And I am sorry.
I'd like to think he is, as well. But I'm not sure Joe'd ever say so.
Thinking about having to be sorry is far far worse than feeling it
- genuine remorse is so liberating.

Long after Joe's band, Howl, won that competition for the
second time, the mood of our love affair changed. Their green
and purple bus was sold to a family who painted it yellow with
colourful polka dots over the sides. They toured around the
country as The Family Singers, playing country music.
Howl broke up and everyone played with different people. Some
went overseas.
One rainy night outside another gig Joe did with a TV singing
star who toured every year, I told him we'd be better off apart.
'It seems like you've already left, don't have any time for your
baby, or me.'
He murmured, 'It's not that, I....'
Rain pelted down on my car. In the downpour, the evening
appeared as black as outer space, without stars. Joe tried to tell
me something but endless disappointments put a snap in my
tone. Rain pelted down, on and on and on, drumming away on
the car roof.
I told him to get out, before I changed my mind.
He opened the car door, ran off through the rain to pack gear in
the van - off to another town to play back-up for a celebrity.
I was left with an empty feeling and something like amazement
but, also, I told myself surely I'd known all along he'd leave that
easily. I'd gambled, wanting Joe to say he needed me to change
my mind, and to beg to let us stay together, but he didn't push it.
I've often wondered what Joe tried to say, why I cut him off, and
why he didn't insist on having time to state what he thought best.
Joe could've explained that he needed to work, to play up and
down the country. I needed to be patient, to understand. That
would be his version of asking to stay with me.
But perhaps solitude would do if I couldn't have passion and

commitment. Neither of us were thoughtful or kind enough. Joe
never offered financial support for our child, nor offered to move
in with us. We were barely together. I had a empty space inside
me where something like love and attention throughout my
childhood should've been held in memory, but it wasn't there. I
expected far too much of Joe, without realising it.

Occasionally, for years afterwards, we'd see each other some
place. An attraction remained, like the memory of a song, a
hum. He saw his son Coltrane as much as I could finagle time to
get them together. Then he moved to Australia.
Joe worked as a tour bus driver who played in a band once a
week, Best Blue, at a club in Melbourne. He got married to
someone in Europe, a traveller he had met on his tour bus. Now
he lives in Poland with his wife, who's also a musician. He always
wanted to play overseas. They tour sometimes. Joe sends
Coltrane presents or postcards from Paris, Rome....
I'm glad I did my best to make sure my son saw his father, but
Coltrane's dad never encourages his son to be kind to me. When
his sister once suggested Joe could support his son in this way -
make sure my child contacted his mother - Joe simply said, 'O, it
never comes up.' Maybe men really do not take an interest in
fostering relationships, or Joe's just incapable of reaching out too
far. Maybe I was too mean and furious for too long to be worth
thinking about kindly. People can go on hurting you as long as
you let them.
Occasionally, I talk with Joe's aunty. No one told me at the time
how his father beat him all through his childhood. Joe never
mentioned this. How we keep on going anyway. Our miracle
selves.
All that attention from adoring fans must have felt like bliss to
Joe.
No one told *him* either that I couldn't recall being hugged as a
child. I remembered blows, hurts, and the horror of being shut
in dark places. I remembered isolation, teasing and bullying,
and some dire episodes I cannot discuss in public even here with
another writer telling my story; much of my time was spent far
too hopefully searching for someone who'd care for me and

make me feel complete inside - so I'd be truly safe - whatever
that means. It makes me weep to think about it but words also
capsule it all up. Now I know it's up to me to make boundaries,
too, so people do not cross them and hurt me. And I know I can
live with how I truly am, can learn and grow from there. My
therapists help me reveal these things. Writing reduces the
overwhelming infinite world within to something visible too - in
the light. Illumination changes so much. Shadows are too easily
imagined full of things which are not there.
We had pain and trouble in common - which we never
discussed. It never came up.
Joe cared for that cat, Pirate, like he cared for me, as consistently
as kind as possible. When someone got close I tended to run, or
cause a fight so they'd see I could fend them off - in case they
attacked later. Anyone I met inevitably would cause inexplicable
pain, I believed - we learn so much from our families, not all of
it true. Causing trouble was a rest for me. There's so much I
know these days I never knew back then. Blankness fills my
mind more frequently. I say it's so wisdom can arrive.

One Toke over the Line, Highway to Hell, Lucy in the Sky with
Diamonds (LSD), Number of the Beast.... Many 70s songs
caused parents near-heart-attacks. Lately they are played over
shop sound systems to induce buy-trances, wander nostalgia -
forget the budget. Choose a can, the old music segues on.

There's a rented juke box at an old friend's party. We're
seventeen again swimming those sounds. Music conjures vivid
memories almost as strong as a whiff of perfume, or the taste of
certain foods - original cola, marmite on toast, lamingtons, roast
beef with gravy and three veg, candy floss, and banana splits.
Songs insinuate: Grand Funk Railroad, Led Zepplin, Joe
Cocker....The Shack packed with friends, our pow-wow jargon,
jokes and nicknames, Joe's cat Pirate purring.
Choosing what to keep.

Funk and False Eyelashes

A puzzle needs every piece babe,
like a song's gotta have melody.

But you weren't singin' no, no,
you just hid in the long grasses.

Not rattling that tail but growing it.

- from Devil Game by The Fast -1981

'Shoulder pads, sh-sh-shoulder pads.' Heather laughed, lifting both hands above her ears, showing how high they got. She repeated her extravagant mime. We collapsed against each other, laughing again, in stitches over the 70s and 1980s on her jazzy red settee. A page then opened to Madonna, with black lace gloves and crucifixes. 'The religious scaaandal, daaarling.' We laughed and slapped the sofa. The B-52s. 'O how big our hair got...didn't you twirl yours round a whole pile of feathers once? Humongous.'
'Sure, big hair, along with our heads. Didn't we think we were hot chips.'
'Those enooormous shoulder pads and all that hair. A wonder we weren't crushed.'
'What?'
I giggled and barely got the words out, 'Someone could've thought we were some strange new kind of armchair and sat on us.'
'Ooo, I had a great sofa then, bright blue reupholstered art deco. An'a zebra print coolie chair.' Heather flicked through pages. 'Wish I still had a perm sometimes.' I tugged my straight bob. 'Nooo you don't.' She leafed through the glossy extravaganza, a coffee table book. Our lives from mere decades before now appeared historical enough for this hardcover, big-format, extraordinary treatment. A volume packed and jostling with fashion hysterical enough for Heather to break the coffers open and buy a copy.

Later on, when I sat in my warm car in late sunshine, other 70s and 80s people floated into my mind. These old friends and fiends cruised into view as attractive as a reconditioned Chevrolet, and as detailed as a photograph. I wish I'd forgotten some of them as easily as I threw away geometric knits and bright blusher. At the time I couldn't wait to get to know those beautiful maniacs.
Wanting, desiring to know more....
If I was a cat I'd be dead.

Stripes, glitz, day-glo, so much hair, and confections. Around 1976 extreme jeepster jester garb and make-up masks dominated. Donnie's high notes on stage sounded like it would if light pouring out of a cloud could make a sound - sun turned into music. His flashy smile as unreal as a screen idol's I'd once mooned over. Donnie wore t-shirts and printed shirts. Wavy black hair past his shoulders flicked back when he talked. Donnie's long locks perfumed with green apples. Him and his Pepsodent smile.
Moxie played original hit singles to hordes of fans. They bought their records, too. Famous. Rare. Talented. Arrogant. Nutty. Scarce. Few mega-bands in our teeny-weeny nowhere country ever found stardom playing their own material at home.
They rarely sang their uber-famous number one song. When they did women squealed and grown men grew sickly green with envy and jealousy. Someone pirated t-shirts with the single's name on it - Legal. Parents were shocked to learn what this term meant. Some tried to have the song banned. Stories surfaced about confiscated t-shirts that had been ripped up, burnt, and then buried. No teenage daughter was going to wear that like an advertisement for quick sex.
Donnie had a boyfriend, Patrick, but no one we knew said *gay*. We didn't call same-sex lovers anything in particular. People who were homosexual said *queer* or other words sometimes, but we didn't mention those. The illegal aspects of their happiness and practises were probably the reason why. It didn't matter - Patrick charmed everyone, Donnie included, and he also played keyboards and sax sometimes. Patrick would laze about making

eyes at managers' girlfriends or various bartenders. He liked anyone pretty.

Through weeks off the road, when he missed the manic attention and excitement of touring, Donnie often refused to leave his room. 'O magnificence, a pretty pot of tea just in time,' Patrick danced in to his lover with treats and dashed away to find modish music or tempting snacks. 'The dear pet's yearning for deli delights.' Off he'd go to the one delicatessen closer to the city, run by a somewhat bewildered German man. Patrick also dragged Donnie back off the roof. Donnie lay out there saying he'd just roll off to die in the shrubbery. 'Death by hydrangea. Let the branches pierce me. What use am I?'

People laughed over those ridiculous lines, but never where Donnie or Patrick could hear them.

Their big Auckland house beamed darkly, in spite of the messy kitchen and the perennial dramatic re-enactments of fights and tantrums. It gradually evolved into an underground attraction for an ever-changing cast of sometimes annoying or hazardous strangers, hangers-on, friends, lovers and fans who wandered their place.

Other musicians (girlfriends or boyfriends in tow), camp followers, dubious substance seekers, and fashion models in stunning clothes with excellent hair constantly arrived with the latest music, fresh slang and strange concoctions.

Some days we did nothing but lounge about and listen to the stereo pumping out mind-angling wonders. The drummer's girlfriend baked wholegrain bread, made foreign and unspellable spreads from dried legumes, herbs, oils and secret recipes from her Lebanese grandmother - completely delicious. Usual life slipped and expanded. You could pick globes of extra time off the walls and light the way with them.

Three suburbs and fifteen bus stops away through dreary suburbs, far from the precarious wonders of crumbling inner-city villas, I lived in my own tiny shared flat - in a block of four, orange brick places with white wrought iron railings along the front of them. I kept a store of my excuses at the ready, and abandoned my flat more often than staying there. Waitressing work was undemanding - even if my feet did hurt. I had no

boyfriend to entertain. Coltrane, my son, lived with my parents
after yet another eviction. The landlord had wanted his
extended family to live in my place.

The idea was that I'd find work in the city, get settled, and then
Coltrane could stay with me again. A couple of childcare places
operated nearby. Waiting on tables paid barely enough to cover
expenses, however. I needed a better job.

About once a week one of my flatmates would complain that I'd
not done the dishes, or not cooked dinner on 'my' night, or I'd
find a pile of soggy towels in my room. I'd forgotten to wash
them. The tension felt like a rubber room - you'd bounce off it
and smash something if you weren't careful.

One Friday night, the flatmate with the curliest blonde hair
snapped, 'Just do your roster. How hard can it be? Are you
retarded?' Her hair wobbled furiously.

I smirked at her. It was nerves more than anything else. When
people got snarky I kind of floated away and an automatic
response of looking like I didn't care emerged. I guess now it
was to stop them thinking I was involved, to somehow make
them go away, but it was a poor strategy.

She erupted, 'No joke. You utter cow.'

Finally found my voice, 'I'm hardly ever here. Why cook for you
when I never eat what you cook?'

The other flatmate dashed out of her room. The two of them
faced me in the tiny dining-lounge-kitchen area, 'You hang out
with those freaks. They all look like druggies.'

'You told us you liked cooking when you moved in here. Never
do any.'

'Leave your stuff everywhere. So bloody messy. And the
swearing.'

'*You* just swore at *me*.'

'We think it best you move.' The tallest put her hands on her
hips. 'Go live with those weirdos.'

I muttered to myself, 'You're only jealous.' I packed in a tempest,
then stalked out again. I trembled for the whole bus ride into
town, a few tears running down my face.

I'd been kicked out of my place for refusing to cook every three
days, or so I told myself. The way my flatmate's boyfriend

laughed with me, how I touched his arm rather too often when we swapped news and views, the way he walked into my room and sat on the bed to talk I more or less forgot. To be close to someone else a yearning deep inside me, but I'd no real idea what that meant, not then. Barely house-trained, an incorrigible flirt, terminally unable to control my need for stimuli, rude, lazy and as messy as a natural disaster. So I can say now. And I did wear the best lipstick and knew what shoes totally went with fun fur or vinyl, or anything. I could accessorise astro-turf if I had to.

In the back of the city bus, a suitcase I'd hastily packed sat beside me with other bags, bits and bobs. With make-up tumbled on my lap and a good sized pocket mirror, my gloss to mask misery took a good fifteen minutes. Evicted and blank with worry despite my polished appearance, I navigated myself over a suburb or two, and told a friend there my dire eviction woes. Rex said they had no room in his flat but I could sleep in his van. 'We've got a gig. Come on, you'll love it. New club.'

I stared blankly at a shiny bulldog clip on his desk where he designed band posters for a moment then made up my mind.

In a tight leatherette dress and towering black and gold platform shoes with ankle straps, I sat backstage at the gig Rex's trio would open for, with Donnie's band, Moxie. They strutted backstage talking loudly to each other. Nerves.

Someone entered the cramped backstage area, a flash of bright green and yellow shirt. They groaned with admiration towards me, over-acting. I blushed. But Donnie leaned in close without mentioning my discomfort, and murmured, 'Your platforms, they're epic.' Then he kissed me on the cheek and stared into my eyes saying, 'Skin so soft. And how do you get your eye make-up like that? Are you an artist?'

A few heads tilted, people listened surreptitiously. Not that anyone could be secretive - the area backstage was so small barely nine people could fit in there at any time, even if two decrepit sofas sat jammed in like mangy old over-sized pets. Donnie's jokey lightness with his flattery made it sound like he was kidding, but his flippant lines spun and caught in my thinking. A fisherman dips in a net to catch a fish, after it's snagged on the line. The angler places the net under his catch to hold its weight away from the hook.

Later, I hoped the sharp looks (so pointed I almost fell to the ground the way an animal does when an arrow hits it) that Patrick, Donnie's boyfriend, threw at me didn't mean much. But, Patrick simply told my friend Rex that if Donnie didn't stop flirting, Patrick'd hit *me*. Rex snapped this at me with his arms folded, 'Our band wants to go on tour with Donnie's. You only look like trouble. Sorry. Someone else has a place you can stay. Ask around.'
Outside, darkness had settled over the city. Now shoved into a bad soap opera, I wished the cameras would stop rolling so I could go home. But without anywhere to go, I clambered around in Rex's van, and hid.
The back of the van smelt of old beer and damp cardboard. I tugged my new duvet and pillow, with my other belongings in a huge plastic bag, towards myself. Rex had already half-made me a bed with his single mattress kept for padding their gear, on a clean tarpaulin behind his spare drum-kit. He'd told me no one would see me there during the show if I needed a rest.
Warm from a couple of whiskies previously, I giggled over silly Donnie and jealous Patrick. While at first it was vaguely distracting, after five minutes of crossed leg discomfort, I decided I could sneak out to the ladies' then back before the band loaded out their speakers, instruments and amps. Soon I needed to be on board and hidden. Patrick was not to see I was still there.
Halfway out of the vehicle, someone grabbed me from behind. I squeaked and they let me go. In whiffs of patchouli oil, the mother of pearl buttons on Donnie's Hawaiian shirt were right in front of me. He hunkered down. 'You look great in that dress.'
Gone, he moved fast for such a tall man.
I checked the alleyway but no one else stood near. A few people stared from the far end. They appeared to be smoking a joint, passed around their tight circle, taking deep drags. Everyone

looked quickly away – they didn't want me wandering down for
a toke.

My face felt hot.

The bathroom was the best place, definitely. I didn't want
Patrick appearing now and noting my blush after Donnie's
flirting yet again. He'd figure out why I looked flustered, if he'd
noticed that Donnie had just darted back inside. Anyone else
could gossip if they'd seen us, too.

The bouncer let me back in and I edged along the narrow hall
at the back of the stage, past chipped black and green painted
walls, old posters, and stacks of chairs, sliding between them and
a fire extinguisher to get into the smelly backstage toilets. I chose
the booth furtherest away and wiped the seat down with loo
paper. A sad little block of lavender air freshener sat on top of
the cistern.

I washed my hands later, warm water going over my skin 'til it
felt really clean. I thanked goodness for paper towels – there
were plenty on top of the dispenser. Now I lived in the back of
Rex's van. How many more public toilets would there be, how
much more backstage grunge?

After my ablutions, I found the van again, clambered inside with
my heavy shoes and edged in behind the drums. A large foot in
a dark boot stuck out. Donnie lay in my secret cubby. 'Hey,
gorgeous,' he purred.

'Sorry Donnie. There's only room for one,' I tried to sound
resolute.

'They've kicked me out of the band,' his voice cracked and he
looked away.

In the van, away from passers-by or anyone else, I crouched
back from him. How would he feel? The band going on without
Donnie. Moxie's new album recorded but not yet released, a
tour offered around Australia, and they'd received an award only
the week before.

Once, months before, when I was in favour with Patrick, he
showed me Donnie's gold records displayed around his room.
'Donnie calls them his galaxy. Don't tell anyone. He lies in bed,
looks at them at night. They gleam in the streetlight coming in

that window. He says they're his...yes, his galaxy.' Patrick so
proud of his rock star.
Lifestyles of the really-quite-famous. So many parties at their big
old house. Someone christened the place Bacchanalia. A few
jokers called it Genitalia. Someone draped the front porch
tracery in fake grapes and small plastic cherubs with little red
horns painted on their heads. Devil angel children, gilded and
flying through the air.

Now Donnie could lose his room on the second floor in their
cool Grey Lynn villa. A singer without a band, a star without a
home, an adored performer exiled to everyday life. I tried to
imagine Donnie in an office or working in a restaurant serving
food, on the factory floor placing transistors inside radios, or
anywhere but on a stage charging the air with golden sound.
His dark head swung around again and he smiled, still somehow
sad.
'Oh poor you.' I held out my arms, despite a thudding ache in
my guts. Fear.
With his dark curls and warm cheek against my chest, it felt like
I held a prized cat. Donnie poured out his woe and wonder for a
good ten minutes. 'If they only knew how hard I worked. I
practise all the time. Been taking singing lessons. You know, if....'
I'd had no idea he could talk so much. When he looked up and I
smiled, he inched forward. His warm lips found mine and he
tasted of something sweet like oranges. Someone wanted me. I
was okay after all; it made me feel good.
Outside, through the stage door, down a hall and up some stairs,
Rex's band played my favourite song while Donnie gently took
off my clothes.
Stunned, I felt like I was watching a fancy foreign film with
myself in it. It was unbelievable that he wanted me - this man
who lived with a man. As unreal as a mythical animal, half lion
and half eagle, as if a chimera suddenly appeared in Rex's van
and spoke. His hands so warm against my skin. He stroked me
gently at first, then gripped my waist and pulled me closer,
kissing my arms, my collar bone.... His fingers worked between
my legs and I arched my back, groaning with pleasure, 'O

Donnie.'

'Here, undo my shirt,' his voice deepened. He let go a little so I could undress him, then slide up against his warm skin, my breasts against the curly hair between his muscled pecs. After a flurry for a few moments, he took down his jeans and laughed. 'Isn't this great. C'mere,' Donnie's liquid voice, growling against my neck, tongue in my ear - tickling, enquiring, darting in and out.

I groaned again.

We explored each other, our breath faster and faster - nothing else existed.

Streetlight at the back of the club shone into the vehicle. I thought for a second I saw something insect-like running about in the profuse hair across Donnie's groin, but ignored that idea. Only the movement of light, surely.

In seconds, after I cried out in my throbbing ecstasy he came, too, with a massive shudder.

Then he'd gone again. I'd never seen someone dress so fast, but then he'd only half removed his pants and undone a few buttons on his shirt.

In Rex's van, fogged with afterglow, I lay back on my few belongings. Abandoned in some alley like a homeless hooker refused payment, coldness crept over me. The van door slammed behind Donnie and the sound kind of rattled round in my head, something broken.

Then, his band started up - familiar music, Moxie's new single. I'd heard them practise it many times. And Donnie's voice poured light over the dirty grind of guitar and raunchy bass. On and on he sang, Donnie moaning, too. It didn't sound one iota like they'd kicked him out, ever.

Then I realised I couldn't hear the keyboards or any sax. In the back window of the van, Patrick's face snarled at me.

Quickly, I clambered around the drums and locked the door from the inside. My state of undress was forgotten for a moment. I skittered back behind the drum kit, grabbing clothes. Patrick yelled insults from outside the back of the van, through the window, and pounded the vehicle with his fists. The van rocked from side to side. I worried Rex would make me pay for panel beating.

Dressed well enough, I slid to the front seats and made sure those doors were locked too.

There was sudden silence, then occasional shouts. I heard the bouncer tell him, 'I will let you go when you calm down. Shit man, shut up. Who cares about some scrubber?'

A few people - a different crowd from before (these were younger) - passing a joint near the van wandered over to see what all the fuss was about. One of them said after a while, 'Bummer. Here man, have a drag on this.' I slid down in the seat but could hear their gossip.

Through our collection of friends and fiends, buddies and back-stabbers, bad news travelled faster than a radio signal. Evil stories passed by osmosis. Press up close enough to anyone with spiky ideas and wicked words are absorbed. In no time, countless people out that night knew what Donnie and I had done. It was as if no one had ever had quick sex in a van with someone who wasn't their partner ever before in the history of humankind.

Donnie murmured luscious words, like a poet, I told Heather days later.

She told me, 'Great words don't count for much unless great actions follow.'

Even later it transpired that Patrick saw his boyfriend Donnie and me get it on, he told Heather, through the back window of the van. One of the bouncers had told him he saw Donnie sneak in there, and then I followed afterwards. So much for Rex assuring me I'd be hidden.

It gave me the creeps to think that Patrick had watched us. But gradually I saw the picture looked flimsy, he'd surely lied. If he'd seen us, then he would've yelled straight away. Yes. Patrick wanted me to feel worse than I did already. He made up that story about watching us. And he took the chance to invent stories about how I performed sexually, too. Almost no one believed him - he was too disparaging.

Heather snapped, 'If you were that useless at making love, you'd never have been able to conceive a baby. He's trying to make out you're a screw loose.' But she also remarked, 'You *could be* mentally deficient if you sleep with fools like Donnie.' Her laugh so dismissive.

I hit her with my handbag, only on the arm – softly - but she did squeal. Quite difficult to shake the thought, however, that I did have something wrong with my thinking. Why did it matter so much when Donnie wanted me, why did I just go along with him? I risked a place to stay and some security for that liar - a man who already had a boyfriend?

Anyway, Rex insisted after their gig that I couldn't sleep in their van, 'If you do, we can't play our
next gig. Patrick told our manager. We can't use Patrick's PA if you turn up at the new venue.'

A van or PA owner held enormous power in musical circles - sometimes they were only in a band because of their material asset; their musical ability almost irrelevant. Beaten by technology's thrall, I stood with my suitcase, make-up bag, a plastic hold-all full of shoes, bundled up bedding and a framed, signed picture of Marc Bolan. Stranded, a stunning waif (or so I told myself) on the pot-holed asphalt alley at the back of the club.

Everyone drove away.

Drunks and druggies slept rough, sure, but what say I tried it at 3am and they stole my belongings or hurt me? The air was extra chilly against my face. One of the bouncers leered that if I hadn't slept with Donnie, he'd let me go home with him. 'But babe, that guy, you could catch anything off his arse.'

I almost told the guy, *I don't just fall into bed with people, thanks*, but having just proven otherwise, I tried instead to look like I had better plans.

In a burst of clattering heels and a toss of wild hair, Mad Martha (real name Alice) staggered outside. She wrangled with a long spangly blue scarf for a few moments, then faced me. Her hands on her skinny hips. 'Luggage? Why?'

'Kicked out of my flat.'

'We've got heaps o'room. Come on.'

In a few minutes we packed into her teal Cortina, with its stretchy leopard-print car seat covers, to nip through back streets and over the leafy Domain to this enormous ancient place, once a boarding house. She parked behind it after jiggling down the dirt drive and trying to miss all the bumps. I clung onto the seat, all a-bouncing.

Inside, she called a spontaneous flat meeting with the five or so people still awake. They each asked me a question, 'Do you read awful books about foreign drugs? You know, someone in a Mexican desert meeting a shaman? Then try the stupid drugs out?' or, 'If I told you I'd eaten a dead cat, what would you say?' I did my best to answer carefully but not too timidly, then left the room while they conferred.

I hoped that my saying eating a dead cat sounded really unhealthy and I'd probably say I thought they'd need a doctor, was not too dumb. But they did appear thoughtful, not whooping it up like maniacs who'd laugh about dining on roadkill.

A tall boy with dyed black hair over his eyes soon asked me back into the long large lounge (sparsely furnished with two clean red sofas, a few large patchwork cushions and a poster of a Goya painting on the wall). A plump, blonde girl with a tattooed forearm handed me a page to choose my task-a-day from, and a list of expenses, too. It was explained straight away by an older flatmate with a shaved head, 'Have a job to do like all of us. You do. If you don't do it, you're out. Drug-taking, you're out. Violence, you're out. Don't pay rent....'

'I'm out?'

They laughed.

Martha's logo for the flat headed the page. A two-storey villa with a guitar coming out of the roof, The Blue House; on a hill near the city. It was walking distance to clubs and pubs, near a few friends, and future work was possibly available in places close by.

She ran a flat with fifteen people in it - Mad Martha only *looked* crazy. I mentioned this in passing and the blonde girl earnestly sat me down. 'A few insecure pleboids decide she's their scapegoat and call her names. Bullies need an outlet for their self-loathing and usually pick on someone popular, clever, or remarkable as a target. But this place works like a well-regulated

business, believe me.'
'You sound official. What do you do?'
'Training to be a social worker. Last year of varsity.'
Someone informed me the next day that five of them owned the place. 'If anything needs fixing, tell one of us immediately.'
When Patrick turned up at The Blue House a week later, three people stood around the spick and
span lounge like guards. He only frowned at first. In a bright red shirt printed with black palms and dusky maidens, Patrick glared at me. With a deep breath, his diatribe began, 'Look, you are a little slut. No doubt these people already know. Your antics with my Donnie have made your name filth, utter dirt, garbage, get it? I want you to know....'
After inventive name-calling and some completely grungy ideas of what I could do now, which I blocked out, we gathered I had to go to the clinic. Donnie had not only crabs (I'd killed them already after an embarrassing trip to the chemist for special cream), but also some awful STD which people generally called VD (venereal disease); Patrick was sent to inform a huge city-wide troupe of probably-infected people. Donnie couldn't face anyone.
The blonde girl Elsie made a hissing sound, blushed, and left the room in a flap. One of the males rang someone up on the phone in the hall and spoke to them in peculiar, urgent whispers, later. I wondered how many lovers Donnie hadn't mentioned to Patrick - or did he simply not know where they all were?
My new housemates almost all mentioned the importance of using condoms, that week.
Condoms were useful but no protection against crabs, or public lice. A condom would've probably stopped the STI, but abstinence was better. If I'd blanked Donnie's beguiling nonsense, I'd have saved myself a place to stay, with my friend Rex. All this embarrassment would never've happened.

Like many people who did the right thing, when I took an AIDS test a while later, I had to wait four days to hear the results; and learnt just what terror felt like.
For days I was simply a wreck of nerves.

On the phone when I rang later for the AIDS test results, the
clinic girl said I had to talk to a counsellor. I took ages to
respond, then shakily, 'Am I all right?'
'You have to talk with a doctor or counsellor. I can make an
appointment for you.'
My insides turned into an empty room. No one could ever live
there - so cold, no future. I trembled when I tried to make a cup
of coffee. Days dragged.
By the following Thursday I'd listed anyone I'd need to tell, in
case I had HIV. Did they know when someone caught it? What
say I got it from someone apart from Donnie or my last
boyfriend? I planned my funeral ten thousand times. My
favourite music was definitely chosen : Sweet Child in Time,
from Deep Purple in Rock (even if it was hopelessly out of date
now), Moon River by Louie Armstrong, and I needed to listen
closely to many Miles Davis albums to choose a track. I couldn't
decide what I'd wear. Did they have open coffins for AIDS
sufferers? Fashion distraction saved some worry the first evening
by a style miracle. I drifted to sleep, considering plaid with
leather for my funeral attire, when birds started singing about
5am.

In my best straight clothes, as if attending a job interview at a
nunnery, I attended the clinic alone. In the waiting room there
were huge safe sex posters. Words danced in my mind. I had to
fill out a questionnaire.
Through the white door, I certainly thought the doctor'd say I
had AIDS. Tense, I held my hands tight on my lap like they
could leap about without my awareness.
The doctor looked kind, with shortish grey hair, crinkly greenish
eyes and a wedding ring on her left hand. 'I see you've
mentioned you have unprotected sex.' She read my answer.
'O, only with boyfriends I am, y'know, going out with,' I lied and
eyed the roses poster on the wall.
'Condoms are the best protection against STDs if you must have
sex.' Her face didn't give away any opinion, her tone of voice as
even as a planed piece of wood.
We talked for a while and I finally blurted, 'Do I have it? Please,

can you tell me? HIV?'

She smiled. 'We make sure people come in and talk with us, so we can see how they're protecting themselves. It is important you know to stay safe. But your blood test looked fine.'

I gaped at her. 'I'm not going to die?'

Her laugh was real, but restrained. 'We all go one day, but no, you're not infected with the HIV

virus. Not right now, and when we stay safe, we can avoid this illness. I'm sorry, I thought you'd been informed.'

The doctor carefully described each aspect of safe sex, 'Be careful who you sleep with. A trusted partner is better than casual sex. Condoms are always needed unless trust is complete and proven.'

We both laughed ruefully over the fact that this could be almost impossible to achieve. Two condoms at once (these days heavy-duty or extra-strength) for anal sex were best, and lube too. And dental dams for oral sex with a woman. 'Do not have sex when open sores, ulcers or abrasions are present. Avoid any practise which causes the skin to break. Don't linger - a man is not to linger inside a woman when he has come. The condom could come off.' She said again, 'We make sure everyone comes in to talk with someone face-to-face. We hope people get the message. The incidence of AIDS is increasing. Heterosexuals, homosexuals, people having their first sexual encounter, anyone may contract HIV AIDS.'

The carpet had a pattern of teeny flowers on it, or were they flecks of colour. I resisted the temptation to stare more closely.

My generation went from free love and flower power to finding out that sex could kill you, and for a long time I felt like murdering Donnie; blue dreams with livid red centres.

He luckily went on tour everywhere except around our city after this scandal; twice up and down the country, then overseas. A spiral of rainbow news reached home, hopeful and cheery – Moxie was touring and selling records fast. They were rarely home for long. It was impossible for jealous cuckolds or embarrassed, annoyed lovers to track him down. Quite a posse could've formed if we'd felt motivated to gang up. Except, with

Donnie, most of his illicit lovers possibly squirmed with such
shame that we preferred the *forget about him* option.
Their fame grew like a plant when it's watered and cared for,
only they flourished in limelight.
Donnie was on the front page of the Sunday paper one
summer's day with a bandage around his
wide chest and a grin like he still truly loved everybody. It
seemed we'd be best to adore him back. Heather had rung me.
Laughing like a mad bird she blurted, 'Go get a copy. You won't
believe it.'
Their business manager tossed back whiskies in a bar and told
me, weeks later, 'Donnie received so much fan mail. They found
an extra staff member at the hospital. Put her in charge of the
mail?' Their manager laughed. 'First off he's shot, shot, bang
with a bullet, having it off with the American road manager's
wife. Nearly dies of lead poisoning.' He roared at his bad joke.
'Then gets it on, fully on, with a hospital chickie, in his sick
room. Supposed to manage his fan mail and instead she....'
Their manager with an admiring chuckle.
'I get it. Sure. For God's sake,' I snapped, and immediately
walked away and out the doors of the club; I needed fresh air
after that story. Someone had tried to shoot Donnie dead in the
States.

Now and then, I bumped into Donnie somewhere like an
exhibition. He always beamed, and said, 'Sorry.' Never what for,
just that he was really *sorry*. Profuse apologies, wicked glances,
and his flashing pearly whites had me feeling as bitter as a cold
cup of coffee. *Something thick*, I thought.
Eventually one night I told him, 'Shut up Donnie. You're a pain.'
His fake smile fell, his eyes did a loop.
It was tempting to feel sorry for him but I spun around, taking a
great interest in the art on the walls.
The whole band moved overseas for good soon after that. Moxie
made it big, or semi-big, anyway.

Decades later, Moxie's legendary number one plays in
supermarkets – piped, an instant memory. I reach for broccoli

and Donnie's soaring voice appears through consumer-land.
Another Moxie single's the theme song for an Australian show,
rocking on TV all through the week for their promos.
Believing Donnie cared about me and needed help, that he'd
been kicked out of the band, had been my choice. My stupidity
and lust led to reckless sideshows where I hurt myself. But I
could leave
this insane stage, stop acting altogether - couldn't I? I could take
off the costume, wrap myself in a grey coat and walk into the
night to be myself. Gradually I admitted the part I played in
these tragedies.
Most of the men I loved or fancied matched my passion and
then some - forces of nature like the sky or the ocean. Our
bonds didn't last, but our time wasn't wasted if I learnt
something. And I'd never be someone who wished they'd done
something they didn't dare. Bundles of puzzle and marvel, so
easily gone. Pleasure held rewards. Decency built something
more pleasing. Where to find it?

Newspapers and magazines ran stories after the crash. When we
discussed the sad news, Heather confessed that Donnie once
tried to sleep with her too, but she laughed at him. He went into
a sulk. It lasted a long time. He never spoke to her again.
In one newspaper he grinned. It was a recent picture. His lush
dark hair thick and wavy like always framing his oval face, high
cheekbones, full lips and sparkling eyes. This promo shot
accompanied an interview from a month before the truck drove
into the side of his car. Little bits of rock star were strewn over
an ordinary suburban street in the early hours. No one had been
around to see. Everyone died.
Donnie was quoted, 'I wish I knew better when I was young.
Lots of people are out there, people who I think I really I hurt.
You don't realise sometimes, at that age, how fragile people
really are.'
Finally it felt like Donnie had said sorry and meant it. It was sad
that he'd met such an awful end. But Donnie would've hated
growing old. Already many stunning women had surely looked
past him to someone younger. It was such a treasure, our youth.

His cousin told me Donnie had so many things wrong with him
he would've died within months, in any case. Blurs on x-rays,
blooms of alien colour, whispers of Latin words.
As much as anything in mind ever drifts away like fallen leaves
on the tide, forgetting occurred. Only a ghost existed to blame,
anyway, and he still had to be the last phantom I'd want to
haunt me.

The twirly colour-slashed book Heather bought - our laughs
over the 70s and 80s - extravaganza times revisited. Something
to show her grandchildren on rainy afternoons - the old days -
exuberant fashion and stars of music. Freak-show 70s and *me me
me* 80s. From peace and love to self-obsession in only a few year-
long steps. Mad shoulder pads, big hair and - so clown-like - our
blusher. Teens attempting to rule the entire known and unknown
universe. In photos we look so innocent.
The large book made a heavy thunk when it closed. On the
cover was an androgynous face with lurid eye-make-up in pink,
orange and green, slashes of pink blusher and a spiky hairdo
with long gelled sides in pure fuchsia. A pop art sputnik.

Band Aides and Gearhead Girls

Beneath the trees I'm a child spinning light
raised my arms to the sun to hold you.

I could fly across the azure
and to every planet
knowing where you are - all I need, all I need.

- Open Palms by Judi Jones 1976

With glam rock, rock rock and pop playing from loud stereos in
the staff quarters of another seaside hotel, my lovely drummer,
Zap, and I shared lip liner in front of the small mirror in his
room. Our make-up as fake as we dared, a mask of pale sheen.
We turned into fully dressed glam dolls come alive, slim, with big
smudgy eyes and dark penciled lip outlines filled in with deep
red or black cherry.
He wore my white jersey silk wrap-over top on stage one night.
His curls bounced in time with each furious beat, and my satiny
blouse soaked up all his delicious sweat.
They toured North Island hotels, playing pub bars; thrashed out
Bowie covers, Queen and a few originals, sneaking in Lou Reed
numbers and now and then The New York Dolls or Iggy.
Majesty performed in silks, satin and leopard prints, hip-tight
shiny lurid flares and heavy make-up. Their sleeves and hems
dipped to the ground. Flamboyant pendants and rings flashed
and sparkled. Abundant, glossy, beautifully tended locks tumbled
or swung down to their waists, or, like Zap's, formed a halo of
curls radiating almost past the shoulders.
In small towns where the most drastic male fashion involved
barely flared blue jeans and hairstyles just over the ears my
darling's band caused brain fevers and knee-jerks to logic.
Occasionally someone tried to bash their heads in. Zap
recognised a guy holding a tree branch ready to slam him one
evening, a face in the mob. Someone my drummer once played
rugby with; they got chatting about the All Blacks. He explained
his escape, 'I told him I hated all the eye shadow and crap. Just

have to do it for the show.'

'The hoon believed you?'

'Yeah, said *he* had to wear a stupid pair of safety specs at work. Offered to buy me a beer but I said I had to get back to the gig.'

'A beer?'

'I think *he* was gay, tell you the truth. Wanted to chat me up. Rough love.' My drummer kept a serious look on his face until I believed him, then he laughed.

We rolled trials, troubles and tension away, rocking his bedroom for hours; the best music wound us up, then we completely unravelled. Fit, romping and sliding over each other's nakedness with the joy and focus of athletes, abandoning ourselves to moans and groans. Both of us were often vividly made-up too - sometimes he appeared more glamorous than I did - but Zap wasn't gay.

Another small coastal town, where Majesty played countless times, and the place appeared much as it had for decades. It held simple shops with awnings, plain houses and early model cars on the somewhat deserted streets. Inhabitants wore pastels, or beige, with shortish haircuts - for decades tried-and-true. A town of light surfaces, brown paper packages and plans sketched in notebooks from outboard engine suppliers and bait merchants. Beachwear for many men consisted of pale bermuda shorts with a blue, grey, or green polo shirt, or perhaps a t-shirt. Surfers wore jeans or cut-off jeans. They rode waves in wetsuits or rather plain togs, sometimes longer board shorts, in plain bright colours. A few splashy print shorts mainly suited kids. Square-edged, plain reason made days and nights work harder. It was a battle to get men to simply apply sunscreen. Few of them wore much otherwise but special occasion aftershave. Drag queens were often seen as strictly for loud lipstick stage shows or on TV - crude tits and bum comedy. Tassles were for curtains only.

We dared expand our collars with our minds, glooped buttons, flaunted bright over-sized jewellery like monsters' eyes and turned into painted operatic sights, we stalked down Ordinary and faced it off. Hair grew in all directions. I keep mentioning

hair, but seriously, I'm not sure there was ever a hairier time.
Flashy ethnic dress, or we looked like gorgeous birds in a tropical
jungle, sometimes we wore those, too: embroidered and
mirrored Indian tops, African prints in yellows and blues, and
taxidermy birds on hats - or using their vivid wings as brooches.
Majesty all rather flamboyant offstage, as well. There wasn't so
much satin then, but they'd wear chiffon shirts with coloured
pants that were tight over their slim hips, floaty scarves, touches
of eyeshadow, dark eyeliner, Revlon pancake make-up and
lipgloss with extra sheen and shimmer from their five o'clock
shadows.

Interviewed on TV, Majesty's lead guitarist (who had a social
science degree), explained, 'Conservatives may believe
fashionable people dress up simply to give others a fright, but
that's *their* egos talking. Perhaps they're starved for attention
themselves? *We* want to look a certain way, in my band Majesty,
because we like this fashion. But I suppose that free thinkers can
make the mistake of thinking "well-behaved" others are actually
like them, underneath. There's too often nothing behind
conservative thinking except narrow-mindedness and frightening
prejudices. Not that we don't all have biases.'

The interviewer tried to interrupt but Claudio kept on,
relentlessly answering what he'd been asked. Afterwards he
exclaimed, 'They were gobsmacked that I had an education!
What a buzz, man.'

'Yah poofters,' someone would call predictably from a passing
car when we walked yet another small town's main drag, or
upon our leaving a pub after a Majesty gig to walk over to the
staff quarters.

Plots brewed in small places, practical jokes and special
occasions would enliven any routine. The hotel staff at one
place took the stage one night, impromptu. The owner, the bar
manager, two barmen, a porter and a few others sniggered in
their summery pale shirts, lining up so everyone could see them.
Two barmaids carried out their special surprise. I sat up extra-
straight to see. They'd made a large prop out of cardboard and
painted it. The item, taller than any of the men on stage, was an

enormous pink jar of 'Vaseline'. Daubed across the label in crude black paint, 'For boys who love the back door scene.' That night, almost everyone who worked or lived there laughed their heads off. We had to join in, albeit half-heartedly, or appear poor sports. But my laughter felt forced - due to disbelief, not delight - and didn't last long. I smoked one cigarette after another.

In this jolly atmosphere the hotel's bouncer, manager, two barmen and the owner all sang a limerick beside the lurid object. It was someone's birthday, or New Year' Eve, something special....

At the band's table, back from the stage, any out-of-towners did our best to keep smiling. We'd seen the film Easy Rider years before, we'd also lived in New Zealand most of our lives, many of us. Small towns could so quickly turn nasty, with nowhere to hide from the mob, or from the self-righteous. When long-haired bikers in the movie got shot by rednecks who didn't like their looks the whole cinema had gasped, but I still wondered how many people in New Zealand carried shotguns in their utes.

I saw that film with our local motorbike gang arrayed in the seats behind; an uncanny coincidence. They muttered horribly after the shooting. That gang could've rioted and ripped out the red leatherette seats, but they settled down to watch the rest in silence. Most of the gang smoked quantities of marijuana by then - this was rumoured to have solved the previous problem of their constant violence.

Music is a jar of keys that can open a time, any time. I'm twenty-one again, slim although curvy in places, six foot in my platforms and lipsticked to the nines, tens and beyond. I needed a soundtrack for my psychology.

On nights when Majesty played my city we trooped along like cool draught horses in clompy shoes covered by wide flares, our feet huge. Boys and girls in green, purple or gold eye shadow with pearly shadow beneath the brow to accentuate it, slashes of blusher, pale cheekbone highlighter and glossy lips outlined in dark pencil. We were glo-paint Andy Warhol screen-prints sprung to life.

Recently, in a film about this man who photographed New York fashion for decades, Bill Cunningham, they said he believed, 'Fashion is like armour for life, you could never get rid of it without destroying civilisation.' Fresh exciting looks protected us from frame-ups.

In the mid-70s, mainstream NZ presented a sea of fashion plainness, a bastion of careful dressing, a way to drown in pastel wandering. Some daring, well-off, older fashion lovers did incline towards eccentricity, wearing bright colours, enormous jewellery, or a mad hat, but such people were forgiven. The rich had the power to quell criticism, in case the tolerant missed out on imagined favours which could come their silent way. Many women nevertheless chose almost identical helmets of hairspray, and male hair was predominately the same short back and sides as if they couldn't wait to join an army. Or a few dared to wear theirs just below the ears at the back, in the daring 70s. Softening up.

A backdrop of sameness proved coincidentally perfect for our displays. We bade adieu to sleep-walking. Some adults gaped at our gaudy finery like at a circus parade. Many staggered, spilled, 'Don't know how to tell the boys from the girls,' perplexed. Stunned bystanders expanded spaces in their minds to accommodate brilliant waves, or invent warnings. The sky would break open, grass could turn to sand, and rivers would run backwards. We never did cause the sky to do anything that we noticed simply with our fashion sense, however, even if Hendrix could kiss it. And now, we choke the heavens with carbon when we could plant more trees, take better care of where we live. In any case, with fierce, young and tender applause for ourselves, we silently clapped while we sauntered and swept along in our fashion splendour.

On any hard surface we went tip tapping, clop clopping and tarrundering along on our enormous shoes, some with heavy wooden soles and heels. With high hair as grand as any mane, we were a herd of glittering beasts, burbling and laughing, invincible youth stampeding. The inventiveness of fashion

survivalists, wives and girlfriends gave almost everyone's high
fashion a wow factor.

To make your orange drum-kit look new, paint a black stripe
around it. If it was impossible to buy satin pants, find someone
to make them. Fireworks for the stage didn't exist in New
Zealand, then. But who now would ever get away with blowing
up a black powder bomb they'd made themselves, setting it off
in a crowded venue like a pub or club, as a special effect? My
lovely drummer was almost blown off his chair one time. They
hadn't tested the explosive at all. 'Set off too close to my kit.' He
laughed.

Zap produced a distinctive wrapped parcel after one of my
visits. 'Of course you'll never guess what this is,' he spoke wryly.
'It's a surprise. Your Christmas present, do not open 'til the day.'
It looked exactly like a wrapped vinyl record. Most of our
recorded music arrived that way then.

We laughed knowingly.

I kept it until Christmas Day. Zap was playing in some pub miles
away, touring for summer again. A friend from varsity sent me a
card she'd written. *Sorry to hear the bad news from uni. Hope you're
okay.* I was on the phone to her as soon as I'd read this alarming
message. Her voice sounded thin, worried, 'O don't you know?
Haven't you seen the results?'

They'd failed me. I felt instantly cold in the middle of summer,
at Christmas. 'I've never failed an exam in my life. God, it was
shooting my mouth off, wasn't it? And what I wore. They hated
those clothes.'

'Don't ever change,' she replied on the phone. 'I love the things
you say. Too many people say nothing at all, even when they
never shut up. And you always look wonderful.'

Later I found myself in a daze in Mum and Dad's living room. I
remembered the wrapped album Zap gave me and tore off the
maroon wrapping paper. It had a grey cover, and a known
figure. My eyes widened, Radio Ethiopia, Patti Smith.

Immediately I crossed the carpet, ignoring splashes and squeals
from outside where the family swam in the pool. I opened the lid
of the stereo, a priestess performing a magic ritual. My
headphones an escape to Patti wailing her incantations and I

submerged myself in sound.

Outside there was Christmas sunshine and lollipops that had been dropped in the dirty shade. But my drummer saved me with that album. Music washed through me and over everything else.

Later that summer, I took the LP with me on a Road Services bus quite a stretch to see Zap in New Plymouth. Majesty set up as the house band in a booze barn attached to a hotel.

I liked how my new spiral perm felt all soft and fluffy, had worn a short skirt, and black underwear, appeared with my new album and in a blur fell into his arms. The album soon on his stereo in his room (they each travelled with their own sound systems) and we tumbled across fresh sheets on his bed. Clothes tugged away, smooth skin on skin, we writhed, listening to songs of our own invention too; playing on any broken pieces until everything melted fine with our friction. Our arms, backs, legs, necks, faces, feet, torsos electrified with touch, sparks coursed through our bodies together - sublime beyond any drug or dream.

Every note and word of music translated to our moves, our breath faster and faster. He pounded against me and I rose to grind with every thrust, arched my back, gripped the sheets. We groaned with pleasure and generated another world, dark notes cascading from his stereo, highlights sparkled and zinged.

Zap said he couldn't take side two, his thick brown curls fanning across the pillow as he stared at the ceiling in wonder. I saw visions sometimes, too. Sensuality such a surreal waking dream. I'm grateful I wasn't born when women had to grin and bear it. Only one or two generations before mine, women couldn't move or enjoy sexual union without being called whores or sluts. Some people still believed that nonsense. But Disapprovers' opinions appeared like gravel on the road. I just walked on over naysayers' sharp dullness - busy contradicting itself like the lumps were acidic. Those taboos burned through sense anyway, if we let them. I walked right on into the arms of beauty.

Still, I annoyed their roadie when I playfully threw his pillow out another hotel window one night. There were no TVs tossed in the pool, however, nor Rolls Royces driven into hotel foyers.

Majesty was not about to imitate The Who offstage, no matter
how much I liked a commotion and letting go of my voiceless
rage and frustration. Any action made me forget how small I
often felt, tearing back the sides of so-called normalcy to see
what lurked there - what it pretended to like, and then destroyed
- or so I imagined.

Looking back I can see the whys, the wherefores. A map unfolds,
but at the time I operated in a hijinks blind. Silliness meant not
needing to think about anything else - not about how loneliness
turned into a dark machine, with the past shadowing me,
waiting to slide in with some extra complication. Many people
found me a puzzle, I suppose, with my mischief. I know I did.
Their roadie and soundman liked to trial remote-controlled
boats in nearby lakes, streams or by the sea, after his dutiful,
expert sound check. Majesty's singer demanded cups of tea
made just so, with a glare for emphasis. There had to be real tea
leaves and the pot warmed first, then turned three times directly
after boiling the water. The keyboard player preferred his
girlfriend to be always by his side or watching him play. They
sometimes wore the same orange lurex or leopard print lycra.
Electric blue coats to the ground, cut so they flowed behind
them, were worn over shocking pink platform boots and skin-
tight black body suits. This pair almost caused a pile-up of
traffic when we swept down to the only burger place in a small
town. But, besides glossy, painted pouts and crushed velvet hip
thrusts, Majesty behaved rather like suburban office workers in
some ways too. With a set routine, they focused, and were
careful to stay with pleasant habits (the kind preferred at home)
as much as they could. A band on the road wanted to tour as
long as possible, they liked a venue to ask them to play there
again. It didn't actually matter how they liked their tea or what
beverage or routine anyone favoured, but this band - as startling
as aliens, although they were - did have their ironies.

Strict guidelines were devised about what was and what was not
"glam rock", amidst churns of discussion. 'Shoes that colour and
shape aren't glam. They're more Mod.'

'You could wear pink jeans in the street, but not on stage.
They're Rock. They are, AC DC wear them.'

'Are sequins bunkum now? Isn't glitter gel better?'
'But sequins catch stage lights. Glitter's for fans, not for stage. It's dance floor stuff.'
'You have to use eyelash glue to stick them on, too. Careful with your skin, man.'
Zap looked so fine in tight, pink satin pants, his green silk top open to his waist; he told hilarious stories and kissed like a dream. Softly at first, then with more passion and his tongue would flicker - a tremor I had to respond to. I also loved to hear him talk. But I wondered when I'd get a chance to explain this. We ate in the hotel's dining room before the general public got a turn. Someone mentioned, 'Management sounded annoyed we've extra people staying.'
A thud in my guts. Feeling like I'd taken a slug of sherry, blurted, 'I can eat elsewhere,' got up to leave, 'that's fine.'
They all protested, 'Don't be silly.'
We ate silently. My position as the occasional girlfriend of their drummer unfocussed for the big picture. We'd never declared we loved each other. I was scared he'd refuse to see me if I got too serious, and maybe Zap was also wary. Flippancy so much easier. It was cowardice and inexperience I suppose now, refusing to dare to reach out and hope for more, desire more, make long-term togetherness happen.
Old cooking oil smells lingered throughout the thickly carpeted pub dining room, but the salad tasted good. I lived mostly on hope and flirting then. I was too excited and too good-looking - overly daring, you could say. *Too much* was, however, a compliment then. Excess meant success.
Watching them, all charisma and talent, electric instruments, thrum, crash, sing, flash; I sang along and laughed like a lovely girl in a shampoo ad. Like I was someone else, not anyone who hid from her brothers - whose mother and father forgot she existed. Reinvented, transformed, a different life shaded in further and further from invisibility.
The latest magazines were as glossy as chrome. I drove them into my thinking.
Always, I hunted my city for tiny back street shops, new designers' boutiques and little places with outlandish music

playing and racks of unique frippery. Or for vintage clothes for
next-to-nothing. I danced later, knowing half the club hated me
because they didn't have my shoes.

In the lounge bar one evening, all the band's friends were
yakking away. Soon it would be time to troop back to the staff
quarters, but my bag was nowhere to be found. 'It's 1940s, boxy
snakeskin. O it's gorgeous, from a second-hand place in
Ponsonby Road,' I wailed. All my money was inside, in cash.
There were no money machines or Eftpos in 1976, and I didn't
understand cheque books (no one I knew ever used a credit card
either). I was a seven hour bus ride from where my parents were
staying for the summer. Such facts swamped my mind while we
searched the sticky pub carpet.

Then Zap dropped his head. Behind the mask of pale make-up
and green eye shadow his face looked so tired, and he said, 'I
know who it was.' He wouldn't say who, just that it would be
pointless to try to get the bag back.

My drummer lent me money for a bus ticket, since that too was
stolen. In the taxi early the next morning, I suddenly asked the
driver to turn back. I raced up the outside stairs, my heavy shoes
going clatter bang, clatter bang, clump. I pushed open his door
and dashed in, gabbling on about how I'd forgotten I had no
extra money, and could he lend me enough for the taxi to get to
the station and catch my bus? Luckily, he handed over some
notes - probably quite a bit to him. With his arms folded, he
shook his head like I was hopeless.

Possibly the pub rejoiced in one less salad to give away.

I felt as interesting as an empty cardboard box, in the rain, in
the dark, disintegrating.

All the way back, fighting soggy sensations of failure, I thought
about how we'd flown through imaginary doors in the night.

Jimi Hendrix taught us how to wield a psychedelic pen. At home
I'd tell myself in the mirror every possible variety of each brand
of nonsense, and on the bus I recalled as much palaver as
possible.

After another spray of Charlie perfume and a slick of extra lip
gloss, I was away to holiday with my family with my head high
after all. I thanked goodness I'd kept my make-up in a separate

bag in the hotel room.

Cosmic doors soon slammed in my face, however, every time one appeared in my mind that day. Driving through farmland or past sun-struck suburban byways, neat or untidy, not a scrap of lurex was to be seen and no drummer in tight pants with curly hair ran alongside the bus to blow me kisses.

It felt like we barely knew each other.

Perhaps a girl who liked him had stolen my bag - got rid of me so *she* could snuggle up when the band took a break? Knowing that if I lost my money I'd have to go home.

I needed a way back to electrified thrills, like when I'd arrived with my favourite accessories and that excellent Patti Smith album he'd given me. But months of pretending we didn't care that much started to feel real. I didn't even know Zap's real name, only the nickname everyone called him. My jokey, light-hearted attitude was a mask I wore that didn't really fit, but I'd left it too late to show the true me, who did love him.

On beach days that were sunny and fine, people were either languid, cheery like families in breakfast cereal ads, or proud to show off their latest looks. There was no one I knew anywhere, except my family. I pushed away nagging thoughts as if they were out-of-date hair accessories.

My lovely drummer told me while I'd last seen him that he wanted to join another band, and asked did I think they'd suit his style? Funk, a new tack; then I remembered a woman I knew sent her guitarist boyfriend crazy telegrams every day, when she worked for the post office.

It didn't take long to create the message. I thought it was fun, exciting, hip and cool. The post office clerk had simply never flown through any velvet-hung doors in other dimensions, obviously, because he asked, 'You are sure you want to send this?' He squinted at the telegram I'd composed.

'Yeah. Sure. Of course,' I replied. I grinned the grin of the fool when everyone but the idiot can see a cliff face about to appear - a drop away into nothingness - the fool staring at the sky instead of looking where they're going. I grinned and paid my fee.

I could've known that when you need four adjectives to feel good about something, you're a complete ignoramus, should go home and not do anything. I could've got a clue.

Exit jumping jack flash, enter funky white boy. Off the same-day message went to the latest hotel my darling Zap stayed in.

But maybe it wasn't the telegram. Maybe that song lyric about rock and roll minds changing sounded like a positive anthem to someone else on Earth besides me - who knows? Disco was a dirty word to some people, however, so maybe I failed the cool test. I feel like I could beat my empty head against a brick wall thicker than the ancient pyramids and hear my pebble mind rattle every time I think about not paying him back the money I owed, though.

And why didn't I say, *I miss you. I wish we knew each other better*, I ask myself now.

I didn't hear back from my lovely drummer.

My cool was in fact only so much thin ice. I pretended I didn't care much, never got too close to anyone, nor slipped too deeply into any meaningful conversation, in case I drowned in whatever lay beneath. Life hurt less from a distance, I told myself then, but I started to see I could be missing out.

Punk arrived to catch up to me, held together with safety pins and desperation, and I went to see the glam band, in its death throes. Glittery and satin thighed, they still played pubs. The bass player's girlfriend wore a yellow lurex dress. Although tired round the eyes, she smiled like a fashion model.

The old city hotel was packed with umpteenth-time losers in the public bar below the upstairs lounge area, which had an enormous stage and a huge dance floor. A small crowd gathered in the cavernous second floor bar, but left the dance floor empty. They were mostly older punters in worn-out fashion : thin long scarves, body-hugging dresses with medallions and a few worn satin bomber jackets that were a little too tight.

Special effects flashed lightning across the back of the stage. The now-balding singer thrust his hips at the microphone stand, but his belly was so plump by then - and it wobbled. Majesty's guitarist grimaced through complex lead breaks. Cover after cover rang out slick and true like the radio playing overseas hits.

No originals. The open, mostly empty bar a yawning room
where they'd packed in a few hundred people many times
before. A long time ago we'd rocked the place.
I'd heard Zap planned to see them too, and maybe rejoin to
drum for Majesty again. I glanced about, hoping to see him,
hoping for some kind of closure I suppose. Eventually it felt as if
I'd picked up someone else's luggage for them and they'd not
come to collect it.
The frilly, grandiose music suddenly felt as silly as the idea there
could ever be dark doorways that lead to light hidden in our
dreams. At that time, bands screamed and railed, grinding up
walls of noise, screaming that no hope existed, no future. My
broken dreams rattled like souvenirs of honour; we danced like
maniacs, even if life was so hopeless. No one and nothing would
stop us enjoying ourselves, no matter how terrifying the world
grew. It felt braver to me.
The decade that taste forgot was almost over, now the 1970s
needed some shade.
We punks dragged ourselves into nightclubs and pubs, faults and
all. Accepting disillusionment felt new, the effort of pretending
things were greater than they were no longer consumed my
time. It seemed better to just give in, then let loose in the
disappointment - which had its own drama.
To a query about my absent friend I got a snappish reply.
'Zap's already heard Majesty play. Before you got here,' their
roadie glared while he told me this unwelcome news. Anger lasts
a long time with some people, and this man probably
remembered me throwing his pillow out the window, laughing.
Any idea we'd chat happily about the old days proved as false as
the hope that Majesty could still excite a huge crowd. Glitter's
sad and dirty when its old.
Their name was outdated, too. The Sex Pistols sang that the
Queen wasn't a human being. We felt the fear in the western
world. But there in that old pub I felt somewhat scared in
another way - and insulted - I mattered so little to these people
once known quite well.
I pretended I didn't care, and drank too much.
After the gig, with my latest boyfriend (who'd turned up later

on), I walked outside into a stumble of drunks. 'Hey man, can I fuck your girlfriend?' One of them leered. 'Hey girlie. Take your top off.'

I told them to shut up, then screamed it, 'Shut up!'

One man frowned, moved back a little, took aim and kicked me in the side quite softly - but I felt his strength. He laughed hard and loud; knew some kind of martial art. The kick didn't hurt, but I staggered in my spike heels, yelled something else.

My boyfriend sprang to my rescue but it was three burly guys onto one. They floored him. His head was kicked while he lay in the gutter and I screamed and screamed.

My love, bleeding because I shot my mouth off to some half-cut muscle heads on the dirty street.

Why had I even gone there? My chaotic life spun me round and a door opened. I stepped through it, not thinking if I wanted to move or needed to go anywhere else.

The rest of the evening was spent in Accident and Emergency, surrounded by injured bods, dazed people and drunks in an ugly pale room with shiny old linoleum floors. I swore to myself never to give cheek to anyone in the street again.

Now and then, I nevertheless think that I could find Zap. I might see him in the supermarket and we'd joke about something, catch up, like old friends do.

Many hotels he played in when he wore full make-up and satin pants have gone with demolition efficiency, in clouds of dust and old stories. Or they've been changed altogether to suit botoxed and lifted people in chic black and cream.

Still, I wish I knew his real name so I could look Zap up, maybe google him and see if he produced movies lately or ran a vineyard. We got on so well and he helped me out when I needed someone to stand with me. Does he also abide in some house furnished with funky this and that, surrounded with souvenirs and art, knowing that doors in the mind do open to varieties of illumination if you believe, but some scenes are best forgotten?

A tribute to someone decent and kind could mention their patience and talent, beyond their curly hair and excellent taste in music. With a fine sense of humour, Zap invented scenarios and said hilarious or touching things in different accents. While we waited for someone to come back with the van keys, he did all the Ramones' Noo Yawk accents.

It made me want to find out more.

He laughed. 'O they're stupid, and geniuses with it.'

Fascinating. I was determined to read up about them.

But the time my snakeskin bag got stolen, I left my white cross-over top behind, and a 30s necklace of pale green cut glass, which glowed in ultra-violet light. I didn't ever pay him back, but said he could keep my top. He told me on the phone he didn't really want to wear it again.

I just remembered that awkward detail, his call. Out of place, out of time. So much makes little sense, is wrong or difficult, then time glides on and memory fools us with the pictures it plays.

On Google, using his old nickname linked with Majesty, I found an old fan site dated to the year I finished this book. A woman said, 'If anyone's got anything we could use for the service, photos or anything, please let me know. He hasn't got long. It'd be great to see those.'

I didn't have the courage to read more. Was it him? Zap smoked so much, he could have cancer or.... But it was lovely to think he had someone close who wanted to do the best she could for his funeral. If that was him. I had no pictures or ephemera in my scrapbooks, and didn't feel I belonged there. Just felt sorry that I lost touch. How do we readily stop making the effort to write or phone when we are unable to pay back money owed, and ashamed to mention it or anything else even vaguely connected...?

Maybe he never received that telegram, but in any case we stopped seeing each other.

Favourite songs make up images and intense feelings as fine as a flower arrangement. And some daydreams dissolve as easily as clouds on a windy day. Other pictures are as vivid as if they happened a few moments ago. He ran so elegant-wild in platform shoes, genuinely cared for people close to him, made an excellent pot of tea, could figure out so many things so fast, and his sense of humour snapped and shimmered - such a grin. Zap was someone I'm glad I knew.

Writing these stories, with a colleague whose name is on this book, helps me. I determined recently I'd do my best to stop just letting go of people as if they were fashion items, easily replaced. I've had years of therapy off and on, improving relationships - my university of self. Recalling Zap and our drifting apart needed to count for something beyond a smile and warm or wild memories. In time I decided I'd build relationships on more than before and keep them worthy of living in, too, somehow. But first, I needed to sort through even more ruins.

Razor Blade Kisses

Our embrace rearranged time,
but cut-glass shouts against us,
fell as easily as water off a roof, girl.

O, we'd better win now and bring this rain
under razor wire in hazy sunshine.

- Triumph over the Asleep by Paul Kutt 1981

Disco's dazzle electronica and sequined everything didn't quite
scrub us of our sins, and punk's smoky friction didn't later
suffocate as many as it could've; some clambered from the 70s
with stylistic sensibilities and political intent intact. Many in the
Western world across most social classes, at one stage, almost
simultaneously submerged itself in black or shades of murk.
Even the most perky or vague took darkness for their preference.
Late eighties' fashion grew overwhelmingly funereal in the end,
despite eruptions of stunningly lurid flapdoodle earlier.
Many older hipsters disguised themselves with conservatism or
tat through the 90s, like returned soldiers after a war ended.
Forget and move on, reassemble known clothing into indications
of laissez-faire or retro witticisms, then buy only classics.
Remnants of divine decadence lingered. The reek and damage
at times unsettling.

A former punk star from a girl band waved her bottle of plum
brandy at a bus-stop one morning. 'My holiday in Sydney was
almost over by then. I stopped to chat but she was honestly
nearly unconscious,' a friend told us upon her return. 'Said I
didn't want a drink, thanks. About 9.30am.'
Other casualties wore old dressing gowns to watch soap operas
through unemployed and recovery days.
A few famous old punks appeared in the news occasionally, one
climbed a skyscraper with rubber suction cups attached to his
hands and feet. A handful found hidden talents, child-care
genius, or wood-turning abilities (an ironic hippy-ish talent),

sallied forth into territory they'd never seen. True punk attitude, adventurous one and all.

Saintly, some turned far too good, religious zealots banging on and on.

Countless friends left the country.

Worries multiplied like rats, while substances and therapists appeared to quell them.

A few chat-monsters stayed. We'd make a time, get together, relive dares and dates, and sing up whatever we did now. Being true originals we added musical flourishes to our bragging. Recaptured togetherness from combat zones where we'd once fought to play and hear zinging original sounds.

Old friends in fashion splendour eating delectable cafe food, we shared in-jokes. Matching slang, echoes of cosy stories, despite our former spikiness; transformed with our butterfly minds. In the midst of questions about who ended up with who, how many children they had, and what stunning men some of the wrecked creatures we saw lately *used* to be, 'How do they get so ruined?'

Well, then someone had to ask me, 'What about that guy, the one in the band? So tall, dark, really good looking. Navy blue eyes. Worked doing something creative? X-man or something?'

Some questions hit like your car just slammed into a tree, but I tried to look vague like I'd lost my way in the conversation, nothing more. 'Oh? A musician, hmmm. Uh, yes, Paxton did have a day job like that, I think. Him?'

'You two were so gorgeous. People seethed with jealousy.'

My laugh sounded driven badly too.

I got up to get a glass of water. Cheeks burning.

A long time since the night Paxton sang Sympathy for the Devil to me, or rather *at* me, when we walked home from a gig at the university, soon after we first met.

Immediately, in the calm of that mid-evening, I could've twigged a whole new branch of understanding and walked in the other direction beneath other trees, towards a more flourishing future. He of the glittering eyes, his curled lips singing that I could guess his name, telling me what was confusing me...his stride almost at a crouch like a scary cartoon character. Smile like a weapon. But maybe I too had the devil in me. We rarely know at the time where we're headed, or why, when we're young, with lessons to learn.

Good-looking, charming, dressed to please ourselves; sexy, young, energetic and confident - or pretending bravery - determined to keep what we called freedom. The glittery rags and lurex extremes of the mid-70s discarded for altogether more alarming, gloomy outfits and attitudes.

This tall young man glimmered. Dark hair, with one long streak of pure white in the side, over his furious dark blue eyes. Stood by a low stage in a pub. When he glanced about the room, he didn't seem to see anyone.

Paxton's angry good looks at a Hello Sailor gig. Couldn't imagine what I'd say to him, desperately wanted to invent something, and tried, through three sets, for hours. Sometimes he whispered to another angular figure; these two young men in plain black early-60's style op shop suits and open-necked white shirts, stylishly dishevelled. Metal badges or something silvery flashed on their lapels.

No one else dressed like that.

We left the pub, my friend and I, and made for a club, Sulky Sue's, a short distance away. She told me I was crazy not to have just gone over and talked to him, but I laughed coldly. 'And said what? That I think he's gorgeous? That's a real conversation killer.' Trotting away from excitement.

Men often approached us with the same line. It wasn't as if she didn't understand.

We negotiated streets and gutters in our towering platform shoes, wooden soles, teeter-totter clop, clop, clop.

Fate, I told myself, *it's fate,* when in about an hour later while we sat there in Sulky's, his taller, rather lanky friend appeared and threw himself into a chair near our table. Floppy, like a bundle of unwanted laundry. Then the same angry young man in black I'd seen earlier tumbled into a chair too. Hoodlum lounging. They'd walked across a few streets like we had, and appeared at the nightclub, the only one we vaguely liked (every other club we simply loathed).

I'd had three drinks and felt sure I'd think of something to say to him, any minute.

When Citizen Band's drummer sat with my friend and I a while, he nodded to the two figures in black nearby. 'They're in this new band, Crashbang. Playing here next week. Punks. This tape playing now? It's them. Wait, it's about to come on. Not bad.'

Wailing from speakers during the break, a cover of Patti Smith's Gloria, loud, male, and shambolic, with massive energy. I grinned as if I'd been flown for free to New York. Music playing that I loved, for a rip roaring change.

Wan patrons absolutely still, in round-back chairs at their little, faux-Victorian wooden tables, while I wriggled with delight on the padded velvet seat that ran along the back wall of Sulky Sue's.

Contemporary music had morphed into pop rock, grown old and lazy albeit gussied up, but doing almost nothing to excite anyone. Regimented dancing took over, dancers in lines repeated the same moves in unison. Mid to late 70s mainstream tunes bland, exhausted dreck and tinkle-flop.

Important but obscure tracks were instead furious, they sparked, pounded out, wrenched us sideways, determined to provoke a completely dedicated reaction, everything aching afterwards to prove it. But rarely anything like that was played in public.

Inspired and decisive, when the band played again I stepped away from our nightclub table, wobbled a fraction on my heels, but knew to keep going no matter what and master those shoes, approaching the two strangers with my best smile. He slumped (back to me) all in black and sneering at the white jeans brigade bopping half-heartedly on the small dance-floor in tight lines. His friend across their table saw me first, and raised his eyebrows. Then Paxton turned and slowly smiled without showing his teeth.

I'd seen vampire movies but had quite forgotten how they watched people in that guarded way, predatory, stunning, such black hair and pale skin. To me, in the quiet, safe crowd barely moving in pastels at Sulky Sue's he appeared marvellously different, a contrast, magnetic.

The vampire allusions only appeared in mind decades later, when a friend was flicking through some old photos. 'Did he ever wear a cape?' She gasped, then laughed uneasily.

In Sulky Sue's I felt the confidence of my youth and the drinks combined, as if I was playing a role in a film. My templates, in action. 'Do you want to dance?' I asked, grinning even more. He inclined his head as if in a bow, and arose, much taller, moving like a strong animal, like he truly was feline and only took on human form sometimes.

This was before DJs took on such a strong entertainment role and their seamless music played. Short spaces appeared between the band's numbers. In such a break I mentioned, 'Great tape they played before. I love Patti Smith. It was you?'

A half-amused, half-scary smile, 'Come to our gig next week.'

'Love to. Who else do you play? Any of your own?'

'Not yet. Versions though.'

We each listed bands we liked. Rare tastes for the times. 'Lou Reed, The Clash, Iggy Pop, Patti Smith, The Damned...'

Although Paxton spoke slowly like he wanted to impress, he also glimmered, a young man with facets, edges. Put me in mind of jet beads. Weapons could've been hidden about his person.

I drank more than usual, probably from fright. Alcohol the trickster, the calmer, and make-believer.

We sashayed away from dancing, sat along the deep-red velvet bench seats at the back of the room, surveyed the twiddly place like we owned it. Faux-Victorian décor, frost-edged mirrors and tiny chandeliers, turned-wood room dividers, dark wooden tables, young people in pale colours with limp manners. If someone kicked the whole place to pieces it'd seem more inspiring. It felt like many of the people there wanted to be more exuberant, but did not dare move too much in case they were hurt or derided.

Paxton murmured, 'Come to our band practise tomorrow.'

Full of cheek, drinks and a fervent belief in the license of the poetry of our meeting, after a short while I spoke with my voice

low, 'But I could get lost if I went there alone, tomorrow.' (This
was true, I was often easily bewildered, sidetracked and lost).
'What say you just come home with me now. Then you can show
me where the practise rooms are in the morning?'
His full lips curled even more wickedly, 'How presumptuous of
you,' he growled, so show-biz.
But a smart line from The Rocky Horror Picture Show wasn't
an insult, was it? Who knew at the time? Not me.
The night clear and still, we staggered together, half-drunk,
laughing, into a taxi then to my flat. At my place, in the leafy
street I eyed his black silhouette just before he walked in the
door. He seemed to take up all the space. Hard heeled boots
thumped the stairs.
I didn't turn on any lights.
My small, dim flat empty except for us, no stereo or radio
playing, a stranger and myself in the darkness.
What now? Coffee? Chat?
What then?
Awkward fumbling at each others' clothes and a few kisses, then
I'd decide he needed to sleep on the sofa? But my sofa was this
tiny thing, wooden, uncomfortable. Would he complain?
Something inside me didn't want to ever let him go.
When I grabbed his lapels he yelled, 'Watch the razor blades,
watch the razor blades.' Then he murmured, 'How cold.'
Still quite drunk I laughed uproariously, had seen a safety razor
blade attached like a brooch with a safety-pin on the outside of
his jacket. Easy to avoid. Ignored his other comment.
Call it chemistry, blame the moon and several clinky clink drinks
too many, but no passion like that existed before, ever. Up close
the smell of him more intoxicating than whisky, summer sun,
and promises. Logic, any remaining careful manners, plans, all
of those vanished.
Desire coursed through my arms, legs, torso, mind, electrified
my fingertips and toes, as surely as if we'd both dived into a
warm ocean and had to accept wetness.
Clothes dissolved without effort. Skin met skin, we moaned,
thrashed. Hair tossed, my spine arched. I climbed onto him and
we moved hugely together. He flipped me onto my back, I

wrapped my legs around him, then held them against his shoulders while he drove into me on and on.

Afterwards, the universe settled over everything and absorbed into our skin. We transformed into planets and stars, infinite darkness and light. I couldn't stop exclaiming, 'O wow, o wow, o....'

Later, near dawn, Paxton looked half-annoyed. 'You didn't get cut when you grabbed my lapels?' He hefted his jacket onto his lap, looked underneath his lapels, examined the blades fixed under there. 'I want those to work,' he muttered, checking each one, seeing if they were sharp.
I stared in startled amazement. Up on one elbow I watched what he was doing.
He'd placed new razor blades *underneath* his jacket lapels too. 'I taped these here to cut any bouncer who grabs me. If they try to throw me out of any nightclub,' he grinned. 'they'll be sorry.'
I muttered, 'Could've shredded my fingers.'
'Maybe you shouldn't grab men's clothing like that?' He laughed and flung the jacket on the floor.
We kissed again and I forgot what we were talking about.

The niggle of worry that threaded its way through my delight later on appeared weak, a sign of stupidity, too difficult to notice. Little idea then how I floated away from anything like confrontation, and had done since before I could talk. I still believed my way of life was normal, and that most other people also struggled with these continual confusions.

In years to come he hid weapons around our house and wanted me to learn how to shoot his gun, when he went overseas, but I'm leaping too far ahead.

A rush and roar, the telling, forever muddled together. My chaotic existence in those days. Shell shock does that to you. The battle of staying alive did so many strange things to me all my days to that point, and for some time later.

Jolts and slips, and always looking for love. Luckily, I often found some.

Drawn together, magnetised, our mutual fascination. A conflagration drawn with us, ashes in our wake.
We burnt our past, started again in this brilliance.
Threw myself into his furious life, daring. How far we could go?
All, everything, for love. Each breath of him intoxicating. Every sight of me he'd smile, immediately draw me closer.

We adored each other. It felt like an island of two, and everything we liked was there.

Under siege, over-sexed, and simply gorgeous - with photographic evidence to prove it. Paxton and I part of a seething crowd packed into shredded marvels or shiny-fright nonsense, ironic costumes, DIY political frazz.
They admired us and we eyed them.
Our friends.
In ripped black and tattered finery we strode the town. Passers-by gaped. We revelled in their rigid amazement. No one truly had ever dressed like that before. Kings and Queens of Wonderful Ruin.
He played in Crashbang and I danced up the front, sang every word. Female fans in ripped fishnets, leatherette pants they sprayed on, tight short skirts made of rubbish bags, and vintage tat eyed him from the edges of the throng. A few danced close to me. I repelled them with a look.
At any party, people stopped talking to stare. An apparent friend told me years later, 'When you were both in a room together, you were too intense.' Annoyed like we'd tipped paint all over her clean floor.
No idea back then that a few in the crowd we knew could want us gone, ruined, apart, to stop being so attractive. How dare we show off and love each other so openly? Some bods like things dim and quiet, as little excitement as possible. Never young, even when they are, perhaps. Or some think they know best and everyone else needs to be like them. Lessons we learn from mis-

friends.

When we stand out, we often have to stand alone.

Conformity never really my bag, Paxton and I fed each other
like neighbouring suns, oblivious to anyone's supposed need for
shade. I loved believing he'd stop anyone who tried to hurt me,
too. Relished the glares and horrified looks that punk provided
us. A smoke bomb of fashion. The cloud of our damned
existence finally mattered.
Paxton and I playing with o so many ways of whimsy and
fierceness.
Seven inch bedroom shoes from France (impossible to walk in),
an arrangement of leather straps to outline my curves, flip skirts,
and peek-a-boo tailoring. He loved my dress-ups at home.
I loved him to lift me.
He needed to stand against the wall. Our extremities flailing or
holding on tight, hips pounding hard, fast. Our moans rose
above everything else.
Sometimes only a look from one or the other demanded we tear
off our clothes, grab each other, to howl into another encounter.
Slick skin slammed slick skin. We climbed and climbed to
ecstasy, divine exhaustion. Visions ensued, beaches littered with
fabulous gemstones and oceans of glittering blue. My mind
generated glory, illustrating where we took each other.
These pleasures saved me, they proved life held some goodness.

Our conversations sometimes, though, cooled too far. Paxton
gave me commands, 'When we're with them, don't say much.
Okay?' Or he provided prompts, 'If I'm talking with them, don't
say or do anything. Just sit there.'
'But it's the band's name. I only wanted to know where they got
the idea.'
'Not your conversation.'
A list of who to speak with and when, what I could wear, how to
style my hair and make-up. He thought feminism, 'A ridiculous
idea someone thought up for publicity. A fad, it can't last.'
I laughed, but he wasn't joking. 'Feminism's centuries old if you

want to really think about it. The Duchess of Newcastle-on-Tyne was a feminist writer in the 17th century. A fad? Come off it.'

He laughed. 'Three hundred years ago. We wouldn't have lasted long. Imagine wearing what we are now and walking through London. All those uptight wankers.'

Easy to tell when I'd mentioned something he'd never have thought of, or did not know, because Paxton changed the subject.

One day, in a roomful of friends, he announced, 'Well, if we had a standard IQ test, I'd win.' Out of the blue, this boom across my bows.

I wheeled on him and laughed. 'No such thing as a standard IQ test. They have to be written to suit every group of people and a context.'

He ignored me, spoke to their drummer, 'Got the van okay for tomorrow?'

Such a swerve-nerve.

Chilly difficulties.

My lovely drummer and I, Zap, we'd conversed like a fun piece of theatre. He often made me laugh, but I'd no idea where he'd gone. My previous love I did nevertheless recall. Zap and I had sparkled.

But after a while with Paxton, our affair gathered more and more disagreeable moments, rolling heavy. Staying close however at least approximated love and safety, didn't it?
I'd lie awake and wish I knew how other people managed to look so content together.

Loose ends, pieces of vegetation floating in a storm, people who get to know each other in a nightclub - these are not so disparate.

My feelings, however, I built on them as if they were the solid timber frame of a beautiful house.
Strange weather threatened to compromise my determined

creation, this imagined stability I so wanted. Inexplicable disappearances occurred for up to an hour at odd times in nightclubs. Sometimes he didn't make a date with me, just never turned up. Then no reason, no apology.

I'd notice him eying other women across the room. He'd barely cover it up.

Pieces of clothing appeared in his flat that weren't mine, a woman's skimpy top, a pair of stockings... 'O they're Jason's girlfriend's...Hey, Jane left that here. Y'know that fat chick who hangs out with Pete.'

Figuring Paxton screwed around, his affairs felt like bruises and blows, wreckage and stench, visceral and damaging. The effects took me over, as if I was in an accident then suffered from shock.

In my condition I didn't have the ability to do much about it. Shell shock, Post-Traumatic Stress, it's somewhat invisible but manifests in many strange ways, in behaviour. He didn't know how I was affected either. Like with the I Ching, this is a *no blame* situation.

Raked over anyway, the ruins and ashes of anywhere exhausted offer clues to what once existed.

Here I sit reeling images of memory like they're movies, but some frames are missing and others catch fire as soon as they stick.

What to make of this?

If our relationship was a smashed building we'd be somewhere once-grand, a stone mansion with carved fireplaces and a courtyard, gargoyles too, out-buildings like stables and a cottage for the gardener. Our life together built to last and o, so beautiful. We truly did love each other, it was stupendous.

But after it fell apart the scavengers took everything pretty or valuable, some destroyed the remaining story with nasty talk. What's left was tattered, smashed, too heavy to move easily, or overlooked. Hints remained nevertheless, and chaos. Step carefully through the wreckage, the way people revisit an earthquake-damaged house, looking for reminders of what mattered before. It also means we accept what's truly disappeared, if we search and find nothing much.

Love based on beauty soon fades as fast as beauty does, the moralising John Donne said, but I'd not read his poetry then. Mesmerised by each others' looks and our extraordinary imaginations revved the rest.

Loving him felt like standing on the edge of a volcano, travelling into outer space, or living under the sea surrounded with tropical fish in some luxurious, glass submarine, then more. As exhilarating as a sky dive, Earth's entire atmosphere just for us, weightless and blessed. Greeny-blue and wonder of clouds, perfect sky. Houses and streets laid out as beautifully as an indigenous painting of spiritual pathways. Trees and land blended, contrasted. Lovely, startling colours. We forgot ourselves. Falling all the while.

We met.

He commanded the stage, punk band Crashbang exploded music. I screamed lyrics in a jostle pogo-ing, flailing. We bounced off each other and laughed, roared and growled, singing too, o we so sang.

My friends in a cafe years later reminded me I lost something valuable.

Can I find it sifting images, walking back, retracing steps, turning the pages of photo albums?

Recalled conversations drift in and out of awareness, as if on radiowaves disrupted....

Held together with safety pins since I first dressed myself. Mum didn't have time to fix things that often, although she would if I'd asked, but I didn't like to bother her. My brothers demanded enough.

To be as far from my family as possible, a discovery of escape. Ripped my skirt or a button fell off, took the fast way to fix it. No need to discuss a repair, asking for help usually wasted my time.

My clothes looked fine on the surface at first, or so I told myself, expert at disguises. No one knowing I'd pinned up half a hem, or a zip was only safety-pinned together. Accustomed to

haphazard and make-shift, worn openly by the time punk
appeared, badly-repaired clothes then miraculously stylish.
Punk like a lost friend returned from somewhere harrowing. We
swapped smeary notes. Punk understood ruin, redressing
tailoring in wilderness and renderings. The relief upon not
feeling alone felt like recovery from a severe illness. The entire
musical canon spoke of unmentionables, dire secrets, fury and
disappointment. Fear, rage and raggedy sadness found words.
Injustice, ruin and tatters translated into grinding noise music.
The New York Dolls, Lou Reed, Patti Smith and later, UK
bands, The Sex Pistols, X-Ray Spex, The Damned and other
exponents of vehement commotion appeared for our frenetic
celebrations. Punk found many in the early days already clever,
despite blows and bullying, and we were defiantly deformed. We
could make our brokenness beautiful, o yes, we succeeded.
A punk unofficially (and officially if you look into the long
history of the word since the 1500s), most of my life, along with
an ignored crowd of kids, beaten or neglected by parents and
family, scorned by teachers, shunned at school for our difference.
An inability to relate well or fit in quietly, tormented by those we
sought for attention.
Predators had found us needy, and took advantage.
But I've no real idea exactly how I ended up that way, except
that I knew I desperately needed some kind of closeness and
almost never received it.
When I did find a lover or friend generally I messed it up.
Did someone teach me distance had to prevail, affection was
unwelcome, too messy to bother with for long?
Socially conditioned violence, I read in a magazine, *is a learned
condition which may be unlearned.*

Open scowls in theatric fits, ripped clothing, spike jewellery, dark
make-up, and birds' nest hair, cropped ragged locks, or gelled
spikes - our bodies looked like weapons. Short hair fashionable
again but more menacing. Damage worn as talismans, reformed
fashion to affront, can opener styles against repression.
Pretensions and annoyances dealt with swiftly too. But we many
times needed to watch what we said privately, and did to an

extent respect others' feelings in our small circle of cliquey
shadows and sharp brouhaha.

Not that anyone explained a set of rules, nor did we know punk
was an ancient word first used in the 1500s.

Now, sitting in the future which we said didn't exist, writing from
a wealth of years and education, I marvel at how we
congregated, in those strangely shiny, rough overcast days.

Went for what we liked and took it. Punk as accessible as a black
plastic bin liner, a pair of scissors to shred anything, or we were
rethinking old garb in ridiculous ways.

Buster Stiggs, The Suburban Reptiles' drummer, owned a
necktie collection stretched across the diagonal of his large
bedroom on a rope, hundreds of them. He often wore five or six
ties at a time.

Jamie Jetson, singer with the Idle Idols, dressed as a tall and
extremely beautiful baby in pink and blue, with an enormous
pink dummy around her neck, a nappy 'pinned' with an
enormous safety-pin-shaped rattle, a teeny singlet to top this,
and her kiss curl forehead.

Jonty Jamrag bawled Proud Scum's lyrics, a used tampon
earring a-dangle.

Inventive where money could never suffice. One lovely younger
girl, Evie wore an open mesh gold dress to dance in, nothing else
except tons of make-up and pretty shoes. 'I'm a classical nude
statue come to life.' Another more curvy creature who called
herself Ali-rat had the first ever bright orange hair in town. It
stood on end with something called gel. A manic grin while
showing off this skirt she'd made, shiny jade green satin with two
gold metal zips, one each side along the whole seam top to
bottom. Inventive, we created what had never been seen before
and only later became ubiquitous.

The Scavs, or The Scavengers were more low key, in worn out
blue jeans, tight plain t-shirts ripped in places, old black suits
and white shirts worn messily. Somehow looking sharp-edged at
the same time. Their bass player wore this 1930s black suit
jacket, the wide lapels dangling with razor-blades, that with the
tightest blue jeans and black down-at-heel boots. He seemed to
always have his long black hair over his face, too. He rather

frightened me. Seemed moody. Their singer Mike Lesbian
sometimes wore a beret, and a striped t-shirt like he wanted to
be French, maybe he was....

Many of us wore whatever we thought looked the part anyway,
only loosely modelled on overseas styles at the beginning. We
weren't slaves to fashion. Some of us said we were real punks,
the first in our country, our DIY styles proved it.

Many already pre-half-way shredded by childhood, then teenage
angst did the monster mash, so abuse and frustration translated
into revolting statements (sometimes nauseous) or loud, crazed
denial. A few also punked up only for fun. But I suspect many of
us held sad or devastating stories to suffocate, destroy and drown
out, to dress up, flaunt and scream about, to strew over the city's
torn, scarred sides like the garbage we were supposed to take.
We threw rotteness back, magnified, amplified, grew to be more
than mere nightfall echoes.

Others took fun to whole new levels. The Spelling Mistakes
played this cover version of We Vibrate, by The Vibrators. One
night they played along, (judder, judder, judder), then their
singer tipped out an entire brown paper Kleensak full of pink
plastic vibrators. They skittered across the half-empty dance
floor. Every one had a battery inside it. People had these pale
pink appliances dancing on table-tops, and did mock passionate
things on the dance-floor with them, laughing.

Mid-city, down some iron stairs by a stone wall, Paxton and I
walked past a dark grey stone place (where a pottery and tie-dye
market had stood beside a once upon a keraaazy psychedelic
nightclub next door). Someone called from the doorway. 'Hey
man, come 'n' see this.' Crashbang's guitarist Jimmy Loud
grinned, announced, 'Been in here for days. It's almost ready.'
NME music newspaper pages plastered over the old brick walls,
pages ripped, daubed with paste, instant historical wallpaper.
The Scavs' guitarist was in there too, helping decorate the place.
'Stage already built.' Paxton took one step up and strode around.
The dance floor roomy with a mezzanine floor on three sides
above. A serving area to the left as anyone entered, once a hatch
for a cafeteria perhaps. Dark stone walls, and old dark red

carpet where there weren't bare floorboards. Jimmy grinned.
'We're calling it Barbz.'

Anyway this guy, Craig (previously a Mormon, he told us he'd
worn chastity pants as a teen), well, Craig served our drinks and
resolutely wore his genuine, heavy, brown leather bondage collar,
chains hanging down his back. Green eyeshadow and spiky hair,
bright yellow lycra tights, flashes of red make-up, Craig so
outrageous. 'Most of my friends refuse to walk anywhere in
public with me,' he said one night and fell into step with me.
City night full of bright lights, the main street teemed with
shoppers. My short-sightedness meant they looked blurry.
'Ridiculous. We'll walk up together. You look fantastic.'
A handful of dedicated punks haunted Barbz through those
early years, dragged some distinguished darkness back to our
world after the garish early 70s threw up on itself too many
times.
Unlicensed premises, but our chained barman Craig in his vivid
make-up served surreptitious special coffees, or a slug of vodka
in our cokes, if he knew someone well. The club welcomed all
ages and about eight or so in the crowd always looked about
twelve or thirteen.
Paxton and I deeply in love, we rarely had much to do with
younger patrons. Aloof, I say it was necessary. Others could've
said snooty. Wary around strangers to a degree anyway, this
collection of edgy youth made me feel I needed to be extra-
careful. Underlying neuroses surfaced, pet monsters smuggled
into Barbz got loose when we drank too much, heard something
we disagreed with, or just felt like creating mayhem to feel at
home.
The boys slammed against each other on the dance floor,
sometimes leapt from the mezzanine above into the melee, not
crowd-surfing, just landing, pushed against others, or colliding,
they collided again, pogo-ing furiously, arms flailing. Manic
laughter, hilarious to almost fight each other in time to the
thrum, crash, smash. Our anthems to feel fearful no more, songs
released our hounds, rhythms to bash by, but all ironic in funny
fun fun.

No one there ever deliberately tried to hurt me in the early days. Much of the pushy dancing playful. But, if the furious dance floor reeked too much of testosterone, some girls escaped outside.
We'd spend a few songs in a car discussing life and all that, hoping the uproar inside would soon die down. Soon girls ventured back. In our latest ripped creation or retro, re-configured with fabulous boots, eying the crowd to see if they met our need for edginess.

Time and people changed, more patrons swung around the lanes to Barbz.
A few black-eyelinered vixens egged the boys on. Eyes flashing, those girls stayed to watch the carnage, licked their lips when someone punched someone else, or got thrown out or subdued by the others. Bashing, smashing, cruelties and jibes.
But I skirted this hardcore group. When things in Barbz started to turn nasty, it felt like eating tinfoil or brushing up against something stiff and prickly, an old broom, a hedgehog. I'd sense it and slip away, sit in the band's van, or find someplace in the alley behind a car, with a cigarette.
My sights set on a fashion splendour future, as if Paxton and I would live in an updated, jaggy version of one of the more engaging romance films which made my childhood bearable. Style mattered. To dress well meant feeling good, in the latest look, albeit ragged and scary, the future owned me; wild clothes elevated anyone from nothingness.
Paxton also disliked obvious displays of machismo, street fighting was anathema. Sometimes we talked about Barbz being the pits. 'I wish we had a better club,' he'd say. 'I want to play other music too.' New albums appeared, music changed daily like socks.

One rainy Wednesday, in the planetarium, we watched stars whirl overhead, zooming to a planet or nebula. I wrote about how we swam outer space together, created our own atmosphere, gathered heavenly bodies into our arms like flowers. So spectacular I almost felt envious of myself.

But the only vivid nebulae at Barbz were puddles of colourful
vomit on the footpath and bruises on the arms and bodies of
friends, turning from blue to yellow and green. A few suffered in
other ways, one adventurer, Jean Jeanie, had three boyfriends at
the same time, all in different bands. She told me, 'I can't
choose. They all hate it. But what am I going to do?'
I didn't say I'd seen her gorgeous lead guitarist holding the cute
drummer she liked upside down over a motorway bridge one
night, trying to make his victim swear to leave her alone. I just
muttered, 'It seems like there could be trouble.'
Little Jean Jeanie, she laughed. 'Everything's a problem. Haven't
you learnt that yet?'
Then someone careened out of the club and swept her away to
a party.
Left in the alley with my smokes and too much to think about,
once again.

Crashbang played our small punk club, Barbz, then also in pubs
like the run-down Windsor Castle as it was or at huge parties.
Loud music with so much dirty grace it overcame any doubts.
Thrashing sound occupied every skerrick of space. No room for
our pasts, our worries, our syndromes and despair. Troubles all
raced for the city limits as soon as the first grinding, wailing
chords flung in.
Between songs and gigs our parents and many others found our
fashion a challenge, an affront, a travesty. Paxton's immaculate
blonde mother in her flowery trim frock would toss her curly
hair and wail, 'But you look like a beggar. It's ugly.'
Paxton laughed. 'The modern age kidnapped me. Pay the
ransom, Mum.'
Old men marched up to Paxton and shook their fist at him. He'd
grin or burst into raucous laughter. We'd stride away.
My Paxton's name, *place of peace*, but hardly calm when he
played anywhere. The crowd slammed into each other, pogo-
ing, jumping up and down on the spot and banging into other
punks dancing. Girls threw themselves at Paxton when he
stepped off the stage. I'd elbow my way to his side. Paxton
hooked my arm through his, we turned into statues of coal and

ice. The girls soon threw themselves at someone else, when I was
around.

Crashbang's sets a grind of layered screeches and drumming. So
loud. A giant approaching and we called it music; living in a
grimm fairy story, bad dreams came to play, but style answered
every single fright with a better angle.

In another club downtown, we were at the door one night and
two young punks started harassing the woman taking the money.
'Hey man, steady on,' she grabbed the bannister beside her
while these two louts dressed in op shop black suits, shredded so
they were almost like fur, tried to jostle past. 'We don't have to
pay. We're in the band.' The tallest punk laughed.

'It's my club. I know who's playing.' She wasn't a big woman but
appeared determined not to let them past without handing over
the money. She wore a pink top and leopard print pants.

They were all in black and shouldered themselves at her. She
held the bannister and they pushed, wanted her to tumble down
the stairs. A strange squeal came from this bundle of people. I
couldn't move, just petrified. Paxton said something sharp.

The two bullies twisted round, stared back at us, and suddenly
dropped their tough act. 'O God, it's him. Pax Never-ever.
Fuuuck, you playing here? Shit man, you know this chick?'
Paxton stared them down like only he could with his best death
ray glare and they pushed past us, ran off screeching into the
night, laughing and in pain concurrently.

The woman on the door a little shaky but she smiled. 'Thanks.
Some patrons complain of getting chain whipped in the toilets
by punks. Maybe those two. Did us a favour getting them to
leave.'

I finally found my voice, 'We like the music. We don't chain whip
anyone.'

'O yeah well, they move between Barbz and us. Last month a
patron of the highest punk ilk tried to punch me while I was
here as usual, taking money at the door. He later turned up and
apologised, along with his best friend. A lovely guy. Son of a
famous writer. Like many punks, extremely intelligent. It's not all
bad.'

Paxton relaxed and held my hand. We both stood awhile talking with the club owner, Josie. Paxton wanted to know if Crashbang could play there.

'Tell you the truth, we aren't booking punk bands. The punks that other time, well, we became quite good friends and they visit me at Cook St Market. I've got a stall there. But lately, we get furniture slashed by punks most nights. It's a bitch fixing stuff. We stay up 'til five or six in the morning so we can open the next night.'

'Sorry Josie, but people who come to see us wouldn't do that.' Paxton tried to sound pleasant. 'We're called pop punk by some people, you know.'

Josie smiled coldly. 'Look, I see this stuff every night. You can't know what the punters get up to, you're on stage. The boot girls are more violent than the guys. Did you know that? Especially on the dance floor.' Josie went back to her little counter. A couple in disco outfits, white pants and shiny tops, who'd just entered, handed over a twenty dollar note and waited for change.

'I *heard* they were down here attacking disco kids,' Paxton muttered to me.

We went back into the street, looked up and down the road where a few people walked to and from. I tried to think of another club or pub, for Crashbang to get a gig. But we'd been to three places that night. No one booked punk bands any more. Hardly anywhere else was open.

We discussed the idea of them changing their name to something more amusing.

Everything rather brittle like when things get scorched and fragile. 'Those girls have to stop making eyes at you,' I demanded, although neither he nor I controlled the bright-eyed lingerers and lollygaggers, hoisting their PVC skirts to just below their groin. They hunted men like part of a survival game. Perhaps it was.

Paxton took up boxing, 'For sport,' he said, 'to keep fit.' The boxing I didn't like either, even if it meant he could defend us more readily against increasing numbers of thugs. Some we called weekend punks. Kids acting out brutality they knew in the suburbs and at high school, wearing weekend costumes stapled together for hard fun. No idea of any genuine revolution, not one of them appeared to be first and foremost in love with the furious music.

Boxing produced grazes, bloodied noses, bruised arms and chests, but my boyfriend beamed afterwards, all his words louder, broader. The only sport where you were expected to hurt your opponent. Paxton simply stopped asking me to see him practise punches.

I suspected he liked the way women who did relish the fights fawned over him and asked inane questions, closely watching his full lips in answer. Their low cut, day-glo tops and super-glossy lips, bizarre fish. But Paxton never said a word against anyone at that beat-up old gymnasium. Truly fond of his coach too and he often went to the old guy's house for dinner.

Each time I demanded a change and Paxton refused to budge, I flounced off in one direction with righteous flare all about me and he strode away in the other with fire in his wake. Our togetherness flamed to ashes.

It took me a long time later to accept I had no right to ask someone else to change, no. I could say I didn't like something, or that something else annoyed me. I could refuse to go along with this or that. But I had no rights over someone else's life, as if I was their security guard.

It'd be days or weeks before we calmed down and spoke again, in the meantime he behaved like I didn't exist. We'd fight and he'd stray, repeatedly, or sometimes we just plain fought for variation. I suspected he also strayed without our breaking up at all. But any accusations of infidelity he met with laughter or some quip, and quickly changed the subject, 'Do you like those armchairs with the turned legs? I'd like to buy a couple.'

It's possible my lover also occasionally forged notes from women and left them lying about, to make me jealous.

I gathered this after careful observation. Pictures he hung on the wall after utilising a builder's tape measure and referring to the

Golden Section, vacuuming and dusting every other day, object d'arts arrayed on his desk as if they sat in a museum. He'd never have just forgotten an incriminating piece of evidence.
Years passed before I gathered this forgery probably took place. At the time, I'd see a slip of paper on his dresser in my line of sight exactly, a note from, 'Gloria' one time. No one we knew with that name, but I loved the Patti Smith version of the Van Morrison song. Many slicing questions ensued. I tried to penetrate the padded confidence around his smirks and denials, or his tricky stories told to make it clear I should never fight with him, he'd only find someone else.
We both jumped to conclusions so often, you'd think they were a train we needed to catch.

One night he sneered that I only wanted to stay and admire how good-looking the singer of Hello Sailor was, I didn't really like to hear them play.
Not realising he simply hated me enjoying anyone else's music; I jumped up, so insulted and riled that he'd spoilt my fun. Threw my drink over Paxton. Stalked out of the pub as fast as I could in high heels and aimed to walk home. I rode feelings like surfers rode waves.
He was going to pay for the taxi later. I'd run out of money. Outside chilly, but past Ponsonby Road's dairies, butchers, second-hand shops, old villas looking run-down, as they were then, and just a few little cafes I grew warmer the faster I went. Bad temper for company and a self-righteous determination not to care. High heels ticker-ticking, my flat situated seven or more kilometres of footpath away, I'd get there soon. When I looked back, however, he strode along behind me.
Paxton followed along left to Karangahape Road then right past the graveyard in Symonds Street and over the motorway bridge. Streams of cars flowed along underneath and a needling breeze caught my hair. Legs scissoring up the distance, anger snipped away at tattered sense. I knew he was close behind but refused to acknowledge him and make up. The narrow streets and old Mt Eden houses in view. Almost home, I mentally cursed myself for ever giving him a key.

Up the stairs and inside my one bedroomed place eventually, with Paxton also indoors, I behaved as if he wasn't there and went to brush my teeth. Bed all that mattered.

Things rattled in the kitchen, I thought maybe he could get the bottle of bubbly and throw that on me. Heard the fridge close. Unidentifiable noises followed.

Naked by then for bed, I brushed my teeth, thinking Paxton just wanted to make a snack and had calmed down.

From the bathroom sink I turned, a great whoosh of something wet and semi-solid hit me in the chest and face. The slap sounded like ocean hitting a rock. It felt cold but it was early summer and I'd grown hot walking and fuming, so it felt refreshing too. Stood naked with my hands fanned out and my body rigid with shock. I looked down. Red everywhere, splashes and circles of red over the floor and the walls, over me. Watery blood? Had he cut me? It took a short while but I recognised the vegetable shapes. The contents of a tin of beetroot.

I'd seen Last Tango in Paris the week before and the beetroot reminded me of the blood-stained bathroom in that movie, except this wasn't a suicide. The beetroot didn't hurt either. Despite the shock, the waste of food, and the insult I laughed at the idea we were somehow imitating a film, and cleaned it up. Paxton watched me clean and didn't say a word.

Then, without speaking further, we made wild love for an hour. Fell asleep as happy as we ever were.

My friends gaped, gobsmacked to hear I'd cleaned it all up. 'He threw *food* at you. Didn't it hurt? What will he throw next time?' 'How can you laugh about this?'

'*I* would've told him to clean up his mess and then told him to get out.'

Their assertions and comments on and on.

Our high entertainment factor.

'He only did it to get me back. I'd thrown a drink on him first, in public too. And then it made me laugh. What can I say?'

They muttered we were childish. One girl fidgeted with her keys as if she wanted to drive away immediately. 'Punk rock? You can have it if that's what it means.'

'Some people bring trouble on themselves.' Heather snapped.
'It's like white water rafting, you have to have a death wish.' And
I laughed the anecdote away.
In some peculiar manner the bedlam fights, tension uncoiling in
every direction when we shouted, pleased me or I pretended to
like the tumult. Waterfalls of words, a torrent. Familiar pain and
trouble. Many years would pass before I'd realise how to learn to
enjoy closeness, calm and quiet, that I needed to see someone to
help me. Until then, if pleasant acceptance threatened to form it
felt like a trick. What did they really want? When would
whatever horror was truly planned appear?
My condition also meant I floated away when trouble ensued,
like I was not really there. I read in a book from the library,
'Shell shock, or PTSS, a person disconnects from reality if
anything frightening occurs. It's too much for them to take, so
their subconscious protects them with distancing.' With
hindsight years later, o how simple everything looked, but living
in a trashed, zappy punk of a time was as complicated as any
chaotic mess could ever appear.
When I wished my life had not unfolded so messily I fell into
depression. No way to change the past, not understanding that
memory is flexible. I could learn to forget, forgive.
People with kinder lives may scoff but we each learn behaviour.
Those who've never experienced true, safe closeness, those like
me used to threats, physical force, lies, tricks, cruelty and danger,
we're strange. They're lucky not to understand why.
Antagonistic, drunken, and sometimes violent, we shredded
rules as if they were secret documents we had to keep from the
enemy. Cried myself to sleep at times, but also sailed about some
days feeling so good it was almost religious. Emotional release
covered bad memories, like a fog or a storm hides ruin.
In love, a haze of warm fuzzies and passion, too. Neglect and
hurt forgotten.
Those times when the relationship failed, every one of our
disappointments, most bad memories diminished with romance.
Doubts were rinsed away.
More extreme fights and I fled from Paxton, but always one of
us returned eventually to find our fix. Moon-children, somehow

accustomed to wax and wane.

Extremes took me as strongly as a tide. Others didn't live calmly except in movies or books, it seemed. Some men only pretended to be kind and attentive. My lovely drummer gone and I had to forget him, the few men who'd tried to interest me with quiet lines or pleasant advice didn't count for some unfathomable reason. Someone who's always lived in a concrete prison without a garden wouldn't believe in public parks with fountains playing, either. They'd laugh in disbelief to hear of them. Uncomfortable in open, lovely spaces. What could they expect there? No idea, except that what they already knew felt comfortable. We try to make wherever we are seem like home, to feel secure, so we know what happens next.

In some ways, peaceful days when Paxton and I lounged around to talk (making plans to travel one day, or when we enjoyed an art gallery excursion) felt the best. But we didn't seem capable of creating those at will. Each mood accepted as it arrived, worked with like it was weather. Beyond our control. Swept along as if we were water under lunar influence. Neither with any idea of how to treat someone else intimate with us carefully, but delighted to have found each other. A feeling I knew so well, from before with Mark, with Joe, caught in a mirror, repeating. The need to feel important, that we mattered to someone, this over-rode other desires for safety and security.

Paxton bullied at school, marked outsider with his strange looks and foreign status. He'd been born in Poland, arrived in New Zealand at ten, but soon lost any Polish accent after a few months of jeering from other pupils.

Bonded in exile, determined to grow even more peculiar so we'd truly stand out. Not cowed by those who wanted us to disappear. Paxton favoured lace-up black boots and tight jeans, a short, tight, plain black leather jacket, and his black super-straight hair cut short at the sides but long on top, soaped into a mohawk, or it flopped over his eyes, a too-long fringe, dark and with that white streak. Both hands full of silver rings, one ear with so many earrings it looked like solid metal. Black eyeshadow he always wore smeared like someone had punched him in both eyes.

I'd dyed my hair bright pink by then, a product sent by friends in London. It stuck out like a scarecrow's bob. My eyes black lined and shadowed, winged up to points at the sides. A blast of hobgoblin glare. Short skirts and shredded tights, usually two holey colours over the top of each other, red and yellow, or green and pink, and a black fishnet top over various vintage underwear reworked with spiders, bats and spikes. Bracelets up my arm and often a studded dog collar around my neck. Sometimes Paxton led me along with a chain attached.

We built ourselves a territory this way, an area we knew and controlled. It felt like moving on, a train ride into the darkness, clattering metal, we owned all the hard places and they enclosed us, took us forward in a manner of safety.

Drunks in the street one evening jeered, 'Yah stupid punk-rock, yah wankers.'

One made to grab me but I ran on ahead, thinking Paxton paced fast behind me. The yobbos behind shouted, 'You fucking girl. Wearing make-up like a poof. You're no punk, you're a stupid girl.' The sickening sound of someone kicking something soft.

I whirled around and saw them piling into a bundled up body on the footpath against a wall.

Raced back and hit Paxton's assailants with my handbag, heavy and sharp-edged. A couple of yelps. Two of the three guys drew away, but they snarled mangled words at me.

Sirens sounded, as if police were on their way.

The drunks scattered, one fell and shouted for help but the others ignored him. Another dropped something metal and it clattered to the ground.

Police pulled up in a car with lights flashing and two constables scrambled to grab the guy splayed on the road. I knelt beside Paxton. His leather jacket sleeve tattered, the arm and hand bloody, and his face swollen. 'They hit me with something hard.' He tried to smile. It looked like a snarl.

The ambulance man muttered something to the other one when they were loading Paxton inside, it sounded like, 'That hand's no good.'

His parents moved him to a private hospital.

I had no idea where he was and nor did anyone else who would answer my calls.

It took three days to find out what was wrong. Paxton's parents refused to talk with me on the phone and when I called over there they pretended they weren't home, I'm pretty sure.

Not my fault those out-of-its didn't like a man in black eyeshadow.

Depressed for months, Paxton couldn't do much but adapt eventually. Family and friends lavished so much attention on him. He said he was, 'Bathing in love, every day.'

Without a hand and learning to use a mechanical prosthesis, Paxton developed more empathy. But the bad dreams and his thinking his hand was still there, these caused concern.

Across the news like someone scattered Deadly Nightshade seeds all over it. 'Punk Rocker Loses Hand, Leaves Music.' A magazine interview asked about his still wearing a leather jacket and jeans. 'I like these clothes. Why would I stop wearing them now?' He answered, bemused. In a TV piece he said he bore the drunks no ill will but wished they'd left us alone, 'We just looked a bit strange. It's not a crime.'

Crashbang found a new guitarist and Paxton said he thought he'd try record producing. Mainly, he read books and hung out at friends' places, a shadow of a star.

A relative called him. Paxton told me, 'They want to pay my fare to Europe. A special clinic's there where they help amputees adapt. France.'

I listened to the plan and lay my head against his chest. We unwound on his bed, afternoon sun streaming in from the garden. Lovely trees out there nodded in a breeze, all the way to the back boundary of the large property. Nothing for it but to say, 'I hope you enjoy yourself, Pax. Sounds good. Fun trip.'

'My uncle's found me work in France. Could be years living abroad.'

Through his dark blue sweater his heartbeat felt strong. I'd miss him more than I wanted to admit, but it seemed foolish to say this out loud. His happiness mattered more than what I wanted

and truly, it did. I loved the idea of one of us getting such a
stunning chance, even if in the name of recuperation.
When I turned my head to smile bravely up at him, his voice
went low, 'Come too if you want.'
I leapt to my feet and asked over and over, 'Do you mean it? Do
you? Really?'

The city became a hunting ground. Three extra jobs found in
two days, plus I sold everything possible including my ray gun
collection and electric guitar (I never did learn to play), all my
shoes except for three pairs, most of my wardrobe and books. I
finished up with only enough to fit in a backpack, and a box of
things to send to Mum and Dad's to go into storage.
Every day since the younger me had discovered the world
contained more than our little street, the static seas of suburbia
or the town where we shopped, I wanted hear other countries'
traffic noises and foreign conversations, listen to their music,
breathe new cooking aromas from strange windows.
In only a month and a half Paxton boarded a plane and left for
France.
For ages I took a sweatshirt he left behind to bed with me.
Comfort, the smell of him. Beautiful chemistry, if we'd been
minerals in a test tube someone could've made a fortune.
My plan to save as much money as possible manifested denial
and abstinence. Holy. A spartan existence, divine solitude, in
control of so many aspects of my life.
At home, I stocked up on library books, read avidly instead of
going to movies or anywhere which could cost, used up every
scrap of my art materials for drawing and painting, took long
walks to the park when I felt skittish or ready to break
something. Fed my magazine addiction with sneaky reading at
lunchtime, in the biggest city bookstore with other guilty lurkers.
Crashbang let me into gigs without paying, every weekend.
One night, I told the bass player's girlfriend how often I wrote
to Paxton, 'I miss him so much. Hope he's warm enough. A
European winter. Must be so cold. It's the worst one for 60
years. He's learning how to use the new hand they've had made.
The latest one. But he hasn't really got any friends, going on his

letters. Wish I knew he was okay.'

She peered closely at me in this hard way then softened and shook her head. 'You're too good for him. He may have had that accident, but he's not really a decent guy.'

Someone may appear with news you didn't ask for. Could feel like they're involving you in a crime. In stories, it's a wizened crone or an odd little man. For a fairy tale they ask a difficult question or hint at a secret. If you ever sense a whiff of their sordid souls in a mere mortal then flee, get shot of them with their acid talk or it will burn through your pretty plans and leave only ugly marks.

She told me about a few things seen when I wasn't around, 'He was down the back of that tour bus with her. I'm not saying anything happened but I could hear them laughing, and other noises. I wouldn't like to say what they did.' She described what Paxton did when I had to stay home from gigs. What really forward girls did, then what Paxton did and the sounds *they* made.

Someone pouring poison over my evening and days to come, thick, sticky and ruinous. Suspicions about his cheating appeared founded. But all I wanted was blue. Shock meant I felt nothing. My dream escape from the ends of the earth to the rest of the world lost colour and shape. A flower long dead finally crumbles if anyone touches it.

Blank anger attracted everything dark gathered over the last years as if it were fuel. I sat by this cold fire and plotted how to feel better.

The calculation involved in this little sum of wrongdoing took only minutes.

Daring sidelong looks, dark brown eyes, a great smile. I didn't have to bear betrayal alone. Someone else did like me, a shy smile, close talk when we met, they often flirted silently with me when Paxton was around, too, and looking the other way.

Survival, someone at least interested enough to draw nearer, so I didn't feel shoved into a blizzard.

Three days later, this handsome acquaintance reappeared, and I drew David into conversation. We discussed what was on that

weekend. He asked me to one of their gigs. We stood only a few centimetres away from each other, as if a kiss was inevitable at any moment. Our embrace took four days longer.
Fell into an affair with the bass player from a band Paxton admired, as if it was an acrobatic trick.
We laughed our way through summer. Saving money, I worked hard and still wanted to leave the country. Heartfelt moments turned into clickity click frames from a film reel, dangerous fun, a few months of fancy time, nothing more. Denial a powerful ally for someone young and selfish. Refusing to register the way David looked at me like he wanted to never let go.
Then the date neared for me to fly away. No light-hearted movie script now, when the man I chose for a fling started sobbing, the night before my flight, and so did I. David and I clung to each other in his bed. I furiously tried to imagine how to stay, yet also travel overseas. We'd never pretended I would change my plans, he'd always known what'd happen, but the whole ridiculous, hurtful exercise now appeared so unfair and wicked. My dream to leave the country then turned into a painful separation.

Youth, it's like driving an excellent car in great working order without a map or any experience, going with whatever you think you can get away with day-to-day, curve to curve. Sometimes the gears graunch, or the car wobbles and getting lost is inevitable. I tried to outrun understanding, but couldn't assume people wouldn't get attached, and I to them. Younger days were one large, unregulated, feral university, and in order not to *only* get older as in time just passing, I had to absorb knowledge, or stay barely formed. Mapped the return to places I never wanted to be again, recognised them in future and refused to tread that pathway.
I go over dire times to make sure I never repeat dreadful patterns, but hope I'm not impressing them instead.
Prior decisions took me away then as surely as if a guard marched me off. Backpack had been ready for days. Paxton's parents drove me to the airport. My own mum and dad there with Coltrane, too, only a boy, he looked cheerful to see me but a bit bewildered, poor kid. I told him I'd send fabulous toys from

over there. Didn't seem like enough at the time but I had to go.

Escape. I'd wanted to leave the country all my life. Forgetting
trauma was possible when I no longer lived in New Zealand,
that was what I believed. Start again. Desperate to get out;
believing bad memories could stop reappearing constantly.
In another place being awake could feel better.

More dangerous at Barbz by then too, boot boys with weapons
had multiplied, beatings for their own amusement, more and
more idiots on all manner of home-made drugs, or foolish
mixtures of street concoctions. Punks turning into a terrifying
page from a Heavy Metal comic, the ink running red.
My excuses look like a rusty old crashed car now, however,
overgrown, never cleared away.
Paxton's losing his hand only the beginning of the injuries some
of us suffered, for no reason apart from looking like easy targets.
Some punks were provocative but we didn't deserve beatings. I
don't include the boot boys or the the boot girls in our punk
circle. They were thugs, criminals, to my mind and another
group altogether. My friends were never about overtly violent
acts, but about expressing our darkest selves in how we looked,
danced, and played music. The initial group who started it all
off, about forty or fifty people in the late 70s, were not the louts
who started to dominate gigs later on.
Although Jimmy Loud *had* tried to stab his girlfriend, he used a
table knife and didn't do much but bruise and scare her. Bad
enough of course, but then he hid. Jimmy told me after they'd
sorted it out with a counsellor, 'We were packing to move the
flat. She just would not shut up. I told her to stop it. Then
everything went red. Had the knives in my hand to put in a box
and jabbed at her.'
Messed up, confused and crazy, any stupid, violent act probably
more due to repressed pain and trauma, and a lack of ability to
problem-solve, than actual sadism or psycho-drives. Waving flags
of white noise, hoping we've all surrendered to better days.
My unstable mental state carried with me as surely as my make-
up bag and plane tickets. Off I went, leaving David sad and

myself confused, along with my family. I imagined a threshold, a
door to somewhere new, stepping over it and into what I
couldn't imagine far easier than staying behind with the
wreckage.

Many cocktails and some sleep; our flight took a stopover in
Singapore. Tiger Balm Gardens a pleasant walk past colourful
statues from local mythology, nice, and so was the air-
conditioned bus. Steamy air as thick as soup. No idea any place
could be that hot. Stepping back in mind, closing down in some
ways, watched life like a movie.

Then we lifted off again for France and my true love who'd
waited to see me for six months. Thirty-eight letters from me,
twenty-seven from him, fifteen postcards from him, eight
postcards from me, one telegram from him, two telephone calls,
and fifty-four handwritten pages in my daily journal.
On the plane for the last leg, I looked forward to seeing Paxton.
He'd stand close to the arrivals door, waiting, maybe holding
flowers like in an airline ad, the romance of long-distance travel.
Soon I changed in the tiny aeroplane toilet, black lacy
everything, cleansed my face, applied make-up and perfume.
Ready for Europe, ready for my darling.
Although I now couldn't get David's stricken face out of my
thoughts. I couldn't imagine how Paxton cheated so often, if all
his other girls haunted him the way David now did me. Did I
make a mistake, leaving New Zealand?

Queues of people longer and longer while I stood wondering
when we'd get through all the checks and stamping of passports.
Officials as methodical as machinery. Surrounded with hundreds
of other travellers, shuffling towards yet another sign, I
wondered if I'd get through procedures without screaming.
They'd drag me off to a French lunatic asylum. I stood extra-
straight, clamped my mouth shut and played music in my mind.
Only sad songs appeared. Tears in my eyes, and I hoped one day
David would forgive my fecklessness. I worried over Coltrane,
my young son too, with his rather forced cheeriness at the

airport. Me on the other side of the world, with regret for
company. Songs say to regret nothing but tunes make the most
difficult things sound so easy.
This avant-garde airport about 100 times bigger than anywhere
I'd seen. A metal holding room with sweeping patterned glass
ceilings, it could hold the population of a small town.
Finally permitted to leave the check-in area, stepping out where
strangers grinned delighted at newly arrived passengers and they
greeted loved ones. Six months apart and now in Paris, in the
airport. I tried to see his face, I looked everywhere around the
airport.

Did my best to forget the look my lover left me with back home,
the way David sobbed the night before I left. Swore to myself I'd
never hurt anyone like that again. Cheating not worth it, no
matter how angry I felt.

But this was what it felt like to be abandoned. No one there to
meet me after all?
Had someone told Paxton about David? Someone certainly told
me about Paxton's infidelities.... Now this was an elaborate
karmic payback?
I'd have to somehow manage alone, to travel around all those
countries without anyone else, or return to New Zealand and
admit I'd been stood up.
I went over everything so far, luggage claimed, passport checked,
hair fluffed up again, and miniskirt straightened. I'd stepped out
of the wide glass automatic doors into France. Paxton to appear
any moment, surely.
Not there.
No Paxton.
I stood as still as a column holding up the roof.
Then I realised someone could see my fright and take
advantage; wheeled the trolley forward where many people
busily walked by, no one recognisable. The air smelt different,
ancient European history's dust. Crowds, so many passers-by,
uncountable this bustle of people who knew where they were
going and who'd meet them there. Open coats flapped, some of

that cloth brushed my legs, like soft waves goodbye.

Every second person so well-dressed, elegant, understated, so *French*. Shoes and handbags subtle shapes and colours, clever hairstyles, beautifully cut jackets, the most stylish shoes I'd ever seen en masse. Everything altogether belonging the way a forest belongs to itself. A dense tamed wilderness of beautifully put together humanity (and no doubt, some wolves).

Stomach churning, I hoped not to throw up with nerves in front of these impossibly lovely international travellers, their family and friends. *No punk jokes or tricks now, please*, I prayed.

Had I told Paxton the correct airport? He knew I'd dyed my hair black again and it was longer, permed? I'd sent him photos, hadn't I, or had I imagined that? Did I have his address, so I could ring? Did I need to talk to an operator to call? How good was my schoolgirl French these days? *Parlez vous Anglais, s'il vous plait....*

A row of figures sat along a wall in those built-in, hard seats typical of airports. Way in the middle of the row of seated people in the immense glass and concrete airport, someone with his dark head down turned and saw me. His fringe with a streak of white.

I let my luggage trolley go and ran.

My high heels clicked loudly on the hard floor. We raced towards each other like lovers in an ad for Valentines Day, we only needed the sound of water on a surf beach meeting the sand. A couple apart for months who half-believed they'd not see each other again.

His new leather jacket creaked and I buried my face in his chest, breathed, inhaled security.

Paxton bewitching. Intoxicated by him, without question.

In the back of my mind I knew I should've felt far more excited and eager when we rolled together naked in our hotel bed, but Paxton didn't seem to notice. His passion as furious as an ocean in a storm.

My disappointment at myself for being as fickle as he was, for sleeping with David, I tried to forget. (I never really did dismiss it however. Mistakes are always an opportunity to learn a lesson. I know now, for instance, that the best revenge is success - not tit for tat behaviour. Apologies to anyone concerned too, of course).

Anyway, after we'd sated ourselves in the funky old hotel room in the Latin Quarter which he'd booked, Paxton told me, 'I imagined white slave traders kidnapped you. It took so long for you to appear.'

I laughed.

Paxton frowned. 'I met a guy in Singapore. Swore he was a white slave trader.'

Each of us with a gift for imagining ridiculous scenarios. Not sure if it was a worthwhile ability, I had to think, but we were very good at it.

Paxton with only one hand meant he wasn't worth much, this slave trader stranger had told him. 'He had a wicked laugh, like some bad guy in a movie.'

My love believed I'd be a valuable slave. Perhaps his worry equalled a compliment but the wild tale made me feel rather diminished. Didn't Paxton realise I'd never allow myself to be abducted?

To ignore my annoyance at being thought gullible, I told myself life was beautiful. Paris. I ran my fingers through his longer hair. Mohawk grown out, strands long about his neck.

'You never told me your flight number.'

'What's that?' I laughed.

Long before email, way before cellphones, messages from overseas took days to arrive in the post unless we sent a telegram - expensive and often hard to understand - as few words as possible. Paxton had waited for me at Charles de Gaulle airport, not knowing my flight number, only the day. Anything omitted then a haphazard sketch, and no expensive telegram needed if someone possessed an imagination. Paxton had decided to watch every flight that day from Singapore disembark.

Oblivious to any mishap, I'd dressed up on the plane and expected to see him immediately, when I appeared in the airport foyer.

We laughed about my foolishness. Hearts fonder, distance collapsed.

On an immaculate sweep of long lawn with the Eiffel Tower
standing guard, we picnicked and planned, kissed, held hands to
watch clouds turn into birds, cottages. 'That one looks like a
dachshund. O an'that one's an umbrella.'
'A train taking us into the future.' Paxton waved his mechanical
hand to the sky. Much less self-conscious, and more able to make
the new lightweight model operate.
'It's not a very long train.'
'Big enough for us.' He rolled towards me. We kissed for some
time, such soft warm lips, and he tasted of oranges. Everything
repaired itself instantly.

We scrimped, subsisted on minuscule savings, lived on ten
dollars a day. Railway expedition á la Europe for months. Our
riches were evident however when we took in masterful
sculptures and paintings in galleries. Enormous renditions of
angels and clouds almost reached forty foot ceilings; startling
cubist murals stretched along corridors giving off previously
unknown light. We strolled through grand and unusual
architecture, Gothic spires, modernist severities, medieval
arches... took in exhibits in museum cases, which we sketched for
hours. Writing journals every day (luckily left-handed, he'd lost
his right in that long ago attack). Hours of walking. We hefted
backpacks from train stations to hostels, ate in small, inexpensive
places or cooked fresh vegetables in hostel kitchens. Noting
where locals shopped. They knew where the best quality and
value were offered, and their language flowed about us as if we
too definitely belonged there.
Wisely, Paxton had researched guidebooks while he waited in
France, and he'd drawn up the way journeys could go, dates and
destinations. He made my dream come true, world travel.

We approached glass cases of antiquities for hours of drawing.
Leather sandals an iron age farmer wore to tend his crops,
artifacts from stone age artisans, human clues in shaped rock
where someone started an adze, or they wrought gold and silver
Viking jewellery, German ceramics, French vintage or antique
furniture and toys. A guard asked if we were archaeologists,

'Usually people do the tour, zoom, zoom and leave, but you've
been here all afternoon.'
Paxton told him, 'No, we're artists.'
Grinned with the fit of it.
Lived on almost nothing.
Delighted us when we were taken for residents somewhere we
visited.
A pleasant path or jingle jangle street, myriad people never seen
elsewhere. African youths in the Latin Quarter of Paris stood by
carved jewellery from their homeland spread on woven rugs,
selling to pedestrians. A Scotsman on Magic Bus to Greece
laughed, swigging wine, sang about a girl he'd left behind and
how he missed her so. A border guard in Yugoslavia as stern as
an executioner, dark uniform, buttons shiny, and demanding
pounds sterlings for fees. A Greek farmer loaded a donkey on
Fira, the volcano island, by whitewashed houses which edged
slowly disintegrating cliffs, some tumbled into the sea. Bright
orange weaving hung on wide, white terraces. Liquid orange
sun, a Mediterranean horizon, blue-green shimmer. In
Germany, a museum empty of everyone but us, crammed with
exquisite furniture, jewellery, china, embroideries, a black and
white chair with a ladder back....

When CK Stead wrote that he liked the fact he was published in
other countries, because it felt like otherwise you could become
a parrot in New Zealand, he knew what we felt like, our free
range. Overseas absorbing, more than we could ever know.
Away from an insidious push in our own country, hints to
conform, to fit in at the cost of a valuable individual point of
view.
We'd redesigned fashion from garbage and waste, displayed pain
like a trophy, made from our ruin something glorious, attention-
getting, world-changing. Fixed ourselves, flaws and all, into
history. A long list of taboos existed where we came from,
however, and at the top of that list was liberty. Repressed New
Zealand, where abuse was fine as long as no one told the sorry,
horrible tale, where a smile and look-happy routine seemed the
best way to behave no matter what, where we needed to all dress

as alike as possible in case someone singled us out (for a beating for instance), where to be excellent at anything or openly delighted by some experience was showing-off....

Finally released, at last, and a wide more promising world welcomed us. This even though I missed Coltrane and sent him letters, postcards, and toys as promised. Every day I wished I could think of a way to get my son to travel with us.
Impossible on our budget. He also needed school.

Paxton enjoyed showing me places he'd researched in his lonely French room.
In a Greek cafe where a crowd of us sang along with locals, a young woman asked me, 'You two, you are together, yes?'
I nodded and smiled.
She replied, 'It is rare to see two people so truly together.' She looked pleased.
Rather taken aback by this out-of-the-blue compliment, I did nevertheless smile broadly. With Paxton I'd hold on, wouldn't easily let him go. We'd learn better, we had to, people needed each other and we'd found something valuable, our alchemy, shared interests, and now this journey.
Just then, Paxton raced in from watching a three-legged dog and a fire eater in the ancient street outside the taverna and ordered more drinks, shouting, 'It's amazing. We've gone back in time.'
Smooth plastered walls, simple décor, golden light and voices warm about us.
Our observations quietly written in a journal after dinner. But, now and then, after breaking into one of our stories, we screeched with laughter over some people, like this cyclist we met. A tourist, he told us, 'They have nudist beaches here, yah.'
Hints we could go there with him, in Denmark.
I found the overly friendly Frenchman in Athens puzzling too, his seeming unafraid of anything. With just the two of us alone, Paxton later pointed out the know-it-all's African metal arm-band hid track-marks. 'He's high. No fear then.'

We wondered if our host on the island of Naxos felt lonely in the winter. He loved summer holiday visitors so much. 'I make coffee. You have. Turkish coffee.' Lambros did his best to explain things with almost no English (he spoke Deutsch, with most of his guests being German). A natural host; grinning with genuine pleasure, he welcomed us to his porch along by plain concrete block rooms on a tiny plot of subsistence farmland. Lambros, an old man, missing half his left ear, showed us both the little communal kitchen, offered Turkish coffee he made in his own small room.

Later we unpacked in the one room we'd share, with a shower off to the side (freezing cold but the room so cheap we couldn't complain).

Backpacking, our chattels folded into restricted luggage. Paxton wore his black leather jacket - too bulky for the pack. Heavy, padded leather, many silver zips and buckles, it looked like it could've had its own engine. In those pockets, compass, pocket knife, notebook, pens. My pack crammed with four different colours of baggy 80s pants (they tapered suddenly from just below the knee like jodhpurs), make-up and swags of jewelry, along with sleeping bag, socks, t-shirts, tops, underwear, bikini, towel, flannels, plastic bags, and a warm jacket.

Always walking in light it seemed to me. Dark places within ourselves we abandoned to ghosts and scurrying errant thoughts. Few worries then over past mistakes, no time to look back. Travel made us look outwards, forward. Every day demanded creative thinking to catch the proper train, find decent food, or claim the best beds in any given hostel; to relate our museum finds to something known or dreamt about, to avoid sly eyes and peculiar locals. Only responsible for ourselves, bunches of belongings and a few official papers, passport, rail pass, and maps kept with cash in neck pouches concealed under our clothes. Relaxed in photos; Pax taller, we stand close. I grin, the grand prize mine; the wide world about me at last, my desire since I discovered planet Earth existed. And this man loved me. Both blessed with agreement, dizzy at sharing so readily; a match, chemical, social, emotional, and physical. Delicious foreign food, engrossing museums, clickity click trains whizzed us onward and hostels accepted our weary needs. Cameras

snapped and our pens adeptly wrote or draw. Then sublime
exhaustion, night descended before distant memories
reappeared.

The moment our concern, this second now now now and where
we'd be next, train chug-a-lug, shoosh-a-shoosh, a grinning,
handsome couple in a stream of activity carrying as little as
possible.

Arguments dwindled to mere occasional snappishness. Relaxed
and secure, I told myself a smile could be genuine, days need
not have shocks or nasty surprises. We'd created a true bond
amidst the pretty trees of Europe's forests. Our travels took in
settled villages and magnificent cities. People did good, the proof
of this abundant.

One afternoon, a pretty foreign girl told us her sorry story in a
youth hostel near the communal lounge. 'Decide to go on
holiday. Helps to forget. My boyfriend and I, we broke up.' Big
dark eyes, she dipped her head a fraction and smiled at Paxton.
Then she took his injured arm, and touched his mechanical
hand. 'You have accident?' Her pout unsympathetic, more like a
cartoonish joke.

I didn't get the punchline just wanted to punch *her*. Resisted the
urge to blurt *she'd* have an accident in a minute.

Paxton paler than usual, withdrew his hand. He almost never
discussed it, nor made a feature of having a prosthesis. As if
angry, he trembled slightly.

The girl smiled radiantly on. Out the window, various
evergreens appeared strong, dark, growing tall in the sun.

Spinning on one foot I went to examine the snack machines. To
my surprise, Paxton stood behind me saying, 'I'm just going for a
walk with Gretchen.'

My Paxton, who I'd crossed the world to see, who'd shared travel
and plans with me for months, he wanted a forest walk with this
young woman we'd only just met, and to leave me there with a
chocolate bar? I took him aside as if a crowd watched us, but we
were alone. 'No. Stay here.'

'It's just a walk.' Paxton glancing away towards her now. She
stood half in and half out of the doorway to the hall from the

hostel lounge, metres away and swayed a little as if drunk.
'No. We don't know her. Could be anyone. This could end
up....' I turned to the machine so he couldn't see me almost
crying. When I pushed in the coin for a treat, the machine's
graunch loud.
When I looked back the girl had gone, and only my boyfriend
stood there. We didn't discuss her or much else, afterwards. We
made and ate dinner, wrote our journals then went to bed.
Hostel dormitories segregated male and female, so I slept in
another place, alone. I'll never know if they met that night
somewhere, ignored curfew, slept under the stars together.
She also could've been a gypsy temptress who schemed to lure a
man with only one hand into the forest. There her crazy
husband would try to steal everything my Paxton carried.
Unbeknown to them, his boxing training would've been handy.
He'd fight, then run, run to the hostel and hide, cover up any
bruises and never tell how he'd been tricked, for shame.
Impossible to know.
Doubts then did hang about sometimes like unwelcome guests,
distracting and upsetting, an annoying hum. A crowd of worries
reappeared. For a long time I entertained suspicion, needed to
keep one step ahead or he'd surprise me with some awful scene,
a betrayal I'd not seen coming. Frazzled with going over and
over this.

The next day, hours of walking meant we stayed reasonably
neutral, without breath to argue. I was learning to let some
things alone. Then, in the Black Forest, he told me, 'We can
sleep here. Well, we're not supposed to, but I figured out how we
could.'
'You're telling me it's not allowed? It's illegal, you mean? This *is*
Germany, you know what they are like so far about rules. How
do you know we would not get arrested?.'
We'd already been far too relaxed for various youth hostel
owners and museum guards. They'd told us off, shouted at us, or
told us to leave when we did some minor, (to us) rule-breaking.
'It's fine, honestly. Come on.'
Tramping through endless dark trees, we spoke only a little but I

tried to talk him out of sleeping there. I think I also said feminism meant he had to do what I said (a weak joke). After consideration, I suspect he wanted payback for my not allowing him to walk with Gretchen. Any tiny thing fits inside a bomb, propelled with force, damaging. 'You don't like this trip, really, do you?' He snarled, 'I planned this for months. It was hard work. Gratitude would be nice.'

We cracked away at each other in the crisp mountain air awhile.

'Listen. I know ...'

'You? You know nothing except stupidity.' He sneered.

'Me? I am NOT stupid, except of course coming all this way to see you. That's stupid.'

'Forget me then. Leave. I bet you've got plenty of men to catch up with.'

'Me? Wha...? If this wasn't the middle of a forest where we are not even supposed to be after dark, I would bloody leave, you fuckwit. It's getting dark. Look, we have to find a hostel or....'

'We're sleeping here.'

'Paxton, we have to ...'

'Stop telling me what to do.'

'Idiot. Someone has to have a brain.'

He stormed off. Took the dirt and grass at a fast pace in his sturdy boots. Setting sun to his left, metal hand glinting, and it swung in time. His long legs then running, backpack strapped on, Paxton, even at the end of the day, could cover so much ground. In seconds, his tall figure in jeans and a khaki shirt, out of sight around the curving mountain track. My darling had disappeared.

Silence.

The Black Forest was mainly dense black spruce for kilometres, some over steep country. Extremely tall, spiky, dark trees reached up. They grew all around, and went on for miles. A wide dirt track behind and before me in fast diminishing light. Below, a valley of yet more trees. No one walked or talked, no sounds except occasional birds now calling to each other.

Anyone could travel in Europe with reasonable safety. Germany appeared especially organised. I only needed a night's sleep, then to re-plan in the morning. My thinking yawned like it

needed more air to work, a blank pale blue in my mind. Then I
felt as if someone threw me out of a plane and I needed to know
if I even wore a parachute, let alone if I could tug a cord to
open it.

'Where am I?' I muttered.

The map, Paxton had left with it.

We'd walked for two hours, by then. It'd been mainly uphill
through close spruce forest. A few roofs below, to the left, as tiny
as toys. So the town lay to the east, in shadows cast by the setting
sun. Air at a higher altitude, quite cold. Hardly sweltering hot in
a German summer, nothing like blazing days in New Zealand
dripping with humidity. How to survive alone in the forest all
night?

Ferns for a bed? Some rocks sat covered in moss and a few tiny
ferns but they'd not fill even a cushion. And was I permitted to
pick anything?

For a short while, I followed where he'd strode the wide track.
The mid-brown earth smelt damp, trees gave off a dense scent
too, uplifting, cleansing. Above and below, tall, black spruce as
before, ten to fifteen times as high as me, over a steep mountain.
No animal noises, not a snuffle nor a yelp. Repeating to myself,
trees, only trees. In gathering dark, a man like Paxton could
disappear and fend for himself easily. A woman alone was far
more vulnerable, an easy target if anyone wanted to....

For years previously, Paxton rowed kayaks and practised boxing,
ran marathons and won medals for gymnastics. Whereas I could
barely carry my pack longer than twenty minutes without a rest.
For the nine millionth time I told myself to give up smoking
cigarettes, but wanted one badly. Resisted.

I needed to take off my heavy pack and sit in the shadowy
resinous air. The rock I perched on cold but my sleeping bag
good padding. This meant unpacking my whole kit. In a
backpack the heaviest things go on top, the lightest at the
bottom.

Abandoned by my go-getter boyfriend, I needed somewhere
hidden to sleep, then to make my way to the train the next day.
Passport, Eurail pass, and money in a pouch around my neck.
Kiosks sold maps. Practising fragmented German, how to ask

for directions, what things cost, how to say thank you, sorry. 'Wo ist der Bahnhof? Wie viel kostet das bitte? Dankeschön. Taurig.' Blinking away tears.

Night approached relentlessly as a hunter who knew they'd catch up with what they wanted to catch. I repacked and set off in faint light to choose somewhere concealed from the main pathway. By particularly dense trees, I hoped no wild animals lived there and looked for raised ground.

A noise behind and I twisted to see, held onto a tree when I almost toppled over. Fright and adrenaline coursed through me, I almost screamed.

Paxton strode up, beaming, a thin sheen of sweat across his lightly tanned handsome face. 'Going to say sorry?'

Anger dissipated entirely by walking, I just laughed.

He put his arms around me. 'As if I'd leave you here. Alone. Miss me?'

Warm kisses in a forest in a foreign land. We only had each other and kisses proved forgiveness. Summer skin against skin, the smell of him a potion, hints of hibiscus, sharp lime, and musk.

Soon, makeshift pillows of jerseys lay under our heads. In sleeping bags, we occupied a depression in the ground hidden from people walking by (not that anyone did pass). We waited for night.

Between dense spruce, high, narrow open spaces to the late afternoon sky (edged by branch tips) looked like enormous, plain cathedral windows. Blue above now faded to grey light shining mistily through. Everything then totally dark. Complete silence. No trafficked road for kilometres and not a bird sang, no animals trotted by or called, no wind arose.

Illegal to sleep there or stay after dark, and I wished we were somewhere else. If found and arrested, could we be deported? My stomach grizzled and groaned with nerves. Paxton wanted to sleep out. I agreed to prevent an argument. This also saved us money. But in our own country there were no snakes and few wild, dangerous creatures could bother anyone sleeping in the bush. One poisonous spider prevalent at that stage back home, or we'd hear a noisy possum at night, or dangerous pigs in the daytime, only. In perfectly regulated Germany, surely, nothing would dare harm us, someone would appear with a rule book and demand it followed the proper guidelines. I smirked in the night.

Sudden, distant screams, like a woman in terror, resounded through the trees, screeches on and on. High, loud shrieks, sharp as vinegar. We both gasped, I tensed and gripped my clothing inside the sleeping bag. On our backs on the ground in sleeping bags, rigid. I trembled. 'You hear that?'

'Hard to tell if they're joking or not.'

We breathed in silence, I tried to slow my thoughts down.

'Nothing we can do anyway.'

'I know.'

A pair of planks there in the vast forest, inert; I hoped whatever it was, they wouldn't draw nearer. Put to flight to any last irksome thoughts about our disagreement. Globs of night seemed ready to smother me.

Exhausted, we soon slept anyway and did not wake until dawn.

Years later, someone mentioned a bear screams like the screeching we heard, a womanly howl. Bears could have been a good reason why people were not allowed to sleep in the Black Forest.

Despite our fireworks and exuberance disrupting plans, Europe and Britain grew familiar and we travelled on, eager to see and record the world. Paxton had planned with dedication, ten countries, $10 a day. Our Let's Go Europe disintegrated in a year, the hefty book's every page rifled.

Eventually, we found legit work to earn our passage home in an English pub. After meeting a few living on their wits, illegally working in other countries, neither of us wanted dodgy arrangements. Paxton could work again in France. But I preferred us both to earn money.

News and tips circulated fast. Young and sociable with membranes that magically absorbed talk, writing, smarts, and I wrote and received many letters. Before email, or myspace, or

facebook, back then we sought real time conversation and
written correspondence or landline phone calls. 'We go to NZ
House, find the local paper and ring up places. Millions of ads
for barpeople.'
My old friend Bonnie had written, 'NZ House has a row of
telephones, payphones. Take some change.'
In London, carefully checking addresses in our A-Z of London
to make sure we wanted to live there. Five calls later we had a
job. No interview.
Stories I'd read inhabited every cobblestone, busy park, historic
site and each character face of passing locals, people in cars,
those working in shops too. The crowd showed more stress and
their inner self in their appearance than I was used to. London
made their faces more expressive, applied extra pressure.
Wrinkles and attitude appeared obvious. They also reminded me
of people in books I'd read.
We pictured an old brick pub, a quaint establishment like in
British TV dramas.
The pub we found near Wembley on the map. Quite a train
ride, then a long walk beside a busy main highway, six lanes of
traffic. Concrete berms and overpasses, tall aluminium street
lamps, strip mall shops and roadworks, bright signs, wire mesh
fencing. I peered about seeking quaint and historic, hopeful.
Would've laughed if I wasn't so weary. 'Look, it's enormous.'
We'd found the one place in the whole of London built like a
New Zealand beer barn. A sprawling 1960s venue, dark brown
and orange, aluminium windows, neon sign already flashing at
only 4pm, set on a gigantic asphalt carpark.
Inside the furnishings attempted Victoriana, but were only about
ten years old. Fake Persian carpet for the patrons but behind the
bar a hard concrete floor. Two pool tables, many pokie and
video game machines, a huge half-circle bar in one room,
another smaller, straight counter in the other, the public bar.

Each morning, I linked my arms round Paxton's neck. He had
to lift me up, hoist me out of bed. I hobbled around for fifteen
minutes until I managed to get going again. My legs ached
diabolically after walking on hard concrete floors all day and

half the night.

Agony.

An income.

Enormous distances across Greater London, a busy, filthy, multifarious, magnificent city sprawl. Every week we searched ads for better.

Then we were robbed.

'These Charlies came in here Saturday night,' our guv told the shocking story.

I hoped the robbers wouldn't return. The pub lost a week's takings. What say the perpetrators then tried to get what little we owned off us, too?

Paxton said nothing much for days then mentioned, 'They keep explaining. Really want us to believe them. Why? What does it matter? Also, said they were here when those three men broke in at 1am. They were out, though. I saw them leave from our window just before one.'

One of the other barmaids came into our room one night and hissed, 'Don't talk loud. They'd hate it if we were meeting like this.'

'Why?' My eyes wide, hunched on our bed.

'Bloody crims the pair of 'em. Heard 'em talking when they thought I'd gone up last night. I'm getting shot of this place, tell y'now. You'd be best to get on too, if y'ask me.'

'I'm scared, what....' I hissed but Paxton hugged me quiet.

'They staged a fuckin' robbery so they could keep th'week's takings. Money usually in the safe until Saturday night? A security firm picked it up, Sunday, see? The brewery who owns th'pub pays them wages. The pair of them wanted more.'

We agreed their story made little sense and their insisting it was so true all the time seemed suspicious. None of us much cared about the robbery as long as we weren't affected.

We already didn't want to stay on. Believed it best not to tell the police our suspicions then find ourselves in organised crime's bad books, either. Our bosses such bad actors, we couldn't believe they were in it alone.

After poring over newspapers and ringing around in
desperation, I felt sure, 'We'll never find anywhere.' A few
nightmares later, I imagined the guvnor and his wife could
blame *us* for something. One night the guvnor dropped a glass
and said I'd bumped him. I just screamed, 'Don't you dare
accuse me.' Ran crying to to the ladies' loos.
Paxton managed to convince them I'd had bad news from home.
For days I insisted we'd be better off to just leave on payday,
'Pack our things and walk out. Come on. We've only got a pack
each.'
'They'll tell other pub owners. How will we get a reference?'
Paxton folded his arms.
Finally, a week later my boyfriend beamed. 'Come on, interview
at midday and it's our day off.' He wouldn't tell me where we
were going. 'You'll see.'
The tube stopped in Chelsea. 'Come on, our stop.' Paxton
beamed.
'Chelsea. Nooo. We're going to Chelsea?' I almost skipped with
excitement.
Out of the station onto a teeming street as if into an enormous
outdoor theatre, it may as well've been one. The King's Road. A
backdrop of small, colourful, or elegant, and ancient shops, and
the most stylish, startling crowd on Earth at that time.
Two foot high bright red or blue or orange hair, punks' mohawk
silhouettes posing while glamorous models in designer dresses
sashayed by, and street people in tawny browns, worn greys like
Dickens' characters.
I almost bumped into a few sharply dressed young men in black
and white, their sneers an accessory, beneath number one
haircuts or trilby hats.
Businessmen in suits so well made the very fabric appeared
about to whisper in a foreign language.
Middle-aged women swept along in camel coats or mink to their
ankles, diamond jewellery and zillion-mile stares.
A crowd diverse enough to look manufactured for some
advertisement, but as real as the grimy air.
Edge of the middle of London, where The Rolling Stones wrote
about the Chelsea Drugstore, where further along Bryan Ferry's

wife bought her frocks, and a short distance on again Vivienne
Westwood and Malcolm McLaren discovered Johnny Rotten's
safety pin encrusted jacket could start a fashion revolution.
We walked The King's Road and prayed the pub would be
great.
'Just do not speak unless he asks you a question,' Paxton snapped
when we neared the place.
I knew my big mouth annoyed quite a few people, but it felt like
he was my minder or a school-teacher. Wasn't sure I liked the
feeling. Glorious sights and leaps of imagination about living
there one day, however, had already stunned me, silent.
Inside the corner place, through narrow doorways, enormous
engraved and hand-painted mirrors covered the walls, ancient
and gorgeous concurrently. A horseshoe-shaped bar in the
middle of the room, teeny seating areas each side, red velvet
buttoned upholstery, small, round wooden tables. My
impressions staccato.
Excitement took over.
Characterful patrons, well-dressed. Drinkers quietly talking or
sipping drinks. Not an overly crowded place.
Paxton charmed his way through a short history, 'Yes, we're
travelling, or we were but now need to work. Hope to stay a long
time in London. Love the place. Only want to move closer to the
city centre, now.'
I managed to keep the appearance of a sweet girl from the
country, throughout our interview, with silence and my smile not
too wide.
The balding guvnor shook our hands, agreed we were hired.
A few hundred years old our pub, Stars in the Sky. Edwardian
engraved mirrors a recent addition.
Patrons from the film and TV industry, with various toffs to
spend up large on expensive cognac, whisky, or pints of lager,
bitter, cider and Guinness. The gregariously antisocial English
merrily insulted each other and everyone else. We served
Italians, Irish, New Zealanders occasionally too, Scots, a
Frenchman who always looked so sad until sipping his cognac,
and a couple of older women who I think were gay, from
Belgium. Distinctly different styles, one, a thin woman, wore

only plain colours, dark blue and green, the other plump, always in florals and brighter shades. This pair arrived at 6pm and left at 7pm, regularly sat at the back curve of the bar and criticised other women to each other. A steady stream of quiet, pointed remarks. I'd hear comments while nipping by on my way to get this or that.

They told me once they were sisters.

Another patron commented, 'Those two. They sit there like judge and jury.'

'O, they're sisters,' I answered, 'just nattering on, you know, I....'

He laughed knowingly, 'They're not sisters. And you're too kind.'

For some unknown reason I mentioned this remark to them, about their not being sisters. Thought they'd laugh. What did that guy know?

They both opened their eyes in fright.

Next evening these two really quite dissimilar women turned up in each others clothes, as if to prove they were related. I didn't think, just commented, 'You've swapped clothes. Wow.' Laughed, thought it was some kind of amusement on their part.

They gaped and coughed, wide eyes again, then their mouths pursed.

I stopped talking with them so much after that. They didn't appear to care and kept up their critical commentary to each other, the same as before, the whole hour they sat drinking gin and tonics.

One regular only about five foot high and a Lord of the realm, snappish. Another, his friend, this bloodhound of a man over six foot, he talked so posh and slow it was hard to understand. They often argued, although old enough to know better (around forty or so). Building up with a few snipes at each other. 'You knew it. You knew it and went on regardless.'

'Moronic behaviour. As if *you're* qualified to judge *me*.'

'Transparently idiotic. It's not nuclear physics.'

'Jumped up twat. Science quite irrelevant. Tosh sir, utter unequivocal tosh and bollocks.'

Their drinks slammed down simultaneously on the bar, 'Watch these, girl.' The tall one would bark.

The Lord hissed, 'Yes. Take this outside. Right now.'

Two ninnies striding out the arched doorways, with a little foyer between to stop warm air escaping, and onto The King's Road. One or another of their friends sauntered out to referee. A few jabs at each other outside in their expensive suits. The first to land a punch declared winner.

They'd return *haw hawing* to finish their whiskeys (Jameson's, Irish whiskey). Whoever landed a punch first also bought them both another drink. 'My round, my round. Fair blow.'

The Lord's rather silly, longish, page-boy haircut, blond, made him look as childish as he behaved. Off-hand or insulting like someone bothered with bad digestion who needs to blame someone else for the gripe. 'Come over here to our fine land, arrive on their damn colonial planes without an idea of decency,' he'd say with a sneer. 'You, you girl, damned colonial. Another drink, another.'

I more or less ignored his jibes. Usually drunk when he railed on, and I didn't care what he thought. This refusal to appear upset made him bright red. 'You, you, girl. Did you hear me?' 'Another drink?' I'd smile sweetly. '*Please* is helpful.' Serving him anyway. You'd suffocate if you held your breath waiting for that one to be kind.

He'd mutter to a friend. They usually got the twit onto a new topic.

Once he made lewd remarks in whispers about my breasts across the counter, as I handed over his pint of lager. 'Luscious globes of pleasure there you've got for me. Under that blouse, what fun.' I ignored him expertly and turned to Paxton to let him know the bitter was off. He needed to go downstairs and change a beer barrel. 'It's that tap there.' I spoke quietly, pointed to where I'd been pulling pints, which also happened to be in front of Lord Purposeless.

Lord What's-his-Name shouted, "I said nothing to her, nothing.' He blushed furiously, stood on tip-toe.

A piercing, disbelieving glare from Paxton and my least favourite customer melted into the three-deep, mostly three-piece suited crowd around the bar.

Lord Mucky Mirth rarely ever nasty to me again from then on.

Bantering with customers, walking kilometres every day around that bar to pour drinks, away to clear tables, over and over. Wash and polish glasses, rearrange measuring cups by the cocktail stand, wipe benches, nip off to hide in the Ladies for an unofficial break....

Late one afternoon, with only a few people in, I selected glasses on one side of the horse-shoe shaped bar, someone else serving. I'd just poured beers and placed them over the taps, onto towelling beer mats.

Lord Idiot gave a strangled screech. He screwed up his face, looked down at his foot, lifted it and found chewing gum stuck on his shoe, picked it off. Such a hullaballoo he made.

Many of us stared at him with aghast astonishment. 'No one cleans properly around here.'

I just stared at him mildly, unused to this talk. He'd left me alone for months.

Then he threw the hard wad of gum at me, over the counter. It hit me in the chest (at close range).

I threw it straight back, snapped, 'Don't throw things at me.'

Even his friends looked shocked, this time.

In seconds I stalked off to serve someone else.

For a few days I expected the guvnor to reprimand me. The Lord and his friends every day lavishing enormous amounts of money on each other in our pub. They'd complain, surely.

But instead a few managed a *please*, occasionally. The funny little Lord with his swinging blond hair behaved like I didn't exist, even when he ordered drinks from me. Quite a feat. I supposed upper class people learnt this skill as part of their heritage. No mere colonial permitted to appear superior. Instant amnesia the best answer to insubordination.

When Lord Thing and the other taller chap, his bloodhound friend, said they'd step outside to sort out some disagreement *yet again* one evening, I didn't say anything against their fighting. His friend appeared truly angry for a change, and not as drunk as usual. The sleazy little Lord getting thumped seemed a glorious idea. He was almost always the one to buy the drinks afterwards. They dashed back in as pale as milk after a few seconds. The barman on with me whispered, 'The Old Bill are outside.' He laughed to himself.

A few bobbies on the The Kings Road beat sauntered the footpaths, evident and obvious in their distinctive blue uniforms and egg-shaped helmets. I guess our patrons didn't want to get arrested. Lord Twit and Bloodhoundman rigid when the policemen looked inside (police never entered the pub, usually). The upper class scaredy-cats only breathed normally once the police had gone. One pulled a dark bundle from under his coat, handed it to someone else who took off outside with it.

I began to consider them truly dodgy.

When Russia invaded Afghanistan the pair loudly proclaimed it'd be impossible to get caviar for years, but they knew a supplier. Over the next months Bloodhoundman appeared every other day with enormous cans of best beluga concealed in his calf-length, cavernous tweed overcoat. He'd whisk out two large flat cans, shove them over the bar and say, 'Pop those in the chiller would you, love? Got someone collecting them in a minute.'

Customers arrived, but not for our drinks. Bloodhoundman'd signal me. I'd retrieve the caviar (with a frown). Wads of money changed hands and happy punters sailed off with a large can in hand or tucked into a basket, briefcase or satchel.

In huddles by the bar often in urgent conferences, four or five toff conspirators. A new face would appear for a short time, they'd hand some item over. More wads of cash appeared briefly like ugly butterflies hatching, then disappeared. The posh posse play-acted innocence, stood more rigidly than usual, chins in the air, refusing to meet anyone else's gaze for a good five minutes. Staff did our best to pretend we knew not what they did, except when they ordered drinks. We didn't want to know. Every now and then I imagined their deals were mere pretense for them to appear more important. Anything was possible.

Their constant bickering and playtime fisticuffs an ebb and flow of tension. Also, with rumoured inbred genes in the upper classes you'd have to think they couldn't take much knocking around. Perhaps they'd developed this method of barely fighting, a show of bluster, to save their class? A pack of nincompoops, not that I met them all.

Red buses meanwhile sailed past the pub, double deckers, reminders of where we now lived. I wished I could get on one and leave, many days.

Only a few of our well-off patrons however were awful. Most eased their way with classy manners and evidence of education. Good conversations, tips for what sights to see and where to avoid, glimpses of history and mystery.

Irish Jimmy always making me laugh, his dark hair cut shortish but not severe, swept across his forehead in a long fringe which he brushed away whenever he saw me. His eyes always kind, his dark eyes. He told me one evening after we'd swapped banter throughout some months, 'O it's an awful story, I have to leave tomorrow. My wife's found where I am. She's divorcing me. Have to fly out tomorrow morning, back to Ireland. Give me a kiss."

So I did kiss him, and enjoyed it too.

He strolled in all smiles again the next morning.

'What are you doing here? You were flying to Ireland, Jimmy? This morning.'

'Was I?' He looked about himself as if someone else must've been talking to me.

I laughed, despite my bewilderment. 'Your wife had found you?'

'My wife?' He looked shocked and turned as if she'd just walked in the door. 'O I hope not.'

I laughed again, while pallid London sun streamed in the open doors.

'If she comes in again, tell her you've never seen me.' Jimmy winked.

'You're not going back to Ireland?' Me mock-annoyed, hands on hips.

'O now, it was only for the craich. Give us a lager then, lovely. Straight glass.' That grin.

He tried variations of his panic about five times and always somehow convinced me he really was going away, forever. Won a few kisses and much laughter.

For all I know he did this along The King's Road at every pub he frequented, whenever he fancied kisses from young barmaids. Another, older, Irishman moaned and complained about the

English with great twists and turns in his rhetoric. 'The bleedin'
English, I tell you what, if they were all killed off right now, no
one would miss them, not even their own mothers.'
Made me laugh. 'Their mothers would be dead surely, so how
could they miss them?'
But he never cracked a smile. 'A good thing if they too were
departed. Lord forgive me.' Great head of black hair and a
massive set of shoulders on him, accent so strong I had to truly
focus. Thought he must've only just arrived and found London
overwhelming, but his wife told me, 'O we've lived here in
London these 20 years.' She cracked a wry smile.
One local, a woman with a fine head of wavy coiffed strawberry
blonde hair and immaculate full make-up, like so many English
women, she told me, 'Once you've gone home, come and visit
any time. We'll all still be here.'
Along the narrow Chelsea footpath to the corner, open one door
then the next, into a cosy interior rich with wood panelling, wall
lights, and painted, engraved mirrors. Regulars in the same
chairs, saying new things in the same way, each minding their
usual drink.
But after all those hours and months of hard work, cleaning,
bar-tending, entertaining 7am 'til 10pm six days a week, the
sniping upper classes, the spilled beer rotting my shoes, our
guvnor fixing prices higher than the legal level and the lies we
had to tell to work there, local fashionistas sneering when I put
on a little weight...I never wanted to return.
Our eighteen months around Europe and Britain engaging.
Then an ever-glorious parade of fashionistas, punks, wide boys
and assorted others along The King's Road as well. Our
excellent jukebox in the bar made work more bearable, along
with various lovable customers, free drinks, an excellent pancake
place over the road, and museums to visit in every direction.
But the o so true reason I headed back was that I truly needed to
see my son, Coltrane.
Home.
For all this time I'd written stacks of letters, found stunning toys,
parcelled to send off to my child, but nothing I'd seen and no
one I met interested me as much as he did. Not the same, unable

to see Coltrane whenever I wanted and to hear what he had to
say. I missed my son, dreadfully.

Our families delighted to see us, glad we'd not been kidnapped
or blown up. Coltrane taller and older. Pleased to see each other
but he'd grown somewhat distant.

People say 'There's no manual - How to Look after Children.'
But while being parented ourselves, we watch adults constantly.
Parenting's learnt from our own family.
My mother often joked we were *dragged* up. If I'd admitted that
wasn't much funny earlier, I could've found a book with better
ideas or a kinder role model, but the way we lived was normal as
far as we knew. Other children in our street, suburb, school, city
also neglected, many were hit, hard like we were too, and
treated like we didn't matter all that much unless we did what we
were told. Some I suspect had the unwanted sexual attentions of
various relatives or visitors to mess them about, too. Crash,
bang, wallop, and memories trailing after the damage a-clanging
along too.
I had to learn better by myself.

Mainly Pakeha, our reasonably well-off street, urban New
Zealand and a cookie cutter life.
A few say Maori treated some children appallingly too,
especially when times were hard. The English however created
New Zealand law allowing adults to hit children. Teachers
treated us like we were idiots, scathing over any little thing, they
sneered. Teachers hit us for looking out the window, *whack*,
whispering, *whack*, forgetting something, *whack*, not speaking
loudly enough, *whack*, speaking too loudly, *whack*, answering
back, *whack*, fighting, *whack*, bad hand-writing *whack*, etc etc etc
whack, whack, whack....
I didn't know much about what to do as a mother, and admit it
now. My own mum exhausted or preoccupied usually, so what
did I learn watching her? My idea to escape to overseas and find
a new life where I could care for Coltrane there, a dream, a silly
fancy. Before I left New Zealand I truly believed it was the

country's fault my life had turned out so disappointing, harsh, hurtful and empty of genuine kindness.

Mum only gathered herself into attentive mode when I grew older. She was probably less tired then with my brothers away from home. Dad behaved like callousness was normal, even wise.

But I had considered my past when I decided to keep Coltrane, and pushed some behaviour into the *never again* basket. I didn't hit my son, at least I knew that much to change. But neither could I imagine precisely what to do instead, just tried explanations for why some behaviour wasn't allowed and some time out. Only knew it was wrong when older people hit me so often, when they didn't listen to us and smiled over trouble like it didn't exist; grasped at another idea and tried it instead.

My son Coltrane had lived at my parents' after I'd found our routine impossible to manage. University and childcare combined an impossible task, with evictions and flatting issues overwhelming. No one else as supportive as I needed. A single parent's life is such a trial. They find you guilty of so much, the public, officials, the government, your family, even friends sometimes. But I did want to care for Coltrane, myself. I did my best. It didn't work out.

So sorry now.

Back in New Zealand, without an income or any savings, I survived at my parents for a while.

Paxton lived with his family, 80 miles away as it was then (100 kilometres north).

A dreary main street pub provided employment for me in my home town. My vast, sophisticated experience pulling pints overseas mentioned in the interview, the manager smiled with delight and I was in. Local bar managers liked bar staff from London, possibly knowing we worked like slaves from 7am til 10pm or 11pm at night. Cleaners and bar staff a combo in London, we vacuumed, polished, washed glasses, served, restocked shelves, lived-in upstairs and even with a few hours break in the afternoon, were in-house servants, daily. One day to ourselves a week.

Life as a barmaid in my home town was bliss by comparison.
Hard yakker in bars in London, and dreary weather, the black
air, the pressure of crowds; Paxton and I also fell out overseas
more than a few times. His flirting an affront too. Once it was
with Marianne Faithful but I didn't know who the blonde in a
fur coat at the end of the Chelsea bar really was, at the time. I'm
not sure that was the point.
Ginger Baker from Cream also drank in our pub. He'd stride in
with a wild stare, tiny dogs at his heels. A long tan overcoat
flying about, and with his reddish hair, a startling figure. Led
Zepplin's road manager drank at Stars in the Sky too. Fierce, a
bearded individual with a plump face who people whispered
about as if he'd hit them if he heard what they said. Celebrity
clientele, rock and roll royalty, a glimpse of a world glossy with
magazine cred.

Then I'd whisked myself away. Disappeared back into
Nowhereland.
A town surrounded with cows, same as usual but so unfamiliar,
living apart from Paxton.
Coltrane's cheery face and the clever, intriguing things he said
made up for so much. My son grown so much in almost two
years. Toys we'd carefully chosen and sent back were great
surprises, but I think I made a better present.
In my down time, I figured Paxton's mother arranged his trip
overseas to make him escape the punk band, to get away from
more street fights she perhaps saw coming, to make sure he
adapted to his shocking injury properly. Possibly also a
relocation to get away from me. She'd asked his uncle to pay for
Paxton's fare to France.
Facts and probabilities slowly revealed themselves like artifacts
left in sand, when wind blows away the grains. I wondered about
such matters, but then, I'd travelled all the way back because of
my son.
Paxton's mother only did what she thought best. Good on her.
Human beings do usually try their hardest and do their best, I'd
decided. It's easy to look at someone else's life from the outside
and think what you'd do, say, or think, but we're each alone in

our bubble of world. Everyone different.

My Coltrane grew up without my visits for months. He lived at my mum and dad's.

Over and over I went thinking about this like I'd lost something I had to find, trying to make sense in quiet moments; no idea at that time that my inability to focus and difficulty with relationships needed treatment, nor that Highly Sensitive People like me require time away from others, out of the public eye. Troubles tossed me around like weather or rough seas, without warning. Inside a clanging, live machine, I'd grow close to understanding something important but an unexpected noise interrupted, a whir took me in a new random direction. If only I could just concentrate I'd plan a way to care for Coltrane and live in Auckland, it had to work out somehow.

Thoughts broke into fragile bubbles then popped.

Imagination couldn't reinvent Paxton and I fighting either. No happy ending about to appear and neither of us pretended to have joyous pathways planned. We liked to fight almost as much as we loved our other passions, art, music, books, sex, and food. In books from the library various psychologists and therapists theorised. I read, 'The more sexual interest exists in a relationship, often the more such a couple also indulges other passions including a tendency to argue and fight.'

In film stories, however, I had to recall, the couple usually fought with both at fault. But often, the woman some day calmed down completely. She kindly allowed the man his plans, his command. Later, when she really needed something, her charm caused her man to comply. Men behaved like a pampered cat, or with the snap-to of a beloved pooch. Women tamed men, but did not use their power too often to get their own way. The School of Old Movies so easy to follow, however real life truly bewildered me. Paxton and I, our best illumination was a full moon.

A lack of discretion also one of my failings. Back at my parents' place I needed to face a few facts, they appeared so obvious there. Many times, Paxton appeared somewhat crushed when I'd received particular letters in London. My friend David back home only wrote and told me about his new girlfriend, however, who sang in a band. 'I found out what it feels like to be a

groupie,' he joked. David always said to 'stay happy' when he
signed off. One or two pages, chatty, pleasant letters.
Reading them, I felt Paxton's eyes on me but didn't care. He'd
created the rule. Paxton cheated first. If he was allowed to then
so was I. And a letter from an old friend wasn't wrong.
Life needed to make sense. My going back over the past, now
that I lived back in a place where almost nothing happened, this
served me with material to sort, rearrange and try to
understand.

When I'd only just arrived overseas and we stayed at his uncle's
in France, he'd hinted I probably slept around when he was
away, but I confronted him, 'Me? Never mind me. You've slept
with other women. I know you did. Someone told me.'
In the darkness we lay there a while. It felt like something heavy
pushed down on my whole body. The knowledge I had nowhere
to go if I needed to leave.
A murmur at first, 'Well, I suppose I should say....' He confessed;
every single affair and casual moment of sex described, '... and I
also slept with the woman behind the bar, at this gig out West.
Didn't find out her name. We did it in this cupboard under the
stairs. Then I slept with two girls on that bus trip....' It took him
about a half an hour.
Sobbing, my chest ached like he'd punched me. 'Why tell me?
Why hurt me so much?' Exhausted, I couldn't easily get up and
leave the room.
His reply gentle but with a dig in it, 'I wanted you to know the
kind of person I was, to see if you still loved me.'
Shocked silence. If I said I hated him, what then? His voice so
deceptively light, as if wanting me to believe he cared, but did
he? Sobbing, due to the litany of infidelity, and my resisting a
push to have me confess in return. It appeared so obvious, he'd
told me, now I had to reciprocate.
In the dark, in this narrow bed in a foreign land way away across
the world, knowing Paxton wanted me to *be honest*. But if
anything close to what I'd done in that regard was revealed, he'd
possibly self-righteously kick me out into the alien French night.
Our planned glorious European excursion gone, my dream

destroyed. I couldn't plan or travel alone, would never find a
place to live with my son Coltrane and feel at last free, (which I
hoped for), excited by the world. My focus on anything too
public, orderly or regimented truly weak. My talents lay in
making things, writing and drawing - and disagreements - not
with timetables and schedules, boarding buses and trains on
time, and who would protect me?
Nothing said, prone in the dark, crying until I fell asleep.
The next day a blur. My eyelids the size and colour of sun-ripe
tomatoes. Emotional damage internally crushes your will, cracks
plans, ideas, beliefs, your very core weaker.

Now I imagine Paxton wanted to hurt me for what he imagined
happened or what someone told him did occur while we lived
apart.

Then, I wandered the bedroom saying I felt jet-lagged, needed
to rest, and slept off my injuries. Inhabiting a cloud-land,
sensations produced by pheromones and cupid's mischief. Our
love affair a sports match or hunting expedition, score cards in a
perverse almanac.
Gradually strained and strange overseas, actors in a play we
knew all the lines for but no longer cared about. This theatre of
two travelling the wondrous world.

At home we needed energised lingo, new people to remind
ourselves we spun better yarns than most. I never thought to
discuss what we'd do together once we touched New Zealand
soil again. We needed to see our families and later would
arrange something together, why not?
By the time we flew back, it felt entirely natural not to live
together. My parents, with Coltrane, drove me home and
Paxton's mum and dad drove him to their place. We went in
opposite directions with barely a good bye.
In my home town, I believed we were still in a relationship,
albeit apart. A job to make some money and then I'd move back
to the city. I certainly called Paxton on the phone often enough.
Paxton remarked later *he* believed when I went back with my

mum and dad, he'd not see me again.

His assertion shocked me, but I hid my reaction, disliked Paxton knowing when I felt hurt. My pain seemed to give him a perverse satisfaction. Possibly he only said such a thing to see me blanche. I grew to expect that was how men behaved and we women apparently took it, but that knowledge wasn't conscious, it took up some foggy place and simply clouded me at times. When I eventually moved back to the city, we did go out to see movies or a band sometimes but didn't move in together like I wanted.

The mania for everyone possible dressing in black had not quite yet enveloped the 1980s. It was only 1981, many women piled on asymmetrical geometric knits in yellow and red, or green and white, pale pink and white, striped red and pink leggings, or cutesy bright pale pink or lemon or pale blue fluffiness matched with dark lace. Men in powder blue, baggy dress pants or harsh deep reds and blues, and red or blue zipped leather jackets with pointy lapels and shoulders. Teens and daring twenty-somethings imitated characters from Star Trek (the original). Nightclub crowds lived on a planet where angles mattered more than elegance.

Occasionally I saw someone who looked like a punk but didn't know them. This felt strange, we used to know everyone who dressed that way. But we'd changed, and maybe our old friends had too, those who hadn't moved overseas or been lost somehow? Neither Paxton nor I looked much like punks now.

Only a few weeks after I'd moved back to Auckland, a group of friends dressed up for Halloween. Paxton had celebrated the festival overseas. 'I like the costumes. Y'know, witches, goblins....' No one else knew much about it.

He gave us pointers, 'Vampires, that kind of thing. Darkness allowed to reign. One night a year.'

Eight or so of us in witch, vampire, and ghost costumes drank beers in my flat, then someone suggested, 'Let's go into town. We all look so fantastic.' Vampires chomping fangs, or witches holding on pointy hats for the most part, we trooped off to the

London Bar. A change of scene, about 9pm.

Striking in full costume, smiling, nine of us through the door of the pub. Warm air hit, the place jam-packed. A crowd four deep along the bar waiting to be served. At the back, we stood more or less together. Almost the entire pub of several hundred people turned to us, glaring, not a laugh or interested quizzical remark, but blatantly repulsed. Some muttered insults or angry complaints.

I looked around frantically. Had someone walked in who these people hated?

A man in a white shirt with folded arms stated he was the manager and we wouldn't be served. 'No punks, not allowed.' Everyone scowled, a few shouted furious comments, 'You filth. Scum.'

Used my best loud voice as cheerily as possible, 'It's Halloween. Goblins and witches?' I watched the man look around our motley crew and take in a witch in a black pointy hat. She smiled, revealed her two blackened front teeth. My flatmate put her fangs back in, and he could see her spider brooch at the throat of her white shirt, under a black jacket with the collar turned up. I laughed and went on, 'It's not celebrated here, but maybe next year have a promotion in your pub. Could be a real money-spinner. Halloween.' Elocution lessons years before. Made myself sound posh.

He leaned a little closer and his face softened but he didn't unfold his arms.

My smile had to work.

Then he nodded. Most on-lookers didn't care about kids in costumes, no one watching us now.

Drinks in hand, but only one each. Soon we abandoned the beige, pale blue, and souped up brigade. Everyone remarked on the uptight crowd. 'Like we walked into a redneck bar in an American film.'

'When did punks become enemies of pubs?'

'O, there's been some trouble since you were away.'

'That crowd's not even straight-fashionable. Did you see them? So conservative.'

We'd returned to a population who loathed punk rockers. In our absence, the infamous boot boys, boot girls, and other violent fools made punk fearful. Attack without irony. A few victims died, some attackers went to jail, others wrecked by drugs, excessive drinking, whooping concrete acrobatics, fractures and splits. Soon, no pub or club in the city allowed anyone in dressed in anything black or raggedy. Not one darkly clad figure gained entry for a beer or G&T. A blanket ban, enacted in only just over a year and a half while we'd been overseas.

Paxton left his black leather jacket (all zips and buckles) at home then unless going to a private party.

I hung up my bits of black and vinyl bondage top for good, retired from the dark circus; clothes reduced to novelties. Batty old things at the back of my wardrobe.

Fashions changed but we stayed together and resurrected silly moments, reminisced. Our history, we wanted it to mean something.

The heady summer before, we found an hour to kiss and red ants bit his knee, by the shore of fabled Loch Lomond. Lake waters floated with swans. Sunny grasses and shrubbery, summer flowers bloomed, hot kisses and half our clothes half-removed, skin on skin after weeks of sleeping apart in hostels. Urgent cries, moans pushing desire.

Afterward his knee red, raw and we looked for cream in the first aid kit. 'Could feel them biting but didn't want to stop.' He grinned.

And Paxton left over twenty Easter eggs for me around our room at the pub, Stars in the Sky. He took an early shift and I slept on. Awoke to a trail of coloured foil-wrapped eggs, pale blue, pinky-red, deep yellow, a couple mauve and a few patterned with swirls, a scattering of treats around our attic. A row of teeny eggs followed the line of an electrical cord to a lamp. We shared them later, kindness wasn't always rare, I need to recognise that fact.

One night, I dreamed we lived King Arthur's legend. Stag antlers suited Paxton, a fire ceremony while I mixed potions.

Avalon had long ago disappeared into the mist, but now reappeared as real as a kitchen, as true as a fresh piece of motorway, as fine as blown glass.

Eventually my hints, plans and demands back home in New Zealand effected a decision. 'It's a small place close to the city, but you'll like it,' Paxton told me.
New paint for our kitchen kept me busy.
Time would alter the feeling of dislocation, I told myself.
I asked Coltrane to stay the weekend a few times. My secret hope that Paxton would one day say he could live with us.
For weeks or months we'd talk, joke, share plans, Paxton and I. Then I'd not like how he treated me and say so, or suspect he was scheming to have another woman, or that he was sleeping with someone else already. After every crackling fight or spat, Paxton slept with someone else or disappeared, or both. Then we'd make up and start over like a corny song, like musak on repeat.
If only it was a movie and someone could just wrap the shoot, send us home. At least I'd have been paid and have something vaguely positive to show for the experience. Paxton soon disappeared for two days with some teenager in a short pink dress. Just walked off from a party at work.

He said later, 'She needed a ride home.'
'A great reason to walk out without explanation, then not reappear 'til 2am and disappear the next evening, wordless.'
No fight as an excuse this time before he'd walked away. I think he blanked out when he drank too much and followed some kind of reflex to only please himself.
Before that work party loomed, I'd put on some weight, and talked endlessly about plans, loved my workmates, and socialised with them after-hours. Not the stay-at-home and do-what-he-wanted version of a slim woman so often mentioned as the best way he thought I needed to be.
Next move, Paxton shopping for a girlfriend, cruising around to find a new one, more along the lines he desired.
One fine Saturday afternoon I explained, 'I'm sorry. You're out

all the time. I don't know where. Off with that girl at our work
party, in front of.... I have to move out.'
Some resistance but then he gave in, seemed not to mind.

In only a week or so three friends found a place for us in the
middle of the city. At night, after work, I packed carefully and it
was like I was getting out of jail.

I mentioned the five flights of stairs at Soho Apartments being a
pain, in passing. Paxton suddenly loved to hear me talk and
wanted to see the apartment. In my excitement I took him there.
My entire load of boxes and bags he carried up the stairs.
We spent half the day in bed.
Closeness our forte. We metamorphised our breath and blood
and sweat into a fantastic drug. Doubt dissolved, our inhibitions
faded. Desire arose. His hands over my silk skin, mine slipped
under his clothing, our kisses sweet, soft, then harder. Breath
faster and faster, a magnificent song, naked and joyous. White
sheets cool, I slid and lifted to meet his thrusts, flipped him over
to sit high and push, harder.

Then he disappeared for a week, he didn't call, wasn't home
when I rang.

A maze of behaviour. My head hurt from bashing continuously
into the same dead end wall. A twisted time we built together.
Blockades everywhere. The familiar dent in this imaginary wall
nevertheless hurt.
My puzzle, I could rebuild it, I decided, but the facts blurred.
What clever metaphor dresses up stupidity for long? The picture
fell apart.
Just us.
There.
Blatant as a pair of abandoned ships.
All our fights were in private, I realised one evening lying awake
and going over the wreckage. Our own perverse entertainment;
others never heard our screaming matches and snarky moments.
They'd hear we'd broken up yet again, or see us glare across

crowded rooms, but not see the actual battles.

In public, Paxton almost always managed to get me to smile around others, when we were together again.

If I ever ranted at a club or party he disappeared pronto. This calmed me down.

Later, he'd lecture, 'Other people do not want to see your lack of self control. Discuss things at home.'

Desperate to get off our sick seesaw. Downtime a life-shaking thump onto concrete.

Every time we disagreed, fully enacted in private, he stormed off, or I did. Paxton usually slept with someone else. But we'd be together yet again in time.

Seamless surface romance, passionate kisses and closeness in public, but something torn and repaired too often for comfort. Our secret damage. Why?

Realisation eventually dawned. A solution often appears following a good night's sleep. Paxton didn't like anyone else involved. Our fights embarrassing, they could make him look bad; the tattered, repaired aspects of our love affair. Therefore, if I thoroughly insulted Paxton in public, he'd never make it up with me again, because he'd look foolish. All the elements added up. Mathematics presented hope as surely as a triangle has three sides and a circle is perfect.

Naturally, I'd also played a part in every nasty word, each screaming match and nut-off., but I was suicidal some of the time. Often so depressed I could barely move. It had to stop. My visits to counsellors off and on taught me that much.

After his terrible public humiliation, I imagined, with the image of true love which he liked to portray between us totally gone, later when I weakly changed my mind and wanted Paxton back like always, he'd refuse me if I'd made him look bad enough. If I'd made it clear to others that we really fought, horribly, he wouldn't want me back.

Fine for *me* to accept back a flawed, cheating, power-crazy man who belittled me in public, but not fine for his woman to insult him so everyone heard, so they knew I thought so little of Paxton.

My plan to open an escape hinged on the fact that when he refused to have me back, I'd simply pass through the ensuing tears the way anyone endures a storm of emotion. Old movie aesthetics promoted hopefulness. Misty violins in mind. I knew it'd be painful, but I was sick of the craziness we called a relationship.

This stunning idea also meant I needed to wait and see. If we didn't grow close to break-up again, we were meant to stay together. But if my man strayed once more or treated me like I didn't matter one more time, to the point where I lost my temper, then the whole mess could be cleaned away, finally. Over, gone, finito, as fast as a film frame passes by. I'd find a real life hero, instead of only wishing I loved someone who treated me with respect, someone to count on who stayed loyal and truly kind. Above everything else I longed for enduring kindness, true friendship, and had noticed mutual respect between others. The mystery of those intimate and happy was bewildering, it made me cry to think I'd never know such a thing.

Kindness looked so simple, why couldn't I have some? Desperation as urgent as if trying to elude a kidnapper to save my life, but I'd trapped myself. My own kindness to Paxton could've perhaps saved what we had. But that type of realisation was difficult to see when you're tying yourself in knots and excuses.

One night, listening to music at the Six Month Club, both standing close near the dancefloor, I felt Paxton stiffen. He'd seen someone who alarmed him? I hoped we weren't about to get attacked and looked about.

Then he slid well away past a couple of people standing nearby. Amazed at this glide, I watched him, all in black, side-step through the fancy lights.

In The Six Month Club (six months before it was demolished to make way for Aotea Square, the name changed by the month as a countdown, but it'd just opened), a long dark hall of a place with heavy red curtains framing an old-fashioned low stage at the other end, above a wooden dancefloor.

The DJ box at right angles to the stage (where bands sometimes played). Snazzy dressers and super-freaks crowded on in. Young designers clutched their notebooks. Musicians patrolled their turf or kicked back. Office girls pretended super-stardom and suburban boys in the latest clothes prayed they looked hip enough for someone to love them or even like them, just a night would do. Eyes everywhere, a crowd of wicked or wishful watchers and conversation sensationalists.

In a few improvised steps he'd made himself alone.

My stomach felt like someone had punched it.

A dark woman in a bright lemon tulle-skirted dress smiled at Paxton. Ga-ga for a few moments, Paxton simpered at this stranger who ruffled his black hair, ran her fingers through it and held out the long white strands at the front as if about to lead him away by them.

The DJ played on, music flowed from one track to another, speakers pumping. An animated crowd matched the beats. In the bright seethe of young things and older famous we stood together only minutes before, watched the DJ. Both looking fine and as far as I knew feeling happy, together. Instead of smiling at this woman from *beside me* so we'd all talk, Paxton took sidesteps. Instant single man.

Mysteriously out all night recently too I had to recall, when I'd been waiting for him to come home. Excuses as glib as if rehearsed, 'O, passed out at the guys' flat, Why Street. Watched a video....'

Now, this slim brunette in sunny tulle. Daring femmes lately wore that ironic twist on 50s style. She messed his hair like she'd already been close enough to nibble his ear. He leaned in as if to nuzzle her neck, but writhed on the spot instead like a delirious puppy. The fingers of his mechanical hand clenched and unclenched at his side, catching the light.

Thoughts spat, my frying pan mind heating up. But those two simmered together. Some kind of tongs could've been an asset, hooked into her high heels, flung over a fence to a pool of crocodiles. She'd tumble over wrapped up in tatters of finery to disappear in a gulp.

Drunk, admittedly, it took very little alcohol to affect me. And Paxton had already sunk twice my intake.

All those many nine years of this infidelity – our true love
bipolar affair disorder. One moment up with heavenly bodies in
our own galaxy of wonder, the next crashed and bewildered,
knee-deep in murk with painful injuries. This did make me
nastier.
Hurly burly music and dancing surrounding us, while I watched
with disdain. Feline detachment and a need to pounce, to rip.
Ancient Egyptians believed cats can enter the realm of the dead.
I prowled a netherworld. Whatever died in Paxton's nightclub
encounter could be easily dragged way out of sight.
Dismembered rotten ruin, a pile of forgotten debris left to form
dust and be blown away after I played cruelly with it for a while.
Certainly, the dead-end in my maze, our blocked thoroughfare
needed knocking completely down.
Wriggling on the spot, coloured lights swirling, Paxton an over-
sexed, juvenile animal. A few people pointedly looked at him,
laughed. The dark woman tossed her curly hair.
A choice existed. I could leave.
Eventually when Paxton tired of this latest fling, he'd call. We'd
meet and I'd forgive him. The path of our life ahead lay in that
pattern, forever. Our old dead-end a landmark, familiar, blood
patina on bricks where my head pounded infinitely, Stupid Alley,
No Exit, Fools' End.
Decided to pretend I didn't care.
He could wait.
To the bar; I ordered another drink.
Sister Sledge cruised from the sound system, We are Family.
Made me smile. Music my saviour. I did a few dance-steps on
the spot. How cool someone had such a great family they wrote
a song about it. Not everyone was like me. And I could find
happiness too, surely.

Off up the stairs a few hours later, a short walk from the Six
Month Club, in my apartment building, trailing after Paxton,
who took off ahead. I for some reason took a side door and hid.
Maybe he'd just go home? The thought snapped into my mind,
foolishly.
In the dim corridor, smooth old concrete walls gave the place a

run-down castle atmosphere. The Soho building dated from the 1930s.

Relaxing to think I could be alone soon, just go up and into my place, cleanse off my make-up, get into bed, sleep. Smooth white cotton sheets against my nakedness. I leaned back against the wall and closed my eyes for a few seconds.

'Where are you?' Paxton shouted. I heard his footsteps, running up and down the stairs. He chased around. The gothic old place echoed, people could come out of their apartments and complain.

Futile to believe I could stay hidden, so I walked up the stairs and into the flat.

His pale skin and furious glare. 'Where were you? Don't just walk off from me.' His leather jacket creaked with gesticulating, zips jingled, his feet stomped in new black boots.

I flounced into my room and he nipped in after me.

I shouted, 'You walked off from me tonight. You're allowed to, but I'm not? You just slid away to fawn all over that woman.'

Instant calm, his eyes hooded. 'She was a friend. I wanted to say hello.'

'Yeah, right. Friend. How many other benign words have you got for screwing around?'

'Shut up,' he snarled.

'No, you shut up. You disgust me. You have the manners of a dog. A dumb, filthy dog. Sniffing up women's skirts like some animal, you....'

For a good half an hour that evening, Paxton and I shouted at each other. Upstairs boomed, we railed and screamed. My volume and diction surpassed his, my extraordinary clarity and noise dragged out every insult ever considered. Swearing, graphic details, 'Your pathetic need to stick yourself into any hole you find. What a bloody shameless piece of shit, pure excrement with a sex-drive. Animated sewage, that's all you are, stinking like the worst hell....'

The windows of my top floor flat wide open to the summer night as still and open as a stage set. Flatmates often shouted down to friends some greeting or instruction, voices carried as easily as a leaf in a breeze. Anyone passing now would hear us below in the street, each furious foolish word.

The fight to end all fights, a true city melodrama.

Trembling in danger and excitement, not wanting and wanting him to be gone, at the same time. Too late now.

Shouting about the girl in the club, into his face, my mouth wide, snarling, 'I suppose you were sleeping at her place the other night? I bet you wish I wasn't even there this time.'

Paxton shoved the heel of his hand into my mouth.

I fell backwards.

It hurt.

On my back, mouth on fire.

Ink falls into water. Nothing clean then unless the colour's used for words.

My mouth swelled and language roared forth, as if hatred was lava, consuming just like the entire night was eventually dark.

My room dim, Paxton stepped back against the hallway light. Huge, a dark shape against the pale wall behind him. Startled, like his solid frame could shatter at any moment.

Beside me two sash windows wide open to the still evening, to nighthawks walking home from clubs and parties. Many passers-by we knew so well they could've written books about us. In days to come they'd say enough to fill several volumes but we'd never want to read them. We weren't in the future however, we were caught in a fully present storm.

A stream of invective flew from me, a volcanic lake burst upon an ancient town below, a town that thought itself safe with stone walls and history. Fire engulfed everything and kept on burning. 'You'll never touch me again. Never enjoy me again with your pathetic tiny cock and your stupid slobber. You disgust me. I'm a woman, all woman. I need a man, not a grizzling little thing who wants all the lollies in the shop. Throws up when he takes too many. Want me to clean up your vile puke? Take your selfish, disgusting, ugly self away and never ever come near me again.' More too, far, far more, on and on. Refusing to stop in case he stepped back into the room from the doorway. My mouth hurt and I felt scared he'd really hit me next. A boxer, he knew how to wallop someone. His metal hand, would he use that?

My lip throbbed where he'd shoved me. Voice manifested against every brick of any dead-end and collapsed those traps. Sound blasted the room, blasted him and blasted the city outside, strewing great crashing bricks of noise everywhere, tumbled what we'd built down and down and down.

Paxton tugged on his leather jacket in the doorway, light behind him. He fled when I wouldn't shut up. Probably realising at that point that almost everyone we knew would hear about it the next day or knew already.

Every night-club closed a half hour before, city streets below teemed with clubbers walking home. Our people. Musicians, fans, record shop girls, journos for the entertainment pages, fashion-crazy kids and music buffs. My cool apartment building, Soho, held DJs, band members, fashion designers, shop girls, artists, and hairdressers until kingdom come, and my voice really did carry righteously to all. They'd certainly horribly discovered the hell Paxton and I lived in.

When my flatmate arrived home wide-eyed and asked if I was okay, she told me, 'I heard every word from a block away.'

Most friends soon told me I was well rid of him.

In the fashion-extreme shop where I worked, a few nights later, we enjoyed staff drinks around closing time. The large mirror by the counter gave me a head-to-toe view when I picked up scissors and started cutting my shoulder-length black hair off, close to the scalp. The other designers blinked in alarm at first but soon murmured encouragement and made sure I did a reasonable job. Nice sharp scissors from our workroom.

Snip, off with the long hair. Snip, a hank of it in hand. Snip, lighter and lighter, so light I'd levitate and hover just above the ground forever.

Off.

Hair about two centimetres long. The shortest since being a baby. Turned into a pixie.

Reborn, I ran a hand across my head and knew times had changed, enjoyed the feeling of air around my neck and ears. If I did regret insulting Paxton later, if I stupidly thought I could retreat from this decision, then my haircut would remind me. No return.

My lip went down after that horrific night, didn't bruise too much. Also, when sober after the headache wore off, I realised Paxton really had gone. He would not appear at any fancy wild club with his me-only smile, nor call with some smart remark to make me laugh. Close to a religious experience to feel so free, finally. Holy originality, blessed. Nothing could change this situation.

Quite as I knew already, Paxton detested my insults in public. He remained silent.

I took stock. Together more or less for nine years of stylish fiery passion, pleasurable insanity on occasion, a definite pleasant routine in any lull. Paxton once upon a good mood or fifty bought me lovely things and cooked spectacular brunches, sent flowers to my work, and talked me up when I felt down, many times.

All gone.

Our petty arguments and his stray dog ways also vanished. Put-downs directed at me which Paxton laughed over in crowded rooms, not ever going to happen again. His threatening looks at any male friend I ever had also stopped. Recurring pain and emotional labour to make things seem good when they weren't, done.

My extraordinary persistence in staying, meant I could endure. Now I knew I could bear trouble and make good most of the time, even with the worst. Stronger.

We'd also shared countless stunning moments, visited truly fabulous places, owned photographs and souvenirs to prove it. Paxton's mother probably did a victory dance in her designer lounge to think that at last he could find someone relatively normal, to marry and provide grandchildren who *he'd* fathered. I like to think the joy was spread around.

After hysterics faded to a mild obsession, I recovered. Stopped calling him, then saying nothing, just breathing like some insane stalker. Soon I turned to writing dire poetry and burning it. That passed, too.

I refurnished my mind, like a house after an earthquake.

Not sure what Paxton thought, except he finally took up with someone quite unlike me. She loved sports and had long red hair, lovely freckles, and a horse. Her parents owned a stud farm, and she married Paxton there under a gazebo hung with white muslin and lilies.

They later divorced.

When Paxton and I met again years later, on the night I'd opened a new business, we spoke briefly in a nightclub. Black walls and chrome furnishings, two bars made from the shiny silver grills of 1950s cars. DJs played in a glass cube above a black dancefloor. Almost everyone in black or white or grey. The beautiful cool congregated to listen, watch and shouted genially at each other over the incessant music.

My friend saw him first, 'Look, don't get upset. It's Paxton.'

She took my loud groan as interest. But it took a while before I noted he stood only a short distance away. Close to a plain-looking woman who appeared kind and, of course, attentive to him. An ice bucket between them held a bottle of champagne.

I'd just opened my new boutique that afternoon. Four hours of the fashion-possessed talking non-stop, wine clink clink clink, guests trying and buying. Wanted to dance, not talk with someone I needed to forget.

He saw me and smiled. Still so handsome.

Fascination in gear long enough for me to pause and readily slide a little closer (or maybe he did, or we both did). Wanted to see what he'd say, I guess.

He whispered to his female companion. Soon he left to go upstairs, then she blurted at me, 'I'm not his girlfriend. His girlfriend's in Australia.'

I noted the French champagne and smiled, wryly. Either she lied for some reason or he intended to seduce her, either way I didn't much care. Somewhat numb.

Music oonst oonst oonst on and on. Plain pale lights played across the empty dancefloor, early evening. Berlin Club enjoyable before he arrived. No reason to leave.

My friend and I danced a while, then returned to our spot by the long, high, black and chrome built-in leaning bar which cut across the middle of the room.

When the woman Paxton was with went to the restroom, he walked down and stood facing me, the narrow bar between us. We regarded each other.

Same as ever, I liked his face. Nothing else seemed to matter except the soft way we looked at each other. He leant over and kissed me on the mouth, really kissed me. Soft lips exploring a few seconds.

Although I kissed back since I liked kissing him (could kiss Paxton now and not mind it in itself, as if a kiss is isolated like a lovely island), fury also arose.

Something lay there cooked for a dinner he'd arrived too late for and it had boiled over. I pulled away and I said with a sneer, 'It's still there, isn't it?' Meaning my anger. I really wanted to hit him and have it hurt.

He nodded and looked at me in this thoughtful, regretful way. Maybe he was agreeing about something else.

Then he left in a hurry.

Someone at the club told Paxton, I found out later, he needed to ditch the woman he was with and spend the night with me, as if *I'd suggested this.* I told them they were wrong, certainly mistaken. Angry, I shouted and they apologised, but the evening bleached out, frayed.

I went home.

It's shameful how I stage-managed our break-up but I meant what I shouted at him. My lack of strength to blame. If I'd been capable of simply leaving and never looking back, or living with his lusts, insults, and attempts at controlling me (as if they were not my concern), it could've all been far more civilised.

Our story still makes me cry occasionally. I so loved to love him. But emotional abuse involves blows and pain no one else can see, however, they hurt too much. My tears brief nowadays, nothing like my past weeping for hours and hours after our fights when the next day dissolved in recovery and bruised feelings. My swollen tearful face, the dazed places my mind ran away to.

Some memories bring smiles. Europe, when he carried my pack for me up a mountain, for instance, or there's real alarm when I think we could've been eaten by a Black Forest bear in our sleeping bags. Thinking about our possible escape from a wild animal, I did want to call Paxton, but never tried to find his number. A feeling of wanting contact too, after our Berlin Club encounter, phased in like music from a passing car, then dwindled away to nothing because I let it pass, the traffic of my desire.

Paxton and I enjoyed scintillating places, met fascinating characters and loved so much, for nine years. Not everyone sits in the butterfly house and sings opera. True love finer than any film, play, book, or music, and we held some genuine regard for each other beyond admiring what we each looked like, great fashion sense, and how well we danced.

Our selfishness, and my belief in being irreparably broken, halted development. To be simplistic about it, no idea then that fear of intimacy stopped me building relationships, nor realising that I deserved happiness.

It took years of analysis to discover it's a lie we damaged people are not able to be well, that we can bear another close to us, may reject fear of pain. Lies are still pushed by bullies who want to isolate their targets. We can be happy and own our sadness too. Anything can be fixed. It just takes some work.

These stories are my labouring at the mending, and it's working too. The truth does set us free. The fresh places I now find myself in are travels in themselves, even if I never leave the country.

So, it worked out that in the cafe where my old friends wanted news of punk days gone by, possibly for a laugh, I couldn't speak about Paxton like a joke on a whim. Our love wasn't to entertain anyone asking, as if it was a mere script or a soap opera.

Truly too, all cruelty springs from weakness, as Lucius Annaeus Seneca, born in 5 BC, wrote. Paxton lacked the strength to resist his lust and pride. I lacked the strength to sustain our

togetherness, and it was horribly cruel to us both, what I finally
did.
We loved each other's beauty, loved music, dancing, travel, loved
to talk, plan; falling, always falling. If we'd waited a few weeks
after that first night, after when I saw him gleaming at The
Globe, if we'd slowly discovered more things in common, if
we.... But it's futile to play the 'if game', Tony Fomison, the great
artist said. What's happened has gone.
Our crash and burn.

In the beginning both Paxton *and* I could've sung Sympathy for
the Devil, our own forked tails perhaps were concealed most of
the time but grew evident when we exercised our selfishness.
We forgot that love accepts imperfections, undoes the devil, love
stops the punch, the snap and stab. Love makes hopelessness
dimmer through gentleness, a filter. We both could've been
kinder to ourselves and each other. Faith, a leap, hovering
together, breathing underwater, travelling through outer space
without machinery. Everyone wants to fly, just like the Prince
song, even though planes and rockets do crash. But nothing, no
words, no thinking, no length of time makes how we treated
each other acceptable. My narrow vengeful behaviour, albeit in
desperation, only made things worse. The awful clarity of
hindsight a lesson in planning ahead with love instead, in future.

Paxton told me once he wasn't someone I could keep throwing
myself against, and he was tired of being the villain. So Paxton
has his wish, now. I deliberately slept with someone else when I
found out he'd cheated. I lost heart. Later, I ruined his trust in
me on purpose in public, to make him stay away, because we
were both too nasty together, too often. Completely sick of it.
We're both wicked now, gothic bookends of our at times
fabulous story with too many words between us to count or find
our way back to the tale in common that we shared. Friends in
places where sleep reaches.

Fib Street and BJ's Safety

U can turn me 2day like a planet
2 find a better orbit, 4 a betta way.

I kno u kno hot melts cool,
the fierce way u get 2 me, girl.

> *- Heat by KingKing1986*

Ten blenders in disarray along a table in the bright, scarred kitchen. Mega-cocktails for hours already obviously drunk while an infamous skinhead band played in the garden. In a black vinyl and leopard-print fake fur Secret Service minidress, I strode through the Fib Street party, realising how late I was at a glance. Bodies piled on huge sofas in the lounge, a tangle of arms and legs, bleary faces, and hair awry. A few managed to stagger around the house but most bumped into things or could barely talk. The fantastically inebriated state of almost everyone matched the extreme violence of the fast loud music from the sloping back lawn.

Their last gig, someone told me, the riot squad broke up the crowd who'd spilled into the street and wrecked vehicles along the road to the corner, where they threatened to attack a car sales yard. If a sound could be furious red, they played it.

Fib Street. Waiwai Street - no one bothered to correctly pronounce Waiwai. They'd say, 'Why Street? Ask me no questions, I'll tell you no lies.' A lie was a fib so there you are, Fib Street. Sometimes they said Why Street for variation.

Most of the boys lived in denial of liver and brain damage, and my hysterical stage of heartbreak demanded the stupidity of lying to myself. Their party a perfect disaster, superbly suitable. Late, but I walked about the huge old house and smiled towards a few recognisable faces.

By the back door, alone looking down at the band and their screaming screech, I wondered why I'd bothered. Someone raced up beside me, I heard their panting. A tall guy with black hair held a cask of wine without the box, we called them bladders. An ugly way to carry drink or take it. He looked wrecked. I smiled at him anyway.

In a second he stood far too close, slobbered all over my ear, and spluttered with rancid alcoholic breath at my profile, 'I saw you first. Anyone asks, I saw you first. Okay?'

Wet slime over my ear made me want to run, to find something to wipe it off. Hid my revulsion with an inane smile, but edged away, said I had to find the loo. Got out of there fast.

Waiting for my taxi home by the corner away from the party, I wiped at my ear with tissues. Queasy as if I'd eaten bad food. What a disaster that had been, I should never have walked in the door.

The riot squad arrived again and I thanked God I'd already left the place. 'Hup. Hup, Hup,' they chanted down the road and into the broken concrete driveway. Ranks of clear visors and black helmets looked like a costume. If I hadn't heard what they liked to do with their batons, I would've laughed.

The next time I trotted along to a Fib Street party, an early arrival, much better. In a long red dress with a full circle skirt I sat on the front verandah. Two sofas, one comfortable enough. Could've been a lone good-time girl from a wild west saloon, playing a part set back in time, living someone else's days and nights. Strange hope in others' laughter, the stereo rockin' sounds from inside and the crowd already tossing smart, light remarks around. I dimly recalled feeling the same way once upon a happiness.

Without saying, and only half-admitting it to myself, I also knew Paxton could attend. Wanted to see how I reacted, faced with my ex's charisma and doubtless bravado. He no longer needed to cover up any flirting to save my feelings, not that he often did before.

The stereo pounded on in a room by the porch. I kept imagining Greek Gods playing ancient instruments in the evening sky and them laughing at me.

What was I doing?

Paxton and I had parted in awful circumstances. Nasty things I shouted at him so everyone outside could hear, and he'd shoved me in the mouth, so I fell onto the bed. In the months since we didn't speak if we did happen to be in the same place. I usually avoided anywhere he'd prefer. My ex tried to get me kicked out of the flat I moved to when we were evicted after our apartment was gentrified.

My friend told me she'd told him, 'They've been asked to leave their great rental in town. Soho Apartments are being renovated. She's nowhere else to go.'

Our funky, if run-down, apartment block being prettified and fumigated. Arrows and lines scrawled on walls were directions to builders. Gussied into a 50s idea of New York with a blue canvas canopy trimmed in white over the walkway into the foyer, and an elevator that worked.

Not swish or rich enough to stay there.

Only just settled into the new house near Paxton's flat, so I could've stayed home, sorted bookcases, and avoided the party. But I sat there, a freak in a cage of people we knew. *See what she does. What she says when the handsome muscle man walks by and hisses some nasty name, or sticks his lovely nose in the air. What she does when the acrobat refuses to do a double flip just for her.*

A street of parked cars, but no one passed along the footpath. A still night on the edge of the inner city, and warm. I could take a taxi down the road at that late hour. Just hail a cab.

To my right, a few footsteps loud on the porch. BJ (Boris Janovich), sat down and handed over a beer. Freshly opened, cold, it tasted good, malty and dry.

'You sitting out here all night?' His green-eyed smile in every word.

I laughed a little and whispered, 'Not necessarily.'

'You know, sometimes I see you, and it's like you're on a mountain. So far away. Now though, now I feel like just holding you and keeping you safe.' He spoke my name and it gave me a warm feeling.

'It's been strange lately, BJ.'

'Yeah. I heard.'

Sat in the evening summer air like a long married couple, watching the world go by from our front porch. A few moths bumbled in light spilling from the open door. The stereo played something easy now, reggae. 'Thought you could do with some company,' his husky voice tender.

I smiled by way of reply but didn't look at him.

Cheeky sod; maybe a year since we'd met. The only one in that flat who didn't regard tall, confident Paxton, my ex, with awe or fear. BJ often teased Paxton, called him silly names, challenging things my ex said, making fun of his ideas. In the pub, strong, healthy, facing off against each other. Paxton indisputably handsome and square-jawed, BJ also tall, but heftier and with more of a sparkle than a gleam about him. Without Paxton's model boy charm, instead, BJ carried extraordinary intelligence and kindness in his green eyes and cracking remarks. Paxton relied more on looking handsome and his velvety voice for persuasion.

BJ spun me that line about wanting to hold me, my needing company, waited. Fishing. I could sense his intention but didn't feel like it was a threat or a push, I believed he did care for me, and it felt pleasant like late afternoon sunshine on a free day.

Sometimes he flicked through channels on the TV so fast, images and sounds made a crazy kind of music. BJ plugged into some genius cut-up with the remote buttons and played it for whoever happened to be in the room. Laughed at things we couldn't see, but not in any crazy way. He didn't make me feel afraid. Usually he drew people in with his smile or humour. Even Paxton lit up when BJ walked into the room, no matter what he'd said or done before.

Now, next to him I mused on what he'd said...wanting to hold me. Turned the idea around, measured it against what BJ usually did. He never annoyed people cruelly (even with Paxton he was witty, not cutting), people didn't talk behind his back, saying he'd ripped someone off or done the dirty. 'You want t'just hold me?' Turning sideways to see him more clearly, I smiled. 'That's all?'

'For now. Whatever you want.' Almost purring. Big smile.

'Okay then, why not.' I shocked myself, but it felt better to walk down to BJ's room than to keep sitting out on the porch by myself.

We walked down the hall and BJ murmured, 'I think Paxton just arrived.'

'I don't care,' I replied.

The front door opened, it creaked, I guess Paxton saw us walk into BJ's room. My bright red skirt flowed behind. Paxton shouted, 'BJ. Man, I thought your driving was bad. But look at your taste in women.' Jovial but with this split in the words, like he'd broken the sentence and put the phrases back together in a hurry.

I lay my forehead against the cool wooden back of BJ's door now shut tight, and closed my eyes.

BJ stood by my shoulder and his hand hovered near my arm. 'O, don't cry,' he said.

'I'm not crying. I'm just waiting for him to go. I want to use the loo.'

We both stood there.

Fine to be inside BJ's room while Paxton strode about the rather echoey hallway. His heavy, loose walk and the way he swung his shoulders, I knew it like a song. Could see him in my mind's eye. Willed the picture away.

After a while, I asked BJ to check the house and Paxton had gone.

Soon undressed completely, I got into bed. So did BJ. A high bed, sheets clean and white, soft duvet on top and the room clear of anything ornamental, pale walls, plain wooden shelves with books, and a chest of drawers.

Warm against my body, BJ held me until I fell asleep, held me like he really did want me to be safe. Another's skin against mine, warm, some smooth. Hair on his arms and chest a contrast, his soap and musk smell pleasing. Maybe it was his size, maybe the way he usually joked all the time and now didn't (this evening he simply smiled), I felt protected.

Safety existed after all.

Drifted off.

Slept better than I had for weeks.

Early morning, my whole body energised and tingling, he

trawled his hand over the soft skin of my thighs, arms, stomach,
and then my back, drew me closer. I moaned, kissed his neck.
We growled together.

It surprised me that someone overweight would throw off the
covers in the bright light of morning to seduce me so openly, but
BJ didn't care if I saw his large belly. We enjoyed each other for
a good half hour. Sunshine beamed into the plainly furnished
room.

Paxton had said if he ever put on weight he'd hide in a
gymnasium until he lost it all. If I ever gained a little, Paxton
acted repulsed. But I refused to think about someone who'd hurt
me so much.

The bedroom brimmed with light.

After we arose, BJ behaved like he always did around me,
friendly but not too close.

I wondered what would happened next. *When in doubt, dress up.*
Applying make-up on the porch with a hand mirror. BJ
appeared and watched me for a few seconds. 'Painting your
face?'

I gathered he didn't like my wearing make-up but ignored the
hint to feel self-conscious, just replied, 'O yes.' Stroked on more
purple eye-shadow, tried another coat of mascara, lined my lips
with a dark pencil and filled in with red shiny lipstick.

Then he left to see his dad. 'It's Father's Day.'

I wondered how to suggest I tagged along but somehow it
seemed a foolish idea.

Unusual, someone I knew quite well had slept with me then
walked away the next day as if nothing much had happened.
Puzzling. We made no arrangements.

My flatmate's eyes round when I told her where I'd been that
night about a week later. 'BJ has a girlfriend. You know, that kind
of dreamy girl?'

This shadow through all the time I knew him. Tall, dark, with
long light-brown hair, she wafted into rooms and hovered there,
no definite silhouette. Even quite still, on a chair or the sofa she
appeared to not ever sit fully in light. I'd never realised they were
together.

Easy to imagine BJ used this to his advantage when he wanted to sweet-talk someone recently heartbroken, or he had a loose agreement with her and could sleep with whoever he wanted. No idea exactly and somehow I never got around to asking him. Gradually, the message appeared clearly in focus. BJ didn't want a permanent position caring for me.

Then he moved away. Gone to another city. The Fib Street flat he lived in disbanded too.
So many of those noisy young men found steadier work, better cars, a few married. One went sour and I saw him a few times here and there. I'd be walking along the street, but usually he was entering some seedy bar. Old suddenly, too old, his grey skin and tired eyes. Then I didn't see him anywhere again around the city.

A few of their girlfriends knew Paxton and one dated him for a while. She told me he was too intense, 'Only went out with him *once* and he sent all these presents, flowers. Too much.'
Another told me he'd married a woman she knew and I questioned her further, 'O, what was the wedding like?'
She folded her arms and refused to talk about it.
I laughed to myself. Paxton's eternal fan club protecting him. Some part of me glad.

One night, home in front of the goggle box and there was BJ presenting on this TV sports show with his eyes sparkling.
My previous flatmate again knew the story, 'O yeah, stardom from the edge of a cricket pitch. An announcer asked him some bystander questions. BJ wisecracked his way through a good fifteen minutes. The network offered him a job. Didn't you know?'

We met again by chance in a restaurant, my table next to his table. BJ grinned and I smiled back, arose before I thought about what anyone could think, went over and kissed his cheek. We both caught up later together at the bar for a half hour or so. His strange green eyes the same, dark and piercing but paler

when he laughed, dark lashes, BJ's one stunning attribute, unless
you counted his mind, and that big heart when it suited him to
show it.

Kicked myself sometimes the way someone kicks a car tyre
when it's flat. I could've asked him to cradle me in his enormous
arms every night. Persuaded him we'd be good together. These
thoughts my foolishness since BJ convinced others, they rarely
ever talked him into much at all.
Words floated through my head like fish I could tickle and tame,
but ideas dissolved into vapour. I didn't realise not everyone
contended with a fog of muddled thinking, not then. Just
laughed at his comments about life in TV-land when we'd met
again and I answered questions, too, in a vague way. Smiled as if
I'd won a happiness competition.
Three cocktails later, we walked along the quay to a hotel and
messed up their fine linen with enthusiasm.
BJ the big star. He ordered hamburgers from room service. They
said they'd happily go along to the White Lady caravan parked
in the city (usually a place for hungry clubbers and shift workers
to buy snacks, on the side of the road, all hours). The room
service waiter walked down there and bought our burgers,
handed them over at the door with a grin.
Monster meals with fries, onion rings and cheesecake. The pair
of us in a huge oval bed, like a sultan and his sultana on a day
trip to Ordinaryland for supper. Although the room was hung
with gold curtains and a picture of the Taj Mahal on the wall
opposite the bed. A long way from a scummy flat where no one
made many definite plans, and skinhead bands caused riots at
parties.
Parted in pale morning light with the city awaking around us, a
kiss on the cheek and a smile. No addresses or phone numbers,
he just said, 'See you next time.'

BJ's sweet-faced girlfriend kept his bed warm at home, or
someone like her, I supposed later. It never occurred to me I
behaved like one of the girls who Paxton cheated with, it didn't
feel that way.

So many of us looking for a little warmth and kindness, anywhere we can.

Realised eventually how easily people fall into difficult places, and how much we need closeness, sometimes gladly taking whatever's possible instead of nothing at all. BJ also rather threw himself at me, a steady movement forward until there was nowhere except into his arms.

He threw himself at a story, threw himself at players after they'd won or lost and asked them outrageous questions at sports matches, he threw himself into life. Guaranteed a good show, BJ the sports commentator star and his big beaming face, a tall broad figure raving in the middle of a sports crowd. I hoped he felt as happy as he looked.

One of my old flatmates, Angie told me the way they'd drank at Fib Street seemed like youthful silliness to her. Some tried other mad things, three or four dragged off to hospital with poisoning, overdoses, and injuries from fights. 'They read some stupid book, tried all these herbal, uh.... Almost had liver failure, almost died.' Then she realised many of her friends really had a problem and BJ looked like he'd never stop over-indulging. Older now, a handful of the Fib Street crowd joined AA, found God, or married and abstained, but not BJ.

We met over coffee, Angie, who I'd known when I was younger, and I. Talk about people who'd gone too far. 'Friends who drink a lot? They don't realise. It's like people who wander into the forest without warm clothes or water. They forget where they are, what they're playing with,' Angie said.

'It's fun too. People like to enjoy themselves.' I laughed.

She looked stern. 'Ah well, I've got a family now. No way we can afford to drink like BJ even if we wanted to. Such a laugh, but...' My friend returned to her twin boys and the suburbs.

Through a few years, BJ appeared on various TV drama shows. In one he played a hard-case stock car driver and in another, a farming town veterinarian. In a film, he was a carnival owner with snazzy waistcoats. A bit wider each time. I wondered if he needed someone to tell him to slow down with drinking, or maybe television added a few kilos.

Idiot wastrels, birds of a feather, damaged sensitive souls. I
needed to seek help eventually and did so. BJ and Paxton and
many others, maybe that's what we had in common. A crazy off-
note we all recognised which others didn't have, or didn't like, or
wisely didn't want to ever know. We hoped this whacked tune we
all seemed to hum in common meant love could be ours, like
anyone else could have some, but maybe it was discord in the
way, all the time. Shared ruination, anything agreed upon would
do, whatever togetherness we could find.

The same ex-flatmate, Angie, told me the story after I heard
what happened, briefly on TV news.
Laughed his way through an hour and a half of a party, through
a bottle of the best bourbon, then just fell backwards like he
wanted to lie on a big soft bed.
One of his friends explained it like that, 'Just lay down in the air.'
Partying on a yacht in dry dock not the best idea and he
weighed so much. I suppose the yacht would've stood about
three stories above concrete, if it had been a building.
The tarpaulin shown on TV, a blue plastic sheet over his
remains in the ship yard. Bright blue over a grey expanse; keels
of boats floated about the reporter relaying this sad news.
BJ's countless jokes gone.
Tens of thousands loved him, maybe more.

At one of the lowest points of my life he convinced me someone
really did care for me, even if it wasn't for long. Feels good to
this day, how he held me all night, safe.
If BJ could comment on his demise he'd say something like, 'I
always wanted to go out with a splash.'
A laugh and everything else disappears, light pours in, anything's
possible.
Wish he knew how to keep himself safe like he made me feel
that first night. Not for me to see him again necessarily, just so
I'd know he was still about the place. Somewhere.
Despite his philandering and drunken nights, we need men who
understand how to hold a woman so she can believe nothing will
ever harm her again.

Part Two

Athena

Blue True

Y'Know You Got T'Find Ears for This Wikid Noise,
'Cos Y'all Poisoned By Pretend-Honeycoated Tunes

This Bee Stings When He Hits Your Daze with Truth
Run Screamin' My Name t'Explode Walls & Off th'Roof.

               - StandUp Real Life by D'StanMan 2000

Across the road, sometimes through rush hour traffic I thread past cars like I'm a wisp of silk and they're the steel of a needle's eye. Stitching time, mending a plan so it all hangs together, knowing any life shows a few frayed edges no matter how well anyone mends anything. When the day's felt calm too long, or I've done something so spectacular it starts to reinvent music, I may easily take the opposite tack.
Told my blue eyed trickster once that he could watch me turn the day inside out and into night, if he waited long enough for me to tire of the sun. He said, 'You could turn over a pancake and I'd watch. I'll never leave you.'
When later I asked him to tell me everything would be fine, he did.
Completely convincing.
I'd waited all my days for someone I cared for and believed to tell me that. Once my heart broke so many times it made a mosaic firmly set into a kind of inner concrete, I believed I truly fell in love.

Away on a weekend for music fans, in a run-down hotel where famous TV, film and rock stars' photos lined the lounge bar, and the barman kept a lizard on his shoulder. It stared out at the patrons like it wanted to eat them in the same way it snapped up flies.
In a red vinyl-covered booth, with a wooden table in front of me. 'You won this and so did I, I take it.' A blue eyed stranger slid into the booth seat across from me and passed over a name

tag. 'We're supposed to wear these. The woman in mauve asked me to give you yours.'

'Won? Oh yes, I did. Listener of the Week competition, on radio. You too?'

'Guilty as a pantie thief with lace in his teeth.' His eyes crinkled.

'Whaaat?'

'Oh, sorry. This is supposed to be fun. Just having some.' He grinned.

'I thought talks from people in the music industry could be useful. Fun?' I replied.

'Yeah, some fun.' His voice flat then, 'But, I want to know how to tame a typewriter too.'

The hotel cafe area filled up steadily with people, most wore name-tags and talked together. I guessed those attending usually went to music conventions with someone for company.

'They want us to read the piece we sent in? Our winning entries?' I almost picked up the folder with my writing in it that lay beside me, but didn't for some reason.

'My name's Bardon, by the way.' He spoke like I hadn't said a thing.

I went through all the where-I-came-from, where-he-came-from, polite tennis conversation for a while. Three beers and much music talk later he grinned. 'My parents wanted to call me Pardon, then they just made up my name. You know why?'

I waited for his punch line and he twinkled at me. Finally, I asked the inevitable *why*, and he grinned again. 'They said I interrupted their morning when I decided to get born, so they wanted to call me Pardon, but then I was technically a bastard so they thought they could call me Bastard.'

'You are *kidding*.'

'No. But, not allowed to use swear words, for a child. So they combined the two, Bardon.'

A woman in mauve with a name tag that seemed to say Myrtle, flapped around at that point, wanting prize winners on stage. 'Both ready to read your reviews of headliners' classic re-releases?'

Wobbly though we felt, Bardon and I both managed to nod.

He read his 500 words in a slow, assured way considering he only looked about 25 or so. In a growly, wry voice he made a rather dated album essentially about war sound somewhat amusing.

Bardon told me later, '*You* read like a pro.' Not a wink or a leer from him, so I gathered he didn't mean 'pro' like what what we used to say about hookers. That was slang when I swanned about the city at his age, over 20 years before.

'I've trained to be an actor and public speaker,' I explained.

'Hey, me too,' he replied.

When I tried a weak joke about diphthongs he didn't laugh though.

Then Bardon asked if I knew they had a dance on for the last night, a formal dance. Did I know how to waltz and all that? Big band revival, 1950s music. Soon he roped me in to show him how.

A long weekend and we met on the Friday, by the Sunday some people started to call us 'you two.'

A week later, he called me and I felt like someone let the sun into all the rooms of the house, even though midwinter chill inhabited every corner of my place.

Our phone calls devoured nights for a week. Then twice we met for coffee. Friends around his age were with him. We conversed like we'd known each other for years, ranged over every manner of subject from religion to music, from travel to fashion, and saving the planet through planting trees.

Soon afterwards, I went to my friend Marigold's house for our weekly marathon game of 500. I told her it felt strange to have a young friend like Bardon. She looked a little sour, as if she'd got a slice of lemon from that sip of her drink, but red wine rarely had citrus in it. 'He's a *friend*, already?'

'I'd say so. We get on.' I laughed. 'His best friend's girlfriend said something the other day. That she thought Bardon wanted to get it on. With me. Mad.'

'I hardly think this Bardon tells his secrets to his best buddy's girlfriend.' Marigold scowled.

I just smiled, nodded, pretended I loved the excitement,
although it rather scared me. 'It seemed odd. I'd only just met
the girl. But maybe it's true what she said, Marigold. I'm going
to find out.'

Despite my friend Marigold looking like she wanted to tell me
off, I got tingles to think this young man could really like me.
At this time in my life I'd accepted that the old movies I loved on
TV when I watched from only ten years old or so fooled me into
a false idea of romance, and I'd probably never get any sense
about it. Mainly feeling ignored or hurt by my family, and others
close to me, in the past, this meant I developed an inner
blindness around security, and looked for it anywhere I could.
Any sign of love and I was there, hungry. Feeling I cared for
someone, wanting them, diverted me from far worse sensations
like abject despair and loneliness. Then a grand carry-on ensued
and I entertained myself with hope.

Logic and Reason turned into dried up old maiden aunts,
Victorian throwbacks. Sat with their arms folded on the porch in
my mind to watch the Great Love Parade pass by, a stream of
cheer and sexiness with loud great music. It frolicked along,
screened out every single sensible thought or remark. When you
got the chance to enjoy your life, you simply had to - so I
believed.

Phone calls between Bardon and I epic, one conversation from
7pm til 2am. Shaky afterwards, exhausted. For the next fortnight
after that call, Bardon took lots of overtime at work. He couldn't
travel, not even for the Music Buff Dinner that we had free
tickets to as part of our prize. I suspected he felt scared too,
involved with an older woman, but mainly I thought about how
he made me laugh.

By the time I saw Bardon again it felt like he'd been overseas, we
were parted by war or something dire for love to overcome. The
way he looked at me, open face, laughing, it felt like he did want
more than our endless chats and banter. When we walked along
together he kept bumping gently against me, and leaned in close
to talk or listen.

In the cafe, this eccentric younger woman, head to toe in lilac
muslin, whom I knew from university since I was an adult

student, well, she raced over and uninvited, sat with us. I felt I couldn't be too obviously interested in Bardon. Soon, she flirted with him shamelessly and when she got up to get more coffee, he looked like he wanted to go. So I said I could give him a ride home. He jumped at the chance and we took off.

All through the city he went on about this and that, agreed the woman was a pain too. The car took the road easily, lots of green lights. I asked if he'd like to talk in the park for a while. He agreed.

About 11pm, and the night at peace like we sat in a photograph or the opening of a film. City lights ahead, a dark sky above, trees on the edge of the road along one side. Without thinking of time, we sat up all night conversing in my car by the scented gardens for the blind. He told me he liked birds and I suggested we could go to my place, 'Meet my hand-reared cockatiel.' While the bird walked along his arm, I made hot chocolate. Light looks weak when it gradually arrives at dawn, but when the sun appeared completely I felt so tired I could've cried, my brain hurt. Somehow I anyway drove him home.

Halfway there, he told me to drive down this side street past a few closed up factories. I stopped when he said to and turned to him.

'Something's going on, isn't it?' I smiled. 'Bardon?'

'You say. I'm not going to.'

'Well, I like you, it's good to talk with you. Now, now I want to find out more about...' I touched his arm,' this.'

We kissed for at least an hour then he insisted I take him home. 'My family has to attend a wedding. I can't be late.'

At his bright yellow weatherboard place out west, his mother (or I guessed that was the tall woman with his long nose), she flew out of the house like someone on a mission to save a life, threw a dark blue suit on a hanger at him, and he grabbed it. I turned the car around and could hear her shout, 'Get that on. We're leaving, leaving in a half an hour. Shower first. God.'

He told me later on the phone his mum was so furious she didn't speak to him after the wedding for a whole day. Bardon said he'd overstayed there, and was only between flats. Wanted to move out.

We rang each other, talked for hours like teenagers, every other night. Once he asked me to his friend's flat for dinner and made it all himself, hand-made fresh pasta, a sauce of wilted spinach, ham and cream, then home-made avocado and macadamia nut ice cream, with this shortcake covered in liqueur-drenched berries. I gathered he liked to cook.
His friends, bewildered, said they'd never seen Bardon make anything like the meal we enjoyed, ever before. I just thought Bardon went to extra trouble, for me.

One night, at this club we both liked where they played the most eclectic music, in the lounge area, I was walking back from the ladies and heard Bardon say to an acquaintance, 'The way you get a girlfriend is, you don't sleep with them straight away.'
I ignored how his statement made me feel like part of an experiment, sat down, smiled and nodded.

The therapist I'd been seeing, her receptionist told me she'd moved away when I'd called the week before. I wished I knew where she was, to discuss this situation. I wondered if I should see someone else, a new counsellor.
The idea of changing my name still appealed to me. I thought it could help me change my life. I'd always felt like my name meant nothing, my real one. It was like I never even heard it, at times, or didn't want to.

Two more beers and I didn't think about therapists again. We talked about an African band on tour and a movie. I danced with friends. Later, Bardon yet again directed me down a side street where we kissed and made out for ages. Then I dropped him at his place.

My flatmate moved on to find themselves in Argentina and I told everyone we had a spare room at our place. Bardon heard me and almost shouted, 'I want to live close to town.'

My friend Marigold insisted she'd never stand in the way of a young man.

I replied, 'I'm not forcing him to move in. He just wants to live near the city.'

To me, it felt like I sat in the Formula One of affairs, gunning the motor and winning something grand. He did everything in a hurry - talked, ate (meticulously, but fast), paid rent, drank beers, and promised a future more elaborate every time we talked. We would go to South America and farm vanilla pods, hand pollinating once a year, at night listening to bands playing ancient songs on wild brass and drums. Then he said we could work near the British Museum, go to gigs every night and write for Time Out magazine. He knew someone who wanted him to move there.

We'd zigzagged into bed, eventually. Two months of starry-eyed blindness but soon, I gathered he hardly ever took his turn to make dinner and at last Bardon told me he hated cooking. 'Just had to impress you. Worked, didn't it.' Only laughed when I told him he knew how to fool himself, not me.

Often, Bardon forgot his wallet or needed extra for something, and after three months I realised he borrowed around about all his rent back every week then only repaid half, or none at all. The tiny notebook I carried for phone numbers or lines I liked that someone had said, it soon showed pages and pages in the back full of other numbers. The record of his debt in ballpoint pen with dates like a spell, but the magic leaked out when I added the list up.

Over the next three years, I lived one of those con games people play on big city streets with three up-turned little cups. Passers-by guess where the marble goes, the con artist shuffles the up-turned cups so fast, one cup supposedly hides the marble. Few ever guess where the prize is to be found.

Money represented a tool to me. Bardon used it like a great pool of liquid elastic. Sometimes I fell in then bounced around until I felt ill and forgot things.

Years of 500 card tournaments I'd played with lists of numbers I added up on the spot however, they stood me in good stead. If I checked the lists, I could see what had happened. When he knew I spoke sense asking for money back, Bardon shouted or refused to listen. Then, once in a while, some money was returned, so I felt like I'd won for a few days.

Sometimes, too, Bardon read aloud to me or I'd hear him singing, or he'd say when I felt bad some days, 'You know you're the best. Do whatever you decide to do. I believe in you, love. You believe, too.'

He raced about organising friends to visit and cheer us up, or took me out to a movie and talked up a storm the whole way there, blew everything else away. Music filled our days and nights. New excellences every week which he discovered. We both wrote CD cover blurbs for a while and listened to so much new music I started to dream in a completely fresh direction. Young again.

Often enough I forgave him, easily distracted by inspired sounds and ideas.

We recorded a CD with instruments we invented, put out a book of our lyrics but Bardon told me his supposed *friend* the producer swiped the master tapes. Never did sell that many of those.

Then, our business making t-shirts, selling them at a local market. Soon I sold them alone. He said I talked to people more kindly. He couldn't keep it up. 'I'll write the slogans though, love. You sell them.'

He never paid attention to the t-shirts again, except to get his cut every week from sales and then try to borrow my cut from me.

Quick, quick, slow, quick quick; Bardon usually went at a rate of knots and only hung back now and then to let me know what his next move could be. Then made a different move entirely, so often. I learnt to smile and nod unless I felt like a fight.

On summer Saturdays when I'd given up the market, we sat on the porch in the shade of a tree there and drank beer, which I usually bought. Talking, laughing, time eaten up with enjoyments.

When I gathered the CD we made *had* been released, anyone could buy it on the internet, Bardon swore he knew nothing about it. I felt as stupid as a honey-drunk bee but went back to university to do my Masters. He worried I'd find someone smarter than him. I tutored there, and he'd arrive unannounced to sit sometimes at the back, half-asleep, like a sturdy guard dog. Bardon worked in a record store, or a CD shop as they'd become, and managed the jazz section like a fanatic. Some days, he said he refused to let anyone buy anything. 'They didn't look like they loved the music enough.'

When I mentioned he sounded like a character in this film I knew, he snorted, said, 'You have to know they base those films on real people.'

His lies sounded real until I questioned them too long, whereupon his characters looked like inept actors in cheap costumes. But I just smiled, nodded.

In his shop occasionally, I'd visit to browse the magazines. Bardon conducted behind the counter, or pretended to play the saxophone, eyes closed a few moments. Then he'd smile so his face shone, booming towards me, 'Hi there gorgeous, how's things?'

Year after year went on and on.
Busy.

At times, we fought, and I kicked him out about once every six months, but he reappeared. Head against the door glass as if cooling his thoughts. The way he said sorry, the way he sat down and reeled off what his future would be without me, 'I'll have some cockroachy room above a scummy takeaways in the suburbs. My cat'll have three legs and people will call me names like Nutman, to my face.'

Funny and sad.

It felt like he made me see an aviary of coloured birds set free to line rooftops along a city skyline, the cold full moon above, strangeness gobsmacking and believable. Bardon rolled out assurances, 'If you ever want me to go, say you don't love me. I'll go. Truly.'

Mixed up, shook up, so many songs, such attractive lunacy. People mix their own love cocktails, quick drunk on a taste of something muddled, revealed in a tinted glass of romance. Feels so good, anyone would want more. One more day, one more chance, once more for the memories.

Around the fifth year, his parents divorced. He spent weekends at his mother's place, consoling her. By then, I gathered he reeled out stories to suit whatever he wanted. Maybe Bardon also thought if he stayed away awhile I'd forget half the lines he hooked me with, so he could start all over again. My exhaustion difficult to describe, mainly from never knowing what the truth could be and having no definite plan. With Bardon gone, things grew clearer, easier, I dreaded his return home.

I told Marigold she had to help me get him out of my house. By then Bardon owed me thousands and I'd written off a pile of money. Fights over who said what, and what was owed now, confusion made me feel like a boxer hit in the head one too many times. He screamed at me when no one else could hear him too, frightening. When he stayed at his mother's I realised how often it happened, concentrated with the fix of a cross-eyed fool.

Before, I kept forgetting things when Bardon got home every day from work, but now with him away for days at a time a great deal returned.

His mood swings alarming too, how he could threaten and yell when no one else was around, then turn utterly sweet and charming.

Marigold said his family needed him. 'You have to understand.' She wouldn't help me plan to move him out.

I couldn't imagine how to do this alone.

Our garage stacked with CDs and music vinyl along the old workbench, in cardboard and plastic. I checked them while he was at his mother's. On his income, Bardon could not afford so much music.

Late at night, someone rang for him then asked me if I was selling for Bardon now. I hung up.

Bardon said, 'They only called about my old stereo for sale.'

I didn't dare push the question. Anyway a local paper gave me work. I reported on suspicious smells from storm water drains and schoolchildren's efforts to raise CanTeen funds. They let me review albums, a new CD every week. My nose for a story kept pointing towards Bardon, but the thought of his temper kept me wary. Our editor gave me so much work then, and my cheeky young man sidestepped out of sight. I dutifully pretended he'd disappeared, suspicious moves and all.

His mother found the editor of a national music magazine played golf at her club. Bardon got a chance to write for the rag, every month. They gave him free concert and movie tickets, promotional caps, badges, jackets and mugs. I still have this t-shirt from the film American Beauty, with a quote on the back, 'Never underestimate the power of denial.'

The fraud squad arrived on a Tuesday morning, so tall. Detectives stare into your face like no one else would dare. They took away boxes of records and CDs. Luckily, believing me when I said I didn't know Bardon took them from the record store. It was true, I had no proof, only suspicions.

Since only one hundred and fifty or so were counted as missing at that stage, Bardon's bosses said he could get away with diversion, if the court let him. He lost his record store work too. I think he gave up selling the stolen recordings when he got his writing job, too busy; but he refused to discuss it.

At this council park, where Bardon went to do his thirty hours community service, the gardener asked what he'd done to get diversion. Bardon called it recycling music without a license, 'Recycling from my work to my friends.'

Then the guy told him if Bardon helped him take (steal) plants from the council's nursery, and sell them at the market, they'd call it quits after a couple of weeks for his hours he needed to do, supposedly as punishment.

I tried telling Marigold this, and how one day Bardon got annoyed with my money talk again. He, in a fury, busted down the door to my room to keep on shouting at me. I told this story in a panic, but she said, 'People have to put up with a lot, sometimes. To have someone.'

I didn't tell her everything, I'd sound hysterical if I did. My door hung on one hinge, and to stop him rushing at me that day, I shouted, 'Get out. I don't love you any more, now leave.'

'You don't love me?' Confused, all the red vanished from his face and he hovered by the window, looked out to the fine clear day instead of glowering over me.

In a second, I could tell the story about his leaving if I ever said

I didn't love him was just another story. He turned slowly, looked like he wanted to hit me. I had to say then, 'O, I was scared. I just blurted out something, anything to stop you. I do love you, Bardon.'
Fright wrecked me. I shook for hours afterwards and did the dishes to cover up my trembling.
I did love him? This my lie. Someone held me captive, I simply had to say what they wanted to hear.
The door I fixed myself; ashamed to see it hanging there day after day.

Months went by, he'd stopped staying at his mother's. But the room he used as a home cinema and music studio started to look like a horror movie, spider webs and dust everywhere in the gloom. Bardon never opened the curtains. He felt afraid someone could steal his plasma TV, stereo, camera, and fax machine, his vast collection of music.
Tired of demanding he clean up his act and stop behaving illegally, I became the most cheerful woman on Earth.
Women did this while I was growing up in our small town. They couldn't change their husbands' excessive drinking and any propensity to fight, so they changed themselves.
Every Friday, I went to drinks with my fellow journalists. On Sundays I played cricket or indoor bowls, depending on the season. Marigold saw a great deal of me, we attended concerts, watched movies, and played cards. I researched jokes, learnt to tell funny stories, and volunteered to help others with their garden or renovations.
I rarely had to be home.
When we did happen to see each other, at home in bed Bardon rarely had any energy and I told him he needed to stop smoking. Then, I found a peculiar, scraped part of the wallpaper by his side of the bed, as if someone scratched it away. I asked Bardon what it could be. He felt sure it was the mattress rubbing against the wall, which made no sense but I just said, 'O, I see,' and left to help the local school with their playground gardens.
No slowing down.

We celebrated seven years together and I wondered if we'd get a prize like sports people do for endurance. This thought silent, I rarely made jokes with Bardon in those days, because he could snap or snarl. I never knew why. To my surprise he delighted in the anniversary, and chanted the year, 'Seven, seven years. We did it. We stayed together.'
I didn't say he simply would not leave.
One night I went to his friend's place where he visited sometimes, to see if Bardon had my $50 . I wanted to go out. Bardon sat on their fence looking along the road and when I pulled up, he jumped back inside their gate. 'Oh, hi love. Gotta get in, just waiting for a pizza, uh, having a smoke. They want to play a DVD. Better get in.'
He handed over my money without a murmur and dashed inside. I drove away wondering what he reminded me of, his guilty moves slippery like something trying to wriggle through a space, escape. A fish, a cat, a lizard caught in the light, finding a quick shadow, concealment.

Sun often got me cheerful, truly, so I sang around the garden one afternoon getting things pruned and weeded. Admired my handiwork afterwards, but Bardon walked around the house, sat down next to me and without stopping for breath blurted out how sorry he was but he had to leave me.
I eased my bad leg by stretching it out and smiled a bit, tried to stop him sounding so sad. 'It's okay, you are so much younger than me. Of course, you could want to leave one day.'
Bardon cried and I smiled. Strange to be breaking up, especially on such a glorious afternoon, monarch butterflies in the tops of trees and dancing across the blue sky.
He looked angry, asked why I wasn't more upset, so I tried not to show my delight, thinking he could really soon go.
Messy business when someone moves away, even if you are supposedly good friends. I made a pretense at getting on with him before so kept it up. Soon dust blackened various cleaning cloths. We moved his things. CDs into boxes.... Money talk escalated, and secrets came out like prisoners set free.
I walked into his room one night while he sat in there,

supposedly packing. He held this glass pipe in his mouth. I
blurted, 'I've seen those on TV.'
'Want some?' He leered.
'It's P, isn't it? Methamphetymine. That's dangerous, Bardon.'
He tried to frown. Just as fast he laughed. 'Oh save me. Got it all
under control. Been taking it for three years. You never knew.'
'O, I see. The mess in your room, all that. Your mood swings.'
'Crap,' he snarled. Then Bardon bundled me out of there.
I rang my editor and asked him to email me all the articles so far
we'd done on P. I thought it could make a good feature but
wanted a new angle. Someone suggested it at our staff meeting
but no one took it up. They said people called it Crack now, but
it had nothing to do with cocaine.
I researched the drug solidly for a week, while Bardon moved
out. It made holes in people's brains. The pictures looked like
melted plastic. I cried to think the bright young man I met could
now have brain damage, wondered if it was my fault.
No way to say if living with me made Bardon take the drug, or
the drug-taking simply moved along with him like his freckles
and laugh.
Frightened, I made sure he knew to never come back. The
courts issued a trespass order without any fuss.
Sometimes I wished we'd never met.

On a Health and Wellness website I saw a link to Survivors of
Relationships with People with Narcissistic Personality Disorder.
Our love affair in lists of symptoms. Constant, compulsive lying,
obsession with attention of any kind, addiction to drugs
including alcohol, often strongly identified with a cartoon
character (Bardon loved Batman so much he wore the costume
for Halloween every year), an inability to be organised since they
lived in chaos, unable to just be quiet and listen to their own
wheels... alarming, but I read on and took part in some online
discussions.
'To stop a person with this disorder annoying you, treat them
like they are boring. They equate love with attention, if they get
no attention they will leave and go find some elsewhere.'
Bardon packed but he also tried to leave things behind, and tried

to steal things of mine. Almost caused a fight over money in his
last attempt to get me to notice him. I affected a barely
interested attitude, did not react much to anything he did.
Refused to smile and nod, refused to complain or get angry,
behaved like I used to in school when the teacher wanted to
excite us about things we learnt the year before (and had found
dull then, too). My gaze drifted, I mumbled and didn't show any
good humour or annoyance. Bardon moved every single thing
including ten huge bags of rubbish in a half a day, and I didn't
see him again.

Reading about P addicts who chopped off people's hands
because they saw demons, who killed someone to stop the devil,
got me thinking it could be best for me to move, too. My house
close to friends' places and the shops, I cried to think I'd need to
pack up and go.

Someone said I could move reminders of him out, instead. All
my music played for the last seven years friends helped me pack
carefully into his (scoured and disinfected) old room. For two
years other songs played, my fears left with nothing to dance to.
That and my standard poodle puppy, Barney, got me close to
feeling safe again.

When I berated myself for handing over so much money, so
many gifts, a male friend told me a young man would never ask
for money from someone as old as me, but they sure would
expect it. I supposed I got off lightly, never bought him a car or
his own house.

Wondered how things could go so wrong when we had so much
in common. Another friend explained, 'Con artists always have a
lot in common with you at first. It feels like they're already part
of your trusted circle.'

In the end, all that we meant to each other disintegrated into a
pile of dusty lies.

Hard facts built a steady wall against the past's fantasies, just as
playing some of our old music started to help me feel better
after a while away from it. Now, a few good times dance in mind
when I think of Bardon. But when I heard he moved to an
island near South America, I hoped he didn't travel thinking the

cocaine there could be cheaper.

For a few years, I trawled the internet, I would vaguely hope to
see his myspace page, then facebook, or note he'd written
something in a music e-zine. No trace, and no one I knew told
stories about him either.

Eventually, I didn't look that hard, and found I could sell my
double copies of vintage vinyl for a fair whack. A market for
platform shoes too. One shop sent someone from down south for
suitcases of my old clothes. Retro fashion I'd kept like some
people keep a scrapbook. It meant so much to dress up and
forget my life on weekends, years before. The selling bug took
hold. I forgot wallowing in nostalgia or man trouble. I often
spied places to pick up vintage tat cheap and sold it for a great
deal more, online, or at this market. Thrilling. Success,
something done well, without disappointments.

Some collectors wrote lovely thank you emails and a few took
me out to dinner or lunch, after they'd picked up something
rare, an op art chess set, a chunky quartz bracelet.

Kindness saved me from rage, and music's always such a good,
reliable friend. For a long time I listened to songs about people
alone, how they enjoyed the strange safety.

My going to therapy again helped me change some things,
attitudes, habits, I gained a truer sense of myself.

Reached into all the places I forgot when someone else was there
to distract me. A new danger then, since I found I often
surprised myself and sometimes what I thought and felt scared
me too.

Bravery for Ordinary Days

...Come on Sugar, we twirl fine so fast,
all our love's just got to pass the test.

Our eyes meet and our feet smooth,
y'know baby, this dance's so sweet, yeah.

—   Red Ricky 1960

'Don't die wondering.' A tattoo of a question mark on his head
near the crown. A number one haircut, his tatt highly visible.
That catch-phrase, laughing dryly afterwards, an old friend of
mine.
Mind boggling to think 'why' constantly like a three year old.
How can we ever know everything? Mainly reflex, following old
patterns and hoping for the best. Edit in mind what happened so
it looks as good as possible for memory's slideshow.
Many times after Bardon, my last partner, left, I breathed in
relief after recovering from the shock, and wondered how to
alter my routine. The new counsellor I saw for a while helped
me go through what changing my name would be like, what it
could mean. Names I wanted to consider were listed in a
notebook I carried with me.

In the paper one morning, a couple smiled on their golden
wedding anniversary. He said a sense of humour helped. She
said they both enjoyed their family. This ancient couple, lovely
as a pair of tortoises in their best clothes for the camera, what
emotional athletes, diplomatic saints, such staying power.

'Wasn't I special?' Someone asked after insisting they were
leaving.
'*Special* means you stayed,' I shouted.
One blink after another, this time machine flickers on. The
future our only setting, the present proof it works, and all we
ever have.
Snow globe mind, and something shakes me up. Mind-snow

settles, obscuring or revealing different memories each time.
Never everything at once. Discoveries every day, forgetting partly
what went before.

On Antiques Roadshow the Human Edition, then I'd be a
slightly worn out pleasure-seeker, with some talent as a
raconteur, lately turned to artistry, attractive in funky style.
Bright lipstick, a fetching smile. Many stories to tell and how
marvellous that someone looked after me so well. Evidence of
intelligence and some damage, almost mended.

Boundless couples married, appearing somewhat content, the
evidence surrounded me while I grew up. The 1950s and 60s
optimistic; obviously someone famous from TV or a movie
would step in, rescue me from confusion and dull routine. My
dazzling dress and all the guests agog, a husband to kiss, soon
away in a cloud of laughter to varieties of paradise.

Messed about by *something*, disaster shredded holes in my mind
and heart until they turned into mesh, sensations and memories
streamed through me. Many times later I readily walked into
familiar, comfortable trouble and worry.

I grew up partly in a horror movie, but what I took in wasn't
what most could see.

Wishing I'd known what it'd be like to grow up without
extraordinary damage, quite futile. Once something soaked
through, no use pretending it was dry. Although when whatever
it was dried out, then some new form could emerge. I grew to
understand I could heal. Therapists for decades helped me see
that, kept me alive, made me believe in other choices.

I don't know what they did at first to me, whoever hurt me so
badly, or who *they* were. So young. Only the awful effects
obvious, living nightmares, bewilderment. Then, I did various
careless things, only half-connected, gawky, or I froze behind a
wall and stepped back behind it when someone again tried to
hurt me or did so thoughtlessly. I floated away while they kept
on.

Slowly, I understood the maelstrom, tangle and hurt was not my
doing and could dismiss behaviour and people and memories. It

was then like I directed the true-life movie I lived in, the others were less likely to push me around, they never even got to think about it a lot of the time.

My three brothers had before developed real expertise in broken toys, smashed tea parties and crazed days. As a child, crying silently, hidden, because if I was found upset sometimes I'd get smacked or ridiculed for making a fuss. Rarely comforted.

Way behind these memories in caves in mind, shadows move forwards about to find the light. I wait to see, to know the truth, to at last point the finger at family, so-called friends, a stranger, *anyone*. But the light perhaps is kind enough only to hint at a shape, a face, a figure, so long ago now.

They hurt me before I could even talk, that's all I know.

Then there was more, from others.

My tormentor brothers learnt such carelessness, where? Some adult hurt us all? They showed children in my family how pain was simply to be accepted? Or maybe many of them did this? Dad hardly ever home, and when he *was* there our father barely spoke most of the time, except to yell at the TV or to mutter with my mother where we couldn't hear what they said. He also roared with laughter at some of the things my brothers did to tease me. It followed then, violent or distant men grew familiar, and apparently attractive. Explanations exist. They're not enough, but they have to do.

Children may not listen but they always watch you, absorbing a world they think they need to know about.

Earthquakes of ordinary days, disaster-zone routines, toys turned into debris. Emotional aftershocks. Out of the blue, I was saved by movies, books, music, magazines, and conversations. Then also, I felt sure, entranced and transported by the magical wedding day, we'd turn into other people.

The supernatural ritual demanded you wear white to get married, look fantastic, a well-behaved princess, then stay like that in mind. Older, I'd learn grace, transforming like in a fairy-tale from a caterpillar to a butterfly, an ugly duckling to a swan, a fairy godmother provided every single thing needed in secret. A gorgeous frock pristine through an entire day, then a lifetime living up to the photograph.

My mother displayed her wedding photos like religious icons.

One night, in my teen years, I lay in terror in a friend's flat where I'd stayed the night, listening to three drunken flatmates roar down the hall. They fought and broke things. 'Take the telephone to hell with you,' screamed the loudest and threw the phone. It jangled on impact.

Pretty pictures of wedding days and careful plans broke into disordered music. I wandered from shattering event to wrecked evening, then into the arms of boys and men who couldn't wait to share their own chaos. Our disjointed dance.

Then I covered with hard humour like a battle-weary soldier, any pleasure felt welcome. Indulgences smoothed away the cringe, dispelled monstrous thoughts and allowed better memories like a lovely garden in mind, where hope lived.

Desiring more than hope took a long time to come about. Building strength, learning to master my own thoughts, and to desire a better life then drive that yearning towards my goal, this all took enormous amounts of time and effort but it worked, eventually, gradually.

Life a combat zone. Young, I proved resilient. Older, changes were needed or I'd die, at the least be damaged even more. Curious, desperate, I found therapists, meditation courses, and fitness classes. Attending a gym religiously for a year, my rather unfit body altered, and new vigour appeared. One therapist, a favourite so I like to recall her, May Belle, told me, 'Many Pakeha abuse and neglect their children, even if media bang on about Maori and Pacific Islanders. You were a child from a Pakeha family who people respected. Money coming in and a complex social life around you. But neglected for decades and hurt so young it affected you in ways you couldn't figure out at first.' She smiled. 'Struggled bravely against the dreadful effects all your life. Your family won't admit this occurred and you've lost contact with relatives to a large degree. People who were supposed to love you would rather live a lie than admit something went wrong.' Her kind blue eyes, sincere. 'Your pain is not your fault. Needing comfort and love like anyone and seeking it in clumsy, or out-of-the-ordinary ways, has to be

understandable. Escape into fantasy and imagination assisted for a while. It's astounding how well the human mind can care for us when nothing else is offered.' My therapist sat back in her chair. Sun streamed in the window, covered in net curtains with large flower-shaped holes so a pattern of sunny daisies lay over the blue and white furnishings, the pale yellow walls.
'Yes, that's what I meant.' I nodded. Yet more talk therapy.

Now I know I could've found these people earlier and improved my life, but better late than never.

May Belle also explained Post-Traumatic Stress Syndrome, PTSS. 'The sufferer disassociates when anything deeply upsets them. They kind of float away, watching from afar, uninvolved. Also, they may relive a past trauma instead, so the present trouble is never solved. Whatever upsets them may not be something another person finds strange or troublesome. Triggers can be smells, sounds, particular colours, sights or tastes, and more.' She showed me a book she'd quoted from and spoke kindly, 'Read, research this. Knowledge truly is power.'
I noted a description on the page she'd opened. 'O look at that. They were seeing things that weren't there. O, before I could talk, uh, my childhood dreams stayed in the room. Lurid shapes floated around my bed and followed me down the hall to my parents'. Spiders and two grinning men, bright red on a motorbike inside a huge blue whale with a dropped down side like a railway carriage for horses. I believed this was normal but it felt deeply disturbing. Hoped if I crawled into Mum and Dad's bed the shapes could be explained, but neither of my parents seemed to be able to see these bright objects floating in the air. Little me just lay there watching the sideshow until I did fall asleep. I couldn't talk or explain and ask for help. My height relative to their bed, shorter than the bed was high, or only just above it maybe.' I held onto the psychiatry book as if it was a hot water bottle, in her therapy office. 'Thinking about it makes me feel helpless.'
May Belle nodded. 'People hurt terribly may relive past pain or terrors, as soon as they're reminded. When something triggers

us, we can learn what that is and how to avoid the trigger so we don't get thrown back into those memories so much.' She also explained that feelings did pass, even if I went rigid in shock and desperately tried to find a quick way out, it was better to allow the feeling to be experienced and then go, they would change. Trying to stop the feelings could cause depression, or other difficulties.

Years later I came to the point where I could say, 'So I have this sadness, insecurity and instability, inevitable, a part of me. And I can be sympathetic to myself. Never thought of that before. It's easy to be kind to others, to sympathise when they say someone's died or they're unhappy. But I've never been kind to myself about these feelings, this turmoil. Now, I feel that kindness for me.'

Our therapy sessions explained and explored rafts of information, I made them my getaway vessels.

A luxury to know what I saw wasn't madness. People like me may keep being triggered if we don't learn how to stop it, never really engage with what's going on right now. Numbed by trauma. But I learnt to free myself of it.

'They used to call it shell shock,' she said.

An affected soldier would hear a loud noise and think bombs went off, relive the war they'd been through.

Whenever I felt hurt or afraid, I relived some past memory vividly and felt sure someone would hurt me again. Tried to get away, or lashed out wildly, flew into rages, said things I regretted, and all along felt attracted to people likely to hurt me - it was familiar, it felt oddly okay. Closeness, when I was just tiny, often meant pain. If the hurt didn't soon follow then sometimes I would try to *make* it happen, to keep that familiarity. How lucky I'd been not to die.

A highly sensitive person too, this meant I felt things more strongly than others. But I could also work adeptly at selling records in inventive ways, and truly loved music so this got customers enthused as well; and I helped my friends in bands with lyrics sometimes, or made them posters. Original ideas flowed from me. It was me who'd suggested the colours to paint

Howl's bus for instance, and how to decorate the interior. All through my life I've liked styling other people's clothes and so on. Then when I took up buying and selling retro and vintage it was like I'd been working at that all my days. Proved I had a real eye for it.

Anyway, I had to think myself lucky to be able to work at anything. I'd put myself in terrible danger at times....

Past hurdy gurdy noises, fun rides and prize tents, one time at the Winter Show, early evening, in my just-teens, I slipped away. Escaped a boring boy who would not stop talking about his new car.

By a striped booth, a man in a sparkly vest told a waiting group of twenty or so, 'Inside, I shall cut a woman in half.'

Behind the painted curtain we sat on worn wooden benches set around a red, wooden ring. The man stood in the middle.

'Todaaay Ladies and Gentlemen, todaaay witness some astouuunding sights.' Changed into a black cape, shiny blue lining flashed every time he spun about. A steel trolley with shiny struts pushed into place, he picked up a long saw with a bright yellow handle, flourished his hands after every object's display. He insisted he'd reveal how flesh and blood could be cut without injury. This went on for some time til a youngish guy with greasy hair near the front told the magician, 'Get a move on.'

The crowd shouted, they wanted to see this trick. 'What are y'doin' mate?'

His hands over his face, the caped man sobbed. A gold ring glinted and fat tears plopped from between his fingers to the ground, wet the dirt and sawdust inside the striped tent, faded and tatty.

I'd never seen a showman weep. Eyes wide, I prayed he'd stop. My stomach churned. Music started up and three clowns raced in. A woman in the front row shrieked with laughter. The man got led away by a performer in a white leotard with high, white, ostrich feathers affixed to her head.

On the way out later, after clowns had performed magic tricks with candles, balloons, and buckets of water, making us all laugh, a large woman in orange and white polka dots hissed to her thin friend up ahead, that she reckoned the magician's assistant had up and left him without warning. 'These show people. Can't be trusted.'

Outside amongst clashing colours and noises of the fair, the plump woman and her heron-like friend in grey, met with two men. Walked off arm in arm, picture couples.

Every step charged with mystery, I regarded the gaudy side-shows. Wandering past the Wall of Death where two, three, or even four motorcyclists dodged a crash, roared about a circular cage. Fabulous in a swirl of satin cape, I imagined talking loud enough to keep any audience's attention. Mad music rinky-tinked on and on, sideshow machinery clanged and whirred, the smell of frying hot dogs in batter and candy floss sweetness wafted by. Eyes watched the crowds, men called from booths, 'Try your luck, only a buck. Impress the lady, sir. Everyone wins a prize.'

A short step to ask if anyone needed an assistant. I wondered if the girls on those spinning wheels ever felt ill, if I'd scream when the knives were flying towards me. What would everyone at home say when they found out I'd run away to join the circus? Maybe they'd never know? Could I disappear?

Just an hour before, I'd slipped away from the boy who took me to the fair. He wanted to see the hot rods, all thirty-nine of them, and then the racing cars, all fifty-six.

Ahead, beyond the red and yellow sideshow gate, two enormous hangars stretched off into the night. A banner stated, 'Hot Rods & Racing Cars Motor Show.' Mainly men and boys milled about outside, then streamed through the wide doors, towards shiny vehicles on stages and in rows, inside. A few women with male companions, they stood out the way an exotic bird does against green foliage. Most of the men wore green, dark blue, brown, or black.

I'd walked away from there.

Smoothed down my orange skirt as if I'd left the crowd nearer the sideshows on purpose for this activity (not to see if my friend was looking for me over near the hangars - he wasn't), then I strode away from the gate again. Back towards open-mouthed mechanical clowns in a line, above ping pong balls in trays. For a while, people took turns, aimed ping pong balls into particular numbered chutes under a glass counter via the clown's mouth. Everyone aimed for the big prize numbers.

Then the guy running the booth flicked his dark hair back and smiled. 'Go on, does the place good when a pretty girl has a go. No strings, baby.' He offered me a free turn.

I'd stepped into an Elvis movie. No one ever called me *baby*. Older kids liked Elvis. I eyed the hand he held out, glanced at his face. He didn't look that old, maybe twenty-two. Not that much older than thirteen. Won a fluffy-skirted kewpie doll with glittery hair on a long, thin stick like a shepherd's crook. 'Come on, I'll buy yah a hot dog,' he said, then shouted something to a man at the next stand, stepped out of a half-doorway in the counter, stood beside me.

I took a long slow breath, he smelt of soap. Humour in his eyes, warmth too like when a spark shows just before a fire's about to roar. The cheek of him made me a bit breathless in a fun way, even if my mother had told me many times to never go anywhere with a carnie, never ever.

His crisp cotton shirt, cherry red against his skin, along with his swagger made him look darker and older than he really was. Maybe this boy was only a teenager. 'Call me Jake, okay? What's yours?'

I told him my name but he kept calling me *darling*, and once, *love*. We walked past the hot dog stand, a white caravan painted with giant hot chips and an enormous version of the sausage in batter (dripping with tomato sauce on a stick), that I expected he'd buy me. I slowed. 'Come on darling, my mam makes the best hot dogs. At our place. Step this way, no trouble.'

If I'd just wished to be in a show and then achieved almost instant contact with a showman, a taboo carnie, why couldn't I wish for a great boyfriend and get one as easily? My car-mad friend from school cared more for overhead cams than me. But this bodgie boy seemed intent on behind-the-scenes for some reason. He didn't chat like other boys did when they wanted to get to know you. My fists clenched, one firmly around the kewpie doll on its stick while we walked through dim light, away from the flashes, clangs and calls of the carnival.

Momentarily, I reminded myself what to do if he grabbed me, how hard I'd jam my knee into him.

We stepped over guy ropes and behind coloured tents or booths until we stood by an enormous caravan, white and maroon with an Italian name in gold along the side. My stomach churned but I kept on. I lived for behind-the-scenes, wanted to know what show people did in their every-day lives.

My car-mad friend loved it when I watched him take one of the three old cars he owned with his father apart every weekend. I listened to him explain each cog and piston. He didn't know I simply liked to see the insides of almost anything. If we were going to lie *underneath* the hot rods on display at the fair, or take their engines apart, I could happily have stayed by his side gazing in wonder at the greasy machinery, the brilliance of engineering, marvelling at the way things worked.

Suddenly, the caravan door opened and we stepped inside. Violin music played from a red radio with sparkly silver cloth over the front, then a woman with masses of long, red curly hair embraced me and kissed both cheeks. 'You are Jake's friend? I am Anna-Lucia.' She smelt powdery, of lavender. The interior of the caravan looked so clean I almost remarked on it. Surfaces pale or wooden except for the bright orange and white curtains, numerous ornaments about the place, dustless and neat.

'Where's mam?' Jake's eyes darted about.

Dark, and they spoke with English accents. My new friend more obviously English now he wasn't out in public. The older woman's inflection stronger than Jake's. She grinned and two gold teeth to the side flashed. They talked together for a while. I sat on a low red sofa and something made a noise. I leapt up with a squeak. We all laughed when Anna-Lucia's hairy little dog barked. High yelp like something from a cartoon.

In seconds she left us there, her little dog in her arms.

Jake sat down next to me. 'You're brave, laughing at Aunty's dog. You walk off with strange men a lot then?'

'How strange?' I sat back a little from him, drew away, but smiled.

He laughed and showed his white teeth, no fillings. Everything adding to a plus, as if I had to keep a score about this new acquaintance. Noticing what made Jake, Jake. Movements liquid but not so fast that I believed he was trying to trick me, Jake made us a hot dog. Somehow, no lingering fat smell in the small space, and I didn't mind his lack of chatter either. Then my treat sat in a perfect crunchy batter with a cap of sauce, on a plain white plate.

We ate one each at the little fold-out table in the caravan, and the radio played instrumentals softly. The whole place smelled lovely, fresh furniture polish and lemons.

Jake took a few moments to explain his aunty ran the dog show, and he shared this caravan with her and his mother. He spoke slowly like he wanted the next statements to last, even if only a few words, 'I want my own show one day. Working on it. Horses.'

I explained how I knew dogs, 'You have to make them understand who's boss.' Then after I told a story about our pets over the years, I also mentioned my three older brothers. He sat straighter, smoothed back his dark hair with one hand, said we ought to get back, 'Only a short meal break.'

Outside, the night as soft as dark make-up on a young woman's eyes and I stood a while to take in the coloured and striped tent tops, pennant flags, many garish lights of rides beyond us which flared against a deep sky. Various squeals and roars floated over. Jake put his arm about my shoulder lightly, then turned me to him and we kissed. A touch of sun, close and warm for a few moments. 'You're too young to be here, darling, ' he whispered. Then he walked me back to the fair gate. 'You go on back to your parents or whoever brought you here. Tell them you wanted to win a doll,' he indicated the prize I still carried, 'that was all. Say you're sorry for worrying them.' His voice regretful, as if struggling with something he wanted to say but dared not. Jake looked old then, old enough to be my father, and I gasped but he just laughed that bark he had, throaty and strong, turned on one heel like a matador and strode off. Back to calling out to pretty girls and the men who wanted to impress them.

His aunty walked by. Anna-Lucia winked at me. 'You've got him charmed my girl.'

I returned the next night with my best girlfriend. We walked slowly. She said, 'Don't look too keen.' Past booths of bright plastic windmills on sticks and glittery dolls for children, past the guns and targets and a man with helium balloons bobbing on long threads, the clowns ahead. Backwards and forwards with mouths open, their bright faces eternally merry.

Only a fat old man with tired eyes worked the clown booth. He said Jake left that morning for the next town. They'd all move on in a day. He laughed. 'Jake has an address. Forgot to give it yah?' I walked away. My friend hung back to tell the old man off, it looked like, when I stopped and turned to see where she'd got to. He didn't seem interested in what she said.

My girlfriend and I walked about eating candy floss, the last time I ate the sweet sticky stuff, talked about what we'd do that year at school.

Jake the carnie in his cherry red shirt, his surprisingly good manners, unlike the usual rough reputation of carnies. Not many like Jake out there. Recalled him while going over ways to make a picture of my story, romances which gradually faded or turned into some kind of scary ride at a circus. A jumble in many ways, my days and nights, then something good appears, whole and functioning, like a lovely machine, or a living thing, a flowering tree. All the way along, whenever I found good luck, it was a glimpse of a better way - which I wanted more than anything.

No matter what I determined, luck stepped in but eventually I could control how I reacted, too, could think about what could possibly change the probable outcome. It was lucky I'd thought to mention my brothers to Jake in his caravan, I had to think.

Living alone, collecting vintage and retro, selling tat or treasure online and at collector fairs. Music my best companion. In a river or stream of words and songs, they carried me along. One afternoon with sun flooding the lounge, it was obvious I'd stepped into my dream. A young girl star-struck over old movies, their ballrooms, their venetian blind shaded rooms.... In a few clicks I did live inside the screen, in cyberspace. After a good trading afternoon I'd surf the net, read websites, joined

discussion groups and avoided most creepazoids. Our language
shows who we are. Sequences of words, any images posted
provided clues to character, attitude, beliefs and manners.
Anything that seemed too good to be true, usually was.
Solitude, a good income, and the world wide web. A few articles
mentioned what happened with a therapist. I'd tried quite a few.
Online sites recommended articles and books. The internet
didn't precisely have the keys to elegant ballrooms, or perfect
romance, an education awaited there instead.
I changed. Sounds far too simple, but as plain as one day after
another, while I absorbed more and more ideas, words, I
examined who I was and why, like how I pored over a great retro
teapot or vintage handbag. Thoughts were replaced the way
furniture may be. Learning better quite a charm.
Uncomfortable at first, but better to change what I could than to
think that one day I would lay dying and wish I'd tried other
ways, but know I had not.

The Palm Tree and the Real Estate Agent

Cash, cash, gotta dash for some
smash it up and grab it all.

Where's my warm baby in this pile of gold?
Cold riches and a throne but so, oh so alone.

        —   *View from the Top by Blue Abigail 1999*

Puzzle days, some memories as thin as a page or a pressed
flower. My house in the city needed spring cleaning, then I got
to the garden. Outdoor work felt worthy, and the place looked
spruce eventually. I hosed all the bright green paintwork, the
cream trim.
The three metre Phoenix Palm near my letterbox looked
dangerous. Spikes on the leaves stabbed and hurt if someone
brushed against them. I liked to get out there and cut them off,
when the palm fronds drooped too low and long. With a sharp
chef's knife and looking like a serial killer out of my hiding
place, I proceeded to saw away at the thick end of the leaves.
Bright sun, a little winter chill to keep me cool, not hard work
particularly. I soon had a good pile of the spiky things lying on
the concrete area by the lawn.
A voice sounded from the footpath. 'Hello. The palms are a bit
of a nuisance, aren't they?'
Through the archway covered with roses and geraniums, I spied
a man in a cheap grey suit, who told me, 'I chopped a palm
down at my place only the past week.' He held a pile of papers.
Not a religious evangelical smile, friendly enough. 'I'm just,' he
held out a flyer, 'selling this place, nearby.'
'Oh yes.' I smiled back but kept on cutting away at the tree.
'It's a good property.' He held out the flyer again.
I sawed on. 'Can I put it in your letterbox?' He gestured as if
about to post something.
The sign on my orange letterbox stated in large black letters,
Please No Advertising. Why ask? Especially considering the
enormous knife in my hand and my powerful build. I thought he

could be a bit blind, but the power of denial and hope are greater than our everyday six senses, or logic.

Chopped away and thought about the price I could get for my house. Considered moving somewhere smaller. Mortgage-free in a small town. Cutting away fronds, I planned a sign out the front, could sell the place myself online. No agent's fee to pay. The smiling estate agent looked like he *would* slip a flyer into my letterbox. I protested, 'No, please. I get enough of that kind of thing. Don't like them.'

He smiled on and I cut away with more determination thinking about junk mail, the way it filled up rubbish tips. Papers never read. Almost none recycled, the ink removal posed too many problems.

I wanted this man to know my sign meant what it said, but he seemed certain to stay there.

After a second, he mentioned the price of the house up the road. This valuable property I could like to view. I had to explain, 'Not in the market for any other houses in the neighbourhood, thanks.'

No idea why I spoke. Possibly all the extra oxygen from pruning my exotic tree, tossing the fronds around, got me thinking and talking too much. Maybe I felt sorry for the agent in his flimsy suit, trying to gain interest in a house up from the motorway where noise had to be an issue.

Unperturbed by my disinterest he smiled on, slightly more engaged. I realised too late, I'd said I didn't want *another* house. Now he knew I owned mine. 'You must be pleased. The way your house value has shot up.' He rocked on his heels, sure we could now agree on something. 'Yes?'

I clambered round the front of the tree now, it leaned back, rather onto the lemon tree. I tugged out grass there. Shook my head, disagreed. 'Prices are terrible. Lots of friends want to buy a house. They'll never get one 'round here. It is against community, all these high prices, if you ask me.'

'Oh yes, I see.' He stopped smiling at last. 'But what can you do about it?'

I sawed off the last low branch. Spikes rustled together when I threw the palm frond taller than me on the pile behind the

letterbox. I turned and replied, 'O, stop loving money so much?'
'Hmm, yes, I suppose so,' he muttered and stalked off, back
along the road to the next letterbox, or maybe to sit in the house
up the road and wait for people to view the place.
Then again, while I sat waiting for the kettle to boil for my well-
earned cup of tea, perhaps he did not do those obvious things.
Maybe around the corner he threw all his flyers up into the air
and strode off along to the park, then up the hill from there to
the library.
Perhaps he sat and read a book about Chile or Rome, then
walked out of the life he'd had up until then and into a new one,
where I would not recognise him again.
People could change, they found God, fell in love with yoga,
found a cure for a stammer, or stopped accepting advances from
hopeless lovers, grew entranced with a place, decided to be a
pilot, teacher, or rally driver after all. Swerved away from a
business they hated, found they could love their life.
The thought of the estate agent throwing flyers in the air got me
thinking about what I would throw away. So many friends
moved on when rental places sold or were priced out of their
range. Two sailed off on a boat, and a couple joined a collective
up North. They specialised in organic farming and heritage
orchards. My friends loaded me up with monster lettuces and
the tastiest fruit on earth.

My house worth even more once I painted it universal grey with
a lighter trim. 'Now, anyone can imagine this is their place, to do
with as they please.' My real estate agent beamed.
So busy I found someone else to sell the place; my new mission
out of town. On drives I told myself I could buy somewhere
cheaper, use spare capital to start up a business.
My youth spent in flats or backstage, places no one inhabited for
long, waiting for someone who looked like they could love me.
Necessary friends in a make-believe world. Otherwise the
magnificent unreal could sweep us into oceans of unbelievable,
as quick as a real wave claimed fishermen on the rocks,
drowned. But movie moon dust soon scattered away in what the
world blew in. The eight year old who believed another world

existed inside the TV, where films played for real, she disappeared. Left on the roadside, she walked away into the bluer than blue sky. I wheeled along in glorious weather or rainy days, past beaches or farms, and grew to believe I never previously thought about much but the next short while ahead. Around the coast a few small do-up places well back from the water's edge, up reasonably high. No tsunami for me. Much cheaper than anything with a direct sea view. Bach after bach in forgotten countryside. A regular online customer told me about a sweet place, emailed pictures. Lovely.

All the while that real estate agent had spoken to me while I pruned the palm, this plan formed without my really knowing it until later. Sometimes I think I could owe him something.

How the Wind Blows

The family rocks, the family rolls,
we all gotta know that bell surely tolls.

Touch and dance, sing out this love,
but nobody said it was all kid gloves.

- by Brother Snow 1982

'Nothing serious,' Samuel insisted from four hundred kilometres away. 'Dad just felt dizzy. Hospital insisted on tests.' On my fifty-somethingth birthday, my eldest brother Samuel rang to say he'd just driven Dad to hospital. He gassed on, quite breezy. Months between visits and older, we both did a reasonable version of getting on, especially on the phone or in emails. Between catch-up remarks, I mulled through what could happen if we ever conversed face-to-face, in depth. The Americans call it *closure*, addressing outstanding issues. Heated debate boils down to what? Edging difficulties, our sleeping dogs.

Anyway, that evening, a knock at the door, and my grown son, Coltrane, stood there. He wished me a happy birthday. Told me Samuel also called *him*. Afterwards, Coltrane drove for hours to my place.

Since my rather small house held late summer heat as close as an overbearing aunty's smothering hug, we sat outside in cooler evening air. A citronella candle lit to repel lingering mozzies. They floated back into the shadows when the porch security light came on, which it did repeatedly.

Dad a healthy man, he never took time off work. Had only recently developed a few health problems.

'It's a shock, him in hospital,' I agreed with Coltrane's expression of surprise.

Years before, Dad found Coltrane shared his love of combustion engines. Into the upper realms of bonding with every spark plug cleaned, each mag wheel attached. They grew closer than layers of the best car enamel. While we talked, mother and son in faint light on my porch, away from the fierce glare of the security bulb directed onto the steps, Coltrane mumbled, 'I never said much to Granddad about how, well, I really do like him.'

I pointed out no boy spent time with a grandfather unless they really wanted to and Dad knew. 'It's fine. He's clever. Knows we care for him.' How I *did* care about my father struck me as odd. He barely communicated while I grew up and unfairly encouraged my brothers' bullying. But I treasured any of our conversations, pleasant moments finer than favourite snapshots. In the seaside air without traffic noise, I wondered what a close family felt like instead of the far-flung version I had to be thankful for. Thoughts fleeting as the flight of moths past us into the light.

'Good of Samuel to ring me.' Coltrane shifted in his chair. I missed them too, curiously, my brothers. We each lived in different towns. Absence made the heart grow fonder and all that. 'Yes, Samuel rang but the others almost never do. It's like they're scared or....' I sometimes wondered if they worried that one day I'd list all the tortures, put them on the spot, but didn't mention this to Coltrane.

'They say they *don't know* you.' My tall, grown, child's handsome profile against an early evening sky. One star hung in deep blue, with the moon low and almost full. He stuck out his chin like Dad did sometimes. I felt like hugging him, but just sat there, searched for clever words or some platitude. Memories crowded in. As usual, under pressure I rarely stayed in the moment; allowed this blurry effect lately, like someone who lives on a houseboat knows their dwelling will always be a little unstable. Life easier if I didn't fight myself. Nothing to say about this illness to my son. Or perhaps I did need to? Maybe holding back served our forebears, alone in untamed country, but now we needed connections. Didn't we? 'My brothers, your uncles *could* ring. I leave *them* messages. They make no effort.' Despite my complaint, I laughed.

Then Coltrane said my brothers felt puzzled about how little money I made, when they had plenty. I reminded him, 'I make quite a stack, thank you. And since I bought my little house mortgage-free, its selling price has doubled. I don't show it off, that's all.'

While Coltrane talked about how my brothers helped him, describing projects, I thought about Dad. When he fell ill the first time, a year before, phones rang frequently for a change. Wanting to know what the doctors said, to swap opinions. Then, this grown child had turned up unannounced from hours away. Sat there in serious conversation for once. How important. My muscles tensed. It felt a little dangerous. I asked my son Coltrane if he ever read much about the Romans.

He ignored the question and ploughed on to ask about his grandfather's health over the last year.

Remembering what I could, a few facts.

My immediate family sometimes asked straight questions, but they often seemed to want to know something else.

Did Coltrane expect me to discuss my own health? Why drive all this way? But what good would it do to mention Post-traumatic Stress Syndrome? All the decades of therapy had changed me so much, I preferred to think I no longer suffered from it.

A mild chuckle. My family usually dissolved whatever I decided with *their* ideas about who I am. I'm the aspirin and they're the water, fizz, or I'm a letter in the rain, fizzle. Didn't think aloud. If I openly admitted discoveries through years of therapy and reading, they'd pooh-pooh the theories as if *I'd* invented them. *You're not sick. You haven't got anything wrong. It's effort, that's the issue.*

Coltrane said, 'Growing up middle-class like I did, it's hard to get to know someone like you.'

I leant forwards, 'Love, just because I live in this funny old house and most of my money's invested, does not mean I forget where I came from or who my family is.'

Coltrane stared into the distance.

'I like living alone, and simply. You live on your hill, too, Coltrane, dense bushland around your family.' I took a good breath. 'We each may choose our place in the sun.'

We just sat there. Evening, warm and quiet. Thoughts arose about how Coltrane rarely mentioned his absent father, Joe, the guitarist who tamed a stray cat and now lived in a foreign city. I'd decided years before that Coltrane needed to stay with my parents, one last time, when I was homeless. They'd kindly cared for my only child before. This last stint stretched years without me there to make him school lunches, to listen to how his day was, to know all his friends' names and what he hoped he'd get for Christmas. Thoughts of what I'd missed like a stab in the guts.

Coltrane and I both needed far more attention than we ever received from anyone. He grew up with my stupid brothers' pushy behaviour too, then me, his mother, a visitor, and his father, Joe, overseas. My parents looked after my child. They also made it clear they'd give me no help if I just took him, which I wanted to do. We discussed it for an entire weekend. They stuck to their opinion, 'He's better off here.'

Samuel, my brother, visited in the middle of that weekend and took their side, 'His friends are here. He's settled in school. You're all over the place, always were.'

Yes, Coltrane and I shared difficulties. My mother distant, especially when I was young. Dad rarely home, not present when he was there. Joe and me, far away. Coltrane in a repeated pattern albeit with my parents mellowed by age. I could only see this looking back. Neither had I known at the time I acted in this cold, rather careless manner. My thoughts not sounding like anything to say aloud, it felt like thinking in a foreign language I'd never learnt.

In any case, my son and I both moved recently to live quietly, with few people around. We also lived a long way from each other.

My old cream bach with a blue roof and a faded yellow door in a forgotten seaside town (the place recently died when the beach collapsed in a storm). Not the dustless orderly life Coltrane and my brothers aimed for, he was correct there. Coltrane's new place glass, cedar and stone, solar power on the colour steel roof. A reed garden for their waste all the way down to native trees. The driveway immaculate pale stones curved to a pillared atrium and carved front door. Good on him.

Secretly then I thrilled a little, felt like I'd helped my son eventually escape to an extent, to get free of the awful life I'd endured, then struggled to get as clear of as possible. For years when he was a youngster which he couldn't recall, I *had* cared for him, never smacked my boy, devised careful consequences instead. Discussed issues, my son had a right to be treated with respect. Some good foundation. The old saying about a child's first seven years being the most important? I'd mainly cared for him throughout those early years.

My son also may've lived with my parents but they'd grown more sociable by then. My brothers older, a little less wild, and sometimes well tempered, rarely home either.

Lately, I believed my brothers wanted to appear perfect to cover up their diabolical bullying.

People too clean and tidy, completely cosy and well-off, beautifully-mannered to the extent they never really said much even when they said a great deal. What lurked behind easy, pleasant smiles?

I'd written in my journal which I still kept - Everyone has something to be careful of, a side we'd rather not show or bad behaviour which may appear like inclement weather. When anyone behaves like their dark side's nonexistent, how terrible are they when no one can catch them or see?

Myself, I didn't learn what closeness meant, simple as that. Neglect produces recluses, suicides, neurotics and desperadoes who'll take any affection they can find.

Some nights so pressured, despairing, I wished certain freaks had never existed. Fruitless, bare branches of thinking creaked away in storms. Sooty pictures in a gothic story book for halfling grown-ups to imagine happily ever after, even the hope of belief. But few ever gathered by looking at me how my inner world was so fractured and then painstakingly put back together.

A mobile, made of pumice collected from the beach in the next bay, twirled quietly against the darkening sky. That night, I'd originally wanted to watch Antiques Roadshow on TV, but the ancient line of ourselves appeared afresh when Coltrane knocked at the door. He mattered more than any entertainment.

'Growing up seems, uh, it's a mess somehow,' something trembled behind his bass notes, like when an extra instrument such as a flute chimes in with an orchestra.

For a while in the warm evening, I explained relevant events as recalled, from meeting his dad in the days when Joe lived in The

Shack (his rather rundown flat). Psychedelic days when we reinvented freedom, opened inner doorways; tried not to rush the details. But I didn't like to recall the struggle just to get by as a lone mother. 'Mum and Dad took you to live with them when my flat got burgled, or I was evicted and had to sleep on someone's sofa, or other calamities appeared. One place caught fire. Luckily, we'd gone away that week when my flatmate set off fireworks inside. Again, no place to live. But I looked after you a lot when you were young. Then I couldn't cope and you stayed with your grandparents quite a while. It seemed like they'd not talk to me again if I insisted you had to come back, Coltrane. They said you had friends in their neighbourhood. Best to stay somewhere stable. Sam backed them up, your uncle. Angry about me wanting to take you away.' I almost reached out to touch Coltrane's hand. 'I wish now I'd asked you about it all.'
'It's interesting to hear your version of what happened,' Coltrane's flat, cold tone made me quiet.
In mind, I searched for likely explanations, wondered if my family constructed a history without my story. A weight settled, just like when those brothers locked me inside cupboards. Did they say I never cared? Did they lie to stop Coltrane wanting to see me? One final, horrible betrayal I never even guessed until this moment? I imagined such a lie, invented from how I didn't desperately fight to keep my son, didn't demand he came with me. Never mind how exhausted and broken I was. They never listened, ignored my weakened state after years of bullying. I had to learn to give in, to ignore the fact they basically didn't want to help me feel better or care for my child.
They did everything 'by themselves.' Not one of my brothers ever admitted someone else assisted them. They loved to make out they created everything alone, brilliant and independent. Didn't want me to recall the hurt I suffered either, and wouldn't want me telling Coltrane horror stories. Their perfect lives suddenly messy. How neat and tidy to make me someone without a heart, shove me aside and forget, as usual. Someone outside of their lives who was to blame for everything possible. A shell of a person. Easily smashed. Gone. Only a cracked actor. A friend of mine, years ago, hissed, 'Your parents stole your

child off you.'
'It's pointless to get annoyed. That would only upset me, and
they wouldn't care.'

On my porch I did my best to smile. 'O, they did what they
thought best. People usually do, even if later it seems wrong. At
the time I think most people do try to do the right thing,' my
light tone surprised me, so convincing. But anger would not help
anyone. I knew that as well as I knew how to tell the weather
forecast by picking up a piece of seaweed from my gatepost.
Poisonous thoughts threatened, but if I concocted vitriol, mixed
a foul recipe in mind, then I'd only feel like a piece of rotten
debris in the tide eventually. Not for me. Hatred may feel big,
dense and overpowering. But hatred's like the inside of a golf
ball, wound up small, tight and solid, best not tampered with or
it unravels. Instead of upheavals, I preferred to feel hopeful and
involved. Days opened where I planned practical results, sold
treasures online, chatted to locals, and walked along the coast. I
soon looked forward to striding along. Wrote my journal to keep
control, gave thanks every day for my life, my trials, my pains
and joys, my work, food, health, friends and family. My
thoughts, I could now control those too to some extent. Cried
when I had to. Tears pass.

Anger descended once upon a younger me and I rampaged, like
bush fires across vast tracts of land, roaring into and reducing
houses, furniture, food, books, trees, fences, people, pets, tools,
cars to ash. Door slamming at home and often I ran away. But
my brothers teased with the devil, got me in headlocks, hit me
on the arm too hard for, 'A pinch and a punch for the first of the
month....'
Night drew in, cold and moonless, long ago. Chilled, but I
refused to call for help. A possum walked across the grass so
close to my foot I almost kicked it. My brothers had tied me to a
tree. Shivering, I'd thought in the morning they would find me
dead and blue. *Serve them right.*
My mother came out to the letterbox, she'd forgotten to check
the mail. Saw me in back porch light spilled across the lawn.

Stood as tall as I could, a ten year old girl held to the apple tree
with twine. It'd cut into my skin where I'd struggled to get free
and the binding hurt, but I said nothing.
Mum set me loose and said my name in this angry way. My fault
I'd been tied up and left there.
Once at the doctors, he found this ugly school sore behind my
ear. A huge weeping thing, it ached. Mum said, shocked, 'O no.
O, terrible. How did you let it get that way?' Again, I'd done
wrong. Six years old, supposed to stay whole and clean by
myself.

Wondered what Coltrane would make of such pitiful stories
now, but I said nothing.

Going over the past, putting myself in other people's places, for
years this helped me understand. It took three exhausting days
for my birth, and our mother almost died. She'd already had my
three brothers with some trouble. Then this late addition, me.
Easy to imagine no one asked Mum if she needed any help with
recovery. A baby to care for was all a woman needed. *So get on
with things. Box on. Chin up. Made of the right stuff. No complaints.*
A bright, energetic little girl, I didn't know Mum'd had such an
awful time with my birth. How could I? Mum frantic when I
rarely slept and wanted hours and hours of someone talking,
smiling, singing…. Perhaps Mum resented this new baby despite
her best efforts, disappointment hidden behind smiles. 'O yes, a
beautiful baby girl, what we wanted.' What people expected. All
my teeny clothes hand-knitted, hand-washed, carefully aired,
neatly matched, just the picture.
My mother too could've had blue depths where she sunk awful
secrets. Some so far drowned she didn't know what they were,
but their weight dragged. Life perpetually bizarre. Difficult
doesn't even halfway explain it. Everything happens for the first
time, as Jorges the poet wrote.
The past couldn't have been any different. I had to forgive my
parents for lacking the energy and focus to believe in me as I was
and be kind, had to forgive doctors and everyone for not
knowing what to do when Mum experienced such agony having

a baby, forgive my lunks of brothers for behaving like I was a
challenge or a game, too, forgive myself my own limits, forgive
our flaws, we're incomplete without them.

I'd little idea how to care for a child, my growing up with such
neglect meant that was what I believed was normal. Acceptance
a kind of peace, and I could concentrate elsewhere. Forgiveness
for myself. I deserved a life after all, and I could at last learn
better.

Easy to take Coltrane's hint that we all had our views, now we
could move on. I'd already worked through so much on my own.
'Let's have some dinner,' I suggested.

My son set the table. A Clarice Cliff plate in the centre,
Fantasque's bright colours, stripes around an island in a
shimmering, swirling sea. 'This is old?' He ran a finger over the
design.

'Oh yes, sixty or seventy years. Clarice Cliff. Her vivid colours,
angular shapes, lovely aren't they? Art deco, you know?' I served
peas on more recent orange and yellow plates from Japan.
Placed cooked, marinated chicken (pan-fried in olive oil with
garlic, cumin and coriander), some roast kumara and parsnip on
the serving dish. 'I never use her plates for food,' laughed easily
while I spoke, 'they're too expensive. Just put a Clarice Cliff on
the table to admire.'

We discussed choice items he'd noticed. 'This school fair near us,
I found an amazing glass vase in an old cardboard box,' Later,
he nodded at pictures online. 'Yes, it's like that one. Crazy
colours.'

I explained, 'A good price if the glass vase or any china's in good
condition. But at times the bid's below reserve. So I add them to
my collection here. If you can't live with it, don't buy in the first
place.' I settled into my chair. 'Wait years at times before getting
what I want for some items.'

Like rediscovering a favourite perfume after years bereft, we
talked about Italian art glass, fairground, and green and pink
glass, picture mirrors, black mirrors, and china.

Soon, he drove home. His twin daughters had a sports match
the next morning. 'Fathers and children, they tell me.' He

grinned. 'Three-legged races and such.'

While I walked the shell path to the road and kept on waving, I
said a silent prayer of thanks for my son learning better than
either his father or I did at his age. Feckless, we were in a whirl
of anger and sadness, a trial to reach out to anyone else.
Coltrane possessed more bravery, perhaps. I hoped he wouldn't
hold anything too much against me. Forever sorry that I'd never
got Coltrane from my parents with their blessing, and because I
never could, wished that in future we'd create some kind of
peace around those stark events, the definition too obvious.

My own childhood memories growing at last indistinct, someone
walks away and gradually blurs. Writing laid much to rest in
finite words, whole episodes, entire decades transformed into a
story, with an end. Books close. People move on to something
else. I could too.

The book my son had said he was writing sounded frightening.
'Someone isolated, having to rely on themselves alone. Little
food or water, you know, real survival stuff.'

I wondered if the book really existed or if Coltrane still liked
scaring me. He'd inherited some of my brothers' ideas about
humour. Younger, my son hid and jumped out, to see me scream
in fright. Then he laughed, uproariously. I'd never asked him
why. My son and my three brothers, their alarming noises as
unfathomable as the deepest oceans. Way down there, fish grew
monstrous, were transparent and carried their own lights.

A quiet life such as I'd managed to find, it helped focus, and
safety appeared possible. I sang while gardening or just smiled
for the joy of another day. Riches to me, unusual, but I felt
myself growing accustomed to secure feelings when they did
appear. Who knew calm felt so dramatic, so enormous, so
satisfying? I learnt to welcome peacefulness and hoped it'd last.

Great to talk with my son, but later I sobbed without warning,
from exhaustion and fright. Unwanted memories pushed in like
a half-drunk crowd demanding attention. Other people got too
close, as if they could steal my bones, or what they said tried to
take over my skin. Grappling with what it all meant the way
someone would try to take off a sodden knitted jersey after
falling into the sea. I did what my therapist had suggested I do

when these bouts of tears took over, told myself I was doing the best I could and the sadness and fright would pass, soon. It did. My diary that day - So much which others take as normal, ordinary, events they can shrug off, I find as strange as a dream in a foreign language.

This house, its shell pathway and small porch, the worn yellow paint on the front door, my three main rooms and the carefully arranged collections on sturdy wooden shelves around the living area, steady, real, touchable. Myself in a mirror or photograph. A need for time alone. My hopes are flowers, or balloons floating in dawn air where no breeze disturbs them.

Thoughts about my past, the rigours of childhood....no wedding for me. I'll never get on that well with my family, either.

Glug, glug, a glass of wine for my birthday and a queen olive stuffed with garlic. Hartigan's our local shop ordered them from the city, kept them in their fridge until collected. (Some days I went away on china-buying trips and didn't return for a while). Accustomed to expect little family celebration for anything I did. The lack of attention a relief. If they did notice I cared about anything then they could quietly or obviously work to take it away, wreck it or make whatever I loved far less. A happier state, left alone.

My last therapist had thankfully explained, 'You can need a lot of time alone to recover from the stimulation of the wider world. This is due to sensitivity. If you're troubled by visions of faces torn apart or violent acts, make the effort to think of something benign. Summer blue sky, patches of flowers in the garden, the way a cat's fur feels warm when you stroke it.' Years of one-on-one meetings in pleasant rooms, re-patterning my startling stories. Darker elements faded, associated pain diminished. Sorrow and regret snarly and dangerous, a bundle of barbed wire hidden in a garden. Me caught up by accident. But I didn't need to keep barbs with me. The loss of drastic, caustic memories as welcome as a sunny day to step into, instead. 'Of course memories disturb you. A terrible time. But now it's over.'

For a long time I just wanted to die when life pushed me around.
Falling into relationships with men who took advantage, or with
such terrible problems themselves they had no idea of empathy.
But beauty wonderfully distracting. In hindsight quite obvious
that love affairs and dalliances provided some blessed relief.
Could anyone anyway plan never to fall in love again unless the
object of desire was sure to provide security and kindness,
respect? Did we control chemistry?
Sometimes in bed unable to sleep, I silently apologised over and
over again, like a prayer.

Alone, living in a quiet settlement. Comforting, like taking out a
hand-made quilt stitched from the fabrics of childhood clothes.
Lovely handiwork in a chair by a sunny window.
Around my living room, collections of china on shelves, in
cabinets, a few plates hung on the wall. Rich, vibrant colours,
Red Autumn, Bizarre and Circle Tree, bright glazes, distinctive
geometric Clarice Cliff shapes, 19th century Japanese ceramics
like Imari bowls, subtle yet often dense shades of blue, deep
orange, and grey - various patterns, and dynamic. Tall,
voluptuous William Moorcroft clematis or pomegranate vases
c.1950 and earlier pieces, a leaf and berry vase from the
1920s.... Provenance and descriptions ran through my mind like
a list of friends I'd invite to a party.
Cool and smooth to the touch, created by someone who loved
their work. A bowl or plate admired for decades, whole and
lovely. How naturally controlled each appeared, apparently
effortless and simple. Human effects from someone's hand
moving, an interaction of eye and gesture influenced by
thinking, talent, and skill in the pattern. Evidence of care.
Bach on the stereo played softly. One large bedroom window
towards the headland and a patch of sea below just visible, from
my elevated site. On the hill some distance away, a solitary,
ancient tree on a promontory. Sightseers sometimes walked up
there to regard the ocean. A path led along, lit by street-lamps.
And the tree at night such as it was caught the illumination.
Already with leaves appearing fresh green once more, the tree
grew streaming away from the prevailing westerly wind and

looked like a woman with her hair flowing forwards. She walked with her arms outstretched, surely to wholly embrace the future.

Restart

Across the street and through the park,
we ranged this suburb wild as crows.

Hear us call, watch us fall but believe we rise,
wings in mind while eating what you sowed.

- Childhood by Jonah Anubis 1997

'Just pop down shall I?' Sam asked over the phone, as if he lived
a street along instead of four hundred kilometres away. The day
after the day when I decided I'd never get along with my
brothers, all three called me, one after the other, and said they
could visit if I liked.
Pleasure and surprise in my laugh upon hearing they'd visit. So
much time had passed, I told myself. Surely we were different
now and could enjoy conversation, even a trip out on the water?
Sun streamed in the window from a blue sky outside, as uplifting
as a happy song.
Eldest brother Samuel told me he'd already heard from Peter.
'Booked a motel, only a few minutes from your little house. We
don't need you to take us in.' It transpired that Roland had
suggested Sam presumed too much to think they could all just
turn up. 'Anyway, always wanted to see that coast, find out if the
fishing's any good.'
A pleasant idea to go along I supposed, and tried to see us on a
boat, fishing, even if something like a dark cloud appeared in
mind. I hadn't offered them a trip on my boat, either.
In my little house on the top of a good, high slope close to the
sea but not too near, the phone rang about once a week usually.
Gave me a fluttery feeling when it wasn't expected. Did most of
my business online, knew someone was about to call when they
rang, as a rule. Unaccustomed to phone jangle, then hearing
Samuel, jolly with it, too.
It'd been a trying few days. Family carry-on, dad not well, my
son just appearing at my door without a call first, and now my
three brothers ringing, one after the other. Any minute a piece

would slip then something could spin and I'd be scattered to the four winds like errant seed. Intrusions.

I could fly apart.

Something loose.

But online I'd happily describe something offered for sale, typed, 'The bowl is in perfect condition and has a lovely deep purple lustre with a light blue glaze. The effect being like shot silk.'

I needed to talk only enough with local people, when we saw each other, to have them feel like I'd passed on some news, and to ensure they knew I was content, or annoyed for good reason. My garden, and fishing, luckily offered various highlights or occasional issues. 'The broad beans are taking off, but I see there's a bit of oxalis to get rid of, smartly.' We'd nod and frown in the sun, agreeing weeds were a nuisance. 'If I get out in the boat again and find that spot, I'll drop you in a snapper. They were everywhere. Good size too.' Never exact about my favourite places to fish, I'm not a fool.

Quiet days at home online, trading, or writing, sorting bits I'd picked up, weeks without visitors or unexpected calls. My past lolled about like something heavy washed up in the tide, undulating kelp in the shallows, or memory slept, an old dog lying on a porch. Any odd noise and my gone days, my doggone days (I have to laugh even if this is alarming), those mongrel times snarled, snapped, bit or tore something up.

Many people could find me annoying, not believe I had a condition I hadn't much control over. Some lack compassion or are unkind. My wishing they cared didn't make any difference. Now I knew why I gave my son when he was younger such satisfaction, the times when he jumped at me from hiding places. Most people didn't screech and collapse when a child leapt at them from behind a chair or a tree.

Writing from the battlefront to my fellow survivors. Told to shut up, sit down, stay still, grin and bear it, not to bother anyone. We're weak, stupid, over-reacting, sob sisters, hormonal, insane, unstable, and on and on and on. Doing what we can to stay alive after a secret war, a fight that may stay hidden, because it too often seems, at first, like no one wants to hear what happened, or how it affected us. Battles at home, familiar tortures, every

day pain we believed normal. Standing strong with our
therapists, friends, the few trusted people discovered so far.
Knowing my condition I grew calmer. The new me. A label. An
actual syndrome, a condition, a studied effect of abuse, not
imagination or weakness. A few clues about how to live more
steadily. A shell-shocked child from the pummeled, disputed
territory of family. Some wanted me less bright, less demanding,
quieter and out of the way. Not my fault. Their ignorance.
Their intolerance. Their impatience and inability to engage.
Highly sensitive, I noticed things others didn't, or details they
thought unimportant. Those who nodded and smiled to look
understanding were only *acting* clever. At last, the terrible effects
of my neglect and abuse weren't nothing, anyway. They could
be managed, controlled, even erased.

A therapist explained, 'Old soldiers may slowly readjust to life
away from bombs and guns. Others have no idea they're
suffering from shock, they muddle on, become addicted to
drugs, alcohol, work, fall victim to those who disregard their
fragile state, may grow anti-social. Any dramatic experience of
hurt, brutality, abuse, or trauma may produce Post-traumatic
Stress Syndrome (or Disorder). People disassociate from the
scene, float away or think of something else, then find it hard to
come back. Memories of the shock however can flood through
the mind constantly, or when someone's reminded of the
incident or period of trouble. Loud noises, a particular smell,
food, music, scenes of violence, the sight of blood, many things
can trigger those who suffer in this way. Terrified and unable to
escape those effects while the shock occurs, later, shattered, some
people piece themselves back together, hopefully with assistance
from a health professional like myself.'

Not looking particularly sick, no piece of skin had changed
colour or been cut away, my hair didn't fall out (some people's
does) no leg or arm missing, my eyes looked bright. But when
something disturbed me, even a momentary fright, I froze inside
and relived past trauma, couldn't concentrate, would rush off
without warning or act like I could see something about to hurt
me when nothing was there. Often I muddled people up,
thought one was another due to the same colour hair or their

face shape. Sometimes I appeared stupid, easily taken advantage of, lost control of my ability to make decisions. I agreed to go along rather than make a scene or cause disagreement.

Now, in the calm of a house surrounded with small town predictability, little noise or fuss and a known routine, I grew kinder. Solitude saved my well-being. I visited yet again a new therapist once a fortnight in a neighbouring town for years, and many websites offered assistance. The world wide web my saviour. Research. The unknown far more frightening than apt knowledge.

Some days I sat by the window which looked out to the rather patchy asphalt road edged with sand and those bright Ganzania, large daisy-shapes in bright colours which tumbled across lawns and banks, edged the roads and pathways. A view down the hill to a glimpse of the sea. Sky changed day-long from lilacs and greenish-blue in the morning, sometimes pink or scarlet like a fabulous evening dress left behind, transforming to cheery blue or devastating grey, perhaps various miracles of clouds in complicated yet lovely formations. The sky reminded me of nothing but itself.

Over and over I carefully turned the news of a family visit, like a package someone sent me that I didn't want to open yet. My brothers sounded on the phone like they really wanted to see me.

Family sixth sense, surely. As soon as some family member loosens their grip on whatever tension they're supposed to hold steady, even if it is maintaining a taut sense of distance, the others rush to tighten things again. As soon as I had believed none of us children now grown and my own son too for that matter, could ever be overly friendly towards me, my brothers converged for contact. And so considerate, booking a motel. The unfamiliarity made my heart beat faster.

Catch hold of what's known and be saved from drowning in a sea of strangers. Familiar, families, fate, safety in numbers, and blood thicker than water. On my porch, on the small swing seat to listen to crickets along with distant surf on a truly still evening, I wondered nevertheless why we siblings had to be close at all. Each with our own families. My youngest brother, Roland, supported two households, including four children, since his divorce five years before. My son didn't mind me phoning as far as I could tell, although sometimes tension arose, but we discussed his work and their twins at least every month. One liked to climb, the other to sit and 'read', chanted half-recalled words and made up the rest. Every anecdote of Coltrane's encouraged me to ask for more, but I tried not to sound too delighted in case he got annoyed (accustomed to my family not liking me enjoying anything too much). Always pleased to hear his voice. The world lightened considerably.

Grandchildren growing so fast. I wished I knew a way to see them in person more often. Coltrane discouraged my visiting. Distance did the rest. It'd take me a day to drive there and another to return. I had to stop and get out every hour or so, or my legs seized up. Age encroaching.

My brothers with families hours from my place. Could picture them in their various abodes, at a table of some kind, wooden or glass. Breakfast, lunch, dinner, snacks, talking about daily whatever. Children needed help with homework, a ride to a sports match or concert, endless shopping for food, clothes, visits to the dentist and doctor.... Gleeful displays of some picture made at school, or a new dance step learnt, someone building castles or fancy houses with tiny coloured blocks. A neighbour's child and my nieces or nephews in some altercation, a scraped knee, someone caught shoplifting or cyber bullying. Or just sad, a deceased pet on a patch of lawn, a friend moved away, disappointing days at school where nothing ever went right, then the flu, a cold, something mysterious. Celebrations too when someone won a prize or had a birthday.

We could every one of us stay busy without the need to visit siblings, ever. But the pattern had vastly changed. Dad in hospital. I dwelt on this - it was not enough to have shifted how things usually went. It felt like coming home and seeing your whole lawn removed, or half the house demolished, or a gigantic billboard erected over a gorgeous view you once enjoyed. The *three* of them coming here to see *me*? My brothers? My stomach churned.

What would make it impossible for them to come and see me?

An accident? No, they'd visit hospital and find the lie.
Something mysterious? No, they'd find a way to discover and
dissipate any nebulous carry-on. Be firm, refuse to see them? My
hand sat on the phone. Nothing urged me to move.
Not that long ago I'd be happy, and remain so, to think they
wanted to visit. Some faint hope would flower like a seed pushes
towards the sun after rainfall. I'd imagine us all at long last like a
family in a story book, reunited, talkative, laughing, like others
did, with pleasure. Costing nothing but time, we'd finally
discover much in common agreeable and forget the rest.
But nothing like hope bloomed anywhere near, now. My new-
found disinterest curious, the feeling examined the way I'd
puzzle over how a pair of trousers suddenly did not fit.
Emotions akin to clothes, but worn even closer. Now it felt as if I
regarded a walk-in wardrobe of styles too big for me or too
strange, thinking about Dad ill. I sighed.
Great hulks of brothers, tall, sporty, noisy. Could picture them
broader, but were they? Each with their own style but somehow
quite alike, how they walked, and dressed, muted, new casuals,
nothing scruffy. Imagining this, it felt like I had nothing to wear.
My hand jumped from the phone where it'd been resting and
knocked the instrument off the little side table. Sharp pains in
my chest, and coloured patches of light swam in front of my
eyes. Had to sit back with my eyes wide and wait for the sharp
pain and special effects to subside, then scrambled for the
telephone less forcefully. Tested to see if it worked, picked up the
receiver, a *brrr* sound.
Panic. I could say I felt too ill for visitors. But they could all three
still just turn up. *O we thought you'd need a hand. We'll order in home
help.* They loved taking charge. Weakened, I'd be seen as easily
pushed around. One would say I needed to sell the house, get
into managed care, never mind I wasn't anywhere near old
enough. They'd argue over the pros and cons of a visiting
housekeeper.
But what would happen if they found me in the garden, digging
away or hauling pruned branches down the back? Their
supposedly ailing sister as healthy as anyone.
Nervous, I'd made this visit ridiculous.

A positive spin necessary. Therapists encouraged seeing the
bright side and it worked to an extent. It'd be good to see the
boys. Mum called them *the boys*, even when they grew taller than
her.

The smallness of my house comforting then, like when I hid
under the table in my childhood home to escape rough games.
An easy, small world under there, manageable, distracted by
minutiae in the one spot. Absorption in surfaces and textures,
obsessive. I'd gaze at the underside of the tabletop and examine
every line of wood grain. Some shapes looked like animals or
landscapes, stories invented for each one.

Yes, as a child who wanted so much to run, to leap, to shout and
laugh, to comment and question, I learnt to sit very still and just
stare at something for ages. Knowing all the lines and shapes of
it, only my mind allowed free reign. Even then, not to speak of
that much, not to anyone at home. Relaxing in the manner of a
hunted bird who knew how to imitate the branch of a tree.
Nothing could harm me when as motionless as possible.

This arrest happened eventually without thought. I'd slow, find a
corner, sit, inert. Something reminiscent of pain or danger, a
pattern I didn't like in the battle zone, I'd grow zonked out,
staring into space. Uninviting, unlikely to do much, no reaction.
The old days. Now, times had changed. I still preferred the quiet
life however, my house repainted or repaired to a certain extent,
but not overly, anything that I approved of shabby, I left alone.
Not to stand out or draw attention, just to blend in. If no one
knew I had anything, they'd leave me alone.

Our childhood home was rather run-down on the outside in
later days. Dad refused to paint it with so many other bills to
pay, but Mum made him wash the place down at least once a
year. My mother also redecorated with new curtains and
cushions, small affordable items rather than whole walls of paint
or new lounge suites. She also cleaned the interior so often it felt
as if she'd like us to disappear so she could keep it perfect. I
caught Mum once with a cloth behind me, wiping over the lino
where I walked in my slippers. 'They're new, they drop fluff.'
She smiled her half-smile, as if she didn't feel like she was ever
allowed a real grin, then frowned again at the floor. Nowadays I

knew what obsessive compulsive disorder meant, years ago she was just weird and annoying.

Reading books the perfect escape. One day I read three, all the way into the night. Under the table, for a while a pile of books kept there, and a packet of biscuits, but Mum soon tidied them away.

Luckily tall by the time I reached eleven, the boys stopped throwing me about so much. Then the pinches and punches started, jibes and teasing. Apparently innocent albeit painful exercises, without forethought, ignorant behaviour where they didn't seem to realise they did actually hurt me. It's easier to forgive them even if I felt deeply injured and often horribly bewildered, if I think they never planned their attacks and remarks.

Now, those days under the table with my books and soft toys provide happy memories. Finally blank, hidden and camouflaged. No need to watch out. Sat against the far wall, with the tablecloth long like a curtain. No one teased or grabbed. My toys away from ridicule or vandalism, too. Christening the cuddly items occurred secretly, away from cruel laughter. A blue bunny named Sydney, a knitted girl doll suited Twitchy, and then there were three teddy bears. The biggest bear, Ro, perversely named after my youngest, shortest brother, Roland, who behaved like he knew everything, the middle bear, Pep, just like my middle brother Peter, with his short brown hair and rather bossy look; more vague than Roland, eyes a little too close together. The smallest bear, pale fur rather gingerish, a cheeky grin, and one missing eye from when I left him in the basement for months and something tried to eat him, that little bear I named Sam.

The eldest, Sam could take punishments I dealt out when the bears misbehaved. Cheeky animals, each indulged in name-calling and at times answered back. Sometimes they pinched Twitchy or kicked Sydney. I never lost time in telling them off either. Sam the ringleader, I could tell so with my special powers. Poor Sam bear, he sat in the cobweb corner or under the feijoa tree in the rain, until the others were truly sorry.

When those brothers of mine saw me talking to these toys they'd jeer. So I hid my play away.

Nowadays, some well-informed neighbour or family friend
would notice the way I punished my toys (sometimes I jumped
up and down to flatten their stuffed soft bodies). Someone over
the fence would now report our family to some trained person in
an office. An educated woman or man with shelves of folders,
their official desk, a computer, a cheery pot plant, and a photo of
their own well-adjusted family in a frame. Accoutrements by a
large jotter pad for official scribbles while they talked on the
phone to many concerned people who rang in. Children put on
a list. Maybe they'd already have a file on our rag-tag, raucous
family. New information added. Someone we'd never seen
before would call, in a late-model car with a logo on freshly-
washed paintwork. An interview with our mother, and maybe
both parents. They'd inspect the front garden after they knocked
and waited, like someone looking for a leaky drain.

But we can't go back in time and make this happen. The fact
that something observed changes because it is observed, wasn't
in evidence in my childhood, more's the pity. It was like my
troubles were invisible to others, imaginary. Anyone who
possibly did surreptitiously notice how unhappy I was did
nothing much affecting me for the better. Various parents
possibly did mutter to one another, or took their worries along to
another suburb or town to tittle-tattle in that way people have,
talking about *unfortunates* or that *odd, rather wild little girl,* as if we're
characters in a soap opera they like to discuss. They'd soon move
on to boasting about a new car or discussing a favourite recipe.
No one liked to *dwell,* or to seem *too involved.* No neighbour or
relative able to help, except of course if they could've had me
taken me away. But I'd possibly have hated that, too. I think all
of this now.

But other help could've appeared. Someone to help my mother
would've been a start. A friendly home help for two hours a day.
A thoughtful stranger who became a kind of friend. I say this
hoping someone will read my idea and take it along to a meeting
somewhere. Suggest it, try something new so a test run of 'home
help to stop abuse' starts up and other children are cared for,
instead of shunted about and hurt, over and over. Crying while I

write about the past has to be for more than simply words on a page.

When a family is set adrift from others in their street, when their mother barely speaks to anyone else or the people she does speak to never really say much, isolation breeds illness, cruelty and pain. The family grows used to mayhem, depression, pain; adapt or die.

Learnt to do well enough, change to endure the most extraordinary circumstances. If someone had transplanted me elsewhere, *for my own good,* I'd have had to fit with their foibles and habits. My best friends along with me. The three bears. Survivors.

At the risk of my siblings seeing the old toys displayed and thinking me even loopier, I retrieved my childhood bears from the box in the back of my wardrobe. Sprayed them with fabric refresher, set them in the sun outside for a few hours then displayed these bedraggled-but-cleaner-than-just-before items. By the front door on a little table, which sometimes held flowers in a vase, my bears sat looking out. Ro, Pep and Sam inside the glass by the sunny front door. Festive.

Odd to realise then I mostly didn't mind what my brothers did any longer, fear faded like how thoughts lose sharpness on a really warm day. *My* house. Could display old toys, could set out furniture in any manner I pleased, could throw everything onto the front lawn and spring clean, or send it away and buy new. Mine.

From the garden I took vegetables and herbs, soon prepared dinner. Chopped coriander, baby celery, rocket and baby silverbeet for a salad, grated carrot. Emptied a drained can of cooked chickpeas into a bowl to mash them with chopped fresh parsley, cumin, coriander, chopped onion and garlic for falafel. Added some flour and egg at the end to make the smooth paste needed, a little water. While falafel fried in olive oil I looked out the little window. Intense greenery out there, on and on. Thinking about nothing much, breathing in the delicious aroma of my cooking.

Voices outside when they were due, a man called, 'What are you

hooligans doing here?'
Another shouted back, 'Pot calling the kettle.'
They all laughed. Was it all three? I looked out the lounge window.
My brothers arrived at the same time. Coincidentally parked separate cars outside my property, that identical minute. Time gathered them together the way a tide at random groups driftwood, shells and seaweed. Not that my brothers appeared dishevelled, they all wore new, casual clothes, with their brownish hair recently cut, and well-styled, just as imagined. All three going a little grey.
None of the boys knew about the driftwood image which floated into my mind. Anything close to a metaphor uttered and they fell silent, conversation failed as if they thought they needed to watch out in case I threw something, or they could catch some kind of creative-talking disease. Unfamiliar lingo worried them, like a companion using a foreign language. I could've been saying something against them but they'd never know. Took me a long time to realise this.
Before they could get to the house I was out the door, smiling. They each hugged me on the roadside, awkward elbows and shoulders in close proximity.
All four together for the first time in years. Beaming; our feet crunched on broken bits of gravel at the edge of the asphalt road, where sand blown up from the remnant of beach met my lawn. Air fresh with a hint of salt along from the sea. Sky blue and sun shining, late spring with quite good weather expected, if a bit changeable.
For a few moments, it felt like we could need a cake and candles inside, some kind of presents to give each other so we'd have something to do besides smile. I resisted the urge to say so. My voice stayed calm when I said hello, and their names, in turn, no squeaking with glee nor fanciful remarks.
We patted each other on the back after our tangled hugging. Sam surrounded with the aroma of fresh baking like he'd been eating pastries in his car, the others soapy mixed with a kind of old man smell, a little musty.
These grown brothers with the newly more confident me. Now

they'd appeared I felt rather shy. Questions simplest, 'How was your trip here?'

Roland raved on about a car he'd seen, 'They're sleek like a space ship. I'm sure they're Italian.'

Crunching along the broken shell path towards my front door, ajar above white steps to the small porch. Resisted the urge to tug out a tuft of grass, in the middle of the path. I'd missed it in my quick tidy-up around the house. This moment had never been before. Alerted to the import, hyper-vigilance set in. I often made mistakes and they mocked errors. But more usually (now we were older), my siblings fell into a shared, disapproving silence. I repeated to myself, *I don't have to care.*

Each brother murmured about their work, a way of saying nothing while speaking anyway. Their banal chatter made me feel pushed aside. No one asked how I was. They didn't mind either if I noticed they didn't think anything I'd been doing was worth asking about. My brothers probably didn't know how much their stupid, sub-normal sister ever noticed.

Impossible to change someone else, only yourself (then others may change but it's unlikely they'll do what you want). I chanted theories silently to myself.

We walked inside. The boys each with their own mantra. Sam hummed, Roland tut-tutted lightly and Peter sang little snatches of songs so quietly they were like a music box in the house next door, the wind carrying over a few bars. 'Putting the jug on?' Sam smiled.

To stop winding myself ever tighter, I did so and set out cups. Clatter and bustle. I mixed up a batter for pikelets - flour, sugar, baking powder, a pinch of salt and an egg. Placed the large frypan to cook them. Beat some cream. I'd already made fresh jam with frozen blackberries and strawberries combined. A sizzle of pikelets rising in hot butter in the frypan, showing little bubbles. When the bubbles popped it was time to flip them.

The last time what remained of our family enjoyed a party in the city, I'd arrived late, without a dress. My protesting, 'I thought we were only eating at your place,' met with concerned asides, as if they'd never forgotten a thing in their lives. My

wearing a perfectly clean, but rather plain, top and pants could cause a riot. Sam *had* called and told me we were going to this new, fancy place, 'I called and told you twice. Twice.'
'Of course. Apologies.' I laughed but no one else did. 'O well, I can wear what I have on.'
'Let's just pop along and see what I've got. Shall we?' Sam's wife, beaming, propelled me to the hall.
Proceedings more careful than usual, I reminded myself to appear as if our family were always calm and barely spoke about anything contentious. Forbidden public topics well known but unspoken. No politics, religion, anything difficult about the past, any ideas new to anyone, any issue anyone has in mind about anything at all. A kind of bus ride dinner, amiable strangers. So I'd blocked the planned restaurant dinner from my mind.
Dressing up in this case also usually involved wearing polyester or nylon sweat tanks. I refused to splash out on fine silk or wool jersey, some expensive outfit I'd hardly wear. We relatives rarely ate anywhere swept-up, and I never patronised such places alone; formality constricting. Within the next five years when a similar occasion loomed again, the dress would be out of date, no longer fitting me, or both. With people I knew, comfortable attire was worn anywhere special. No friend minded.
Sam's wife, in a frantic hurry, blurted, wild-eyed, 'I have just the thing.' A wardrobe in their spare room, where last years' clothes or impulse-buys on their way to a charity shop hung, in exile. The fitted blue-green brocade dress suited my dark hair, but pinched my upper arms. I had to wear it. We ran out of time. I suspected she knew when she pulled it out with a flourish that it wouldn't really fit.
I needed an invisible friend such as lonely children adopt. They'd tell me, 'These clowns aren't so clever as to think of a dress to annoy you. They're dim. Forget their stupid arses.'
The restaurant crowded. Our huge round table in the centre of the room. Music plinking in the background tinny and light, or as cloying and gooey as cream cake sliding off a platter. People slower than usual. Lights muted on the periphery but we sat beneath a huge chandelier. *Stay quiet unless asking for something innocuous.* 'May I have the basket of rolls, please?' Or *be polite with*

a comment. 'The duck's delicious, isn't it? Thanks so much for thinking of this place, Sam.' *No asking any question which could lead to some interesting, truly unknown reply.* I wanted to know if anyone had tried eating sparrow or crickets in China (available in markets there). When the menu arrived it reminded me, some dishes looked mysterious. I stayed quiet. In this group, if I mentioned ideas I found intriguing, they'd say, 'That's strange,' (meaning *conversation over*), or nothing at all. O for an open window.

Our long-past and last Christmas altogether a terse gathering, six years before. Roland still with his first wife, although his marriage showed cracks. Some rules they forgot. He and his wife leaked snide remarks and sighs at each other the whole weekend, like bad soap opera scripts.

If a marriage creates a structure which the relationship then inhabits, they'd forgotten to include doors. A tragic play of trapped ugliness for our dubious entertainment. Each sought some of the family to take sides, or needed to share their misery. We may trick ourselves that pain and trouble lessen when we involve others in a mess, but really it usually just makes a bigger mess. And anything like a fight or the possibility of one made me twitchy. In my ill-fitting dress at that overly well-behaved table, my thoughts mushed into a muddle.

The brrr brrr endless bland talk and formality samey sameness lulling eventually. Then Roland or his wife hissed something and I'd sit up extra-straight. But determined not to ask what they'd said.

Dad in fine form with silly remarks. I chuckled occasionally. In a pink suit Dad called his *feminine side,* he eventually put me at ease. Five glasses of bubbly. I laughed too loud, told talkative people at the next table they looked like a real family, 'No, no really. I mean look at you, just chatting away. Genuine smiles. How do you do that?'

They all fiddled with their hair until I looked away.

A drive back to my brother's house in a cab seemed best. I'd not have to speak to anyone. Nor would I need to endure the fierce looks Sam kept shooting across the table. He looked like a stern teacher trying to control unruly children in assembly. His furious

eyes flashed, stiffness around his jaw made me worry he'd
damage his teeth, grinding them.
Difficult to hold onto the moment when memories catapaulted
me back to something horrible, the present a brand of diabolical
machinery. Living inside a demonic pinball game.

When major flashbacks occurred I needed to reason, they were
only memories, often exaggerated. My condition did this in
overblown self-defense but I could resist it, lately. Gradually I
came back to the present, less affected by imagined troubles.
The most surprising response in how I missed the excitement,
the challenge of trying to think around flashbacks. But gradually
I grew accustomed to calm and staying in the moment, foreign
and spectacular though it certainly seemed.
Now, in my little beach-town house for this latest reunion, the
boys' noise and boasts filled the place. A volume control
somewhere? Behind their rather large ears, a knob, a dial to turn
them down? Wondered if I could joke about this. Decided not.
Pikelets warm and piled on a plate. Jam and cream in little
dishes besides. Eaten faster than anyone could manage to talk.
Satisfied sounds. Every brother gulped two cups of tea each, too,
and sat comfortably, legs stretched out, deeply satisfied, replete.
Someone started humming, another stood to peer out the
window. Were they were getting ready to say something? It felt
like sitting in an orchestra pit with people tuning violins who had
no idea how to play them. I left the room. Two steps to the
kitchen which only barely held two people.
A glass of good wine and I imagined then I'd feel less put upon.
But I resisted and instead ran the tap. Water fell into the stainless
steel sink, then filled a glass. I drank it with a couple of
painkillers.
The stereo played quietly, Joni Mitchell, and summer lawns
hissing. Sprinklers, the shhhh of fine water in a vanishing dance.
Peter busied himself with a check on my windows, opening and
closing them in the living room. He bellowed about security
locks, 'Get the whole place fitted in a day.'
I stepped again into the main room. His mid-blue pants looked
expensive, but he wore a cheap polyester-cotton shirt. Expensive

clothes altogether could've made him appear more knowledgeable. In this judgmental frame of mind, I also realised he probably wanted the pants to last, they got more wear so warranted a higher price tag. Peter looked at pretty well everything in that practical way, but unable to see his image mattered. Not that I cared much about image, living on a forgotten corner of coast. The best look possible to look like such things were of little importance.

Peter shouted again, 'You were in the kitchen! So good at hide and seek, Sis.'

Lurched me out of musing on his clothes and into jagged memories. The spiky feeling of being hunted in your own house. Sometimes my breath came so fast it hurt my chest. He always led the others to find me when I hid, years ago.

Peter led others against me to give me a message. The handiest target, small, and they didn't want a girl *taking over*. Peter had behaved as if girls possessed secret powers. He didn't ever catch on that I could've been helpful to them with their schoolwork and far more.

They didn't need to be clever I suppose. Greed and selfishness served fine if you count fancy cars and new houses as successful. They rarely gave anyone else anything. Their business-life secretive as far as how much money they made, or what enabled them to get the best deals. No doubt each fell asleep every evening thinking they were brilliant.

Our springs of bubbling discovery. My extraordinary life, great escapes, excellent fashion, then discovering this eye for the best tatt to on-sell. Music and other wonders also revealed, devised and played a part, because I'd been there. Paxton not the only one who said I inspired him.

A deep voice, a question, my name. Someone with their hand on an enormous deep blue and purple vase on the sideboard. Sam smiled and asked again, 'Is this porcelain?'

'O yes, it's a lovely glaze that one. It's called Orchid.'

'Great tatt y'pick up these days.' Sam strode off to peer at Clarice Cliff, Bizarre, oranges, red and yellow in the cream room. He pronounced this china, 'Fun.'

Roland booming, 'You've nothing to steal, have you. Why get

security windows? My mistake.'

The others agreed, nodding companionably.

Antique glass and plates arranged in shelves around my living room, worth thousands. One little dish I'd sold for a few grand, only that morning. I smiled smugly. The less people knew about prices, the better. The burglar alarm no one seemed to notice, with it set high in a dark corner.

Roland never thought anything cost much unless it had a plug and lit up the instant you flicked the switch, displayed the known and unknown universe, or it flashed gold and marble, or had all of the above and no one else could get one. His four living rooms, massive kitchen, foyer complete with wide staircase, every ludicrously expensive centimetre modelled on a Donald Trump monstrosity.

Despite a promise to myself not to ever drink in their proximity again, I poured a glass of wine. Carried out the bottle and extra glasses. No one else wanted any.

In my favourite teal blue armchair, sipping wine. It tasted of oak and gooseberries.

Sam grinned. In a pale yellow t-shirt, his reddish face even more flushed than usual, he boomed, 'Well, we have great news.'

My glass heavy. I placed it carefully on the side table.

Someone coughed.

The room felt smaller. I turned to look at Sam.

He refused to meet my eyes. But Sam had forced a smile into his announcement, as clearly difficult as someone packed too tightly into a car with their arms squashed against the back window.

Surely I needed another slug of chardonnay? I told myself, *If you do not drink, then they can't say anything upsetting. Just resist the wine. Sit still, Stay really quiet. It's a magic spell.* I almost shouted, 'Want a drink? You're sure? Have one.'

Sam blathered on about how I need not celebrate just yet, he hadn't explained.

Roland didn't drink alcohol since his op, he reminded me.

Out of my chair, the spell of stillness ruined. A few curses rampaged through my head while I rummaged in the kitchen for orange juice. If I dilly-dallied enough they could give up and go on with something else. The colander utterly fascinated me for a good minute.

I'd heard the word 'celebrate', however, maybe that meant something good?

'Come on, let's get the planning done,' Peter boomed.

Easy to pretend I didn't hear him but avoidance couldn't fill an entire evening. Reluctantly, back into the lounge, carrying juice, I felt like a messenger with bad news in some ancient court.

Orange liquid slopped backwards and forwards. Someone surely was aiming something deadly at me.

Sam beamed on like a demented creature desperate to please, or escape.

Unable to imagine why he looked like that, so wildly jolly, I gulped down my wine. Poured another.

Peter clapped his hands. 'May as well just say it. Dad wants to live with you. Obvious choice, unmarried daughter. So you'll have to move back to....'

Sam let out a huge breath of relief.

The room burst into brilliance, blinding. I butted in screeching wordlessly. Everything wobbly, shimmering, haywire faces ballooned. Sound kicked in. Was I screaming?

They all stood well back, aghast. My three brothers pale, then red, soon greenish.

My screech failed eventually and I sat down, tried some actual words. Nothing sounded like language. I smiled faintly for luck, coughed, and shouted, 'It is impossible for me to live with anyone, sorry.' Grabbed my glass, gulped all the wine as if toasting myself then slapped my hand on the table for good measure. My palm stung. I plonked my glass down, and nursed my injury with the other hand.

'You'll like the old town. Two picture theatres now,' Sam grinned, his words mangled.

I thought he meant we'd go to a cinema in my town, where I lived. They'd all descended upon me like policemen in a raid, or like religious cult leaders after one of their errant members. Now they wanted movies? We had no cinema. Stared at him as if he was insane.

Sam burbled on, 'We talked to Dad. Decided you're the best idea. He can't manage otherwise, so...'

I stomped a foot hard on the floor and a few things rattled on shelves. I eyed my Claris Cliff vase, a recent treasure, and still not quite in the best place. It thankfully stayed upright.

One good deep breath in and I stood, tall, like in times past when forebears fought for women's rights outside parliament or something else extremely worthy. My words arrows that I aimed for their hearts, 'Good to see you, my brothers. Been years since we got together. All my brothers, yes. O yeees. I suppose you think this is like when you lot pushed me 'round when we were little?'

They said nothing.

Roland hunched his shoulders.

The others just watched me as if waiting for someone they knew to return and I'd just said they would be a while, this absence being my fault.

I spoke more firmly, 'I'm not able to live with anyone. Impossible. Something wrong with me. Just gave up trying to be any different. Have to have peace and quiet. I *have* to.'

'Oh Sis,' Roland smiled and shouted, 'you like your privacy. Dad won't be any trouble.'

'He is trouble though, Roland. Dad yells at the TV and the radio. I had enough, quite enough, when I was little.' My second shout made them all jump and I felt glad of it. 'The gang of you terrorising me, the racket you all made. Enough. Dad's mega-rowdy. Both TV and radio at full volume. He's so deaf. Drags in dirty shoes and boots. Wants cooked breakfast, lunch, and dinner. That's why Jo-Jo left him.' I insisted on that last statement.

The boys shook their heads.

I reiterated, and backed this with the fact that Jo-Jo, (his old girlfriend, companion, whatever you want to call her), told me, 'She got sick and tired of the grand productions every meal. Endless dishes and not being allowed to buy a dishwasher. She also hated all the mess and noise.'

Such wide eyes. Distracting. I couldn't recall them ever listening so closely before.

My luck blossoming, I spoke more calmly, 'Look, I read things online about relationships, and...'

Sam interrupted, 'Bullshit.'

My eyebrows almost caught fire they raised so fast.

The boys all talked at once. They each blamed Jo-Jo for Dad falling ill. When accusations dwindled, I held up a hand for quiet. Effective for some unknown reason. 'We all know thirty cigarettes a day did him wrong, you boys. At least the shock of a stay in hospital stopped Dad's smoking. Now, a marriage is give and take, and good habits help love stay. We could think about that.'

My platitude suited my brothers, they stopped gibbering, trying to get a word in. Each sibling now misty-eyed.

We sat quietly enough, but my mind churned. Outside, the road deserted. Instantly, I saw myself race past other rundown baches like mine, but none with a garden except for bright daisy-shaped flowers by the road. My feet slapped still-warm asphalt. I flew by a newish yellow and green bungalow, and the old dairy now closed down, leapt past Monkey Puzzle trees to the sea wall and foaming ocean.

A car revved past the house. Sam coughed and the others threw each other sidelong glances.

Obviously, I couldn't run. Knowledge held me back as surely as an anchor stopped a boat drifting.

'Dad's got it made compared to this.' Roland snorted and gestured around my treasure-packed lounge as if it was a junk-filled hovel.

'No, shut up.' I glared.

Peter's mouth wide and ghastly with strings of saliva, 'Don't speak to us like that....'

I broke in fast, 'How dare you come into my house and tell me anything without asking first what my plans are, thank you.' I glared at them; Roland with a tiny ship's wheel logo on his t-shirt.

'Stop shouting!' Sam shouted and folded his arms.

Roland sneered. 'This childishness.'

'What the hell would you know about being grown up?' I peered at him.

He looked away.

Peter foamed at the mouth, 'We have children, wives, houses, and businesses. You have nothing, nothing. Zilch. You stupid woman. Be thankful.'

Small, various coloured bands of light swam across my vision. My voice low, a growl, 'I own two properties thank you. Stupidly paid off completely. So far doubled in completely foolish value. Besides a stupid flourishing business which is stupidly none of yours and I know, even more *stupidly*, many friends. People who stupidly care. O yes, stupid, all right!' I fixed Peter with a wild stare. 'Sorted myself out after the appalling way we were brought up. Never ever push me around again.'

Sam coughed in the corner. The others stared at their shoes. A good old shouting match so we remembered who we all were. About a half an hour of silence but maybe it was only a few minutes,

Roland suggested, 'Fish and chips for dinner?'

Shakily, I stepped into the kitchen and ran the cold tap. Gushing water, the sound so calming.

Thwarted, the boys usually did want fast food. Many times called by a parent for dinner just as they were about to throw me out of a tree or worse, they stepped back then dashed inside. And they demanded something from the corner hamburger bar (which Mum said had cockroaches). Never got their wish, but wanted it. Grease and salt, fast and convenient. No idea about good food.

In the lounge I smiled with some effort. 'The next bay runs the closest takeaways.'

Sam loped over the lounge rug, past the big table, and to the front door smartly.

The rather warm house cramped and my hands and legs shook with adrenaline. I suggested in a squeaky voice that the rest of us took a walk through native trees I'd planted. 'Some stand twice as high as me now.' No hesitation, I left the house through the back door.

My two brothers kept apace just behind. Sunset birdsong and Roland on about the cacophony when James Cook first dropped anchor nearby. 'Strange, crazy noise. Bird whoops and echoes,

real odd. They must've stood on the Endeavour and felt amazed.
Thought of monsters.'
'Yes, monsters,' I whispered, but my brothers didn't seem to hear
that remark.
Peter expounded his theory about sailing ships making men
more adventurous, 'Creaky old things, uncomfortable. You'd
want to get ashore, anywhere at all. I would.'
Roland pointed out the ships were not old, *then.*
The boys eyed each other. Peter broke off their silly staring-out.
'I'm hungry. I know that.' Peter clapped once, loudly.
Roland put his hands deep into his pants pockets.
Two gold star impressions, coincidentally, of behaving like I
wasn't there. Taking the fresh air, probably still plotting (our
disagreement would only be me overreacting).
How the boys might've forced me to live at Dad's place became
a speeded up cartoon in my mind. Three on a kidnap mission,
rope and balaclavas, a canvas bag over my head. But too many
people hereabouts knew me for them to get away with anything
untoward. Already, curtains had twitched when I'd greeted the
three of them outside, that day. Half the town would know I had
visitors. A few people could've figured out who they were, too.
Was I crazy? Did I think my own brothers would kidnap me?
Would they? A blue frame, and unable to focus on my own
failings. Thinking underwater, backwards and sideways.
Hedgehogs many evenings rustled in the garden, noisy rats
romped in my roof if I didn't keep trees clear, and the awful
cries of possums at night alerted me to the need to get out there
and trap them. Now, I could see Roland tempting me to Dad's
in the same way he laid a trail to trap animals around *his* beach
house. A haphazard line of treats along the paths or through
flower beds. Tidbits led to cages, traps. Perhaps he'd scatter new
books and imported DVDs as temptations? Smiling vaguely but
not for the boys to notice, I weakly imagined they'd make
speeches or sing some soppy tune to persuade me where my
duty lay. Those last ideas as improbable as the sky turning green
and sprouting daisies instead of stars, but they'd soon try *some*
new tactic.
Even if I felt shaky after our arguing, I now found myself

grinning at nothing much.

Roland and Peter happily took a diversionary walk and discussed history with each other, segued on to the trees further down, whether they were millable. Both rubbished what the other thought, fnally wondering where Sam had got to. Neither acknowledged my part in any of the garden or grove of trees I'd planted, they didn't address any remarks to me directly either.

A good walk cleared my mind, pertinent thoughts racing. Probably, Peter would sabotage any plan Sam made, and Roland never liked anything the other two did (united only *against* me, not *for* anything else). This while Sam offered jokes. Squabbling; one making rude signs behind another's back to make the third brother laugh. Two against one, name-calling. Mad as a Marx Brothers' movie but not brilliant. They'd warm up, remember I was crazy and try to convince me I needed our father's company to stay sane. Yes, I could predict the future, sadly.

Silence my best strategy. Bullies often tried to get rid of any target who stood up to them, and abusers almost never listen positively or at all to the abused. I'd only just absorbed that information from a red covered book ordered the month before, recommended by my therapist.

Peter whispered something to our brother when I giggled to myself.

I tried saying nothing, as a test. They both paid me no mind. We walked back to the house, along the rough earth path through a dense grove of natives at the base of a gentle hill there. My well-tended track sloped towards the house. Soon we trudged up the steeper lawn, towards a large flat area near my back door. Birds continued to chatter and call. Air a little damp, but low clouds, a pleasant pale pink, red sky at night…no rain due.

Peter strode off here and there, criticised the guttering, shouted I needed better drains. 'A good plumber handy?' In the next breath, Peter spoke softly, as if advising Roland about an ill child, 'Heard your engine sounded not quite right when I pulled up in my car, earlier.'

Their mild bickering fell into the background. Darkening hills beyond us edged with gold. Midges swarmed in misty air. The ground not yet warmed enough in the daytime for evenings to be close and humid. Instead a nip crept in.

My two brothers, a short distance away, peered at my outdoor summer shower, a large, black plastic tank above it for rainwater to warm in the sun. They murmured together.

I sauntered inside. One of my favoured tricks, act like nothing was going on, and they behaved like I was invisible. Inside, divinely alone a few beats. Did a dance. Rag rug tousled, I straightened it.

Took my three teddies down from the little table by the door. Without thinking, slid under my big dining table. Their names whispered, 'Ro, Pep and Sam.'

Roland and Peter, their feet sounded firm on the floorboards. They talked for about half an hour in this desultory way as if they barely knew each other. Sam returned and the smell of fish and chips filled my bach. Crunchy newspaper noises while they unwrapped the parcel on the table above.

Feet in various trainers and their trouser hems visible below the edge of the long tablecloth, but I didn't focus. If I ever looked hard at someone, even at an elbow or their knee, they often felt my gaze, like I'd touched them. What could I say if they bent to peer underneath my dining table, to find me there with teddy bears?

The aroma of shark and taties, as Dad called fish and chips.

Mum said, 'I won't be cooking. Dad, do your duty with the treats' kitty.'

He cycled to the fish and chip shop, fifteen minutes on a fast trip (the scungy corner place only did burgers and chips or mixed grills, no fish). They double-wrapped our treat so the food wouldn't get cold on his way home. Dad also wrapped them in an old jersey on his bike carrier.

One time, I asked why Dad didn't drive our car. He said, 'I like to build up an appetite.'

But he probably didn't have money for the petrol and it took a month to save for takeaways.

Now, we grown children each owned at least one house. We more or less enjoyed work. Money rolled in faster than dad's bike wheels ever went. My trading online a *bonanza*, Mum would've said. Anything good was *mighty* and any trouble was *fireworks*. 'You kids making fireworks again?'

It pleased me to profit from trading, but I hadn't explained this to the family precisely, except for Coltrane. Enough competition already. The boys anyway would only start telling me ways to improve. I figuratively fanned away endless suggestions, questions, criticisms, their hot air.

A children's book I wrote, Henrietta and the Bad Dream, also sold in five countries. I'd used my mother's maiden name and my middle name, Rita Appleby. Henrietta had five brothers, each different degrees of awful in the book. An anti-bullying book. Best as a secret.

On and on thinking about my antiques' trading and investments as if they were a gigantic flower to admire. I owned a boat, plus my other bach on a good three acres of cleared land. Native trees over ten acres of bushland besides the large paddocks, all further south. A small camping ground planned for eco-tourists. Quite a bit in the bank to play with too, possibly nowhere near the riches my brothers enjoyed, buzzing nevertheless with events as they'd turned out recently.

Our dad owned three houses, and a block of flats. Roland's advice.

The teddies lay on my lap and I idly stroked their worn fur, while I thought of how Mum and Dad worked and saved, rarely spent on anything extravagant. But some of the brothers now preferred lavish home decorating, or their wives did, and whizz-bang gadgets. I wondered if they saved.

The boys would insist they didn't have anything in the bank possibly, even after a vague enquiry. They'd also no doubt bluff about knowing nothing of when they scared me senseless, or would make out it was just hi-jinks, silly. The past a slippery thing and likely to swim away, malleable too.

Writing an escape into other places, times, and lives. *The bears,* I'd write about them. Teddies, they'd...the bears would care for Sydney Rabbit. That toy long disappeared. Rediscovered on a quest. Dad Rabbit. This name appeared in my mind unbidden. Dad a big blue bunny?

No idea what happened to Sydney, my toy, just like I didn't know

much about Dad. Day and night he worked, often away on
selling trips for weeks, barely spoke, and when he did he
shouted. Stopped hitting me when I got to about ten, I'd
reached a certain height or something. He still laughed
uproariously when the boys teased or grabbed me, but no more
wallops from my father, or attacks with the stick kept behind the
kitchen door. He'd occasionally hold this wooden bookend
carved with Celtic patterns, intertwined, clung to it one-handed,
if he growled at me. At first I believed he'd hit me with it, but
later I gathered it soothed him in some fashion.
I blinked, remembering, refused to cry. *Didn't know any better. In
those days people hit kids all the time, everywhere. Teachers hit us,
neighbours did too, some.* We whacked each other for that matter.
Bruises turned into jokes, kids showed off the worst like trophies.
My mother gone, and Dad had lived alone for a long time.
Once Jo-Jo, his girlfriend, appeared with raucous jokes, her
scatty brash manner, my visiting Dad lost the little appeal it'd
ever presented. Every time I did appear she complained about
my father, as if she and I were friends and he was an annoying
old man, a mere acquaintance. I wanted to join in, then felt such
shame it seemed I could die of it, burn to a crisp like bacon left
under the grill. I never wanted to sink the the level of the others,
to attack family members like it was sport.
A sandy-haired joker a bit too long in the tooth, as he referred to
himself. Tall and rugged-looking with a long face rather like Sir
Edmund Hilary. While Jo-Jo lived with him, Dad turned into a
true shed man. Dad out there making home brew or
hammering. The shed rough-sawn pine, he creosoted the outside
every few years and the inside was never lined.
Pungent aromas of linseed oil mixed with sawdust, strong tea,
and something like nugget rushed out when the door opened. A
little potbelly stove lit all winter, the roof insulated, so it was
never entirely cold in there. Shed framework served as shelves,
bits and bobs on four by two wood horizontally between joists.
Much younger, I'd found a matchbox, a cowboy and indian
logo, red, yellow, blue and green, black outlines. He placed the
box at eye level, by a window. 'They'll keep watch for outlaws,
those two.' A tiny cowboy and an indian facing bleary window

glass, side-on.

I hoped not, didn't like the idea of a matchbox cowboy or indian coming alive to shoot my childhood hero Robin Hood, but didn't dare ask Dad to move it.

In a khaki or check shirt, long, baggy old pants and clumpy brown boots, Dad dug over soil for veggies at the back of his shed. Carefully sifted it through the prongs of a huge garden fork, raked in compost. Birds landed as soon as he repaired back inside. They feasted on worms he'd disturbed. We'd string up foil milk bottle caps or bits of sparkly packaging, hung in rows along sticks to scare the birds off, as soon as he planted seeds.

Mysterious creature, my father. Together so infrequently, it was like meeting a fascinating character from a book I hadn't yet read. In the shed more often when Jo-Jo took over the house, Dad told me to *leave him to it*, if I ever ventured out for longer than a few minutes. Breakfast or dinner, talking was bad manners at the table. My father racing away to, 'Get a wigwam for a goose's bridle,' or 'See a man about a dog.' Lunch I ate outside or in my room with a book when I visited them (not that often). Evenings, he certainly shouted at the TV screen but directed nothing much towards me.

Once or twice, Jo-Jo said Dad didn't like what I wore, or she made offhand remarks, 'Been here long enough? Aren't you bored?'

Reminded me of school bullies with their flinty eyes. Grim-faced girls flicked their shiny hair, hissed snide names in my direction. I soon stayed away from Dad's place.

Evading hurtful situations, avoidance meant new experiences and those I often chose too, made me feel stronger, happier. I learnt to enjoy calm and carefulness, pleasant remarks. A step at a time away from mayhem as if it could notice and haul me back into the melee. I moved apart from my family. I stopped throwing myself at men for energetic sex and particular flattery - pleasant diversions but, ultimately, the shallowness resulted in dissatisfaction and pain. Change proved also excruciatingly difficult. Drastic switches without precise instructions, me longing to give in and have another passionate affair, take illegal drugs again or overdo prescription pills, drink excessively, fall in with another marginalised creative bunch who could like my cooking and sense of humour, blank out as much as I could. Instead I resisted. Maintained focus. Learnt to grow accustomed to kindness and good habits, quietude.

A few regulars, or irregulars really, at the pub in the next bay would've accepted me. Their cheek and swagger. But I resisted. Accepted solitude, my trading regime, and writing. Refused to pretend my childhood involved a wonderful tradition worth maintaining. Truth kept me out of harm's way. Perhaps I'd never be accepted by well-behaved people, those without a history of wreckage (or whose scars didn't show or bother them much), but neither would I continue a habit of ruin.

I told my old friend Heather on the phone, 'Such a lie, the idea we're broken and unable to be mended. We can change and fix ourselves. Every human's flawed anyway, and of course troubles appear but we each deserve kindness and a good life.'

She sounded thoughtful, 'I guess so. Glad you're thinking about things.'

Not that I regretted my glam rock and wild days, provocative scenes with bunches of exotic creatures, some of them lessons and a few such stars. We invented, supported, promoted, criticised, reached for more mystery and history than ever thought possible. We broke the monochrome drone rule. Raced through sameness like a mere paper screen, burst into colour, tall poppy glittering wonders, exaggerated, sound tuned, bloomed and distorted, true. An exotic swarm of rock and roll survivors, queens, kings, deposed or otherwise, rare sparks and larks.

Tears, fears, and frights too. Some over-dosed, were killed, died of cancer, AIDS, caught diseases or tangled with accidents. One young woman, always beautifully dressed, horrifically strangled by her boyfriend - she'd refused to share her drugs with him. I could recall how she once demanded I embroider a dress for her like I was a servant and then, bought a dog she neglected. But a violent way to go - still in her thirties.

Still, canny musos found session work, some rocked their own band and toured. Hello Sailor recently inducted into the Rock and Roll Hall of Fame, away on another tour, dusting off their

leather trousers. Some moved into selling vintage and retro.
Familiar faces more lined, balder or greyer, noticed at auctions
all over the country. A punk singer from Barbz days ran a
puppet theatre. One of Crashbang's guitarists had his own
recording studio, a guitar collection filled a room. The cracked
drummer who believed he was a possum, and made people
stroke him before he'd answer any question, went into IT early
on. Tried to join the Foreign Legion later but, 'They told me
adjusting to life there'd be really difficult.' Now, living in Europe
with his vivacious Swedish wife, they collected animal bones.
I sold precious china and glass, occasionally other goods. Liked
to think of the artifacts' stories, hidden, rather like people's
stories are concealed (except we can tell ours in words, pictures
and music). Each object cared for, tended well to remain useful,
admired. But toys also held meaning.
Sydney Rabbit, a little like Dad kind of peering out from under
bushy, fair eyebrows. He'd fetch a good price with a collector. No
idea where he'd got to. The knitted girl doll, Twitchy, I guessed
then with a pang in my guts like fear, represented Mum and her
nerves. My mother loved to read and also to care for the house,
but noise made her jumpy. Sometimes she cried so easily. It
shocked me to think I'd identified my quirky doll as being her, in
the back of my childish mind. Hot with embarrassment seated
under my table (although I also told myself I could sit where I
liked in my own house). Mum so nervy and who'd blame her? O,
how the boys and Dad shouted and carried on. Days and nights
and weeks and years of it, rowdy, skew-if....

People watched her that day from their house on the hill.
Thought it strange to see someone in a dress and shoes just slide
under the water. They ran down to help, too late. She'd sewn
heavy things around the hem. Officials told my father, and I
overheard them. He sobbed like he'd lost his breath.
Pinstripe trousers can easily bring back that sorry day. Dad wore
a pair. He kept plucking at them like they should change into
something useful, for this impossible situation, to shift things
back.
My guilty dry throat; I'd snapped at Mum sometimes or refused

to do as she asked. As a teenager, I didn't really get it that Mum probably felt hurt when my hard words slapped the air, or when I did or said something thoughtless. Mean of me to call my old girl doll Twitchy, even if I had no idea at the time why. Could've been kinder, wish I'd learnt it somewhere, earlier. *Sorry, sorry, sorry....*

That knitted doll also lost in various moves from house to house. Head aching, playing the futile 'what if' game again, but I'd crossed a line. My heart beat faster. Imagining's momentum. *What if* I was kinder and did what Mum wanted, helped her in the house more and agreed with things she said? What if I was quieter near my brothers and admired them more, didn't ever fight back or be cheeky? What if I just accepted things were the way they turned out and stopped imagining any different, now? (Usually, I managed the latter, but my brothers' visit clicked open locked doors, resentfulness crept in like a mangy pet supposed to stay outdoors).

Socrates said change is law and no amount of pretending can change that reality, and I had to believe he'd known something if people kept his quote alive for millennia. After years of therapy, mysterious meetings, talk, drawing, rituals, meditations, essential oils, reading philosophy, study, I *could* now make myself switch my thinking.

A happy day memory when the family visited this sunny city park. A rug on the lawn for a picnic. Families smiled and played cricket or tossed a coloured ball to each other, not one person hurt or caught up in some overt mishap. Chocolate cake perfect on a plate, soft chicken sandwiches Mum had made and refreshing orange juice kept cold in a chilli bin.

Sitting now under a table to hide, however, since the boys had turned up demanding I live with Dad. Some sharp bitter taste in my mouth. Great rolling thunder thoughts. Mum abandoned us. Swells of feeling churned like vomit. I'd choke on my thoughts. But by some miracle under that table I recognised my mistake, took a deep breath. Shut off the memories.

One hand gently stroked the old teddy bears on my lap. A

couple of tears rolled down my face. Anger and sadness
compelling, like watching lava boil, but my mind-shift worked.
Change into fresh clothes after a sweaty run, have a wash and
pull on something more comfortable, easy.

Others who've never suffered memory shocks may find my story
something to sneer at or disbelieve. I think so at times while
writing this. But it's horribly real. I was addicted to feeling sad or
furious, because possibly at least I was *doing* something. Anger
felt like moving on but was more like being cooked or baked
hard into the same shape over and over, in a kiln of stupidity.
Words make it all something apart from me, manageable shapes
and colour on a page, gone away, transformed.

Younger, I'd searched for an answer to Everything but
Everything got so big and words floated away, so I wandered lost
in a Great Big Everything. Looked for *something*, instead. A chair,
a book, a pen, a toy, anything concrete, holdable. Wished for
nothing but found something more useful.

Nothingness doesn't exist. Nothing as annoying and problematic
as Everything. The numeral zero invented long after the others,
an experiment, something people tried to see if it had some use,
but really, only the idea of nothingness exists. We can't go
nowhere unless we die and even then we've no proof that there
really is a big blank void. No.

Anyway, finding something, I chose a quieter life. The novelty
stunning at first, now my routine, and yet it was still threatened
by these siblings. My hatred peered about balefully, ready to
wreck and rip. I'd felt cornered. Pointless however to allow a
disturbance, so I crawled under the table. Concealed by the long
tablecloth in my own house. But I couldn't forget staying in
charge.

The boys murmured on in my living room, by the table where
they'd spread the fish and chips. The aroma of freshly cooked
food wafted freely, I resisted the temptation to reappear. A
clatter in the kitchen. No one knew where I kept the tomato
sauce. Finally, they called for me.

Silent, motionless.

'Found it. She had it in the fridge.' Sam walked back in with the
others.

I silently mouthed Sam's words but with a sneer, mocking. My therapist told me I did this to diminish others, to make them unlikely to get close, avoiding hurt, choosing isolation instead. Someone switched on the radio and music filled the room, classical, Mozart.

The boys ate with various appreciative noises, above.

An old shoe box also under the table. Teddies fitted inside, perfectly. With tender care, I patted them like they could enjoy a long sleep now. A child again, pretending.

The boys rolled on with innocuous comments, ate their way through the last of their takeaways.

Still hidden, with my back against the wall, I slumped a little with my eyes closed. 'She's so off the wall.' Sam laughed. 'Bet she's down the road at some crony's place.'

Not one started up with how I had to go live with Dad. No one mentioned *crazy* again. They didn't snipe, much at all. I grinned. They *weren't* truly cutting behind my back. Roland tidied up. 'Better get sorted.' Sounds of the wrapping crumpled, then the lid of my bin in the kitchen opened and closed. Water ran in the sink, the few dishes were washed and dried.

Peter thought the bright rag rug looked like it needed a wash. Sam could not figure out why I liked so much clutter. Then Roland spied a picture of all of us when we were little, kept beside the small TV. ' Oh, look at us kids.'

I risked a quick look from under the long tablecloth and saw them in a huddle, the boys in their pale trainers, and variations of neat grey, green, faded yellow and mid-blue casuals. Backs to me, they peered at the old framed photo. Smiles in their voices, each remembered the day we went to the studio for a family portrait. 'I had a haircut. O bay rum. That barber.'

'Yeh, he was a character. Mum wanted us all smart.'

'My shoes so new and creaky. They shone.'

Dad in a new dark blue suit, his ears stuck out a fraction. Hair newly cut too, and mum so pretty in a pale floral dress, a sparkly rose brooch on the starched collar. Each child peculiar in new clothes as if transported to another country without warning. I wore patent leather shoes, loving their novelty shine. Hairclip with a tiny flower, pink and white stood out against my dark, naturally curly hair.

They each spoke my name in unison then, 'Patricia,' such a soft way.

My chest ached and a tear ran down my cheek. I slipped back out of sight. They had no idea I'd changed my name. And that was the first time any of them had said the old name this entire visit. But then the family hardly ever said it unless it was to call attention to something I'd done wrong. Her name, not mine. Patricia was dead, gone forever.

After a while, they left and turned out the lights. Calling *cheerio, hooray* and *see you later*, to each other in the early evening the way birds call familiar sounds to each other. I wondered why they were so friendly, each driving to the same motel in separate cars. Maybe they imagined I could hear them.

I clambered out from hiding.

The place felt like it needed a bit of time to settle back into its usual, welcome silence.

Soon off to bed. Teddies left in the box under the table. Words said and the way I felt a vast ocean where I floated until darkness took me into a good, long sleep the way a boat slides into still water.

A last thought as I lost consciousness, *I won. They stopped trying to tell me what to do.*

Whatnots and Knicknacks

Gotta bop, gotta roll, gotta sing-song,
need a laugh, need a drink, need a not-wrong.

You know it, you got it, you give it,
come on 'n' play give 'n' take, all along the get go.

- Doll Trolleys 1999

Heather, she owned the most extensive collection of ridiculous
earrings on the planet, and a library of spectacular coffee table
books. Open a multitude of doorways and step into glorious
buildings, countries, landscapes, and fashion shoots. Her 1960s
flat red brick, with a white wrought iron bannister up the stairs
outside and around her balcony overlooked a park. Zig zag
white lines, up and down, jazzy. We still knew how to laugh at
almost anything. When I needed a change, I packed essentials,
then drove myself to the city to see my old friend Heather.
Concerts or art exhibitions opened our enthusiasm in the city,
but in the tiny place I'd made home it was rare to entertain a
crowd. My brothers had appeared en masse the day before.
Sam, Peter, and Roland staying nearby for the weekend. Oddly
like another jaunt, as if *I'd* left to see my old friend, Heather.
Disoriented in a pleasant way, even with their hidden agenda
revealed. They'd tried to convince me to go and live with our
ailing father.
'Tell them to *get stuffed*.' Heather would say, 'Come and see me.
Great film on at the Lido.'
A stick figure I'd drawn of myself, green, smiling, eco-aware.
Words floated around this character, *free* above my head in blue,
knowing what I do not want at my feet, *an ability to love others well*
across my torso. Other words suspended as if I'd catch the
concepts at any time, *clearer thinking, good riddance to anyone who
hurts me, able to stand up for myself.* My art therapy sessions lately
drawing pictures with crayons, to reinforce what I'd learnt and
wanted, needed, discovered.
Decades of therapists, countless hours of talk and work.

Language changed me as surely as eating or drinking something potent, those images seen, words heard and written.

The day after my three brothers motored in, a short-notice visit, I woke up as cheerful as someone who'd been told they never needed to work again, whatever they pleased lay ahead for the rest of their days, despite my brothers' bossiness. Other people's expectations and judgements had stopped affecting me as adversely. After a good sleep, almost bouncing while I talked to the neighbour's cat who called in, 'You hungry, puss?'

Black and white, the sleek animal mooched round the kitchen then ran off as if it heard a can of Supreme Majesty Cat Treats being opened next door, metres away.

Examining a can of bamboo shoots, wondering what to plan for lunch, I had to think it an unusual circumstance seeing my three siblings alone without their families. Grown up, but like being young again too, except now knowing so much more. Liberating to tell them off the day previously; I couldn't recall shouting at my brothers before and getting away with it. But, maybe I did in younger days? So much a blur recently, and apparently it's normal to forget things which trouble us. But it surely took a while in younger days before I gathered resistance was futile? Shouting in defense, running to hide, my retorts shocking enough to get free enough, a get-away. An outlaw in my own family, the renegade position, concealment and plotting against them in some cubby.

Making breakfast I consoled myself with that brave idea, a child who had fought back.

Rarely did grown children see each other without their children or partners in tow. The hubbub of normalcy, familiar faces, voices, concerns, questions and remarks quieted for once.

I could also let my trading online slow down, didn't have to keep it up every day. Spare time manufactured had possibly given Roland the impression I never worked, hence his assured comments about my having nothing valuable to steal.

Sam loved outings, always the least interested in anything torturous. 'Let's see what this town of yours has to offer,' he said when they all again converged, about morning tea time.

'I think it's a settlement, not a town or even a village, Sam, but sure.' I put on a light coat and made for the door before anyone demanded tea and scones.

We ate ice creams on the wharf. The boys talking about how calm the water looked. Roland checked the weather on his smartphone. No one wanted to take my boat out. I imagine they worried about being alone with me somewhere I'd feel so secure and in charge. Peter bluffed, 'Have a rest from that, Sis. We'll do all the hard work today.'

Soon we were at sea on a large white launch, hired from Hartigan's General Store. Someone brought the vessel around from a couple of bays south, with only a half hour's notice. 'Lucky we had a cancellation,' Mrs. Hartigan said, when she passed over forms to sign and safety instructions, along with life jackets and fishing gear we'd hired. The boys didn't want my gear either.

Was this my own country? Someone at any moment could speak in French or Greek, announcing they knew a fine story about ancient ruins visible from the deck. Blue sparkling water in every direction, scattered faint islands near the horizon. Coast apparent the other way and more familiar, mainly lush green, dark rocks a jumble near the small outcrop where a bent, ancient tree grew. Basic, rather elderly houses and two motels in our little enclave now mere rectangles, faded colour upon intensely green land. A national flag waved above Hartigan's store.

Mr Hartigan, a retired army man, liked to raise the flag every morning and bring it down at night, flew it half-mast for any major tragedy and, once, upside down, a sign of distress and needing help.

A local share milker went bonkers and kept the Hartigans captive inside the shop. Mr Hartigan insisted he needed to raise the flag, to show things were as normal even if the *Closed* sign was in the door of the shop. The flag slyly upside down this time. A local, Fred Fielding, spotted the anomaly and called the police. They were all saved. The share milker went to rehab. He'd been knocking back home-made hooch and taking some illicit drug, worried about bills. His wife'd up and left him for a travelling salesman. No one local wanted to see him in jail. Mrs Hartigan explained to me at the time, 'Touched in the head, poor lad. Sickness you know. Drugs 'n' that.'

I mused on this story while we stood on the launch, rocked gently in the tide. Slap slap slap, water against the side. Sam stood at the front of the boat, smiling as if in the throes of a religious experience. 'This is what it's all about, guys. This is living.'
We laughed with delight, even if Roland looked tempted to ridicule our brother. Gulls wheeled and cried over the shimmering sea as if they agreed too.
Sam called my old name and I refused to answer. He said it again and I turned, surrounded by the shimmering sea. 'My name is now Athena. She's the goddess of wisdom.'
The boys all gaped. Roland spluttered, 'What's wrong with Patricia? Perfectly good name. Our grandmother's name.'
Peter swayed as the boat rocked, he frowned, focussed on a point near my feet.
I reeled my line in, let it out again, turned away from them, then back. 'My name's Athena now. My life's changed. My name's changed. Athena.'
'*You* changed your life?' Roland sounded scathing.
'We were neglected as children, all of us. You bullied me and I wandered around half-there, like a ghost girl. That girl's gone. Patricia is not here.' I'd spoken without looking at them, terrified of my own story and the effect it could have on my siblings. When I looked up they were all staring out to sea, refusing to meet my gaze. Nowhere to go on a boat, they'd floated away in mind perhaps, too, like I did. Nothing for it but to go on. 'I searched the world for love. Found some wild affairs and crazy times. But yeah, Dad, well, he grew up thinking thumping kids was a good idea. He'd been thumped and his father before him. You took out your pain and fear on me, the youngest. People hurt others to feel some power, then fear disappears briefly. Mum was kind of cowed, shut off, worked day and night in a daze.' I took a deep breath. 'I now accept all that as history. Not

the terrible pain and fear inside it once was. If you all have
issues these days then go to therapy like I did. I still do, every
month.' It felt like my voice was never going to be silent, but, at
last, I found nothing to say.

Sam looked at me briefly, his eyes wide, then away again. Bright
blue sky behind him made his fright all the more apparent.

I gained a kind of peace from his fearful look. He owned the
terror now. Each brother regarded the sea, the sky, the brilliant
warm day. The boys couldn't pile me up with pain, to make
them forget their own momentarily, any longer. If they tried,
they'd remember this day, my speech, or so I consoled myself.
What I'd said echoed in mind, hoping it wasn't as fierce as I now
recalled it. Told myself to stop worrying. Watching waves surge
and fall instead, the glittering reflections.

Sam laughed. 'We're grown up. Can do as we wish. Not illegal to
change your name.'

Despite seeing how Sam wanted to brush over this lecture of
mine, out there on the ocean, I kept going, 'Mum, well, I think
she had Post-traumatic Stress Syndrome, like I did. Shell shock.
It was hard caring for us. She made do with keeping the house
so spick and span. Cleaning. But I've forgiven all of you. It's for
me. Forgiveness makes me feel better. I recommend it.'

The others as silent as if someone had died.

'Patricia hid herself so well she wasted away and turned into old
writing on crumbling paper. Patricia died. Athena was born.' I
spoke more quietly now. 'Looks like someone's got a bite.'

Roland's line bending and he struggled to reel the fish he'd
caught in. My brothers all exclaimed at the size of the trevally
on his hook.'

Out at sea, having spoken our dire story aloud, I felt free of
some weight or pressure.

After a half hour or so, Sam called, 'Athena, you checked your
bait? The fish could've nibbled it away?'

I did need to rebait my line.

Sam and I started hauling them in. The floor of the boat
gleamed with fish. Gurnard slithered everywhere. Sam tossed
them in a white plastic bin.

When Roland and Peter also used my name they began catching

more fish too. We reached our limit in only an hour or so. Sam
whispered to me, 'You've proved you're lucky, Athena.'
'My uncle *is* Poseidon.' I laughed.
He looked blank but Roland interrupted with a Greek God
lecture, impromptu. Set us all to rights. '...and so you see,
Athena gained the city of Athens, with an olive tree.'
Peter mumbled we could need some olive oil for the fish then,
perhaps? We laughed in that way people do, relieved to have
reached a high point at last, after wandering lost, or fighting to
get there. A broader view, it felt good.

Hours later, after a feast of pan-fried gurnard at my place, we
visited the pub two bays across. Roland offered a solo version of
Moon River, '...crossing you in style, one daaay ....' Old heart-
breaker and dream maker, a song from childhood.
'Louis Armstrong you know, he really was going to cross that
river in style.' Sam nodded over his bottle of lager. 'From the
poor side of town, New Orleans. Off to make his fortune, and
he did.'
'Terrible, what they did to that city,' I began to speak quietly,
thought no one would care, but the others nodded. My voice
strengthened, 'If only they'd looked after the place and not
drained those wetlands. That was the other problem.'
'O yes, 'Roland broke in after his karaoke song and leaned back
in his chair. 'You got it, Sis. Wetlands along a coast act as a
buffer. Mad policies. That government was about to set up their
country to be one big concentration camp, too. Way they were
going. Bad decisions, *I would say*....'
'This *beer* is a buffer,' Sam interjected with a laugh and raised his
empty bottle. A hint that someone needed to buy him another.
'So thirsty after all my eeexcellent singing, 'specially to entertain
you plebs.' Roland smacked his lips together. 'Peter. Gone deaf,
man?'
In the old pub, surrounded with varnished wooden walls and
plain, dark tables like *the* most manly man-club, they bantered. It
took a good half hour for anyone to buy another round. Just as
well, I didn't want to see anyone drunk.
Peter whispered to me later, 'Good to have it all out on the boat,

Athena. I've been in analysis for years, but don't tell the others. Y'learn a lot about changing, ay?'

I shot a look at him and Peter smiled, looking like he truly meant it. Tears came into my eyes and we hugged each other. Roland announced loudly that we'd all sing. He insisted on, 'We are Family' by Sister Sledge. Every time for the line about 'sisters' the boys jammed in 'brothers and sister and me', then roared with laughter. A rollicking, swept-along song, music and us an ocean together.

Even if I enjoyed this shared ebullience, I guessed they'd try one last time to get me to move in with Dad. Give me a good day and a bit of friendliness, use my new name. Next, whammo, hit the old maid with her duty. My stubbornness ready like sandbags in store near a river that flooded. Dad could go into a home before I'd be there at his beck and call. Dad with money in the bank and properties. If the boys worried about their inheritance, then too bad, it was Dad's money and it could go to pay people to care for him.

After we'd had lunch the next day, a bacon and egg pie made with Roland's help (he'd developed skills as a baker between marriages), Sam checked his emails. Sunday at my place, Sam sat there laughing. Tears into his eyes, he couldn't stop, gasping for air, wiping at his face with one hand.

Some funny story to get me softened up. Now they'd hit me with what I needed to do. Dad wanted me to look after him. I had to obey. I was thinking that anyway.

The others crowded around, because in a three-room house (not including the tiny cupboard of a kitchen or minuscule bathroom), you hear everything anyone says or does. Sam blathered on and peered at the screen.

For a minute I thought he'd said, 'Dad's under a curse, he's heaving it.' I wondered, 'Who knows a witch? And Dad throwing up means a hex is on him?'

Roland frowned. 'Witch?' He repeated what Sam'd said, 'Dad's *marrying a nurse*. Can you believe it?'

The boys riffed raggedly on the news. 'She'll cure him of aches and pains, all right.'

'Always did like the fancy dress-ups, Dad. Hey, what say we ....'

The room crowded with their laughter. But I loved their noisy carry-on for a change even if it was too loud and crass. I could've lifted off the floor and flown a few metres.

My brothers shifty and sheepish after initial surprise dwindled to realisation. Our father had, after all (we seemed to recall en masse), tried to marry a widowed woman in our street, then another widow when the first refused him. Each he chased in unseemly, fast turnaround turn only a week or so after Mum passed away. Locals started calling him Casanova. One woman took a trespass order against him. But in the supermarket he asked this complete stranger how to roast a chicken. He'd never tried to make anything so complicated. She took pity on him. Dad proposed the very next day. Not that they ever married, but Jo-Jo loved to tell their story.

Dad, desperate for someone to cook and clean, and who... well.... Dad's love life loomed in the conversation like the proverbial, peculiar elephant in the room which no one really wants to talk about seriously, nor in jest. My careless brothers suddenly appeared to realise bawdy jokes didn't fit, even if the topic was so obvious. We didn't want to think about our father's libido. I wondered what happened to privacy in our family. Roland muttered the old man was hopeless.

Despite agreeing, I couldn't stop beaming with joy, free of any obligation now. One of the boys muttered that I could think about the old guy's heart, couldn't I? Just then a knock at the door, which opened, and a dark, grizzled head appeared. 'O sorry, you got visitors?' My neighbour, Bill with his son, calling, as arranged, to collect an old stove.

'O yes.' I showed them to a sheltered, square back porch. The appliance covered with a tarpaulin.

In the balmy air, we talked about any fishing we'd each done lately, and my further plans for the garden. Kitchen door slightly open, I could imagine those brothers of mine listening in as if my visitors and I were hiding, but it was an everyday conversation. 'Lulubelle still running steady?' Bill knew my boat was fine. He'd seen me in it only five days before.

'Just lent it to the mechanic, that's all. Called in not five minutes ago, I heard him hooking it up. A favour. Got it for a week.' I

smiled. 'I guess you saw him and thought it needed more work?'
'She's eye-catching,' Bill growled.

He and I agreed, my Lulubelle was one for the photo album.
His brother's runabout nowhere near as big as mine, and Bill
wanted his own fishing vessel; yearned after my Lulubelle.
Craggy face creased with mostly laugh lines, Bill frowned,
however, when I said, 'Last time I went out, caught lots of
trevally.' Great to boast, especially knowing no one now intended
to bundle me away to nursemaid the father I barely knew.
Instead, at ease on my backdoor step, building up a reputation.
Why *couldn't* I just enjoy life as I wished? Collecting various
treasures here and there as I did, then selling lovely things
online. I could also write every day, get into the garden, pay my
bills, see things fixed as needs be, start my eco-camping ground,
employ a manager, go fishing, and please myself. Why not? How
did single women become likely slaves for hire? Except that I'd
erred there in thinking that. No, I'd not be for hire, Dad
wouldn't have paid me a bean. 'O there's a spare woman. Get
her doing something for us quick. She can't possibly think of
anything by herself, she'll mess it up or go nuts.' Roland would
reel that judgement off without a blink.

But sunshine splashed the back lawn, a landscape daubed with a
huge celestial paintbrush of brightness. I spoke strongly, 'I think
I could trade Lulubelle in soon for something bigger, maybe go
after deep sea game.' This a teasing lie, since I hated deep sea
fishing, but wanted to see his reaction.

Bill coughed, like any words he wanted to speak just choked
him.

I took a step back, hoped the reddish-purple colour he was
turning didn't mean anything was really wrong. 'Whoa Bill, I'm
kidding, I am. You'll get the first bid if I sell her. Truly.'

His son asked just then, abruptly, when I needed paths laid,
'Y'know, I offered to help with concreting?' I think he winked at
me. Then his eyes went soft. I recalled that someone told me
once, 'A man will make all manner of signals and say they're
nothing. But if you make them into something, watch out.'

The sun warm, lovely for a wander. I suggested, 'O, there are
pegs in already to show where you'd need to dig.' Took a good

breath of gorgeous air, some kind of spring flower fragrance,
Early Cheer, freesias....
We walked across the back lawn. For the life of me, I couldn't
recall the son's name. I dreaded my brothers appearing, asking
to be introduced, but soon I blissfully forgot that and mentioned,
'My brothers are here.' My walk became a stumble, for a
moment. Why mention them?
The son however quickly told his dad, 'We'd better get on.'
Then, as if the three of them were eavesdropping, the boys piled
out the back door. Shaking hands in every direction like a badly
choreographed but jovial dance, each introduced themselves.
Too cheery, but no one appeared to care. I supposed it was
normal to feel at least a little awkward when first meeting
people. Accepted this like realising new food would taste
different to what I'd eaten before.
My brothers hefted the appliance, helped load the stove onto
Bill's truck. The clear day quite still and us with it, suspended in
a cosy bubble. Bill did an excellent imitation of a man who
didn't mind what anyone else said, nor even if they answered at
all. Nevertheless quite a few questions curling close in his
roundabout way, 'Good to see some new faces. Guess you'll
holiday here with your families, you boys? Getting a bach, or
one each, close to your sister?'
Roland laughed nervously, clearly worried that Bill could take
offense if he didn't want to stay nearby, 'O, we have a place,
further north. Just visiting.'
The blue and gold day as benign and welcome as kindness itself.
Bill nodded and patted the side of his red and grey truck, like it
was a beast needing reassurance. 'Got my son here. The
daughter only a half hour away. Her old man's a farmer. This is
good land, in this district, for that, wouldn't you say?'
None of my brothers knew a thing about farmland and said so,
with a keen edge. Bill cut to the topic. They discussed the dairy
boom. Bill asserting too many people wanted to get into it,
'...without a bloody decent idea about dairying in their townie
heads.' He finished with a kick at the ground. 'Fishing's the best
thing hereabouts. Your sister, she'll tell y'too. Been out?'
Dimensions of the launch we hired discussed in such detail it

was as if they planned to custom-make furniture for it.

Bill's son, meanwhile, got me talking about a box of tea sets and whatnot he'd picked up. I mentioned, 'Be happy to take a look.' Animated, he got onto embroidered tablecloths. 'Dad has drawers full at home.' His son loved them. 'I think my mother sewed the finer ones. Have to show you those too. Not to sell, just for ....'

I laughed, agreed, 'I don't want to raid your heirlooms.'

We both wandered back inside to examine *my* collection of embroidered linens. Sam wandered in too and listened for a while, then the three of us ambled back out to the roadside. After we'd stood there long enough for the sun to radiate right though every layer and reach our hearts, Sam watched them pull out in Bill's red and grey truck from the front of my place and murmured, 'Nice old guy.'

I spoke warmly, 'Certainly can talk. Really need a cup of tea, now.'

Freshly painted green trim and deep yellow kitchen cupboard doors cheery with all the rest of the paintwork cream. A tiny room, better now it was pale, I had to think. Stainless steel bench and little window to the back garden; freshly wiped tidy shelves. Food packets displayed and on the sill, a china cat giving a secretive smile, 60s whimsy. The kettle rumbled, almost boiling. Sam, in the doorway, hummed this old song.

I tried to recall the words, and sang along for a bit.

'No Sis, it's *Love and Marriage*, love and marriage, they go together like a horse and carriage.'

I regarded him with surprise, then remembered earlier. 'Yeh, Dad. Amazing. Dad married again.' Boiling water poured into my best large-cube, novelty teapot, I pulled over a bright blue, green and red cosy with yellow flowers on, embroidered so it looked like a red-roofed cottage with a garden.

Sam shook his head. 'You live in a dream world. Didn't you see how that guy looked at you? Biff? That his name, Athena?'

The tea cosy needed adjusting. What was Sam on about? Bill? Since he'd had his teeth out, Bill's face appeared lopsided, those wrinkles sometimes looked grubby and, anyway, he smelled of pipe tobacco and wet dog. I laughed. 'He's too old for me, Bill.'

Roland laughed too , when we walked into the lounge, talking, but in this corny way as if rehearsed. Sam had to offer the solution, 'Yeah, he liked your funky plates and things. Saw him gazing around when we were inside. But mainly he just admired you. The son.'

I laughed again, but pushed past Sam and the others back into the kitchen, then returned with funky 70s mugs, a plate of biscuits, and the milk in a jug, on a tray. Completely involved in practical matters, my off-hand chortle hopefully convincing. Romance in the middle of nowhere? A teeny town, if you could call it that. Mainly old people, my neighbours, all wearing peculiar mismatched clothes at this time of year. No holiday-makers about much. Locals liked to discuss fishing, television programmes, weather, tabloid royal family news or major political events and sports, a few boasted about grandchildren. The idea of any serious love-making turned into a silly paperback book in Hartigan's General Store, where a sign reminded customers they did not run a library.

'Lovely outside, still. Out there for our drink?' Roland strode through the kitchen and then out the back door again. He took tea mugs and the teapot on a tray, without waiting for any reply. I got another tray. Sam soon carried the remaining crockery and food outside.

The wooden picnic table cheery with tea things, on the back lawn to the side of the house, where it flattened beautifully for a view down to native trees. Last sunshine caught the lawn at that point. A fine afternoon, no mosquitoes. Cicadas quiet, so it would rain soon.

I had long planned to park my boat on site. Tried now to get the boys to help me decide where I could build a shed to cover it. 'In the sun, where the shed would warm up and dry the boat out after I've been fishing, or in the shade of the house so's not to block the view?'

No one even slightly interested in these plans.

I was used to them ignoring me but it hurt for some reason. I decided to pretend I didn't care. Easy to concentrate on pouring the tea, then I gazed about and silently planned new flower beds.

Roland humming, sipped his tea in this decisive way. Peter blurted, 'You need company, Sis.'

The others nodded, desperately pleased someone'd broached the subject.

I just raised my eyebrows and regarded birds flitting through trees to settle for the evening.

Sam spoke loudly, 'Looks like a good chap.'

I didn't react.

Each brother drafted solutions, even when I tried to change the subject with talk of real estate prices or car questions. Peter, no messing around, 'Any man would say yes if you asked him to dinner or something.'

'I don't like the idea of just *any man*.' Almost set my tea cup flying when I emphatically thumped the table, or tried to, and missed the part of the table I'd aimed for.

Peter swore and shouted, 'Didn't mean it like *that*.' He stood up to pace a while.

Roland blurted, 'You could wait to be asked.' On his feet, too, he held a finger in the air like an ancient prophet in a painting, only saying slowly, 'An air of mystery and a new dress.'

Laughing, I couldn't imagine what they'd say next.

Samuel thought it could be worth getting Bill's son investigated first, in case he was dodgy. 'What was his name? Can't recall it now. He did say....'

They mentioned these things half-jokingly, but with a settled air as if discussing a house soon to be on the market, before they needed to pay for repairs. I'd never asked for help, but could see they imagined the day could arrive when they'd need to pay for my home-care, or some desperate operation. A husband or partner would take the responsibility away. Or did they just like looking as if they were in charge? Or they could've simply been concerned about me. I smiled.

Biscuits I'd made, and a bought, rich chocolate cake were arrayed on the table. No one had taken anything yet. I broke one of the honey ginger snaps in half and bit into it. 'Delicious. This chocolate cake's double cocoa, three eggs, by the way, moist and rich. Do you want plates? Easier?'

'She's a brilliant baker. Could be cooking something up.'

'It's hot in the old town tonight.'
'The temperature's rising.'
A chuckling competition, and attempts at who could say the most ridiculous remark. Three grown men in fading light, grouped around a picnic table with occasional leaps in the air. Sam laughed so hard at one point he rocked and fell on the grass, did a backward flip, and stood up.
I gaped. 'You a super-hero in your spare time?'
Sam with a hand on his lower back. 'Just hope I didn't wreck something.'
'Maybe he's really a prince, this guy. Make this li'l ol' place into a castle?' Roland smirked.
'Nah, nah, he's the king of second-hand stoves. They'll have a tower of appliances and never have to worry about what to cook for dinner again.' Peter giggled like a fool.
'Just having a stove doesn't make you a good cook, Peter.' Sam spoke emphatically, 'We need to ask him what his intentions are. Where does he live? Joking around's all very well but....'
Silent by then, I sipped tea as if they were some kind of rowdy pet I knew to ignore or they'd only be more boisterous. My brothers' teasing, plans, and ideas were merely to pass the time. I'd've missed some ravishing times if I'd investigated every man I ever liked. Youth the time for such foolery. An age since I considered reckless love affairs could ever end in more than pain and ruin. Stopped myself becoming entangled, an expert at remaining single, no longer desire-driven. Athena didn't live driven by passion. After extreme highs came a severe crash landing or some disaster.
Far away in the distance a dog barked loudly. Some man shouted at it to shut up. It did.
The son's name? We'd met many times, but he rarely mentioned his name, and Bill called his son, Son. He did like my lovely vases, plates, and lamps inside my house. We spent an hour one day talking about a 17th century plate I loved. No idea how it came to be in this country. With conversation recalled, his name appeared too. Griffin. His dad occasionally called him *Griff*.
The afternoon turning colder. Peter saying he wanted to thump Roland, who'd taunted him with a childish sore point. Sam

insisted, 'This guy, how long have you known him?'
I answered, 'Anyone wants to know anything 'round here, we just ask. You want info? I think Griffin just got divorced, about six months ago.' I smiled. 'Probably completely off women.'
Roland roared with laughter. 'Griffin? Some fairy tale character?'
Peter ran a hand through his greying brown hair, reminded his brother, 'What about what kids at school used to say about *your* name? Roly Poly. Yeah, Mr Chubby-chops.'

Primary school rag-tag and exuberant, insults flew from our innocent mouths. If we weren't fighting amongst ourselves, we name-called and threatened, or cried and hid. Roland suffered until he lost weight. Playing rugby, all the running he had to do for training, he'd transformed in a year.
Old stories where another girl had lived, not me. Pictures in mind now like faded photos.

Roland plucked at the grey merino wool jumper he'd tugged on and looked like he really cared about a mark there, which no one else could see.
Someone walked onto the back lawn from the path at the side of the house. It was shaded so no one could see them that well. I stood so whoever it was could see me amongst this gang of grown louts.
Then I smiled broadly, my face hot, and I knew I was blushing. A low flying bird cut across the air between us.
Maybe Griffin decided with my brothers visiting, they'd been so friendly he wanted to get to know them? For whatever reason, in a half hour he'd returned. The wooden picnic table and bench seats quite sturdy, but it creaked a bit with one extra. Sam joked, 'We'd better not get too excited in case this collapses.'
'You excited, Sam?' Roland grinned.
They fell into jokey bantering.
'Just getting some more hot water.' I picked up the teapot and walked away. Another cup and the tin of biscuits found in no time, but I determined not to rush.
In the doorway, Sam smiled. The jug boiling, so he made a fresh

pot of tea, whistling that old song about love and marriage
quietly, in my tiny kitchen. I refused to react, and after years of
practise, successfully pretended he hadn't got to me. Then he
whispered, 'We could all ask him questions? Shall we? Here,
what's your intentions with our sister, mate?'
I raised my fist and made to thump him on the arm, but my
eldest brother scarpered, laughing.
Settled in the darkening day around the picnic table, we five
talked through generalities as if waiting for someone else before
starting on something vital. Sam mentioned the fine weather,
Roland had music he wanted to download for the trip home,
then Griffin discussed the stove I'd given his father. Griffin
insisted I was so kind. Whereupon I seized the chance to deny
any such thing, in as light a tone as possible. Softly, Griffin
reiterated, 'You're one of the kindest people I know.' It seemed
as if he'd just handed over a kitten as a pet, or tried to hug me,
then stammered and stopped.
Tea to drink thankfully, but the mug shook in my hand at first. I
almost got up and made for the house with my shyness.
Out of his seat suddenly, Samuel insisted, 'Chaps, we need to get
going.'
In younger days, Griffin could've sniffed his armpits to see if he
had BO, a kind of a joke.
My face hot again, tediously. Birds flew past at a great rate,
many after insects apparent in final sun rays slanting across the
land. I watched the wildlife with mild interest, but wanted to tell
Roland, Peter, and Sam *not* to look like they couldn't wait to end
their visit. But only imagined words could hiss from me like
steam or maybe boil over like jam, a mad, uncomfortable mess.
Samuel caught my eye and slowed down, thank goodness. The
others took their lead from him, ambling away with more grace.
Griffin stood and shook my brothers' hands, said it was good to
meet them.
A hug each from me. Flecks of grey in their hair really obvious,
more signs of age around the eyes; Roland's frown lines, deeper.
My tenderness toward them due to how fragile they appeared.
Now I also knew I had faults, and had done wrong, too. But we
needed to focus on what good we did, if possible. No longer

invincible giants, my brothers, and me no longer the terrifying mysterious girl who'd magically take over if they allowed it.
Peter told me, 'Hate goodbyes, no need to wave us off.'
I hoped Griffin didn't see Roland's wink, like some bawdy bloke in a musical I'd never go to see.
Out I went, nevertheless, to the roadside in dim light now. They were not telling me what to do.
Three cars drove away. Dust clouds flew from Sam's wheels, spinning on gravelly sand. Birds agitated by the noise arose from a tree nearby. They whirred across the sky.
Silence. Small town without traffic. No one mowed a lawn. Not another voice, nor any dog whining.
Air salty, a touch of pine needles, and a light, pleasant dampness like after a good swim on a fine day. I thought of people laughing on a beach, walking into evening, cool sand underfoot.
Only two of us remaining, and we walked back without speaking much to drink the rest of the tea. The sky beyond a livid orange, with scattered clouds over occasional streaks of blue. Griffin at ease, his large lion-like head peering about. A puzzle, because *inside* my place he always looked like he felt sure he would break something, kind of jigged, tense. 'You like the outdoors, Griffin?'
His smile as sensible and broad as a good rowboat. I felt the distance of it too and didn't mind smiling back. He took a while to answer, then offered another grin, 'Sure, Athena. It's best under a sky, you feel more in place, I'd say.'
'I heard you slept in a tent.'
'No hiding the truth 'round here,' he replied.'I do indeed. A four room tent with a gas barbecue at the door. The likes of which this place has never seen. A few green eyes, I tell you. But it sounds like someone else already did the telling, Athena.'
I laughed. Anything new usually got the twenty-nine inhabitants of our small enclave talking up every kind of weather, until they ran out of wind, steam, hail or heat. I'd see them, locals in interesting assortments of rather cheerful garb (bright hand-knitted jerseys) or practical clothing, (Swandri and gardening trousers), sat outside the one main shop we patronised, Hartigan's. They gossiped as expertly as those many seagulls

scavenged the coast. Sometimes I sat there too. Mr. Fielding
called it *news* with a wink, 'Got any news, Lass? Hmmm?' Mr.
Fielding and his papery hands, the sharp eyes of a professional
information junkie.

Greta Smythe, two doors along from me, reckoned he used to be
a spy and still got calls from the Queen of England. Greta loved
the Queen so much that her cottage resembled a state room, at
least on the inside. Always had her hair permed in the nearest
town, to match Her Highness' style. Mr. Fielding possibly hinted
at royal connections only to impress her.

It seemed obvious, however, to be practical, this somewhat
younger man wanted a roof over his head. I'd provide much the
same if he twinkled enough. Even if cynical, I chatted away
about the retro cups we'd used, 'When you see any Crown Lynn
on your travels, let me know.'

'Sure. I like second-hand places. Reminds me of my childhood.
Dad and I, we've had a good life, you know. Our family. Have to
be grateful.'

'Grateful?' I regarded Griffin wide-eyed for a beat or two, like he
was an exhibit in a travelling show of Paragons to be Emulated.
Entertaining the idea that such a joyful circus could even exist
stopped any more sharp questions about his circumstances, or
my foolishly letting slip the horrors of my own growing up.

'Sure. Why not be grateful for our life?' Griffin's smile easy and
he spoke towards the sky.

No longer convinced my childhood had been so terrible,
anyway. Those brothers not monsters now, and bad memories
cartoonish. Why bother recalling them? A pleasant blur, sitting
close to Griffin.

A little frightened by this previously unknown sensation,
nonetheless, I stood up. 'Best get in. My brothers' visit was just
awash with tea. What a pile of cups. O, thanks. Going to help
me, Griffin?'

While we walked back inside, both carrying tea things, I
wondered why the boys stayed for so long. 'Do you think families
change and grow, Griffin?'

He stacked plates on the bench. One clattered out of the pile
and almost dropped to the floor, but he caught it. 'Well, there's a

Philosophy 101 question. Upsetting the crockery, Miss.'
We both grinned, and tidied.
'What? O, about families? I'm deep sometimes,' I carried on,
saying it felt good to see my brothers.
Griffin mentioned, 'Dad's like an older brother. We work well
together. Our family mostly get along.'
Dishes into the sink, soapy water foamed. They sunk to soak. It
appeared as if I was about to wash up, even if I wasn't. One
cupboard open, then another. 'Sure I had a bottle of merlot
somewhere.'
Griffin spoke up quick with a smile, 'Riesling do? It's cold,
believe it or not.' His greenish eyes twinkled. 'In the car, back in
a tick.'
I smiled, unselfconsciousness. Not the finest strategy, but I'd feel
less jittery after a drink.

Supposed I simply wanted a pleasant conversation, but it felt like
there'd be more. Thoughts crowded in like well-meaning friends
with too much advice, bare questions. Would Griffin try to move
in? Did he think of me as innocent or pliable? No one in our
small enclave knew about my youth, those glitzy adventures. If
anyone had found out even a glimmer they'd invent whatever
they liked from the sparkle. I'd deliberately kept my past low-key,
when I spoke about it.
Backstage at a rock gig as ramshackle and glitter bang as the
storage area of a fair sideshow, a circus spare parts department.
Often hours of waiting. Usually only ruined sofas, emitting
strange smells, to relax on. Assorted hangers-on milled around,
some zombies, others with less obvious hidden agendas behind
sharp glances, fake cheeriness. Guarding your own bag and
person. A few friendly extras also helped temper the scorch of
greedy promoters and weirdo managers. Any band with an
entourage arguably safer from secretive meetings where they
ended up not getting paid. I'd never *aimed* to be backstage either,
didn't keep a scorecard, no matter what gossips and envious
twerps imagined. Life simply sparkled that way and I followed
the light, when I felt welcome. Gifted men, and their impelling,
soaring music charmed me. It had been a genuine pleasure to

know them, for the most part. Risking everything for love, and
needing to learn. That's what I say. My belief. Not sure the
story's allowed to go that way. Do I sound too proud? Too
pleased with myself? How dare I display my sexual life as if I'm
permitted one? Am I forgiven for my experimentation, my
displaying these stories like worthy adventures? Do people care
that I do not care what they think?

Only a few will ever say my story should be told, I imagine. I
can see the tut-tutts and pinched faces now. These narratives
ripe and cooked to condense from me, like I'm a still and they're
vodka. My outlaw tales, my fight to be free of believing I was
worthy only of being a target to hurt and decry. My songs so
complex, and, to me, beautiful, I must sing them. This brought
me to a new place where I could find myself worthy of friends,
and true closeness.

Careful at last with others and myself, a new risk, reaching out
in a fresh and tenuous way.

As far as our locals knew, my grown child, Coltrane, who I'd
mentioned now and again, his existence meant to the locals that
I must've been married. I never contradicted this assumption.
People conversed, built with bricks of meaning an architecture
of personal history. 'I bet you had a lovely family home, where
you used to live?' Greta smiled a few times with that question.
I usually just said the name of the city, then asked, 'Ever lived
there, Mrs. Smythe?' or 'I bet you'd have fun if we went
shopping in the city, one day.' A subtle swerve.

With a wave of one of her immaculately manicured hands, clear
nail polish and cuticles neat, she'd be off with an anecdote,
'Smith and Caugheys. Three hours. They carried my parcels to
the taxi. A swag.' Her sister took Greta to a play. 'A sold-out
show. I think she bribed someone.' Anyone who ever goes to
Auckland, absolutely has to go to ... (her list can go on for some
time).

Once, Mr. Fielding said, 'Lovely to have families here for
Christmas. Who's coming from yours?'

Can't remember what I said but he looked puzzled, as if I'd
misheard him. Dipped to a new subject, like a kite weaving
through clouds, or a leaf on the water eddying here, there,

unpredictable.

Now like a peculiar effect in the sky can take anyone's breath away, a double rainbow. Hope. Alarming. Uncertain. I'd believed myself immune to romance. Men's chat-up lines in the pub rarely rewarded with a smile from me. No one in town ever flirted, but if they did any time I would resurrect Scorn Woman. Imagining higher eyebrows for myself and a hairstyle like Lana Turner's, who starred in now classic films. An icy atmosphere appeared in seconds.

The one glass of Riesling now two, rather like grapefruit with a touch of honey, subtle oak. Griffin's ginger brown curls jiggled while he spoke, his face tanned but hardly lined. My brothers had imagined an attraction between Griffin and me, but it was probably some new cruelty on their part. Nothing to disturb my life unless I allowed it to be so.

We discussed a set of ginger jars. He told me about China. 'Gracious'd be the word. They know how to put a guest at ease over there, the Chinese really do. Mind you, I learnt to compliment people before a question. Circumlocution.'

Oven-baked fries heated up in the tiny stove. Griffin wondering, 'You need a larger cooker in here, don't you? With those brothers calling in and so on.'

'This kitchen's not big enough to even have a cat, let alone swing one. I really only need this little stove. It is only me, and my....' I almost said *teddies* and stopped myself. 'Oh, you know.'

'Not sure I do? Erm... and you do know that expression's about swinging a cat o' nine tails?'

I gave a broken laugh. 'Is it? Well, you learn something new every day. Sorry, bit of a weak joke then, I guess. No floggings here. But honestly, your dad's welcome to the stove, Griffin.'

'Well, okay. O, by the way, Dad reckoned Greta told him you knew that band, um...? All those hits?' Griffin spoke fast. 'D'you mind me mentioning them?' He named their award-winning single.

I tidied the 60s cat on the windowsill, more like three-quarters profile, yes. I wondered how on earth Greta knew *that*. Then I recalled we'd seen an article in a women's magazine, Greta and I. Yes, I'd said the bass guitarist was a good guy. A scrap of a comment, she'd embroidered a whole story.

Cooking aromas, freshly heated oil and herbs along with incense lit to dispel anything clinging. I chopped herbs and readied a fresh tomato dip for the chips.

The past shut into photo albums and silly diaries, made into stories. 'Sure, Griffin, I knew a few people when I lived in the city. No idea where they are now. Just the one friend left who I see a great deal of these days, really good friend called Heath...'

'That a boy's name?' He almost shouted.

I guessed the third glass of wine affected Griffin more than me, his butting in.

'She's my age, and it's *Heather*.'

'Uh, oh yeah, h-h-huh....' He blurted, 'You go out with those... any of those musicians?'

Rather too slowly, choosing words as if making a special dish and needing complimentary flavours, I replied, 'They flatted with a friend of mine.' (Almost said, 'Not that band, didn't go out with any of *them*,' but stopped myself).

Griffin rocked on his heels. 'The singer, he insulted my girlfriend at the time. Punched him. Sorry to say I planted him with more, once he fell. That was when I drank.'

'You're drinking now.'

'Oh no, I really drank then. Bottle of bourbon gone in half an hour.'

'He probably deserved a few punches.'

'Don't know that anyone deserves a smack. Funny, I was planning to be an architect then. Now here I am with five houses and tenants. Not one house I designed. Strange, y'end up in places y'didn't expect.'

I sipped my wine. Griffin was *blatantly* showing he was a man of means? Or lying? Meanwhile I'd held onto a secret refusal to have Griffin move into my place for winter. Prepared a firm statement to repel this acquaintance. To see if Griffin meant his remark to really *mean* something, I took a new tack and talked about my brothers again.

Griffin immediately asked if any of the boys lived in Auckland, because he wanted to, '...buy something there, a house, maybe an apartment block, but I've no idea where.'

So, he'd got to know my brothers better, then let me know he
had means, and some interest in *me?* Instead of jeans and t-shirt,
did I waft about in a long skirt and frilly blouse? Living in a Jane
Austen novel; how minutely we'd changed over the centuries.
My faint smile returned by Griffin, but he'd no idea what I'd
mulled over. And I needn't feel guilty, but did.
A slump. Romance usually turned tragic. Why would this be any
different? Did therapy truly work? Had I changed enough?
Truly stopped wanting to find someone else to save me, to lose
myself in? Could I be independent *and* intimate? I knew the
theory. But did I truly accept that was how kindness proved
itself, and how relationships worked best? Could I trust the light
that I'd asked to live in?
Men who'd tried to court me, seduce me, or impress me
throughout the last years I'd ducked them expertly, the slalom
queen of avoiding hitching posts. Reticence a virtue, wasn't it?
Prudence. Now I was refusing to feel entranced by a small town
prince living rough.
With familiar retro and vintage my customers reinvented the
past for themselves - life back then seemed kinder to many of
them in retrospect when regarding something loved and old,
and, oddly, to me. Reminded by ornaments, furniture; fanciful
stories built in a glance. Beloved, time-worn, or antique artifacts.
Such a long tradition, our cultures of humanity. We truly did
belong somewhere. It felt like an old glove, amongst objects our
ancestors knew. Those favoured and cared for materials, shapes,
they'd been tried and lasted. Now they presented an
undemanding haven, could be trusted to deliver comfort,
delight, (or so I grew to understand). *Things* didn't hurt me, after
all, it was people who'd been neglectful, treated me with scorn
or ridicule, people took advantage, or outright punched, kicked
and tortured me. I found the finer, quirkier and startling objects
from those days, however, strangely comforting. Their beauty
made me want to be worthy of it, and served as a poignant
reminder that nothing was ever all bad.
Tradition also encouraged known rules and habits. My brothers
liked the idea of a man to look after their sister. A local man, just
the ticket. They'd also presumed the unmarried daughter cared

for the ailing father. So nineteenth century. Momentarily, a
carriage could ride up. My chaperone a scold. We'd been left
alone together. Griffin and I with no business to be drinking, too,
scandalous.

Horses did clip clop past at that precise moment. I laughed. 'Just
thinking it'd be great to see horses. Then there they were,
outside. Did you hear them? That Riesling's really very good.'
Griffin smiled with more passion than I believed necessary.

I looked away, shook my head at myself, inwardly. A clinical
version of me inside observed, kept house in there. Any fluffy
ideas quickly brushed off to reveal the clean truth. I was better
alone.

We conversed until I yawned. Griffin shot out of his chair. 'S-s-
sorry, kept you up. Goodnight. Great to see you.' One hand
through his shortish curly brown hair. It stood up even more.
Reminded me of this Irish comedian I liked on TV, in a series
about a book shop. I hummed.

And he disappeared in a few seconds. The door closed, *snupit*.
Definitely two glasses sat on the table, and salty air had entered
the room when the door opened and closed, along with maybe
the scent of his shampoo. Expensive, lemony. So I hadn't
imagined the last hour or so.

We rode in an open carriage around a park in a costume drama,
in my dream about him. The director kept saying, 'Go again.'
Neither of us appeared to mind. Round and round in circles, the
rhythm of the carriage, a man close enough to touch, arms and
thighs alongside.

I smiled, awoken by birds ferociously chirruping outside. My
busy day ahead crowded me like a furiously organised parent
with a shopping list. Told myself off while getting ready - no one
ever found the perfect match. I found closeness difficult, needed
to work with the facts. Adapt, be flexible, live in separate houses,
or insist he went away to see his properties without me, spend
long periods apart. No matter what, time alone, vital.

Practical matters served sanity best. I found the camera before
breakfast, snapped shots of things to sell online. Placed each
item on the porch in natural light, but not direct sun. The fresh

smell of recently mown grass, roses, freesias, and salt. Griffin appeared just as I took a close-up of a sinuous green vase with irises across it. 'Hi there. Maybe go for a drive today? Taking photos for long?'

After a brief hello, I asked if he could come back later.

He looked disappointed, but sounded cheery, 'Okay, Athena. I'm off for the day, that's all. Have to get to see a house. Sure you don't want a drive?'

'My brothers were here for days. Need to catch up with things. Sorry. Have fun.'

He walked away and shouted another good-bye in this light manner, without a hint of annoyance. Made me feel like I certainly *did* want to go for a drive. The most frightening darkness in mind between now and the future however, as if I needed to walk through a Gothic novel's forest before reaching some sunny glade beyond. Still, I waved, but only glanced his way afterwards, so he wouldn't see my soft expression. Caution. What a novelty. I stood before a cold sea and did not want to swim. But water could be warm. Imagined as clearly as I could see the green grass and asphalt road beyond. *Find things to do. A man would just distract you. Stop being so stupid.*

For weeks Griffin appeared, and I made it clear I had to take pictures for online trading or needed to post things to people. Now and then he stayed to chat for a short while, but soon went on his way. The lovely warmth which enveloped me when he'd stayed that time to offer me wine didn't ever dissipate. A base of good memory reappearing whenever he did, but I took care not to appear too friendly. Fear held me back as certainly as a lifeguard by a wild ocean.

After three days without seeing Griffin, I wondered why I missed him instead of feeling glad. If I wanted to put him off, it'd obviously worked. *Get on with things.* As certainly as knowing how the boat engine worked or my password online, I believed I couldn't possibly have a boyfriend, a partner. Where was the room for someone genuinely close, a real person with foibles and peculiarities, someone who could let me down at times, and with issues we'd need to work through, when I'd never truly done that ever before? Naive at my age.

When Griffin called in previously, however, he took something
heavy away, like an obstructive wall collapsed with his talk and
the sight of him. Reddish-brown hair all over the place, his
gentle smile. Now I could clearly see something like the trailer of
a film I'd enjoy.

Reminded in Griffin's absence, mysteriously, about when I
stayed directly on the sea front for weeks, watching large ships
arrive. Gradually they glided over to the harbour further north.
Cargo boats sat almost on the horizon, swung in a little closer
then, around the point. They found the channel to wharves, a
major port, to pick up containers and timber.
One week no ships arrived, not one, and no yachts either. I
believed the ocean itself lay still without tides or surf. Nothing
moved upon it. The sky cloud-free.
Newspapers explained the harbour disaster as unavoidable, then
a tragic accident. A few weeks later, news media announced
heads appeared ready to roll. Ships had to turn back mid-
journey when they were radioed about the accident. Millions of
dollars lost in sales. Some cargo meant for New Zealand was off-
loaded in Australia.

Each morning, without Griffin's visits, I walked briskly down to
our desolate beach, bereft of sand, with craggy rocks below the
sea wall. The ocean could relay secrets. Surf rolled in, gulls
swooped and squawked, a few sparrows pecked at freshly mown
grass on the verge. At the end of our long wharf five boats
bobbed there, nodding together like old friends in agreement.
The sight brought tears to my eyes but I just walked on to the
shop, picked up a newspaper and strode back home.
For a longer time than usual each morning after Griffin stopped
calling by, I looked at myself in the mirror. Hair white at the
temples under thick dark waves. Face oval and pleasant rather
than beautiful, but faces rearrange for a mirror. Never animated
in reflection.
Mainly birds, a few skinks and geckos, and the local cats saw me.
For a short while, I fancied dressing my hair with coloured
feathers, to brighten my day. Purchased a feathered hat, 1930s,

close-fitted, iridescent blue and purple, online.

Two more days went by and I didn't wonder where Griffin was so much as really miss him. But when I looked for their address in the phone book, to ring, couldn't think what to say. Tried lines aloud, 'Just wondering how you are? Feel like a cup of tea perhaps?' My voice thin, ineffectual.

The news relayers in front of the store told me, unprompted, the next morning, their faces long, that Griffin and his dad had disappeared. Someone said they saw Griffin take his dad off in the car one night a while back. No one heard more. Perhaps they'd gone to visit relatives? 'Say anything to you, Athena dear?' Greta Smythe then also sneakily asked why I was so interested. I told her, 'Griffin's been helping me with the garden. Wondered why he hadn't …Oh well, better get my bread.' I thought tailing off would make it sound like I didn't really care.

But when I walked into the shop I heard Greta assert, 'She's got it bad, if you ask me.'

One morning, soon afterwards, with dew on the grass and the sun strong, Griffin walked towards me over my rather rough front lawn. I grinned and waved, but in seconds could see tears rolling down his face.'Dad. My dad's gone,' he spoke quietly. 'Took him off to the hospital last week. In there hooked up to all these things. Tubes….'

We stood there with our arms around each other for some time. His face against my head, my face against his shoulder, warmer than the gradually overcast day.

His sister arrived in a silver Mercedes and bossed Griffin about. Tried her bad manners on me too, 'You, you there, Woman. Uh, where can we get a marquee?'

After turning slowly to squarely look at her short self, I stated, 'If we could get some *please* and *thank you* into our conversation, things could go more smoothly. Thanks. And my *name* is Athena.' Astounded at my own cheek, but I didn't weaken. Since I'd told the brothers off, I didn't seem to endure rudeness.

She stalked off, red-faced. Returned eventually. 'I'm sorry, Athena. I'm not usually this way. Just I feel so fraught with the whole….' She cried.

We hugged. His sister smelt like roses and baking bread.
Griffin's sister, Mags, arranged the funeral beautifully, with our
help. The service was not religious and Griffin said to hold
proceedings on the lawn. A huge marquee without sides, for
shade. The one hour service and day-long wake at my place.
Griffin's dad's property was so full of junk, they'd take a month
at least to sort it all out. Mags told me, 'He thinks a lot of you.
Just take it gently. Okay?' Then she drove off in her big car back
to the city.
After the funeral, Griffin and I saw each other every day, and
some nights too.

Days slide along, nights draw in, light patterns move across the
land. Time changes everyone and everything even if, as scientists
say, time does not exist.
Griffin drives me to markets and auctions in neighbouring
districts. He inspects houses for sale, peers underneath and taps
the walls. I buy retro tea sets and chromed tables, chairs and
sofas, snazzy fabrics, antique linens too. A designer in the city
refashions some into sumptuous dresses. My collection of bears
increases. A few sent overseas. 'Going on their big OE,' I joke.
Griffin likes to pretend he's moving to Auckland every couple of
months, or Australia, or Wellington. Always manages to make
me believe him, until I'm almost upset. Then he grins. 'Just
checking to make sure I'm wanted.'
Usually I grab the nearest newspaper or magazine and try to
whack him. He laughs and ducks away.
If we see each other day after day I'm snappish, soon
murderously annoyed. Start an argument over just about
anything; last time it was a tap turned off too hard. 'How the
hell can I get water, if you insist on making it impossible? Leave
my things alone.'
Griffin's learnt to fix whatever set me off then leave me alone for
a day or so.
I learned to apologise and mean it. A dance with possibilities.
We both constantly wonder what we may give the other to make
our life better, rather than looking for the other to be giving us
what we want. The machinery of our lives in a new pattern. I

have one rule, I have to be nice to him.

Together, we made a bigger shed on my property to store treasures. Set up a shop for my finds on the front lawn, Luck & Liberty. Friends from the city call in to admire the latest stock. Our cars kept at Griffin's, his father's old house around the corner, a double garage quite cleared and tidy now.

We lobbied Council relentlessly. The beach then renewed with more sand trucked in.

Griffin's sister, Mags, started a restaurant in one of the older Victorian houses. Got a manager in after the first six months. The chef and the maitre d' took drugs, nodded off, almost set the whole place on fire. After that frightening start Mags found better staff. Someone wrote a guide, raved about it, four stars out of five. We helped build extra rooms out the back, an annex. Lights float in front of your eyes and you have to sit down or fall over. No brief declaration describes the planning and imagination needed, the months of arduous labour, exhausting hours.... Hard yakker forgotten for the most part, oftentimes like one long romp and a laugh. We must love what we do then other people love it too. Visitors stay more often in this coastal district, nowadays.

Greta Smythe's opened a bed and breakfast at her two-storey place. Murder mystery nights in the tangled garden. A farmer nearby takes trampers into bushland across the hills and they hunt too. Local Maori put on a great hangi, spring, summer and autumn.

When you've got something good, hold tight - a Victorian postcard framed in rimu, with a gold matt. A woman and a man, fully clothed. She's on his lap and they smile, ready to kiss. It's behind my shop counter. We sell reproductions of the original.

A feathered hat, candlelight, an excellent stereo playing; musing on this and that. My glam rock, punk rock, rock, rock (ha), and just plain gorgeous boyfriends maybe helped to bring me here, in some ways. Our dress-ups, we changed who we were to fit a show or fashion. Glitter love, acting the part as necessary - mascara, false eyelashes, satin pants, and tower block shoes, amongst other fine and fantastic accoutrements. Our play-acting perhaps didn't stand true through commonplace hours. But we kept each other sane and happy to a degree. Those lovely men also made me believe I was worthwhile in many ways. They weren't the kind of people who took notice of everybody, but they certainly noticed me. A few tried to point out I needed to change my ways too, be less aggressive, more understanding.... Some never get the chance to enjoy one kiss, not even a single love affair, and I've had many. And I loved, or at least cared about, the men I slept with, admired every one of them. Did my best to support their wishes, hopes, dreams. But how to stay close remained an elusive skill, and I seemed unable to protect myself from hurt. It took a long lonely time to learn the chaos I lived inside need not stay a tangle. I had to keep my identity, my own ideas, my way of doing things and also love them, simultaneously, to stay happy. No need to envy me the struggle. Imagine you're inside a glass tank and can see others outside, close with people they care for, happy, but you always have this glass between you and others. Sometimes the surface clouds over or swarms with colours, the tank fills with strange substances, you fight to breathe and think. Nothing quite presents the true picture of my entire experience shattered, smoking and acrid with explosions, a war zone no one else ever saw, the messy world I lived in from before I could talk.

Now, someone's cleared most of the rubble and there's less imagined chances of attack. Sometimes, more and more often, I believe the sky truly is blue, the sun does shine, the touch of another is not a trick to get me cornered and attacked, unawares. And my voice doesn't disappear, I speak out against those who try to hush, push, and crush. I say carefully that I don't like what they are doing, too. The enormous effort of almost always feeling angry has finally dropped away from me. Grateful for so much assistance and for the chances I found to escape the ruin. Clumsy, foolish, trying to do better. I know many will sneer at me still, but who gives in and gives away any chance for happiness, just to please others who we only imagine care about what we're doing, in any case?

After years of work I grew comfortable with calm, stability, and security. Beauty does exist in everything, even within the most ordinary places.

In my diary I wrote - I held Griffin when his dad died. My friend needed comfort. People reach out, occasionally we connect. My affairs were to offer and find comfort. Love's transformative. We each deserve kindness, even those so dreadfully hurt we can barely believe we may fully care for another or ourselves. Offering who we truly are to another, not a fake, not a stand-in or a best version, requires courage.

Not that I had to roll out my whole story to Griffin, but if he couldn't stand back from the start, let me be alone at times, then he'd only grow disappointed, fast. So I did well to be resolute, not welcoming him too readily. Gave away old romantic movie dreams and accepted a real man as he really lives. Some days dull or strange, trying or bewildering, but all things pass.

On warm afternoons I wear my feathered hat for our retro teas on the lawn, under various sun umbrellas, and we've planned a fancy dress ball for summer. The restaurant's hiring a marquee and a swing band. Greta Smythe keeps hinting at a murder mystery ball sometime.

With true love, you never exactly know what's going to happen next. It's all improvised.

Couples married for fifty, sixty, seventy years in the news. They dared to stay and did endure.

True sunlight so good for my bones, even if only to make some fashion of different mistake in the glare of it; love the most foolish and blessed accident. Amounts of forgetting and forgiveness. We're as clumsy as anyone else may be, Griffin and I, and as careful, amongst other things.

Griffin reminds me of the best with my family. Mum and Dad stayed together as best they could, cared for us, worked hard, and we did share some fine times. It wasn't all torture and distress. New memories surfaced. I'd forgotten many fine moments; being with Griffin makes me believe they happened.

I also stopped believing someone else could complete me. Griffin and I help each other out, we love each other's company, but we're separate people with our own boundaries, ideas, and histories. Somehow through all the therapy, writing, and life, I found protection, alone, inside a gigantic cup where goodness flows in, and out. Sometimes we're delighted, mainly content, and we often need to sort things out so they stay that way. Griffin snores, two extra rooms were built on so we can sleep in separate beds. We can't keep more than one bottle of wine in the house, Griffin can get carried away if he sees too much available. I dislike long conversations before midday and need to be on the computer for hours. Tug of war conversations sometimes, o yes, and I've been known to stand on the street and shout. But Griffin makes me laugh somehow, and the ridiculous tower of complaints tumbles to sand. When I'm at my most gloomy, if he disappears in a huff I accept he couldn't think of anything else useful to do.

Griffin behaves rather like a cat who wants to sit on my lap, but if he has to be alone, then he's so beautifully self-contained. A man at times needs to feel powerful. If a woman does not do what he wishes and sees as reasonable, a man can crumble inside and blame her. So I let Griffin pontificate and not make much sense, don't always correct him. When he goes on about grand plans, a trip to Paris, a better car, or a whole new wardrobe for us both, I sometimes agree it sounds wonderful. Not wound up, I never agree we'll get those things. And I don't tell him his odd ideas about world affairs are correct, but a smile works wonders. Then if he tells me to shush in public I do. Not because he has the right to tell me to be quiet, but because it embarrasses him to have people stare.

Ainsley, my latest therapist, told me recently, 'In the developing world people have to concentrate on basic survival. How to grow or find food, get water, work at some activity....' She rearranged her turquoise cardigan and smiled gently. 'In the developed world, we must concentrate on relationships. If we never learn this skill properly, how to relate well with others, we're held back and it can be dangerous. Yes, this is for survival, the work we do here.'

'O, okay, sure, I see.' I smiled. 'Well, I decided to start seeing someone decades ago, because I could tell I was missing out. Felt so alone, often suicidal. Human beings need each other. Now I

can also see some people really do not want to lose me.' Tears
came into my eyes. I spoke, head down, with a sense of wonder,
'Never felt that way before. It helps me to live a more
considerate life.'

'Only recently, in the last one hundred years or so, has some of
the western world turned its back on therapy. It was once
common to see a wise woman or religious leader for help with
relationships, troubling dreams, or recovery from grief.
Individualisation isolated people and convinced many of us we
could do so much by ourselves.' She clasped her beringed hands
together.

I thought for a while then nodded. 'Easier to control us as an
economic unit, perhaps.'

'But we do need each other.' Ainsley leaned forward a little.
'Kindness means - available for independence *and* intimacy,
together. Remember?' Her face soft she sat back, glanced at the
clock.

'Yes, *independence,* don't feel like I have to let someone under my
skin if I love them, now. A distance of respect, I could say.
Taking some getting used to, this new way of thinking, but I like
it.'

We looked through the images I'd created. A story in coloured
crayons. Then Ainsley handed over my drawings. 'All aspects of
life improve after this work. My aunty was a recluse. Didn't do
therapy until she was 70. Became an artist, sold out exhibitions,
loved talking with people.'

Out the blue front door of the therapist's office and to the gate.
Trees fresh in spring green and a warm, sunny morning. Birds
swooped everywhere.

Found ways to reinterpret the past so it recreated me.
Griffin says nothing when I play loud music and dance around
the house each morning. Sometimes he goes for a walk, away
from the racket. He also never criticises what I cook, or how I
keep house, and assists without a grumble. Close to sainthood,
according to one of my neighbours (I must keep my eye on her,
she may imagine she could have two husbands, and Griffin
could fit the bill).

We've always had separate bank accounts, each pays their share.

I grew up thinking nothing should be thrown away unless it
really was no good.
I doubt Griffin will ever read this, but that's not his real name.
This whole story's been fictionalised to protect the guilty, the
innocent, the best left alone.... The point is, I went along and
learnt better, despite overwhelming odds against me doing so.
It's a great feeling to be proud of that. People change by choice
or time changes us, or both. I was lucky enough to have choices
I recognised for the better.

Mostly, we talk over plans, or theories re films and so on. I moan
to friends online about day-to-day issues like next door's cat
spraying clean washing if I leave it in the basket on the lawn.
Griffin doesn't hear my gripes that often. If I do rave on, he
grins, sometimes offers a solution.
The past slipping into the dark of the moon, where nothing lives
but whatever we dream up. Feelings a barometer. I've learnt to
stay close when I feel loved, and no one's getting hurt. Give me
my diploma.

I saw the news-gatherers a few weeks after old Bill's spectacular
funeral (the wake eventually lasted two full days and part of
another, including an Irish pipe band and a troop of men and
women who delivered food from far and wide, while we roasted
two pigs on spits in the garden). Outside our local store sat the
usual suspects like rather bedraggled old birds peering at me
with bright eyes. Greta Smythe smirked. 'Griffin and yourself
looking cosy these days.'
I replied slowly, with a smile, 'There are worse ways than giving
sympathy after losing a loved one, to make someone a close
friend.'
Mr Fielding grinned.
Greta Smythe murmured, 'Close, she says.'
Their opinion a flower in their garden. No trouble to walk on
past the old gossips and go inside the shop, buy two Choc
Bombs and a bottle of ginger ale, then hold tight to the

shopping bag all the way back along the road to our place. And that's about it really.

Somewhere Else

The hills growl and the night lights up
to daybreak about to snap its fingers.

This 24 hours singing louder than time,
can feel how forward things are gonna get.

> *- Weather for IT by Crazzzy Z and the Ma-shines 2007*

On a vacant section beside an unfenced house, somewhere in
the suburbs a girl walked while she spoke into her cellphone. In
the warm afternoon, she laughed and kicked one foot out a little,
talking with her boyfriend.
'Oh Flavo,' she said, because his friends called him that (then,
with MC, it's his title on the weekends in nightclubs and bars).
She saw him perform the first time only the previous Friday
night. He called her Suze since she told him her middle name,
and he preferred that to Ann. It wouldn't do for his darling to
have the same name as his aunty.
Suze loved the way he took a while to say her name, lengthening
the z sound, Suzzze. First time she'd ever had a true nickname,
rather than some unwanted name other kids called her for
reasons only they knew, behind sharp looks that cut her such a
small space. Now, on her cellphone, she laughed when he told
her he missed her so much, and why didn't she sneak out later?
They could meet at the bowling club, he knew where they kept
the key. Flavo sounded unsure when she laughed, he asked if she
thought he said something funny.
For a few seconds, Suze explained she laughed because it's good
to talk, that's all. In the grass under her feet a few beetles
bumbled about, she saw them when she stopped and looked at
the ground. Trying to think, the girl wondered if it always grew
so difficult to explain what you meant, when you just plainly
showed what you felt. At 17, Suze hoped to find clever, fast
reasons, she waited for her mind to reach a new gear and spill
for this phone call. Flavo laughed too, then agreed with her, it
did feel good to talk and she paced about again in the sunshine,

glad not to have to think so hard.

The couple talked about the sun, since Flavo lived only a few kilometres away and his sky looked as blue as hers. They planned going to the beach or out on Flavo's aunty's boat one day. He said they could take a picnic, and wished Suze would make another chocolate cake, like she did when he came over last weekend. 'Just wicked, that cake. Bouncin'. I mean it,' he said.

In the still, dry day, Suze smiled to think he liked her baking, and paid Flavo some compliments, too. His great smile. His record collection's the best. When he sings she feels like melting, he could be a singer with his own band. By the time her battery ran out they'd talked each other up into where clouds could be, if it were not such a perfect day.

Suze floated inside to laze round on her bed and dream a bit, while her phone recharged.

Later, she texted Flavo. They sent each other silly messages about pineapples, UFOs, and socks.

In her pink bedroom with pictures of tattooed singers around the mirror, she dreamt of travelling overseas in the boat the Owl and the Pussycat (from a poem when she was little), sailed in. A pea husk, bright green on a purple ocean, with pigs swimming past from a bank advertisement. Flavo kissed her and she saw all the stars overhead from the inside.

In her parent's lounge the next weekend, Suze noticed as if for the first time that self-help books took up an entire shelf, under all her dad's books about World War Two and big cats. Just then, she recalled she sometimes read the spines of those paperback books and laughed to herself, because they sounded so fresh. But she never let her mum know what she thought. Suze believed if men came from one planet and women from another, then they'd be different species and unable to have children. The teenager never read the books her mother bought about bringing up only children, nor those explaining what made relationships work. Suze thought the titles made people sound like clocks, as if two people could become cogs and spin each other round making sense somehow, tick tock, ring the hour, tell the time, never be late for your date.

She hummed then sang, 'Tick rock, sick rock.' Played some air
guitar and soon Suze swung herself around to the sliding doors
then out to the deck. Hot wood and bare feet. The girl lazed
under the sun umbrella and wondered if ants fell in love. Maybe
all the ants touching their feelers together were searching for the
real true ant, the ant they could love forever?
Small black insects busied themselves along the white railing of
the deck.
Suze felt a little guilty doing so little. Soon she fetched one of
her mum's books and read it. By the time the sun went down,
Suze sat with a stack of books beside her, all read. She'd laughed
at some of them, but not with derision like she did in the past.
Flavo and a friend arrived the next Saturday in a new white van
and they drove to a party. All the way there, Suze raved how
great it was that Dave drove so well, and Flavo went quieter and
quieter until he could've been a tree, uprooted and loaded into
the van.
At the party, Flavo told Suze if she liked Dave so much she
could always go out with him. Suze smiled and stroked her
boyfriend's heavy, dark hair back from his brown eyes.' I just
wanted David to keep us safe. I care about you so much, I'd be
nice to anyone if it meant you'd do well. I love that hoodie on
you Flav, it makes you look mysterious.'
'White is mysterious?' Flavo asked.
'You look like an Arabian prince. The only one in Papakura.'
Suze smiled at him.
The pair snuggled in a corner for a while and kissed, until
someone asked Flavo when he was going to DJ.
'It works,' Suze explained to her friend Ariana, 'you just flatter
them, and they love it. Then men do what you want, they want
more wins. That's what the book says.'
Ariana stood even taller. 'I'll never tell a man nicey nice, they're
awful hairy things.'
'Then this other book,' Suze went on, smiled, and ignored her
friend's tone, 'it said all these things about this couple. I read it
like a drama. They kept screwing...'
'Screwing? Your mum have books like that?' Ariana sniggered.
'Messing, screwing things up.' Suze spoke louder.

The party faster then, with Flavo at his turntables and the better sound system much clearer, louder. Suze smiled at him and he smiled back. She spoke into her friend's ear, 'BUT then the book showed you how not to mess things up.'

'Dance, c'mon.' Ariana demanded, then walked into the middle of the people gyrating en masse.

Suze followed. The two girls danced for a while, then got drinks from a huge tub of ice on the deck at the back of the house.

'Okay, tell me the secret.'

'Ariana?' Suze looked blank.

'How to get a man, silly.'

'To get a man silly,' Suze laughed, 'you could wear a top that barely covers your essentials. He'd go real silly.' Suze looked inside. 'It's hot in there. Let's stay out here.'

'Tell me about your book. Tell me.' Ariana almost stamped her foot.

'Oh okay, Ari, keep your hair on. It said at the end, anything can be cured by dancing around the stove. You know - forgive and forget, have a few drinks and a romantic dance.'

'That's the key?' Ariana pouted. 'What a stupid book.'

'Nooo, that was what most successful relationships are like, but true love... ahhh.' Suze tried to look mysterious.

Her friend glared at her. 'As if you can read a book and know what to do. Mum says true love never runs smooth.'

Suze smiled and nodded. 'I guess that's why you need this rule I read, then.'

The other girl looked thoughtful. 'Okay, I suppose your ancient guardians are still together. Your mum read many of those books?'

'She's only 42. Not ancient.'

Ariana laughed. 'Vintage.'

Inside the music pounded on, but Suze kept talking, 'I like what the book said. I am putting it in my reading log.'

'Miss will say it's not allowed.'

'No. My theme this year is any book about changes for the better.'

Ariana tried her fiercest look. 'Just tell me what it said.'

'Another dance?' Suze pretended she would walk inside, but

Ariana grabbed her arm and glared at her friend til they both giggled.

Then Suze finally explained, 'The last page was only one sentence I think. No, two. It said, "But true love means the couple are truly honest with each other about all the details, in all they say. But they don't tell each other every single detail." There you are Ariana.'

'But what about all my careful lies?' Ariana laughed. 'I think I would've been sent to a nunnery in another age. Then I could spend all my time hunting and riding, and chatting up young men bored with their roles as the younger brothers.'

'My mum said that you are too old for your years, you know that, Ari?'

'Could be right. C'mon let's dance again.'

Outside, after a few more hours partying, Ariana waited with Flavo for the van to appear so he could load his gear and they could leave. Ariana looked like a snake in her tight green dress. 'You were amazing tonight, Flavo. Really good sets.'

'But you hate the music I play.' His face immobile, he didn't look at her but spoke loudly.

Suze stood behind them, by the door, where she'd just walked out from the house. She watched Ariana try to touch Flavo's hair. He stepped away, sneered. 'If you want to get home before your curfew, better call a cab.'

For a few seconds, Suze wondered if she could get away with telling Ariana that if she wanted to try to get a ride home by flattering a man, she had to mean what she said. Then her friend simply hissed, 'Goodbye.' Walked off up the road, talking all the while into her cellphone, and paced on the corner, where a cab soon arrived to pick her up.

The next day all the seniors shared lunch, and Suze wondered when she stopped twisting the stalk of an apple to see who her true love was, and how she ever thought that could be a good idea.

The school so familiar now, but then in months or a year they'd all be working or travelling to their universities. She could see how the senior girls and boys who knew each other so well, and who had so many grand plans, could disappear into the massive crowds that swarmed through the city. Those self-help books people read, they needed guidance, to feel special, like some teachers made her feel good, clever, able to get something happening.

Suze felt a need to plan and do things right then, before the rest of the world could swallow her whole, and people she knew could forget her.

She wondered how they all got so old. Soon, she'd be 18.

References and Thanks

Some chapters were previously published as stories or recorded for broadcast or zine publication, in Takahe, for Radio NZ and www.writethis.com (USA)

Lyrics from three songs past their copyright, (You've Got) Personality by Lloyd Price 1959; He's a Rebel by The Crystals 1962; White Sport Coat (and a pink carnation) sung by Marty Robbins 1950s. Song alluded to briefly in the introduction is Walk on the Wild Side by Lou Reed, and in the Glam Rock and Teapots chapter, some words are inspired by David Bowie and Patti Smith. The song alluded to in Caught in Music is by Cream. The song quoted as a telegram message in Band Aides and Gearhead Girls is Play that Funky Music by Wild Cherry. Permissions are not needed for such brief phrases or for paraphrasing as far as I know, if they are needed then we will change those sections.
The phrase 'band aides' is from the movie 'Almost Famous' by Cameron Crowe.
Quotes of songs at the start of each story are invented, so are the artistes, even if each is based on a real song from the era, (then those were rewritten about nine times).
Henry Miller's book Tropic of Cancer -
http://en.wikipedia.org/wiki/Tropic_of_Cancer_%28novel%29
Thanks to Julie Payne Williams in Iowa for the phrase for the title 'Gearhead Girls'.
Between 2000 and 2008, at least 9,000 children were abused in NZ, of the only one third reported in the press, most of those were Maori. But many Pakeha children are also part of this statistic. http://www.nzhistory.net.nz/culture/the-1950s
Various therapies can assist those affected by abuse, however the best way to improve society and stop abuse is with a fine education system for everyone and excellent health services, along with a living wage for all. When the gap between rich and poor widens, society always develops more problems.
http://www.stuff.co.nz/national/crime/5331753/Pakeha-child-

abuse-ignored-researcher
Thanks to all writers and publishers I've worked with, to Bain
Duigan publisher in this case and also, Book Launch for their
expert help, http://www.booklaunch.co.nz/faq/ Jamie Higgins'
editing was excellent too, he worked well making this story as
clear as he could without losing Patricia/Athena's
characterisation.
Especially thanks to talented, generous American writers and
one UK writer who helped edit these stories for seven years. The
Americans then showed me around their country for a month in
2012, on my poetic journey there. Your love and kindness has
done so much for me I could never thank you all enough.
Especially thanks to Dean Strom, Julie Payne Williams, Amy
Tucker, Laura Lee, James Browning Kepple, and in the UK,
Stephen Moran. We met through writethis in 2000, which is
now an excellent online zine. Friendship has to be one of life's
great blessings. The Eye Street Poets have also helped with my
writing since the 1990s, thanks to Jack Ross, Jacqueline
Crompton Ottaway, Lee Dowrick, Alice Hooton, Vivienne
Plumb, Genevieve McClean, Ila Selwyn and Rosetta Allan. I
also thank Dr. Olwyn Stewart and David Lyndon Brown for
their excellent assistance with my earlier novels, in a regular
writing workshop convened by DLB, which assisted me later
with writing and editing this book.
Great to work with Geneva Alexander-Marsters on some aspects
of book design. Thanks also to Jaq Tweedie, Peter McClennan
and Jon Smyth for their help with this novel, plus friends and
colleagues who offered advice and support. You know who you
are, love you. The woman who told me the basis of this story is
anonymous, and although this is now a work of fiction I also
thank her for her patience, bravery and eloquence.
Anyone else who assisted, especially those who helped with
research which I had no idea was research at the time in my
luckily long-ish life so far, I am forever grateful. Thanks for your
kindness, generosity and understanding. Arohanui - love all

www.ingramcontent.com/pod-product-compliance
Lightning Source LLC
Chambersburg PA
CBHW050916030726
47503CB00007BB/2314